PRAISE FOR *THE SILVER COLLAR*

'Hodgson once again shows what a skilful writer of historical thrillers she is' *The Sunday Times*

'A brilliant, moving novel that takes us to some very dark places in our history – but which also succeeds in being very witty and entertaining' S. D. Sykes

'Beautifully written and packed with atmosphere, wit and historical details, I didn't want it to end. And in shining an uncomfortable light on colonial slavery, it's also timely and relevant' *Daily Mirror*

'Book of the Year . . . a joy . . . the plot crackles with twists and turns, but it is Antonia Hodgson's sense of humour that I enjoy most, which somehow manages to inhabit both the eighteenth and the twenty-first centuries with equal assurance' Michael Ridpath, *Aspects of History*

'Fourth instalment of the wonderful Thomas Hawkins crime novels . . . [Fans] are in for a treat – this instalment is gripping' *The Times*

'Throws readers right back into the grimy, stinking streets of eighteenth-century London' *BBC History Magazine*

PRAISE FOR *THE SILVER COLLAR*

'Written with flair, sly wit, and a meticulous eye for detail . . . *The Silver Collar* takes us into the dark heart of colonial slavery, making this one of the most topical books of the year . . . thrilling' Vaseem Khan

'A breakneck pace set against a brilliantly evoked eighteenth-century backdrop . . . who needs a Tardis? Read this to feel like you're truly travelling back in time' *Sunday Express*

'*The Silver Collar* is a triumph, a fine addition to a historical crime series that gets better with every book. Antonia Hodgson gives us dark melodrama with wit, and a driving narrative with impeccable research. It's a rare combination, and it leaves the reader hungry for more' Andrew Taylor

'Fans of Thomas Hawkins and Kitty Sparks should rejoice as Hodgson makes a wonderful return with a dark tale of kidnap, slavery and seduction' *i*

'My favourite of the four . . . an intense, action-packed drama . . . This is a very good novel indeed, by an author who writes beautifully and with such empathy . . . a page turner' *For Winter Nights*, Top Ten Books of the Year

The Silver Collar

Also by Antonia Hodgson

The Devil in the Marshalsea
The Last Confession of Thomas Hawkins
A Death at Fountains Abbey

The Silver Collar

Antonia Hodgson

HODDER

First published in Great Britain in 2020 by Hodder & Stoughton
An Hachette UK company

This paperback edition published in 2021

1

A CIP catalogue record for this title is available from the British Library

Paperback ISBN 978 1 473 61515 1

Typeset in Adobe Caslon by Hewer Text UK Ltd, Edinburgh
Printed and bound in Great Britain by Clays Ltd, Elcograf S.p.A.

Hodder & Stoughton policy is to use papers that are natural, renewable
and recyclable products and made from wood grown in sustainable
forests. The logging and manufacturing processes are expected to
conform to the environmental regulations of the country of origin.

Hodder & Stoughton Ltd
Carmelite House
50 Victoria Embankment
London EC4Y 0DZ

www.hodder.co.uk

For my sisters, Debbie, Michelle and Kay, with love

Lord, how long shall the wicked,
how long shall the wicked triumph?

Psalm 94

Prologue

Winter, 1728

Jeremiah Patience begins his journey in darkness, far to the east
of the city. He walks with his shoulders rolled, in a thin coat
made for a milder season. It is mid-November, and bitter: the
wind as sharp as a blade. This is his third winter in England, each
one colder than the last. His lips are chapped and his toes throb
with chilblains.

He walks, and the city wakes around him, bolts drawn back,
candles gleaming in garret windows. This is the hour of servants
and street sellers, rising before dawn with tired faces and smothered
yawns.

A nightwatchman trudges wearily up the road towards him,
lantern pole balanced on his shoulder. Jeremiah lowers his hat
and tugs his neckerchief until it covers his mouth. The gesture
makes him feel like a villain in a play. He starts to sweat, despite
the cold.

It is no theft, he reminds himself, *to take what is mine*.

Jeremiah studies the watchman closely as he approaches. His
vigilance is a legacy of his life on the plantation. Even in quiet,
drifting moments, some part of him always remains alert to trouble.
I should be the one called watchman. A brief, darting look is enough
for him to read the man's expression. Indifference – weary indifference. A man with sore feet, who wants only to collapse upon his
bed, and have his wife take off his heavy boots for him. But still

Jeremiah holds his breath, until the watchman disappears around the corner.

Quiet roads and alleyways now, all the way to Jermyn Street and a house with a green door – so dark a green it could be black. The knocker is a lion's head, lips pulled back in an iron snarl. He is tempted to walk up and knock. More than tempted – he has to grip the railings to stop himself. He has waited three years for this day. He can wait a little longer.

A cart turns on to the street. He puts his hands in his pockets and follows in its wake, head down, scouting for a place where he might watch the house unseen. A narrow alleyway leading to the Bell Inn suits his purpose. Two ancient beggars lie stretched out at the alley's mouth, side by side as brothers. He offers them a farthing and joins them on the damp cobbles, breathing through his mouth until he grows accustomed to the smell. London stinks, even on Jermyn Street: it still surprises him.

He watches and waits.

It is past noon when a chair arrives at the almost-black door. The street is busy – it is not ideal, none of this is how he'd hoped it would be. But since when has life been ideal? He stands, his legs cramped from long hours of sitting, and crosses the road. His chest thrums with anticipation. So close.

The chairmen settle the sedan to the ground and stretch their backs and shoulders, roll their wrists. One says something and the other laughs. German, Jeremiah decides. He has an ear for languages, for their cadence, hears scores of them at the docks.

The door opens and a woman steps out in a fur-trimmed riding hood. She is followed by a servant, a sturdy fellow with a rough complexion, dressed up in gold buttons and lace. The finery doesn't suit him, and he knows it. His face is set in a rigid mask, barely concealing his ill-humour.

There are worse punishments, Jeremiah thinks. And in the next instant forgets the servant entirely.

A young black girl steps out carefully in new shoes. Her tight black curls are wrapped in a stretch of orange silk, finished with a peacock feather. Around her throat, a wide silver collar.

Jeremiah's heart lifts and opens out to fill the world. *Affie. Affiba.* He breathes her name and the word forms a cloud in the freezing air.

She is no more than ten paces away.

Jeremiah's plan is simple: pick Affie up and run. She is small for her age, and delicate (*she was not delicate once, what have you done to her?*); she will be light in his arms.

No one has noticed him yet. There is no need to say anything.

He needs to say something.

The conflict squeezes his heart.

Take her and run.

Speak. *Speak.*

This is what he wants to say to the woman in the fur-lined riding hood:

Lady Vanhook – do you remember me? I am alive: do you see? I am alive. I have come to take back what you stole from me.

His tongue falls heavy in his mouth, his throat closes around the words.

She looks at him, then. No, he is mistaken – she looks through him. He is a stranger, a ghost, air. Nothing. She smiles, vaguely, and permits her servant to guide her into the chair, gloved fingers curled over his hand. Such elegance, such grace. Such wicked charm. He remembers it all now and it chills his blood, colder than the ice wind. She is Medusa and he is transformed to stone.

I have made a mistake, he thinks. *A dreadful mistake.* His simple plan, which had seemed so safe and sensible back home in his Limehouse lodgings, now feels like dangerous folly. What if the chairmen chases after him? What if the servant has a pistol tucked beneath all that silk and lace? What if Affie were hurt? He cannot risk her life, or his own. If he is killed, who will save her?

I cannot do this alone.

The truth hits him like a fist in the stomach. To be so close . . .

He must retreat – but he cannot move.

Affie, oblivious, steps into the chair, still admiring her new shoes. Lady Vanhook lifts her on to her lap, wrapping her arms around the girl's tiny waist. The chairmen pick up their poles.

Three years he has waited for this moment. Now he is trapped within it.

He fights – and at last two words escape from his throat, like birds.

'Affie. Daughter.'

No one hears him. They are gone.

PART ONE

The List

Chapter One

Six weeks earlier

We had no warning, Kitty and I, of the troubles to come. It had been a quiet summer – golden and easy after months of violence and threat. When the hot stink of the city became too much to bear we left it behind, renting a house in the country at Greenwich. Our days were spent on the river, on the bank, in bed. In stolen, solitary hours I completed my account of our trip to Yorkshire, and when my quill summoned old ghosts and bad memories I strode into the yard and pounded a sack of corn until my knuckles bled. It was, as I say, a peaceful time.

In early September we returned home to Covent Garden, and to Kitty's bookshop, the Cocked Pistol – an establishment of such ill repute that a brief glance through its window could tarnish the soul. Half the town loved it, the other half wished it burnt to the ground. And half of the half who wished it burnt to the ground secretly wished no such thing, sidling in when the shop was quiet to buy armfuls of filth. We liked hypocrites at the Pistol – they were some of our best customers.

Over the summer, Kitty had devised a new stratagem to increase the shop's profits. She was very much a planner, one might even say a *schemer* – constantly searching for ways to improve her business. The reason for this was no mystery.

Kitty had been born into middling wealth, the only child of Nathaniel Sparks, a respected physician, and his wife, Emma. Then, when she was thirteen, her father died. Her mother – through a mixture of greed and bad choices – frittered away the family fortune in less than a year. Imagine the misery, the profound shock of such a swift fall from comfort to destitution. I say *imagine*, as Kitty refused to speak of it. I knew that she had been forced to abandon her mother, in order to survive. I knew also that Emma Sparks had died a lonely, squalid death, selling her body on the streets. But I had not learnt this from Kitty.

This much she would tell me: the night she ran away from her mother, she vowed she would never rely upon another soul again. She would be her own mistress, forge her own path through life. And the next time Fate came to 'kick her up the arse', she would be ready to kick back.

Which returns me to her stratagem for the Cocked Pistol.

Kitty had been inspired by the frontispiece of our most popular book, *The School of Venus*, in which a clique of goodwives clustered around a market stall festooned with dildos. We sold the book faster than we could print it, so why not the objects themselves?

From here it was a mere half-step to condoms, whips and medicines for the pox – desire, fulfilment and consequence, all under one roof. Kitty insisted upon the best quality and charged accordingly. Her condoms were made from sheep's gut instead of the inferior pig's bladder and were guaranteed fresh and never previously used. Her fine leather dildos were available in diverse sizes from the modest to the alarming. She placed advertisements in the newspapers, kept the shop open until eight o'clock at night, and within a month had increased the Pistol's profits fourfold. In short, the venture was a triumph. Kitty was richer than ever.

I – alas – was not, having been stripped of my inheritance some years before, following a regrettable* incident at an Oxford brothel. I had perhaps eight pounds to my name, a watch with a stranger's

*not entirely

initials engraved into the case, and a reputation for trouble. Why Kitty loved me was a mystery.

'For his legs,' she laughed, when we were in company.

'For your cock,' she breathed in my ear, as she pulled me upstairs to bed by my breeches.

'For your heart, Tom,' she murmured, late at night, only half awake in my arms. 'I love you for your heart.'

Being a great planner, Kitty was very keen on lists. Sometimes she would count things out upon her fingers, sometimes she would turn a group of chores into a little song ('today we wash the sheets, tra la, today we scrub the floors, tra la' et cetera), and sometimes she would write a list IN CAPITALS and pin it to the wall. These TERRIFYING LISTS were always addressed to me, THOMAS HAWKINS, and involved things I had PROMISED TO DO MOST FAITHFULLY, and yet somehow, *dearest*, they were not done, NOT AT ALL, not even VENTURED.

So I would not be surprised if Kitty had pondered the question *Why do I love Tom?* (perhaps after I drank that quart of brandy and mistook her hat for a chamber pot) and decided to write down the reasons:

> Q. *Why (on earth) do I love Tom?*
>   i) *Legs*
>   ii) *Cock*
>   iii) *Heart*

While I would not argue with her answers – one certainly wouldn't wish to see any of them *removed* – I could not help feeling the list was rather short – desultory, even. I mention this because it dissatisfied me, at the time. I remember thinking, *Tom, you really must find something to add to this list, because those three items are not enough, she will grow tired of you, you will grow tired of yourself, Kitty is now a* very *rich woman who refuses to marry you because she will not be dependent upon anyone, and because she thinks — for some mysterious reason — you will gamble away her fortune.*

My point is that while I was fretting over such nonsense, I failed to notice the one thing that mattered: we were happy. Other people *had* noticed, however — and they were most decidedly *not* happy. Envy snaps its teeth at the heels of good fortune, and there is nothing in the world more destructive than a man who wants what he cannot have.

Our troubles began on Sunday 13th October, 1728. I remember the date because of what followed, but also because of what preceded it. Kitty and I had met the previous autumn, when I was tossed into the Marshalsea prison for debt. I almost died in that hellish place, and while I was recovering, my oldest friend, Charles Buckley, told me that Kitty was dead. He thought he was saving me from a shameful liaison — Kitty was a servant at the time, and I was a gentleman (disgraced, but no matter). I mourned her for weeks, while she thought I had abandoned her.

We were reunited the day after the coronation, 12th October, 1727, just after nine o'clock in the evening, at Moll's coffeehouse in the piazza, by the fire. Seeing Kitty alive and well (and furious with me, but never mind), remains the happiest and best moment of my life.

Kitty and I decided to mark the occasion by returning to Moll's a year later to the very day. I had intended to propose to her by the fire, as the clock struck nine, but on our way to the coffeehouse Kitty squeezed my hand and said, 'Darling Tom, please don't ask me to marry you tonight, I shall only say no and you will sulk and it will ruin the evening.' I assured her the thought had not entered my head.

Our table was waiting for us by the fire, and the first bowl of punch was on the house. Kitty and I toasted one another, and made bets over which gang of drunks would start the first fight. Moll's had a wicked reputation, which drew a particular crowd — men craving spectacle, riot and debauch.

Not that anyone would dare start a fight with me. Six months ago I had been found guilty of murder and sent to hang at Tyburn. I had long since proved my innocence, and received a royal pardon – but my reputation went before me, as the saying is. I was Half-Hanged Hawkins – the man who died upon the gallows and was then returned to life. When I walked into Moll's that evening, men stared and nudged one another. Whether they considered me a miracle or something much darker, they certainly did not wish to provoke me. This awe and wonderment would surely fade in time, but I was content to rely upon it while it lasted. I had spent ten minutes choking on that damned rope, legs kicking the air while the crowds cheered me to my death. If I gained some benefit from that, I had earnt it a thousand times over.

'I shall buy you a pie,' I shouted over the din.

'Not from here,' Kitty said, alarmed.

'Heavens no.' I wished to treat her, not poison her. I sent a boy out to Mr Kidder's pie school at Holborn. Within the half-hour he returned with trout pie, fried oysters and a beef pasty. Watching Kitty eat, I felt very pleased with myself. How many women could boast that their (almost) husband not only remembered the anniversary of their union, but bought them supper to celebrate? A lucky handful at best, I would wager.

When the clock struck nine we raised another toast to ourselves, and then another, and Kitty sat upon my lap and kissed me, as she had done a year ago, and then I may have fallen asleep at some point, as I had also done that first night. I certainly remember Kitty digging me in the ribs as if to wake me, and saying we must go home, as she had a present for me.

Assuming this was code for some wickedness in the bedchamber, I jumped up from my chair at once. But when we arrived at the Pistol she presented me with an ebony walking stick, its gold top shaped like a fox's head, with twin emeralds for eyes.

ANTONIA HODGSON

'Kitty,'I said, dismayed. 'This must have cost . . . I have not bought you anything.'

'You bought me a pasty,' she said, and hugged me. 'I love you, Tom.'

I assured her that I loved her too. 'But this is too fine a gift.'

Her face fell. 'If you do not like it . . .'

'No, no.' I gripped it tight, and as I did so the gold head separated from the stick. The ebony cane was in fact a long case, housing a narrow steel blade. The fox head was the blade's handle. A swordstick. I swished it through the air, appreciating the quality. I had never seen its like. I felt strange and almost shabby accepting a gift of such value, but Kitty looked so pleased with it, and so anxious that I liked it, that I smiled, and swished it again before sheathing it back in its ebony case. Naturally this led to a joke about where I should like to sheath my own sword. It was not very funny, but we had drunk those two bowls of punch at Moll's, and a further bottle of claret.

In any case, we went to bed laughing.

Chapter Two

The next morning – the day everything changed – began pleasantly enough.

I was perched upon a high stool in the shop, pretending to read a novel. The Pistol was closed, it being a Sunday, but Kitty was still hard at work arranging books and pamphlets, her copper curls pinned neatly beneath a clean white cap. She kept the openly lewd and seditious works hidden away, while those displayed upon the shelves were more subtle, disguised as volumes of anatomy, medicine, and firm moral correction. I watched her surreptitiously from behind my copy of *Love in Excess*. Watching Kitty work was one of my favourite pastimes – she was so clever and quick, bending and stretching in a most diverting fashion.

She left the window and moved towards the counter where I was sitting, wiping her hands upon her gown. Her freckled face was flushed red with exertion, and I caught a trace of sweat beneath her perfume as she came nearer. She had bathed in lavender water this morning. I thought of her, bathing. Steam rising from smooth, snow-white skin. The lapping of the water as she moved her legs. Her fingers tracing up her thigh—

'Tom, *dear heart*, have you moved once this morning? Will you not mend the floorboard on the landing today? You promised you would.'

I slid from the stool, as if to leave, then caught her wrist and drew her close, pressing my hips to hers. 'I can think of more urgent business,' I said, nuzzling her neck.

She sighed, and trailed a hand beneath my shirt. 'Tom,' she murmured in my ear. 'The floorboard.'

Damn it.

She pinched me. 'Do you think me so easily distracted?'

'Of course not, sweetheart. But you have worked so hard this morning. You deserve a rest, don't you think?'

Kitty knew what I was about, but she did not particularly mind. I kissed her again, pulling off her cap and grabbing her hair, until we were lost in each other, falling to the floor in a tangle.

I lifted her skirts to her waist and kissed my way up her legs, pulling her stockings down so I might taste her skin. The scent of lavender and the scent of her. Heaven. I licked the soft velvet of her inner thigh in light circles, teasing. Higher. Closer. 'Should I stop? The floorboard . . .'

'No!'

She tilted her hips and I slid my tongue inside her. She moaned in pleasure, arching her back.

I pushed deeper, in and out, tongue, fingers, tongue. 'Do you want me?'

'Yes. *Yes*.'

There was a sharp knock at the front door.

The mood, I must say, was spoilt.

Kitty snarled in frustration, then pushed her skirts back in place as I rolled free.

'Open up!' a voice called through the door. Then more knocking. 'Open up at once!'

I put my finger to my lips, then crept over to the rain-spattered window. A man of late-middling years stood upon the doorstep with three guards, tapping his foot in a show of irritation. He was dressed in an old-fashioned grey coat and long, heavy brown wig.

Oh, *Lord*.

'Who is it?' Kitty shoved on her cap and crawled over to the window to take a look. '*Gonson*.' She spat his name, as if it were a curse.

Sir John Gonson, magistrate for Westminster, hated me with a burning, holy passion. He more than anyone was responsible for my trip to the gallows, turning the town against me and testifying at my trial. Did he apologise for this, when I was proved innocent? Show any remorse? Of course not. But we had not suffered a single raid upon the shop since my pardon. I had dared hope he would not bother us again.

I felt a familiar ache between my shoulder blades, a warning of trouble ahead.

'What does he want?' Kitty muttered.

'Perhaps he's in need of your mercury pills.'

She stuck out her tongue, disgusted by the notion of Gonson fucking anyone, never mind contracting something unpleasant from them. And then we sniggered together like children.

Unfortunately one of the guards heard us. He scowled through the misted window, then rapped on the pane with his knuckles. 'Open up, or we'll break the door,' he shouted, his voice muffled through the glass.

There was nothing to be done but to stand up, and let them in.

Gonson strode into the shop, nose in the air.

'Sir John.' I bowed low, with a deep flourish. I am very good with a satirical flourish, it is one of my great talents. 'An honour to receive you in our modest home, sir. Might I offer you some wine? A bowl of coffee?'

He pursed his lips. Persephone, refusing nourishment in the Underworld. 'I am here on a matter of business.'

'Working on the Sabbath? Should you not arrest yourself?'

Gonson reddened. '*God*'s business, sir.'

By which he meant the Society for the Reformation of Manners, which was growing ever more powerful under his watch. The Society's great mission was to rid the streets of sin, most of all that dread quartet of drinking, swearing, gambling and whoring. For Gonson and his friends, London was a latter-day Sodom, its citizens drowning in a putrid stew of vice. No transgression was too slight, in their eyes: a muttered 'God damn' over a stubbed toe must lead, inexorably, to damnation.

This was why Gonson hated the Pistol, and wished to destroy it. In his narrowed, disapproving eyes, our little shop was a portal to hell itself. As for me, I was the worst possible sinner – an educated gentleman, a student of Divinity destined for the Church, who had chosen instead a life of vice. I might as well paint myself red and sprout horns.

Gonson thrust a hand in his bag and pulled out a slim volume. 'One of our members bought this yesterday.'

The Society was unashamed in its use of 'virtuous informers', who visited brothels, molly houses and other places of ill repute such as the Pistol. It was the duty of all honest Christians to betray their neighbours, you understand.

'*Venus in the Cloister*. It looks well thumbed,' I noted, taking it from him. I opened it to a favourite illustration. 'Was it necessary to inspect *every* page?'

One of the guards coughed back a laugh. Gonson frowned at him.

Venus in the Cloister is a stirring dialogue in which Sisters Agnes and Angelica describe – in commendable detail – their nightly exploits with their monkish lovers. It is tender, cheerful, and instructive to both men and women. I wish I had read it before my first adventures – it would have saved a good deal of awkward fumbling.

Gonson snatched his copy back. 'I have never seen such blasphemy. Such obscenity.'

'My condolences,' I murmured.

Kitty elbowed me.

Gonson was too absorbed by his own outrage to notice. 'I could have you pilloried for this.'

With that, I lost my sense of humour. A man could survive the pillory without a scratch, if the town had no desire to attack him.

But if Gonson had me chained up in the square, then ordered members of the Society to throw mud and stones and worse at me for hours, they could easily kill me. Men had thrown stones at me before, when I was dragged to the scaffold. I still carried a scar upon my forehead from that day. Kitty touched the back of my hand with hers.

'What is it that you want, Sir John?' she asked, in a gentle voice. That surprised me. Kitty had many virtues, but meekness was not one of them. 'This is my shop, not Tom's. He is merely ...' she groped for a respectable word, '... my lodger.'

I stared at her.

'I have prayed upon the matter, Miss Sparks,' Gonson said, with a pious tilt of the head. 'I have no wish to see you in chains, beating hemp like a common harlot.' His eyes gleamed, imagining the scene. 'I believe there is hope for *you*, child.'

Something rang false in his words. Too much sympathy, not enough censure. Gonson was a man of unflagging moral vigour. Sinners must be punished. Doubters must be corrected. How many women had he sent to gaol for selling themselves? How many men had been arrested or shamed over rumours of sodomy?

A *lodger*?

'I could find a dozen men to testify that this is an honest business,' I said.

'No doubt,' Gonson sneered. 'Shameless devil. And I could send informers in here every day to spy upon you both. I could raid this place once a week. How long would your customers support you then, I wonder?' He turned his attention back to Kitty. 'But as I say, I have no desire to *punish* you, my child.' He smoothed the bottom of his wig, and offered her a greasy smile. 'I seek only your redemption.'

I folded my arms. 'And while we wait for that glorious day?'

Gonson said nothing. He was still smiling at Kitty, in such a queer, covetous way that I wanted to shove him from the room.

What was he about? He had met Kitty several times before and shown her nothing but contempt. She was always 'strumpet', 'harlot', 'slut' to him. Not *child*. In any case she was nineteen. A woman. *My* woman. He could not think of himself as my rival, surely? Good God. The notion would be comical, if it weren't so nauseating.

'Your salvation rests in your own hands, Miss Sparks,' he said, in a portentous voice. 'I shall return tomorrow morning, and expect to see a great heap of these foul books, ready for burning. We shall have ourselves a bonfire, a holy conflagration!'

'We shall do no such thing,' I snapped.

'Tom . . .' Kitty warned.

Gonson's smile deepened. 'This is *your* decision, child, and yours alone. Pray to God, and in His wisdom He will guide you.' He bowed to her, and left with his men.

Oh, clever, I thought. *He is trying to divide us, but it shall not work.* Then I turned to Kitty, and caught her quiet, worried expression.

'Kitty. No.'

'We can buy more books. Or . . .' She looked around at the shop she had worked so hard to build. 'I can sell other things. I have plenty of capital.'

'He was bluffing, Kitty. He has no power over us. Think of our customers!' There was barely a single nobleman or judge who had not bought something from the Pistol, directly or indirectly.

Kitty was not convinced. 'He'll find a way. You know how determined he is, when he wants something.'

'Precisely! You can't appease a man like Gonson. If we do as he asks, he will only return and demand more and more from us. We must stand firm. Let him bellow and bluster all he likes – he won't arrest us for selling books.'

'That's what Curll said.'

'That is a *decidedly* different matter.' Edmund Curll had spent the past year in prison for printing such noble works as *The Use of Flogging* and *The Nun in her Smock*. But Curll was a notorious rogue who published private letters without permission and copied the works of honest writers without sharing the profit. Worst of all, he sold false goods. I once paid three shillings for what he insisted was a volume of bawdy poems, only to discover, when I unwrapped the parcel at home, that I had bought a collection of sermons by the Bishop of Gloucester. Some villainies cannot be forgiven.

'Damn Gonson,' I muttered. 'Sanctimonious arsehole.'

'You provoke him, Tom.'

'Oh! So this is my fault?'

'I didn't say that.'

'You implied it.'

She frowned, distracted. 'Let me think, please. Just let me think.'

'What is there to think about?' I grabbed the novel I had been reading. 'We cannot burn books, Kitty!'

'That is not for you to say,' she replied. She was rubbing her face as she spoke, and did not see my reaction. 'Gonson is right. This is my shop. I must decide what to do with it.' She turned away from me, contemplating her stock with a fresh eye.

'I understand,' I said, coldly. 'This is your shop. I am *merely your lodger.*'

'Oh! Don't twist my words, Tom. That is not fair.'

'I'm surprised you did not call me your whore. That would have been more fitting.'

'*Tom!*'

'After all, a lodger would pay rent, would he not? And a husband ... Well, if I were your husband, this would be *my* shop. My decision.'

'Yes,' Kitty said, in a dangerous voice. 'It would.'

'So we are agreed. I am your whore. I fuck you, and you pay me for my services in food, and lodgings, and fancy gold-topped canes.'

I did not mean any of it, not in my heart. Sometimes we are possessed – not by the devil, but by our own worst selves.

Kitty's eyes filled with tears. She blinked them away. 'Get out.'

'Kitty—'

She threw a book at me, a very heavy one – aimed at my crotch. I only just diverted it in time.

'Get *out*!' she screamed.

'Very well,' I shouted back at her, temper flaring again. 'I shall do as I am told, *mistress*. This is not *my* home, after all. Nothing here is *mine*.' I stormed out, slamming the door so hard that people stopped in the street and stared. I didn't care. A pox on them. A pox on the whole world, and everything in it.

I stamped about the piazza, kicking at the cabbage leaves and broken flowers that lay strewn across the cobbles, the remnants of yesterday's market. What a strange, lunatic fool I must have appeared to all the good folk spilling out from St Paul's church. I could feel their eyes upon me, but I could not stop myself, I was in a righteous fury. Three words kept turning about my head, like the chorus of an especially irritating ballad. *Gonson is right. Gonson is right.*

Had she truly said that? Did she believe it?

Damn Gonson. Damn him! This was his doing. We had been perfectly happy rolling about on the floor before he arrived.

There was no use going home in such a mood. I headed east, past new houses half built, and old houses half collapsed, evidence of the ceaseless transformation of the greatest city on earth. If one did not walk through London regularly, one could become a stranger to it. A respectable street might transmute into a thieves' alley, and vice versa. Some people found such reversals unsettling. I took comfort in them. It will not do to become fixed, like a fly in amber.

By the time I reached Spitalfields the sun was setting, my anger had faded, and I felt much better. Running away from problems is a very bad idea, but walking away from them, in a meandering way, can be helpful. I was far enough away from the argument – figuratively, geographically, temporally – to have *perspective*. Kitty was, without a doubt, the instigator of our quarrel ('merely a lodger'!), but I must take some (lesser) portion of the blame.

I passed a merchant's where Kitty purchased her silk. This must be a sign, surely? I should buy her a gift, by way of apology for my (small) part in the fight. (Could one truly call it a fight? Kitty was for ever throwing things at me, it meant almost nothing.) I would find some pretty piece of embroidered cloth, something with red-gold thread to match her hair. Better yet – I would visit the gaming tables tonight, and win enough to buy her an entire gown.

I stopped at a chandler's shop, a butcher's, an oyster stall and then turned for home, to Kitty. The woman I loved.

The woman I had brought to tears, two hours before.

The image rose before me. I saw myself of a sudden through her eyes, spitting curses and flouncing about like a child – when all she had been trying to do was keep me safe. No wonder she had thrown a book at me, she should have thrown twenty, and I should have stood unflinching and taken the punishment as if I really were in the pillory, let them land where they would – save for the crotch, no one deserved that.

There was a time when I would have let my mind drift upon the matter, walking in a blind trance through the maze of streets. I had been in just such a state of distraction a year ago when I was set upon, beaten and robbed at knifepoint by a gang of thieves. It had taught me to pay more attention to my surroundings.

A prickle at the base of my neck. Whispers in an empty alleyway. Feet scuffing against the cobbles, too close to be honest.

Without warning I flung my parcels to the ground, spun about and punched the man behind me in the jaw.

Chapter Three

He staggered back, dazed by the blow. I had put all my weight into it, and felt the shock run through my arm to my shoulder. He stumbled into his younger companion, knocking him to the ground.

There was no time to admire the efficiency of my strike. A third man – a tall fellow with sand-coloured hair – was lurching towards me, fumbling for his dagger.

Three of them. Too many. I pushed the thought away.

I jumped on him before he could reach his blade. We rolled about in the mud and filth, kicking and punching wildly. I am a decent fighter; I had taught myself to box and wrestle. But I had never before confronted such an unorthodox opponent. To be clear – he was a useless fighter. But he moved in such a floundering, flailing manner, it was like wrestling a drunken scarecrow. Every time I thought I had him, he was somewhere unexpected. At last, out of sheer luck, he landed me flat upon my back.

The air rushed from my lungs. I lay in a daze, recovering just in time to see a great flapping hand coming towards me. I snatched his wrist to stop the blow and shifted my weight, unbalancing him. Propelled by the force of his own attack he fell forwards, and smashed his face against the cobbles.

It was not a graceful fight but I had won it, apparently.

I staggered to my feet, then pulled him by his coat to his knees. His head lolled back, eyes rolling, blood streaming from his nose. He had broken it in the fall.

I took the dagger from his belt and turned to face his friends.

The older man lay sprawled on the ground, unconscious, his right arm twisted at an unnatural angle. His friend was kneeling in the dirt, blood pouring from a gash above his eyebrow. A child, I realised, no more than twelve. He was crying.

Sam Fleet stood behind him, holding a dagger to his throat.

'Sam,' I said.

He was wearing his favourite street clothes, patched and faded, the colour of old brick walls and muddy cobbles. A battered three-cornered hat covered a tangle of black curls. I wondered how long he had been following me, invisible. His black eyes were wide and very bright.

'He's a child,' I said.

Sam frowned at me. What difference did that make? Sam was a boy too – only just fifteen. He looked even younger, short and narrow-boned. Sam had grown up in the slums of St Giles, he was cutting purses at five years old, breaking into houses, fencing goods taken from the dead. There were a lot of dead bodies in St Giles, more than enough to make a living.

'Sam,' I said again, and patted the air with a subtle gesture. If I ordered him directly to lower the blade, it would be harder for him to do it. He had a reputation to keep.

I waited, holding my breath as Sam fought a war with himself – a war between what he wanted, *street justice*, and what I had asked of him.

He angled the blade, making the boy wince in terror, then lowered it. He slipped it back in his pocket. I breathed out.

Sam Fleet was my ward. He was also the son and heir of James Fleet, the most powerful gang captain in London. In a deal he now regretted bitterly, Fleet had hired me to teach Sam the ways of the gentry. Not so that his son might join their ranks – heaven forbid – but so he could rob and blackmail them the better. *Know thine enemy*.

An excellent plan – but then something unexpected had happened. Sam became attached to me – almost literally. Kitty called him my second shadow. Even when I banished him from my company he had found a way to steal back into my life. That was Sam's great skill – creeping about, breaking into forbidden places. He had found a secret passage into my heart, that was the truth of it. I could not, and would not, send him away again.

This left me with a singular problem – what to *do* with him, this boy raised by thieves and murderers. Sam was clever and curious, and a great consumer of information. *Facts, facts, facts* – they were his favourite things. I decided to provide him with an education. Not in the traditional sense; I did not stand over him with a cane, I was not suicidal. I answered his questions, and recommended books, and translated things from Latin for him. If this sounds as though I was his tutor, and he was my pupil, do not be mistaken. He was my brother. I loved him.

And yet I would lie awake at night, afraid of how he might put all this knowledge to use. He had told me once, in a rare moment of self-revelation, that he would like to be a surgeon. But when I watched him pore over Vesalius's *De Humani Corporis Fabrica*, his fingers tracing the intricate illustrations of bone and muscle and artery, instinct told me this was not a future member of the Company of Barbers and Surgeons sitting before me.

What could I do? Sam would become what he would become – something wonderful, or terrible, or both. In the meantime, I tried my best to influence and guide him. Pure folly. I could barely persuade him to use a fork. And his hair! Combs fled at the sight of it.

Sam whispered something horrible in his victim's ear. The boy started to cry, very hard, snot pouring from his nose.

Sam was unmoved. 'Who sent you?'

'No one sent him,' I said. I gestured to the man lying unconscious a few feet from us. 'They're just street thieves.'

'No.' Sam waved his free hand towards the scarecrow with the broken nose, who was trying and failing to stand up. 'That's Finbar

Inchguard. This in't his patch. They was stalking you, all the way from the Garden.'

Oh. I scratched my jaw, embarrassed. So much for my improved perception of danger. 'How long have *you* been following me?'

'Three days.'

He was joking. Possibly.

'We don't need all of them,' I said. 'Just the leader.' It was best to appeal to Sam's sense of logic, in such circumstances.

Sam agreed. 'Pockets,' he said to the boy.

The boy didn't really have pockets. His clothes were tattered rags, held together with dirt. But he fished out what he had from nooks and crannies within the cloth – a small pipe, a pinch of tobacco, a couple of farthings – and dropped them on the floor. He looked so dejected at their loss that I wanted to scoop them up and hand them back to him, but this was Sam's business. He knew the ways of the underworld the way a courtier knew the rules of the palace, and it was not my place to intervene.

He whispered something even more horrible in the boy's ear, then let go. The boy ran away so fast I swear I heard the air whistle as he passed.

Inchguard had given up trying to stand. He sat with his back against the wall, hands resting on his bony knees, a resigned expression on his face. Here was a man well acquainted with failure.

He craned his neck, to better view his companion. 'Dead?' His voice sounded thick and heavy through his broken nose.

'Alive,' I said, as Sam walked over to him.

'That is most generous of you, sirs,' Inchguard said, bobbing his head. 'Most civil-minded. Much obliged to you both.'

Sam delivered a sharp kick to the man's bony shins. 'You will tell us everything.'

'Oh, no doubt,' Inchguard said, amiable. 'Would you help a fellow to his feet?' There was a faint trace of Irish in his voice, I thought – by way of Newgate.

Sam rolled his eyes, but did as he was asked. Inchguard lurched up, looming over Sam – not in a sinister way, he was not capable of it. More like a tree that bends with the wind.

'Mr Thomas Hawkins, sir.' He attempted a bow. 'Finbar Inchguard, at your service. Might I buy you a drink?'

We settled upon The Ship, close by Lincoln's Inn Fields. The old tavern was aptly named – it did indeed have the compressed feel of a ship's quarters, narrow and low-beamed. Inchguard might have been Lemuel Gulliver in Lilliput, so out of scale was he with his surroundings. He was not a broad man, but very tall, with a long, pleasant face. He wore his pale blonde hair in a curious manner, straight and loose to the jaw, so that it swung about when he moved, and fell into his eyes. Even at rest, he moved in a jerking fashion, as if his limbs were controlled by a poorly trained, invisible puppeteer. Watching him stuff a pipe was one of the most inelegant things I had ever witnessed.

I lifted my ale and silently toasted my luck. *To ungainly men: may they ever trip upon their swords.*

'You know who I am,' I said. The Ship was busy, but most of its customers were clustered at the prow. We had tucked ourselves in a quiet corner, and kept our voices low.

Inchguard smiled, then regretted it. I'd split his lip in the fight. He had wounded me too, by accident, but I would worry about that later. 'Half-Hanged Hawkins?' he said, gesturing at me as if I were a prince. 'The villain who survived the rope? You're an inspiration, sir.'

'I'm not a villain.'

'Of course not.' Inchguard winked at me, then regretted that, too. His face was very swollen. 'And your friend ...?' He slid his gaze towards Sam, who was sipping small beer and staring at Inchguard without blinking. I had offered to buy him something stronger, but he did not like alcohol. He said he did not like to feel muddled. He was an odd child.

'This is my ward, Sam Fleet.'

Inchguard gave a jolt at the name, slamming his knee against the table. 'Fucking hell. A Fleet. Fuck!' He leant forward to take a closer look at Sam – the black eyes and patched clothes and general air of menace. 'I didn't know, I swear! He didn't tell me. I would *never* . . . Oh, fuck.'

Sam's lips curved, a little. What it is to be feared.

'Who didn't tell you?' I asked.

Inchguard put his head in his hands and rocked back and forth. 'Oh Finbar, you clunch. You caw-handed, spindle-shanked *clunch*.' He reached for his beer and slurped it down behind a curtain of hair.

I tried again. 'Someone paid you to attack me?'

Inchguard hesitated. 'Before I answer that,' he said, to Sam, 'I wish to attest that I did not know that Mr Hawkins was under your protection. I've been away, you understand. Out of town. And really I was not of a mind to do it, not at all. I said to myself, Inchguard, walk away. It's not worth it, not even for ten guineas—'

'Ten guineas?' I spluttered my drink. 'Someone paid you *ten guineas* to rob me?' I would have robbed myself for that.

'Not to rob you, sir,' Inchguard said, rueful. 'To kill you.'

The world stopped. I felt a rushing in my ears.

Someone wanted me dead?

'I am sorry for it,' Inchguard said, casting his eyes to the floor. 'And you have my word, I shan't try again, not for twenty guineas. Fifty! Not now we're chums. We are chums now, ain't we? All square?' He glanced plaintively at Sam.

Someone wanted me dead.

I gripped the table with both hands and took a deep, steadying breath. Pain flared along my ribs.

'Finbar Inchguard,' Sam said, quietly, 'if we was alone . . .'

'I know,' Inchguard said, hunching his shoulders at the thought. 'Lord – I *know*.'

23

Luckily for him, a servant arrived with more beer – a cheery fellow, oblivious to the dark storm cloud that had gathered over the table. I waited for him to leave.

'Who engaged you?' I asked Inchguard. 'What was his name?'

'Strait – Richard Strait.'

I raised my eyebrows at Sam. He shook his head.

'I doubt it was his real name,' Inchguard said.

A fair point. 'Where did you meet him?'

'The Golden Cross. I was to . . .' Inchguard ran a finger along his throat, 'and leave word when it was done.'

Sam frowned at him. 'You're a diver not a miller.' *A thief, not a killer.* He slipped back into St Giles cant around men like Inchguard, it was his mother tongue.

'True, true,' Inchguard nodded, his flat hair sliding over his eyes. He shoved it behind his ears. 'Never murdered no one. Don't have the stomach for it.'

'Or the brains,' Sam muttered.

'I need the coin,' Inchguard explained. 'I was marinated for nimming fish two years ago.' He held up his left thumb to show me the letter T branded on his skin. 'Came home a little early.'

I could translate most of this. Inchguard had been transported two years ago for stealing 'fish', whatever that was. Silver, perhaps? The T was an indelible sign that he was a thief, pardoned and sent off to the colonies for a few years of indentured labour. Well, that was the legal term for it, but in truth it was a form of temporary slavery. Anyone who came back before their time was sentenced to death, without exception. The courts did not show mercy twice. This was why Inchguard was desperate enough to consider murder. His own life was under threat.

'They'll hang me if they catch me,' he said. 'And I'm easy to find.' He lifted up his arms, fingers brushing the ceiling. 'It's a woeful impediment in my trade, a memorable appearance.'

A memorable appearance. I was struck with an idea. 'Richard Strait – could you describe him to me? In close detail?'

Inchguard pondered this for a moment, eyes closed. 'Aye. I think so. He had a rum complexion, bright red and sort of ... scuffed.'

'Wait,' I said, and asked Sam to fetch some paper and a pencil.

I drank my beer while we waited, touching a hand to my side to probe my injuries. At least one cracked rib, I thought. My right hand was swollen, knuckles torn and bloody, and I could feel bruises forming on my legs and back.

'Sorry,' Inchguard said. 'If it's any help, my nose hurts to buggery.'

'What will you do now?' I felt unaccountably concerned for the man's welfare. True, he had just tried to kill me, but he'd made such a wretched pass at it I couldn't take it personally. 'You should leave London.'

Inchguard agreed at once, cheerfully. He should leave. He *would* leave. He had family in County Durham. He liked sheep, he said, and thought he could be quite happy walking the fields with a dog, herding them. This sounded a trifle vague, but certainly an improvement on murdering people.

'Inchguard – why did you follow me all the way from Covent Garden?' I must have been walking the streets for at least two hours. I'd given him plenty of time and opportunity for an ambush. 'Why wait until I was almost home again?'

He tilted his head. 'You seemed a touch melancholic, sir. Never kick a man when he's down, as the saying is. But then you cheered up nicely on the last stretch. You must have a fine woman waiting for you at home, eh?'

'You weren't struggling with your conscience, then?'

'Oh, I'm always struggling with something. Came out clumsy, my mam says.'

Poor woman.

Sam returned with a square of paper, which he laid out upon the table. Inchguard resumed his description of Richard Strait, which Sam endeavoured to transform into a decent portrait. Sam was an excellent artist but even he struggled to capture the likeness of a man he had never met. It took several attempts and many corrections from Inchguard, but at last the mysterious Mr Strait emerged from beneath Sam's pencil.

'There he is,' Inchguard said, tapping the drawing.

There he was – the stranger who wanted me dead. He was a tough, sullen-looking man of middling years, with dark, straight brows and a head shaped like a shovel. 'Never smiled,' Inchguard said, but that was to be expected, under the circumstances. His rotten teeth didn't help narrow the search much, but every man has *something* that defines him. For instance, if I were describing Sam I might say: a short, lean, olive-skinned boy, with a great mass of black curls and *unnerving black eyes that can strip a man bare to his very soul.* Or if I were to describe myself, I would mention my legs, specifically my calves, which are very good. There are plenty of fellows who stuff pads under their stockings in the vain hope of achieving such an admirable shape.

In Richard Strait's case, it was his skin. From Inchguard's description, it was clear he suffered from some chronic affliction. His forehead was covered in dry, crusty scabs, and there were red patches around his eyes and covering his neck.

'Anything else you can recall?' I asked. 'Did he have an accent?'

'He wasn't born in London,' Inchguard said, swallowing the last of his beer. 'West Country? Rough speaking. Not a gentleman.'

Yet able to lay out ten guineas without trouble. A servant, most likely, with a hidden master. I sighed, and tucked the charcoal drawing in my pocket. It had been such a *pleasant* summer.

'Trouble,' I said to Sam, as we walked home.

He looked pleased. Trouble was interesting. Trouble was profitable. Before we'd left, he had shaken Inchguard for all his loose coin.

I touched his shoulder. 'You saved my life today. I won't forget it.'

He smiled again, but said nothing. No need to speak unless there was something vital to say.

We crossed Drury Lane, darting in front of a cart filled with perturbed geese.

'Sam – what does fish mean, in cant?'

He looked up at me, confused. 'It means . . . fish.'

'Inchguard was transported for stealing *fish*?'

'Two crates' worth. That's how they caught him. The *smell*.'

We both laughed. It hurt my ribs.

By the time we reached the Pistol, my right hand had swollen to twice its size. Sam hurried off to buy some ice. I stood in the shadowed hallway, my chest flashing with pain at every breath. I could hear Kitty pacing upstairs, in what sounded like a pair of clogs. I suspected she had slipped them on for my return, so that she might stomp out her disapproval above my head.

'Kitty?' I called up the stairs.

There was a long, hollow silence.

'Kitty? Sweetheart? I'm home.'

Her voice drifted down from the bedchamber, angry and hurt. 'I am not speaking to you, Thomas Hawkins. Ever again.'

I leant against the wall to stop myself from sinking to the floor. I had been too preoccupied in the tavern to realise how badly I was injured. Even calling up the stairs was painful.

'I'm sorry, angel. I'm a knave. A scoundrel.' When this had no effect I cleared my throat – and swallowed any residual pride. 'Everything was entirely my fault."

*I offer these five magical words as a gift. Use them wisely and sparingly, as they are more potent than witchcraft. If you are very lucky, your opponent might even disagree with you, and insist that no, *they* were to blame. Either way, the situation is resolved and you are free to shake hands, clap shoulders or leap into bed, depending on the circumstances. One final warning: speak these words only after a light squabble, where the actual fault is of no consequence. This is not a phrase to be uttered at one's trial for murder.

There was another long pause, and then the sound of a door opening. Clogged footsteps, the creak of a broken floorboard, needing to be fixed.

'Of course it was your fault,' she snapped. She had stopped on the landing, which meant that I could see nothing of her, save for a pair of clogs and about six inches of gown. She had no view of me at all. I was very much looking forward to her walking down the stairs and discovering my *terrible injuries*. She would feel awful, when she saw them.

'You will not sleep here tonight,' she continued. 'Or any night,' she added, with less conviction. 'I banish you from this house. *And from my heart.*'

Oh, that was an excellent line, I was envious of that one. I groped for a suitable response – something wry and witty, and a touch wounded – but my head felt queer of a sudden, and then my legs melted beneath me and everything went black.

When I opened my eyes I was lying on the floor, and Kitty was kneeling over me, looking worried. She pressed a cool hand to my cheek. It felt wonderful. 'Tom! Darling. You're hurt.'

I was forgiven, how lovely. I should faint more often. 'Fight. Lincoln's Inn.' I wanted to say more, but my head was still muddled. 'Ribs.'

'Poor love.' She kissed me, then crinkled her nose. 'You taste of beer. Tom, *were* you attacked, or did you fall over drunk again? I shan't mind either way,' she added, in a voice that said she probably would.

I gave her my best, offended stare.

She sighed, relented. 'Look at you. You have only been gone two and a half hours.'

I smiled secretly at that, because now I knew that she had missed me, and had been counting the minutes (or at least the half-hours) until my return. But I also saw that her eyes were red, and her face was blotchy from crying. 'Kitty,' I said, as she helped me to my feet. 'I am truly sorry. I didn't mean—'

'I know, I know.' She draped my arm around her shoulder and led me through the darkened bookshop, down to the little kitchen area beyond. 'We fell into Gonson's trap, didn't we?'

'We did.'

The kitchen was my favourite spot in the house, save for my bed. Everything I loved was within reach: wine, cheese, bread, beer, tobacco, a small pile of books, brandy. More wine. An old armchair by the warm range.

Our housekeeper Alice was busy at the stove, preparing a lamb stew for supper. Tendrils of blonde hair had escaped her cap and stuck to her forehead.

I pulled off my coat, wincing in pain. 'Well Kitty. Alice.' I paused, but there was no gentle way to say it. 'Someone just tried to kill me.'

'Oh, Tom,' Kitty groaned, covering her face with her hands. 'Not *again.*'

I removed my waistcoat and shirt, standing half naked by the heat of the range. A large bruise was spreading over my left side. I probed it with my fingers as I had done in The Ship, then took a deeper breath. Pain seared through me. Two broken ribs, without a doubt. Damn it. Smoking would be torture.

I poured myself a glass of brandy, and was about to start my tale of Inchguard, and Mr Strait, and the ten guineas, when Sam arrived with the ice. He settled the bucket on the table next to my parcels from Spitalfields. The oysters were squashed and ruined, brown paper soaked with blood. Alice frowned at the gruesome package, then at Sam. She had never trusted him – she couldn't see the light in him, only the dark. It did not help that Sam knew this, and found it amusing.

I wrapped a handful of ice in a cloth and pressed it to my bruised ribs. The brandy helped too, warming me from the inside. I lowered myself down into my chair, and took another swig.

Kitty remained quiet, but it was the quiet of a tight-lidded pot, simmering on the fire. She listened carefully as I described Inchguard's attack and subsequent confession.

'Gonson,' she said, when I was finished.

'No, surely not.' Gonson was a man of the law and of the church. He would not hire a man to commit murder, not in a thousand years.

Kitty disagreed. 'You can't believe this is a coincidence? What! We hear nothing from him for months, and then the very day he returns, you are attacked in the street? By some prick who was *paid* to do it? Gonson *hates* you, Tom. I'm sure he could find a way to justify it. He would say . . .' She thought for a moment, then puffed out her chest, and bellowed: '"This is for the greater good. Thomas Hawkins is a devil, and it is my duty to send him to hell."'

I smiled. Kitty was an excellent mimic. 'Why would he hire Strait, and then order him to hire a second man?'

'To keep himself at a distance. To protect himself.' She clicked her fingers. 'Perhaps Strait is a member of the Society? One of his informers?'

'It is too fantastical . . .'

'He wanted you dead before, Tom – and you hanged for it. Was *that* not fantastical?'

I fell silent, musing. There was a difference, surely. When Gonson had pursued me past winter, he had truly believed I was guilty of murder. And still he followed the law – for the most part. The idea that he would stoop to such ugly means, for *me* . . . Was I really such a threat to the world, that he would risk his own soul? No – it was not credible.

'*He* could have done it,' Alice said, glaring at Sam, who was sitting at the table, smashing shards of ice with his dagger. 'He knows every villain in London.'

Sam grinned at her.

'He saved my life, Alice.' The truth of this struck me again. I could have died in that alley, my throat cut wide, and no one would have known who did it, or why. Another robbery that had turned into murder. Buried at six and twenty, and not much to show for it.

Kitty looped an arm about Sam's neck and kissed the side of his head. 'Thank you, Sam,' she whispered.

Sam did not like to be hugged, but he made an exception for Kitty. 'Welcome,' he muttered.

'He could have paid them to attack you,' Alice persisted. 'So you'd be in his debt.'

To be fair, this was precisely the sort of thing Sam might do.

'No. It was Gonson,' Kitty said again, more firmly. 'I am sure of it.'

I did not agree with her. But we had argued enough for one day.

Later, after supper, I sat by the stove, drinking brandy and trying to ignore the pain in my ribs. Alice had gone to bed, and Sam was out doing whatever he did at night. It was best not to ask – he wouldn't tell me either way.

Kitty drifted about the room, worried and angry – an unhappy combination.

'All will be well,' I said.

'You always say that. And it never is.'

'Come sit on my lap.'

She hesitated, then did as I asked. Pain tore through me as she settled down, her head to my chest, but it was worth it. I breathed her in, the sweet scent of her hair and skin.

'I am sorry,' I said. For the argument, for the cruel things I had said, for bringing yet more trouble home with me.

She kissed me on my collarbone, one of the few places that didn't hurt. 'I know.'

'I adore my new swordstick. I wish I'd had it with me.'

'I broke it,' she said. 'I snapped the case over my knee in a rage.'

'Did you?'

'No. But I thought about it. Infuriating *idiot*.'

'Old *baggage*.'

We both laughed. The fight was over, and we were friends again. We sat in silence for a while, sharing the brandy. I drifted into a half-sleep, exhausted. When I woke, Kitty was staring up at me, her face lit by the dying glow of the stove. I had a sense that she had been watching me for some time.

'I won't lose you, Tom,' she said, softly. 'No matter the cost. I won't lose you.'

'No,' I promised, and smiled at her. 'You won't.'

Chapter Four

The next morning, we burnt the books.

I woke alone, as I did most mornings, Kitty having slid from our bed early and left me sleeping. The sun streamed through a gap in the shutters, casting a white-gold slice of light across the sheets. My body was stiff and sore, but otherwise I was content under the blankets until I remembered – *Gonson*.

I shoved on a pair of breeches and limped down the stairs. Teetering piles of books and pamphlets lay stacked in the hallway. As I opened the door to the shop Kitty bustled out, carrying a tower that rose up to her nose. She gave me a warning glare over the top, as if to say, *start nothing with me today, or I shall tip these over your head.*

The shop was in disarray – furniture pushed to the walls, books thrown to the floor. A thick cloud of dust hung in the air, making my nose itch.

Alice stood upon a ladder, gathering more books from a high shelf.

'Those are good,' Kitty called up to her.

'They are all *good*,' I said.

'How do you feel this morning, sweetheart?' Kitty asked in the bright voice she used to change the subject. 'Shall I make a fresh plaster for your bruises?'

Alice began to slot the *good* books back upon the shelves. Kitty stopped her. 'Let's wash and perfume the walls before we replace anything.'

I folded my arms. 'A well-scrubbed shop for well-scrubbed souls?' Kitty threw me a tired look. 'Have you come to help, Tom?' She knew I had not.

Alice flapped a cloth along a shelf, dislodging a cloud of dust. I sneezed, then cursed as pain tore along my broken ribs. Fleeing the room, I sat upon the stairs and surrendered to an agonising coughing fit. Once I had recovered, I pulled on my cloak and boots and stepped outside.

Russell Street was always busy, but Monday mornings brought a great press of tradesfolk, livestock, carts and chairs rushing along in both directions. As I waited for safe passage across the road, I studied the passers-by with more scrutiny than usual. Inchguard had promised he would not strike again and I believed him – his need for money was easily outweighed by his fear of the Fleets. But Strait might have engaged more than one gang to attack me. He might come after me himself.

I knew most of my neighbours, not only on Russell Street but along Drury Lane and through its maze of alleys, and down to the Strand. It was my village. I knew the street boys and harlots who made a profit from their bodies and from their light fingers, the washerwomen with loads strapped to their backs, the girls who trudged in from the country with fresh herbs and trudged home again before dark. And they knew me, of course: Half-Hanged Hawkins.

An old fellow plodding by on a donkey caught my eye and waved. Then he wrapped an invisible rope about his neck and pretended to hang from it, tongue lolling from his mouth. He did this every time I saw him, and thought it was a tremendous joke. I smiled back through gritted teeth then crossed the road. I would feel better once I'd had some breakfast.

In Jenkins' bakery, Hannah Jenkins was tending the oven while chatting with her sister. My stomach rumbled as I breathed in one of the few agreeable smells to be found in this city: fresh bread, warm pastry, jam and fruit. Mrs Jenkins ran the bakery with her husband, but he had been ailing for months and was like to die before Christmas, everyone said. Her sister had travelled from Staffordshire to help with the grandchildren and the business. Mrs Jenkins' only daughter had died after giving birth to her second child. The father was a sailor, and often away.

Mrs Jenkins adored me. If I had wanted to grow as round as a pound cake, I could have lived solely on her baking, as she refused all payment. She had not always been so affectionate. At my trial for murder, she had denounced me as arrogant and wicked. This had come as no surprise – she was a shameless gossip, and her thrill at taking part in one of the most notorious trials of the century was palpable. I *was* surprised when she paid me a visit a few months later, on my return from Yorkshire. Her demeanour was so altered I thought she had taken sick.

'I am ashamed of myself, Mr Hawkins,' she said in a wavering voice, clutching herself for comfort. 'When I think, you almost died and I had a part in it . . .' She burst into tears. 'Oh, sir! Can you ever forgive me?'

When I was arrested outside my home, some of my neighbours had tried to mob me. When I was pardoned, those same people came up to me in the street to shake my hand. *I knew you were innocent! I am so glad to see you well!* Mrs Jenkins was the only one who admitted her fault, and apologised. I admired her very much for it, and we were now good friends.

This did not mean she had deserted her role as Covent Garden's most determined gossip – far from it. *The Daily Jenkins*, I called her.

'Thomas!' she cried, rushing towards me with her arms outstretched. She was near sixty, with a limp that mysteriously vanished when she was in a hurry. She reminded me of one of her unbaked buns, soft and rounded, and trailing flour. 'Are you well? I hear you were set upon in the street by a gang of villains—'

'Indeed—'

'And two ribs broken.' She closed her eyes and shuddered. 'I cannot bear to think of them, snapping like twigs.'

Mrs Jenkins frequently said she could not bear to think of something, while thinking of it in exquisite detail. If it were ghoulish and bloody, all the better.

'Do not show me your bruises, I will faint,' she said, taking out her spectacles. I pulled up my shirt, standing by the window where the light was best.

'Heavens!' she exclaimed, and called her sister over to take a look.

I pulled my breeches down below my left hip, revealing a long red scrape and more bruising. Mrs Jenkins, eyes shining, declared upon her life that she had never seen anything so terrible. 'And where did this happen, Thomas?'

'By Lincoln's Inn. Near The Ship.'

She gave me a reproachful look, as if I had said, 'In hell, near the lake of eternal fire', then reeled off a gruesome litany of assaults and robberies that had taken place around Lincoln's Inn over the past few weeks. 'You should know better,' she scolded, and she was not wrong.

Sam had made two copies of his Richard Strait portrait. I took one from my pocket and handed it to Mrs Jenkins with a flourish. 'You are the first to see this,' I said, and watched her swell like rising dough. *So much news!* 'Calls himself Richard Strait. He paid them to attack me.'

Mrs Jenkins glared at the portrait. 'The *devil*. This wouldn't happen in Burton,' she told her sister, crowing a little.

Her sister agreed it would not.

I asked Mrs Jenkins if she would show it to her friends and customers. 'In a quiet, close way,' I added. I did not want Strait to know that I was hunting for him.

'Have no fear,' she replied. 'I am famed for my discretion.'

Her sister made a small, strangled noise.

Mrs Jenkins held the portrait up to the light. 'And he wants you *dead?* Mercy. What did you do to offend him, Thomas?'

'Not a thing!'

The sisters exchanged doubtful looks. 'I'm sure you're right, dear,' Mrs Jenkins said. 'But I should have a ponder, all the same. If I were you.' And then she gave me a bun, slathered in butter.

It was good advice, I thought, as I ate my gift. What *had* I done to offend Richard Strait? Or, more likely, his master? If I knew that, I might be able to find him and square the matter. This could all be some ridiculous misunderstanding.

Mrs Jenkins asked me about Gonson's visit the day before. She had spied him through the window. 'You would think he'd leave you in peace after what he did to you. I don't suppose he came to apologise, did he?'

'No, indeed.' I told her of his plans to 'rescue' Kitty from sin, and how we were to build a bonfire in the street this morning.

'So that's what they're about.' She nodded through the open door. Kitty and Alice were piling books in the middle of the road, much to the consternation of those trying to pass by. Kitty stood guard over the heap while Alice went back into the shop for more. 'A bonfire of books,' Mrs Jenkins said with a frown. 'I do not like the sound of that.'

'We should bake some pastries for the crowds,' her sister suggested.

'Oh, we should not profit from poor Kitty's misfortune ... Should we?' Mrs Jenkins gave me a hopeful look. She had lost all her savings trying to find a cure for her husband.

'Of course you should,' I said. 'Be sure to cram a few buns in Gonson's mouth. Spare us all from his honking.'

As if I had conjured him, I heard his voice bellowing up the street. Leaving Mrs Jenkins to her work, I ducked out of the door. Gonson was strutting towards the Pistol at the head of a large procession – at least twenty members of the Society for the Reformation of Manners, plus half a dozen guards. His followers cheered and sang as they marched along, shoving people out of the way with their elbows, drunk on self-righteousness and the promise of fire.

Kitty stood alone next to the great pile of books, her face and clothes smeared with dirt and dust. She set her shoulders back as Gonson approached, one notch below defiance. At the last moment she dropped into a deep curtsy, hand pressed upon her heart. Anyone who knew her would recognise the mockery in it. Gonson did not.

'Praise be to God!' he cried, sweeping his arm towards the books. 'For this is His will! Today, a day that shall not be forgotten, we shall burn these foul works of depravity, and grind the ash beneath our boots!'

His followers brayed their approval.

I pushed my way through the gathering crowds. Neighbours leant from their windows, enjoying the spectacle, but the women of the brothel opposite kept their shutters closed. They used to laugh when Gonson paid his visits, calling out lewd offers from the balcony. In recent months he had sent some of them to Bridewell, and others to the pillory. They did not laugh at him anymore.

Gonson's face fell as he saw me. 'You are not welcome, Hawkins,' he snapped. 'This is a decent, Christian gathering.'

I took Kitty's hand, and stood my ground.

Irritated, Gonson turned to the crowd and continued his speech. 'My friends! Good citizens . . .'

I sighed. Sermons always gave me a headache. I leant down to whisper in Kitty's ear. 'There is still time to stop this.'

'I don't care about the books,' she muttered. 'As long as you are safe.'

'We must root out evil, wherever we find it,' Gonson roared, clenching his fist. 'We must be ceaseless in our vigilance—'

'They're only *books*,' someone yelled.

Gonson swooped on him. 'Do not underestimate their power, sir!' He picked a volume from the pile and thrust it in the air.

38

'Gentlemen! Trust me – this is more dangerous to your wives and your children than the sharpest blade. A knife may cut through flesh. But this – this *perversion* of literature – injures the *soul*. Would you consign yourselves to the pits of hell, in exchange for a few moments of sordid pleasure?'

'No!' his followers shouted. 'Never!' I recognised at least three of them as customers.

'No indeed,' Gonson declaimed. 'No indeed! So I say to you my friends: let them burn!'

His followers surged forward, scuffling for the best position. As the crowd parted Gonson caught my eye.

'Let them burn!' he cried again, sweeping his arm towards me. 'As the wicked corrupters of the world shall burn for ever in the reckoning fire!'

The crowd turned its gaze upon me.

'Villain!' a man shouted.

'Arsehole!' someone called back at him. 'Leave him be.'

The crowd pressed closer. Someone jabbed their elbow into me, catching my rib. I hissed in pain.

'Tom,' Kitty said, in alarm. Someone jostled her from behind.

I grabbed her before she fell. She was shaking – the bravest woman I knew. Even Gonson looked uneasy, and well he should. No one could control a London mob in full flow. They could just as easily turn upon him as me. He beckoned to the nearest guard and shouted at him to light his torch. The guard did as he was told, the pitch catching light in a bright blaze.

The crowd, sensing fresh drama, fell still.

Gonson raised his arms. 'These books are an insult to our Lord, who died for our sins. In His glorious name – let them burn!'

'Amen!' a man shouted next to me.

The crowd began to chant, louder and louder. '*Let them burn, let them burn.*'

ANTONIA HODGSON

Kitty squeezed my hand tightly. A crowd that would burn books would burn people, given the chance.

The guard lowered his torch, and the first pamphlet caught fire. The flames spread quickly, leaping from book to book. Soon the whole pile was ablaze, the fire warming the air as smoke billowed up into the sky. Gonson drew his friends around him and they prayed together, eyes shining.

'See how the Lord our God speaks to us from the midst of the fire!' Gonson cried.

'Good grief,' I muttered to Kitty. 'He thinks he's Moses.'

Kitty, glaring into the flames, didn't answer. She was furious, and doing everything she could to hide it. And that made *me* angry, because there was nothing I liked more than to see Kitty in the raw, unshackled. Even when she was shouting at me, there was something glorious about her rages, her explosions. Yet here she was, restraining herself in order to protect me.

'When this is done,' I murmured in her ear, 'we shall go back into the Pistol and scream and curse and kick things all afternoon.'

Kitty, distracted, did not hear me. 'What's happening over there?' She lifted herself on tiptoes.

I followed her gaze towards a disturbance at the furthest fringes of the crowd. Craning my neck, I glimpsed the towering horns of a familiar antique wig.

'Oh . . .' I said, and grinned down at Kitty. 'Trouble.'

Everett Felblade, apothecary and contrarian, was carving a straight, determined path through the crowd, whacking anyone who resisted with his stick. He was carrying a bucket in the crook of his arm, water sloshing over the edge.

Felblade – our close neighbour – was the most irascible fellow I had ever met. He did not give a withered fig for morals, for authority, for anything much save his own opinion. One could see that in his choice of wig – a unique concoction the colour of cheap tallow, with twin, spiralled horns and long, greasy curls that flowed over his wizened shoulders. He alone had defended me at my trial. If there was a mob, he was against it, if there was a prevailing view, he despised it.

'Gonson!' he yelled, pressing forward until he stood toe to toe with the magistrate. Felblade was the owner of numerous wooden teeth. When they dried out he would run his tongue along them to moisten them, smacking his lips hard. He did this now, before continuing. 'What monstrous conflagration is this? You will burn down half the street, you maggot-pated booby!' And with that, he tipped the bucket of water over the flames.

'Mr Felblade!' Gonson cried, outraged.

'Stand aside, sir! Or I shall throw the next one over your damned foolish head.'

The crowds parted for a team of firemen, wheeling a great engine weighed down with water. They brought the cart to a halt by the bonfire. Their leader saluted Felblade and grabbed the leather hose attached to the side.

'Stop this!' Gonson commanded.

The fireman ignored him. A great gush of water sprayed from the hose.

Gonson leapt back with a squeal, his stockings ruined. 'How dare you!' he exploded.

'How dare *you*, sir!' Felblade roared back. 'What sort of brain-addled nincompoop sets a fire in the middle of a crowded neighbourhood? I will not see my city burn again. Remember '66!'

'I order you to stop!' Gonson shouted at the firemen. 'This fire was lit upon my authority!'

It was too late. His holy conflagration had transformed into a sodden clump of wet paper and charred board. People began to drift away.

Felblade nodded to the head fireman. 'You heard the fellow. He set the fire. He will pay your fee.'

'I shall do no such thing!' Gonson spluttered, indignant.

The firemen, all great muscled fellows, turned as one and glared at him.

Felblade, who liked nothing more than to throw down a tube of gunpowder and walk away, left them to their argument. I nodded my thanks to him.

He paused in front of us, squinting at Kitty over his spectacles. 'Chin high, missy,' he instructed her, in his thin, creaking voice. 'You're worth ten of them.'

Felblade was not in the habit of doling out compliments. Kitty's eyes welled. 'Thank you, sir,' she said, her voice catching.

This was too much for Felblade. He must be at odds with the world, not evens. He hurried away down the street, before Kitty hugged him, or kissed his cheek, or performed some other despicable act of affection. As he passed Mrs Jenkins they shared a complicit nod. She must have run to fetch him.

Gonson strutted over, chest puffed, as if he had not just been roundly humiliated by a Methuselean apothecary with wooden teeth.

'Well Miss Sparks,' he said. 'We have purged your sin with fire. Do you not feel the better for it?' He waited smugly for her answer.

Kitty gritted her teeth. 'I do, Sir John. I have learnt my lesson. I shall be no more trouble. You may forget all about me,' she added, with a hopeful laugh.

'Forget you?' Gonson laughed in return. 'Impossible, my dear. No, Miss Sparks – I'm afraid your soul remains in peril. See how you are beset by devils.' He glanced in my direction. 'But I am determined to save you,' he declared. 'I shall drag you from the darkness, into the light of the Lord.' He pressed a hand down upon her shoulder. 'When the time comes, I shall be a true parent to you, my child.'

The look he gave her was not that of a parent.

Chapter Five

I went to bed early that evening, still aching from my fight with Inchguard. By morning I was feverish, with a persistent cough that sliced fresh daggers through my broken ribs. Kitty made a beeswax plaster for my chest, rubbing it into my skin with smooth, gentle strokes. Her touch soothed me more than the remedy.

'I need some paper,' I croaked, when she was done. I had decided to take Mrs Jenkins' advice and draw up a list of anyone I might have injured or insulted in recent months. I had already remembered three unpaid debts in the night, and a couple of idiotic feuds.

'You need rest,' Kitty corrected me. 'Or the fever will turn putrid.'

I sat up to show her I was well, coughed so hard I thought I might die, then lay back down again, defeated.

Kitty slipped under the blankets and curled up beside me, careful not to knock my ribs. 'I'm half dead myself,' she yawned. 'Why am I so tired? I am *never* tired.'

I knew the answer. She had exhausted herself yesterday, not only with the physical labour of clearing the shop, but with the spiritual labour of submitting to Sir John Gonson's will. And all for nought, as far as I could tell. 'Will you not open the shop this morning?'

After Gonson had walked away from his sodden bonfire, arguing bitterly with the firemen, Kitty had announced to the few remaining spectators that the Pistol would be open for business again on the morrow. Let Gonson raid the shop every day if he chose. He may have burnt her books, but he could not stop her from selling her cures and condoms.

'In a while,' she murmured, her voice heavy with sleep. She nudged her cold nose against my fever-hot skin and breathed in. 'You smell wonderful.' She had scented the plaster with almond oil and rose syrup.

'I smell like a courtesan,' I said, but Kitty was fast asleep, her breath tickling my chest.

I spent two days in bed, and two more wrapped in a blanket by the fire, sipping hot whisky and lemon. While I convalesced, Sam roamed the town, showing Richard Strait's portrait to his friends in the underworld and to those who fed from them – the cheats and fences and perjurers. None of them recognised Strait, or if they did, they chose not to admit it. *Thieves are never rogues among themselves,* as the saying is.

As soon as I could venture outside, I paid a visit to the men I had slighted (or who had slighted me, I really did not care at this point) and made amends. Both were happy to accept my apologies, and we shook hands as friends. After that I called upon my creditors and – to their combined astonishment – paid off my debts in full.

'So there is no need to murder me now!' I said gaily, studying their faces for any signs of guilt. They looked at me as if I were mad.

After a brief stop at Moll's for another medicinal whisky and a read of the papers I headed home, pleased by the morning's work. True, I had not unmasked the Man Who Wanted Me Dead, but I'd spent months fretting over those debts and feuds, and now I was free of them. Back at the Pistol, I made myself a pot of coffee and a pipe, and created a table of my remaining enemies. It proved illuminating, as Mrs Jenkins had predicted:

Name	Cause of Complaint Against Me	Conclusion
~~Charles Buckley~~	~~Broke his nose~~	~~A treacherous, venal arsehole, but not a murderer~~
~~Charles Howard~~	~~Ruined his plot to blackmail the king~~	~~Would murder me himself, not by proxy~~
~~Sir John Gonson~~	~~Believes I am the Devil Incarnate~~	~~A puffed up, joyless hypocrite, but not a murderer~~
~~HM Queen Caroline~~	~~Stole ledger that could bring down monarchy~~	~~Would send one of her spies, I would be dead~~
~~Matthew Lybelle~~	~~The incident in Oxford~~	~~Have written again to apologise profusely~~
~~Allison Lybelle née Rose~~	~~The incident in Oxford~~	~~See above~~
~~Pamela Rose~~	~~The incident in Oxford~~	~~She had her revenge~~
~~Eliza Rose~~	~~The incident in Oxford~~	~~In many ways I was the injured party in all of this~~
James & Gabriela Fleet	I stole their only son	A Fleet never forgives, never forgets

Sam was asleep in his attic room. He had a tendency to nap during the day, being a child of the dark. He woke as soon as I opened the door, scrunching his face as I drew back the shutter. In the past, he had filled this room with collections of clocks, bones and whatever else obsessed him that particular month, but over the course of the summer he had conducted a series of purges. The room was now almost bare, save for a few books, and some sketches pinned to the wall – portraits of myself and Kitty, his parents and his five (five!) sisters, plus some disturbing images of cadavers pre- and post-anatomy. Alice refused to step across the threshold, which meant that the floor was dusty, the windows were smudged and the bed sheets … well, I shall leave *those* to the imagination.

I handed Sam my chart. He read his parents' names with a frown. 'I warned them. They hurt you, we're *done*.'

The thought of Sam threatening his parents on my behalf was troubling. It also confirmed what I had feared: if the Fleets were prevented from attacking me directly, they might well hire a stranger such as Strait to act on their behalf. Even better, have Strait hire Inchguard, and place the whole plot at one further remove. If Sam could not trace the attack back to his parents, how could he blame them for it?

I asked Sam to set up a meeting with his father.

'He's in Liverpool. Sister.'

'You have an aunt? You've never mentioned her.'

Sam shrugged. 'Respectable.'

'*Respectable*?' An honest Fleet? Verily, the world was filled with miracles and wonders. Then again, the definition of 'respectable' might be somewhat loose in Sam's family. Perhaps his aunt thanked her victims after she robbed them.

That evening I was preparing for bed when I heard a knock at the door. It was late and raining heavily – not a night for a casual visitor. I grabbed my swordstick and crept towards the stairs. Kitty came up behind me and touched my elbow. She was holding a pistol.

'Don't answer,' she whispered.

I nodded. I could see no benefit in opening the door at such a suspicious hour. Better to pretend we were sleeping, or away from home.

The knocking came again, louder and more insistent.

I stepped on to the landing, listening for voices . . .

. . . and trod on the broken floorboard.

It gave a loud, wounded moan, then cracked in two.

'Damn it!' I shouted, as a splinter pierced my bare foot. 'Gah!'

Our visitor banged harder, calling out in a familiar, rough accent. St Giles, laced with Portuguese. 'Thomas. *Foda-se*! Open the fucking door.'

Gabriela Fleet – Sam's mother.

I pulled the splinter from my foot and limped down the stairs, trapped between two furious women.

'I told you,' Kitty hissed at my back. 'A thousand times, to mend that floorboard. I wrote it IN CAPITALS.'

Gabriela stood cloaked and hooded on the doorstep, balanced in a fighter's stance, light but firm. She was wearing what looked like a gold brooch at her breast, but was in fact the hilt of a dagger she kept tucked beneath her gown. She had cut me with it once and left a long scar down my arm. I showed her my swordstick as a warning before letting her in from the drenching rain.

'Yes very good, very *big*, Thomas,' she said. Gabriela pronounced my name in the Portuguese way, with the T sounding close to a D. With a slight change to the inflection and a roll of the tongue I was transformed from Thomas into something very like 'Dormouse'. This was not accidental.

She lowered her hood, releasing a cascade of black curls streaked with silver. She too had a scar, much deeper and older than mine. It ran from her brow, dragging down her right eye and scoring her face from cheek to jaw. She had killed the man who gave it to her long ago, and the woman who had let him do it – chained them together in the brothel where they had tortured her as a girl, and burnt them alive.

Never forgive, never forget.

I glanced along the street as I closed the door. Gabriela appeared to have come alone, but appearances counted for nothing with the Fleet gang. Most likely there were men on the roof, in the back yard, in the shadows.

'My God, it is so clean, so tidy,' Gabriela said to Kitty, as she passed through the bookshop to the kitchen beyond.

Kitty had inherited the Pistol from Samuel Fleet, Gabriela's brother-in-law. Throughout his strange and violent life, Samuel had used chaos, confusion, lies and deception as his weapons – and had dressed his living quarters accordingly. When I was thrown into the Marshalsea for debt, I'd been forced to share his squalid cell, filled from top to bottom with festering heaps of clothes, books, papers, plates, elephant tusks and other queer *objets*. It was a clever if disgusting way to disarm and distract anyone foolish enough to visit.

Samuel had loved Kitty's father Nathaniel, and regarded Kitty as his surrogate daughter. He had left his business and a large sum of money to her in his will. (Samuel had not been imprisoned in the Marshalsea for debt, but because – as the old king's most effective assassin – the new king could not decide what to do with him. 'Too dangerous to live, too useful to kill,' as Samuel had put it.)

You might imagine that the remaining Fleets would try to steal Kitty's fortune back. Not so. Samuel was family, and they respected his last wish. In any case, knowing Samuel, he would have left them an equal fortune, one less *legitimate* than Kitty's, but just as valuable.

Gabriela sat down at the head of Samuel's old dining table. The surface was scratched and stained, hinting at old stories and lives now lost. She placed a finger on a deep scratch and followed it to its end, remembering.

I sat down opposite her.

She glowered at me across the table. Such a shame. We had liked each other when we'd first met – before Sam had attached himself to me.

'My husband wants you dead,' she said.

Kitty cocked her pistol and aimed it at Gabriela's head. 'Say that again. I dare you.'

Gabriela gestured to a seat between us. 'Sit down, Kitty. I have come to talk.'

Kitty hesitated, then joined us. She kept the pistol cocked and levelled.

Gabriela smiled, indulgent. Her hatred for me did not extend to Kitty. Kitty had shot Samuel's murderer through the heart – with the very pistol she was now holding, in fact. For that alone she was respected by the Fleet gang.

Gabriela pulled the dagger from her gown and placed it on the table. She probably had another six tucked away but the message appeared genuine. *Parley.*

Kitty lowered her pistol, and poured out three glasses of wine. But she kept her eyes upon Gabriela and the blade. We both did.

Gabriela raised her glass to me in a mock toast, and drank. 'My husband wants to kill you,' she said, again. 'But I said: no, James. We kill him, our son will never forgive us. I tell my husband: Wait. Sam will learn soon enough, this man he calls *brother*,' she spat the word out, 'is a worthless cunt.'

Kitty laughed, then covered her mouth. 'Sorry, angel. It was the way she said it.'

Gabriela downed her wine and reached for her blade, as if this concluded the matter.

'Wait, wait,' I said, waving her back down. 'That is your proof of innocence? I am supposed to take you upon your word?'

'Yes.' Gabriela frowned, offended. 'Dormouse, I have so many ways to kill you. You think I would hire *Inchguard*?'

I shrugged.

Gabriela drummed her fingers on the table. She had something to say, but was reluctant to say it. She poured herself another glass then toyed with it, turning it round and round with her long, nimble fingers. She wore no rings. The Fleets never displayed their stolen wealth – discretion kept them from the noose. To look at Gabriela in her patched and faded gown, one would never guess she was the Queen of the Underworld.

'I love my son,' she said, at last. 'My son ... loves you.' Ahh, how she hated to admit that! She fixed me with a disgusted look.

'You die, this hurts him. Breaks his heart. I will never hurt Sam. *Never.* So I do nothing. I wait for him to come home, where he belongs.'

I rubbed my forehead. I might disagree with Gabriela on many things, I might despise the way she had raised her son, the way she called him her *tiger*, as if he were a predator and not a child. But she did love him – ferociously. She would rather die than cause him pain.

I may have crossed the Fleets from my list, but I did not sleep well that night. I thought about Sam, how he looked up to me and enjoyed my company, for reasons I only half understood. What if I lost his respect? What if I were forced to betray him? *What if he died in my care?* It was not the first time I had asked myself these unsettling questions, but Gabriela's visit had brought them into sharp clarity. Calling Sam my brother came with benefits – he had saved my life at Lincoln's Inn – but there were risks too. He was fifteen. Would he still love me at twenty? Thirty? Without his protection, his parents would be free to enact their revenge. They were not known for their mercy.

Well – there was nothing to be done about it. Why waste time worrying about the future? The present held enough terrors of its own. Somewhere in London, someone loathed me so much that they wanted me dead. And yet I had no idea who they were, or what I had done to inspire such hatred.

That was quite enough to keep me awake till dawn.

———

On Jermyn Street, behind a door with a lion's head, the man Inchguard knows as Richard Strait stands before his mistress.

'You failed,' she says.

A bead of sweat trickles down Strait's back. The room is like a jungle – the dark green walls, the lacquered furniture painted with tangled vines, the air thick with scent. And it's hot, hot as the tropics, the shutters closed tight and muffled with velvet curtains, while the fire rages in the hearth. There is even a parrot, with green and orange feathers. It sits in a corner in a golden cage, silent and watchful.

'He was protected.' Strait clenches his fists, not from anger, but from the desire to scratch. The heat agitates his skin – the weeping red patches on his forehead and throat itch like hell. She knows this, of course, and doesn't care.

He has waited three days before telling her about the disastrous attack at Lincoln's Inn. She has been in a bloody awful mood – worse than usual. And when she's angry, she makes sure that everyone around her suffers. He isn't bothered so much for himself, he can take it, but he does feel sorry for the girl. That is one thing we might say about him – he does feel sorry for the girl. She sits on the floor between them, playing with a wooden puppet, and humming to herself.

Lady Vanhook places a long, slender hand upon the girl's head. At once, the humming stops.

'Could he trace the attack back to us?'

Strait shrugs. 'Shouldn't think so.'

She stares at him.

He corrects himself hastily. 'No, my lady. I'm certain of it.'

She lets the silence grow between them, her hand upon the girl's head, her pale blue eyes fixed upon his.

'Well,' she says at last, pouring all her contempt into the word. 'If you are certain. Go. You too,' she says to the girl, who jumps up from the floor and is gone, before her mistress can change her mind.

Strait bows as he leaves the room – relieved, as always, to be out of her presence. Another week of this, he tells himself, and I'll go back to Bristol. It's not worth it – cooped up here like that fucking parrot.

But she has promised that everything will be different by Christmas. By then, he will have twenty guineas a year and an army of servants beneath him, to do his bidding.

He can wait until Christmas.

Alone, Lady Vanhook rises like a dancer and moves to the fire, staring into the flames. She runs her finger along the edge of the fire screen and frowns at the smudges of coal dust.

She is not surprised the plan failed. She had made the order on a whim – she had liked the way it sounded. 'I want Thomas Hawkins dead. See it done.'

No. Now she thinks upon it, she is glad he survived. His death would have brought a moment's pleasure, no more. It will be so much more satisfying to make him suffer. To destroy everything he loves. To break his spirit. Death would be a kindness then, and Lady Vanhook is not a kind woman. Thomas Hawkins will live on – a ruined, pathetic creature, haunted by loss.

How amusing. How wonderful.

She sits down at her desk, takes up a quill and begins to write.

PART TWO

The Trap

Chapter Six

Two weeks passed without incident. My bruises faded and my ribs began to heal. No one saw Richard Strait about town, and no one recognised his portrait. There were no further attacks on my life, and Sam was certain I was not being followed. I remained vigilant, but believed the danger had most likely passed. One cannot live in perpetual panic.

In truth I was more concerned about Kitty. As promised, she had opened the Cocked Pistol the day after Gonson's fire – but then she had closed it again a week later, for good, despite protests from her customers.

'I've grown tired of it,' she shrugged.

I found this unlikely, and said so.

'It is not the same without the books,' she said. 'And I do not need the money.'

'But you were so excited over the summer—'

'Stop *pestering* me, Tom! If *you* wish to run it, go ahead!' She folded her arms. 'I should like to see you ordering stock, and chasing bills, and managing the accounts book, and sweeping the floor, and standing on your feet for hours and hours.'

'I would bring in a chair,' I said. 'That would be my first act.'

'It's yours!' she said, flinging her arms wide. 'The shop is yours. Take it with my blessing!'

I didn't want the shop. I wanted her to want it. Kitty was born to bustle. But now she drifted about the house without purpose, or wandered alone through the city. As the days passed she grew increasingly careless of her appearance, dragging on the same dress each day and leaving half her curls unpinned. She did not shout, or kick things, or sing (badly) from the top of her lungs. She laughed rarely, and when she did, the laughter did not reach her eyes. She snapped at me over silly things, or withdrew to wherever I was not, as if she could hardly bear my company.

In the midst of this, and with impeccably bad timing, Alice asked if she might take an extended trip to Ireland with her friend Neala. (In truth the two women were far more than friends. 'Playing the game of flats', as Sam would put it.) She left the following week. I missed her kind, steady presence – and her cooking. But when I suggested we should find a temporary replacement, Kitty said we could survive well enough on our own for a few weeks. As I did not have the funds to pay for a housekeeper myself, I could not argue. So the Pistol grew ever more dusty, and I spent half my life eating in taverns and chophouses.

One evening I came upstairs to find Kitty crying silently into a pillow. When I asked what was the matter, she turned her back on me. She was tired, nothing more. Why would I not let her be?

'I don't know what to do,' I complained to Mrs Jenkins the next morning. 'She is not herself, not at all.'

'Is she eating?' she asked, her hand hovering over a bun.

I thought of Kitty cramming her face with pie at Moll's, three weeks ago now. The last night we had been happy. 'Not really. Not as she used to.'

That settled it. Mrs Jenkins made up a parcel of pastries. It was her answer to most problems.

'How is Mr Jenkins?' I asked.

She stopped in her work, and looked sad. 'He's dying, Thomas. Forty years, we've been married.' Tears glistened in her eyes. 'What shall I do without him?'

I drew her into a hug, and she had a good cry on my chest. She was warm and well padded and smelled of bread.

'You should marry Kitty,' she said, when she had recovered.

'You know I've tried. She won't let me.'

'She's a naughty minx.'

'She used to be,' I said, wistful.

I crossed the road back to the Pistol. Gonson's bonfire had left scorch marks on the cobbles – a permanent reminder of that awful day. I cursed him for the thousandth time. How was it fair that he should persecute us above all others? London was beset with problems: disease, poverty, crime and corruption. And yet our celebrated magistrate was too busy fighting his Holy Crusade Against Fucking to trouble himself with such *trifling* matters. *Honestly*. If I were magistrate . . .

It was then that I had my Great and Momentous Idea.

'Kitty!' I said, leaping down the stairs to the kitchen. She was settled by the fire, knees to her chin, her hair loose about her shoulders. 'Sweetheart! I have just had the best idea in the history of the world!'

She dragged her gaze up from the floor. 'Have you, Tom?' Her voice was flat and low.

I dropped Mrs Jenkins' parcel on the table and spread my hands wide. 'A new venture.'

She stared at the parcel. 'Baking?'

'No, no. I am going to be . . .' Not a magistrate – heaven spare me from that dreaded fate. How to describe it? 'I am going to help people in trouble.'

Kitty knitted her brows. 'What sort of trouble?'

'Oh . . . Blackmail, fraud. Absconding husbands. Miscellaneous roguery. Mysteries,' I said, suddenly inspired. 'We could solve *mysteries*.'

'We . . .?'

I dragged a chair to the fire and sat opposite her, taking her hands. 'Yes – you and me, together! Think of our triumph at Fountains Abbey—'

'We almost died!'

'Briefly! But we unmasked a killer.'

She gave a half-smile, remembering. 'I suppose.'

'And Sam can help us.'

'You want *Sam* to catch villains?' She raised an eyebrow. But she was taken with the notion, as I knew she would be. Kitty loved puzzles and mysteries, she loved excitement, and she loved my company. How could she resist?

I jumped up again. 'It's settled, then. I shall place an announcement in the *Journal*. We'll transform the shop into an office, invite people to visit with their problems . . .'

'Not here, Tom. Not to our home.'

'Oh. No. I suppose not.' I faltered for a moment. 'Moll's, then. She won't mind you being there, if we limit the hours and offer her a cut. Let's go there now and celebrate.' I grabbed her by the hand and pulled her up.

'Wait.' She stepped back. 'I can't.'

'Of course you can. Sweetheart, please – we have not ventured out together since Gonson—'

His name landed between us.

Her shoulders sagged, the light in her eyes fading. 'It's a fine idea, Tom. Truly. But you must do it alone.'

And that was that.

I spent the next few days planning my new endeavour. I suppose I should have felt ashamed – a gentleman reduced to selling his services. Quite the reverse. I felt revived. I was tired of lurking about at home – I must be out in company, exchanging stories and meeting new folk.

I also needed money – there's the truth of it. After paying off my debts, I had been left with only a handful of coins, most of which I had spent on an advertisement in the *London Journal*. I could not bear to ask Kitty for help – then I *would* have felt ashamed.

And so it was with a mixture of anticipation and anxiety that I set off to Moll's on my first day *in business*, freshly shaved and swordstick in hand. Would anyone come? Was there any demand for such a novel service? I had no idea.

October had straggled into a grey November; wet leaves on the cobbles, and a grim, drizzling rain. In the piazza, Everett Felblade was haggling with a fruitseller, a basket hooked over his arm. It reminded me of the bucket of water he had tipped over Gonson's bonfire. I smiled to myself at the memory.

'Worm-filled abomination!' he declared, thrusting a ripe, healthy apple under the fruitseller's nose. 'You should be ashamed of yourself.'

The fruitseller, a young fellow called Platt, offered his customer a patient smile. He, his father, and his father before him had all dealt with Felblade and his idiosyncrasies.

'Hawkins!' Felblade beckoned me over. 'Regard this pestilent globe!'

It struck me that a decaying apple would suit his wooden teeth rather well, but disagreeing with Felblade was a singular waste of time. I muttered something diplomatic and tipped my hat.

Felblade, seeing that I was in a hurry to leave, must of course force me to stay. 'Where are you going? What's the rush, boy? Strutting about before noon, fresh shaved and sober – that's not your style. What are you about?'

Platt gave me a sympathetic look and turned to another customer.

I opened my mouth to reply. '—'

'Where's the girl? Are you not *conjoined*? Cteatus and Eurytus, never to be parted?' Felblade narrowed his eyes, suspicious. 'I spied her from my window yesterday, hair all dragglesome. She looked dreadful! Miss Sparks has lost her spark! Hah! What have you done to her? Is she sick? Why have you not brought her to me? Well? Why do you not answer? Come, come boy.'

There were many, many reasons why I had not brought Kitty to Felblade. It was a measure of my desperation that I paused now, and sought his advice.

'Melancholia,' Felblade pronounced, when I had described her symptoms. 'Excess of black bile. Clogs the mind and slows the blood. Bland nourishment and light beer, that's the remedy. Nothing spiced, nothing salty. And plenty of fruit.'

Platt, sensing an opportunity, waved an apple under my nose. 'Penny for three, sir.'

I gave him a pained look. Kitty would not want her sickness debated by every stallholder in the market. Then again, I had already spoken to Mrs Jenkins about her. No doubt the Highland clans were discussing the matter over their morning porridge by now.

Felblade threw his basket at Platt. 'I will pay you a ha'penny for six and you'll consider yourself damned lucky, you conniving thief.'

Platt, who was used to this, deposited six apples in Felblade's basket and balanced a free orange on top.

'What the devil is that? I detest oranges,' Felblade complained, tucking it away safely.

Platt smiled at me. 'I saw your advertisement in the *Journal* this morning, Mr Hawkins. I shall tell my customers.'

'Thank you, Mr Platt.' I gave him a short bow. 'I hope you never find yourself in need of my services, but if you do I shall be sure to offer a discount.' I was rather pleased with this reply, it sounded most businesslike.

'*Advertisement*?' Felblade frowned at me. '*Services*? What idiocy is this?'

I told him of my intention to help people in trouble. 'For a fee,' I added.

Felblade laughed so hard his teeth fell out into his hand. 'What a rotten idea,' he sniggered, when he had stuffed them back in. 'Why the devil would anyone come to you for help?'

There was no point in feeling wounded – Felblade thought most things were rotten: apples, ideas, the world in general. 'I've investigated three murders this past year,' I said. 'I enjoy solving mysteries. At the risk of sounding vain, Mr Felblade – I'm rather good at it.'

Felblade sniffed. 'Solve this mystery for me, Hawkins. Why am I freezing my arse off listening to your twaddle, when I might be at home by the fire, drinking brandy?'

Thus bolstered by his encouragement, I headed to Moll's.

Moll's is a night place, a shadow place of flickering candles, swirling pipe smoke, soft flesh reflected on silver platters. It was not built for mornings. I pushed open the door to find ... nothing. Silence. It was as if the coffeehouse itself had drunk too much the evening before, fucked someone regrettable and now lay in a half-slumber, sour-tongued and listless.

A solitary maid sat perched on a high stool by the stove, head bowed in concentration as she darned an old stocking. *Betty*. I felt a sharp pang at the sight of her, this young black woman who watched the world with her keen amber eyes, and kept herself above the fray. We had always been good friends, but last winter she had used that friendship to betray me. I did not blame her – she had been given no choice – but we had lost that easy way between us. I told myself it was for the best – Betty stirred feelings I should be saving for Kitty. That one kiss we had shared, when I was languishing in prison ... Yes, it was for the best.

I wished her good morrow and asked for a pot of coffee.

'As you wish, sir,' she replied, in that neutral way that suggests a person is feeling very far from neutral.

I settled in a chair close to the fire and opened out the *Journal*, searching for my advertisement.

and thereby hinders the Tooth-ache: It admirably fastens loose Teeth and makes them as white as Ivory, though never so black or yellow, being a neat cleanly Medicine, of a pleasant Scent. Price 1 s. the Box. *N. B.* At the same Places is sold the highly esteemed Lip-Salve for Ladies, &c. of a charming and delightful Scent.

At TOM KING'S COFFEE HOUSE, *in the Square upon Covent Garden, known to the Town as MOLL's*

† † † Whereas MR. THOMAS HAWKINS, *Gent.,* celebrated for his Miraculous escape from Death at the scaffold and subsequent Compleat Exoneration and Pardon from *His Majesty the King,* now gives notice that he is prepared to offer his services to Persons in Distress and suffering from that most Lamentable of situations where neither Lawyer nor Magistrate may be called upon for aid. The discovery of lost Persons undertaken; unexplained Mysteries of a diverse nature resolv'd; Frauds unmask'd, consultation offer'd in neighbourly disputes, &c. A swift, discreet service is Guaranteed, with no provoking Questions ask'd.

Note, He gives Advice Gratis, with a fee to be agreed upon Application. He is *daily about* 12 *and* 2, Monday to Thursday, at the Place abovementioned, and answers Letters to the same address *post paid.*

Newly published,
The Twelfth Edition of,

ONANIA: Or, The Heinous Sin of Self-Pollution, and all its frightful Consequences in both sexes consider'd, with Spiritual and Physical advice to those, who have already injur'd themselves in this abominable Practice. And Admonition to

Betty placed a coffee pot and bowl on the table. 'Sam paid us a visit the other night. He said someone wants you dead. Again.'

I looked up at her. 'He showed you the portrait?' That settled the matter, surely. Betty not only worked at Moll's, but was also connected – against her wishes – to the Queen's network of spies. She knew everyone, saw everything. If she didn't recognise Strait, he was either in deep hiding, or had left the city.

Betty tapped the newspaper. 'Is it wise to announce where you'll be each day?' She often began her sentences with 'Is it wise ...' or 'Have you considered ...' or 'I did warn you ...'

'You would have me hide beneath my bedsheets, I suppose?' *You might hide there with me. No I must not think that, I must not think of Betty and bedsheets, damn it.*

She gave me a level stare before returning to the warm stove and her worn-out stockings. 'What does it matter what I think?' she tossed over her shoulder. 'You never listen to my advice.'

I took off my hat and laid out ink and paper, and a quill. It was a quarter to noon, and the coffeehouse was still deserted. Perhaps Felblade was right. Perhaps this was a rotten idea. I fixed myself a pipe and closed my eyes, tipping back upon my chair.

'Mr Hawkins?'

I opened my eyes. A short, soft-bellied fellow of about five and thirty stood at my table, clutching a copy of the *Journal*. My first client. He introduced himself as Mr P—.* I slammed my chair back down on to four legs. 'At your service.'

He pulled up a chair, launching into his tale before his arse had met the seat. He was new married, he said, and delighted with his wife. 'She performs miracles in the bedchamber, sir. *Miracles*.' She was also an excellent cook. He patted his stomach contentedly. 'I have not eaten so well in my whole life.'

I congratulated him on his good fortune and wondered why – under such blissful circumstances – he might need my help.

'I fear she may have murdered her previous two husbands.'

Ah. I ordered a bowl of punch.

We were soon joined by a young hackney driver, brushing the rain from his coat. He was pale and fretful, and looked as though he had not slept well in weeks. He did not mind sharing his troubles with my first client, in fact they seemed reassured to find they were not alone in seeking me out. The hackney driver was a Catholic. He'd asked a priest to perform a private Mass at his home, in memory of his father. Against the law, but where was the harm? Somehow his landlord had learnt of it and was demanding two shillings extra in rent every week, or else he would report him to the authorities. Nor could the

---

*I disguise his name here for reasons that shall become apparent.

man leave, as the landlord refused to give him a reference. He was trapped.

'I've been working night and day to pay him, but a fellow has to sleep, Mr Hawkins. I nodded off on the ride home yesterday. Almost tipped the carriage into the Fleet ditch.' He buried his head in his hands, the very picture of despair. 'I'm so tired I could weep.'

I squeezed his shoulder. 'Don't worry, sir. Have a glass of punch.'

He peered at me through his fingers. 'You can help me?'

'I believe I can.'

The trick with blackmailers was to discover something even more incriminating in their own life. It takes a particularly foul individual to threaten a decent citizen for his faith. Foul individuals tend to have foul secrets.

I scribbled notes, agreed a fee and shook hands with both men. Meanwhile a small crowd had gathered about the surrounding tables. Some had genuine enquiries, others were simply curious to meet Half-Hanged Hawkins. An old boatman had brought along an inch of the rope that had hanged me, convinced it held protective powers. He placed it on the table between us – a filthy stub of a thing – and grinned at me. I felt the noose tighten once more about my throat, like a constricting snake. I had promised myself that I would not be haunted by my hanging, but there were limits.

'It's kept me alive these past six months,' the boatman declared, and to be fair he was, demonstrably, not dead. A miracle.

As predicted, the blackmailing landlord had a sordid history, and plenty of enemies willing to share it with me. Once I had my information, I paid him a visit.

'Tattled on me, did he?' he said, sticking out his chest. 'He should be grateful I didn't tell the magistrate. These damned papists would have us bowing to Rome if we did not—'

'Rob them blind?' I had no patience for such talk, not least because my own mother had been raised in the faith.

He scowled. 'You'd rather he spent his coin on gunpowder and bayonets for his Jacobite chums, I suppose?'

His mention of coin afforded me the perfect opportunity to remind him of his previous life as a counterfeiter.

He paled. He was living under a counterfeit name these days, too. Clearly he did not expect his old life to catch up with him. 'I am done with that life, sir.'

'That is not what I hear, *sir*.' The punishment for counterfeiting coin, as he well knew, was death. He had only escaped the gallows the last time by peaching on the rest of his gang.

'I swear, I am done with it,' he said again, but he looked so agitated I thought he might jump out of the window and flee into the night.

'Well,' I said, perfectly affable. 'We might test that at the Old Bailey, I suppose. No doubt you will remember poor John Johnson, the coiner from Nottingham? He gave up his friends last winter, and yet they still hanged him at Tyburn. I doubt the court would forgive you a second time, but of course I *may* be wrong.'

By the time I left, he had agreed to pay back what he had stolen, and waived the hackney driver's rent for the next two quarters. He also paid my fee – which I had doubled. I made sure to test every coin he gave me before concluding our deal.

The investigation into Mr P's energetic but potentially murderous new wife proved more complicated. I was able to confirm beyond doubt that, after just six months of marriage, her first husband had died of the smallpox. She had married her second husband, a Mr Q, two years later. It was her account of Mr Q's death that had unsettled my client. Her recollections on the matter were peculiarly vague and contradictory. Mr Q had died of a fever, she said. Another time, when she had drunk too much wine, she claimed he had suffered a fatal apoplexy. Even the date of his death wobbled in the retelling.

When Mr P questioned his wife about these anomalies she became anxious, and declared she would not speak of Mr Q ever again. Shortly thereafter, on three separate occasions, Mr P suffered a terrible cramping of the stomach. He feared poison, but did not wish to accuse her without proof. What if he were wrong, and lost her affection for ever? He was extremely content in the marriage and without complaint, save for this one slight concern that she could be a murderess.

Seeking more information, I paid a visit to Mr Q's old neighbourhood – but his death was a mystery to all. One day he was there, the next he was gone, and his wife dressed in her old mourning gown. ('She was pleased she could still fit into it,' one neighbour confided.)

My suspicions grew when I searched the parish records and could find no reference to Mr Q's death. After further enquiries I called upon his one surviving relative in the city, his great-aunt. She confirmed what I had begun to suspect.

Mr Q was not dead. He was living in Streatham.

I visited him at once, before his aunt could send word. He was at home, and one glance at his lodgings solved the puzzle. Mr Q lived with a gentleman friend, but the second bedchamber had been converted into a workshop, where his friend made shoes. In other words, they shared a bed, and a life. Once I had assured them both that I was not an informer, and only sought discreet reassurance for my worried client, Mr Q was eager to explain what had happened. It was in his interest, after all, that the matter be settled quickly and with discretion.

'Annie was my friend,' he said. 'I felt so sorry for her when her first husband died – she was only seventeen, you know. I convinced myself that I loved her. And I thought if I married her, it would help me to control those other ... urges.' He glanced at his friend, who gave him a playful wink. 'It didn't work,' he sighed. 'Annie grew ... *impatient*, shall we say. A young woman ... She needed things I couldn't give her. She was like a sister, if you understand me.'

I understood. Annie wished to marry again and have a family, but as they could not divorce, they were both in a bind. 'Death' had been the only option. I thanked Mr Q for his help, and assured him

66

again that I would not divulge his secret or his identity. Perhaps his friend did not make shoes, perhaps they did not live in Streatham. His name most certainly did not begin with Q.

This did mean – unfortunately – that Annie was a bigamist, but I thought Mr P would forgive her for that. He'd already told me that he did not care what her secret was, as long as she hadn't murdered anyone.

'Pray send Annie my sincerest good wishes,' Mr Q said, on the doorstep. 'I was very fond of her, you know.'

I promised that I would, if I happened to speak to her. 'One last thing, sir . . . Annie would never poison a man, would she?'

'Poison?' Mr Q looked astonished.

I explained about her new husband's terrible cramps.

He gripped the doorframe and laughed until he could scarce breathe. 'That's not poison,' he said, wiping his eyes. 'That's Annie's food!'

'But is she not a wonderful cook?'

'Oh indeed, sir! It has taken me a year to lose this.' He patted his now modest belly. 'She drowns everything in butter and cream. Mountains of cheese. Bread smothered in dripping. Egg and potato pudding . . .' He looked away into the distance, dreamily. 'Delicious. But very trying on the stomach.'

'I *see*.' We shook hands and I returned to the city.

The next morning I called upon Mr P and gave him the good news: his wife was a bigamist, and he was a pig. 'Breathe between mouthfuls, sir,' I counselled. 'Do not ask for seconds. That should cure the cramping.'

Mr P promised he would, and paid me an extra guinea for the advice. I left with a full purse, and the satisfaction that I had saved a happy marriage from catastrophe.

And there was the rub. I spent my days solving other people's troubles, then came home and could not settle my own. Kitty was still wretchedly unhappy, and I hated it. Sometimes she would reach for me in the dark, tender and passionate. I would think: *there – all is well again.* And then the next morning I would sit down for breakfast and see a pair of blank green eyes staring at the wall, the fire, the table – anywhere save for at me. Was she angry? Upset? Miserable?

'Kitty,' I would say at last, when I could bear it no longer. 'What the devil is the matter?'

'Nothing.'

By which she meant, *everything.*

Winter arrived swift and fierce that year, with slicing winds and glittering ice. Hurrying through the streets, one would hear a scuff and then a thud, as some poor lump skidded and fell on the freezing cobbles. One morning in mid-November, passing under the colonnades in the piazza, I almost tripped over a young girl dressed in rags and stretched out upon the ground. As I looked closer I realised my mistake. She was not sleeping, but must have died in the night. I called out to some fellows passing by and we carried her across the square to St Paul's church. She looked young, and no one recognised her. No great mystery to solve. Just a girl, little more than a child, who had died alone in a city of six hundred thousand souls.

I went home, and described the affair to Kitty.

'She should have found a warmer spot,' she said, 'and wrapped herself in more layers. It's the only way to last the winter.' She didn't mean it cruelly, but spoke as one who had survived upon the streets herself for a time.

'I wish I'd found her sooner,' I said.

'You can't save everyone, Tom.'

'Oh, true enough. I only meant . . .'

But she was already striding from the room.

The next morning I woke to a blizzard, dazzling white and silent. I unlatched the window and put out my hand, capturing snowflakes in my palm.

'It's frozen water, Hawkins. No need to turn poetical.' Felblade stood in the middle of the street, as if he had been waiting for me. The twin horns of his wig were topped with snow, like mountain peaks. 'You'll have supper with me tonight,' he commanded. 'You, Kitty and the boy.'

My stomach twinged in alarm. There was a reason why I walked several streets to a rival apothecary's when in need. The thought of Felblade preparing supper in his squalid home, with his grimy fingers, was not a happy one. 'That's kind of you, sir – but I would not put you to any trouble. Let us treat you to a chophouse meal—'

'No. You'll come to me.'

'Then let us bring something—'

'No. Seven o'clock sharp.' He crunched away in the snow, hands clasped behind his back.

I found Kitty in what I still thought of as the shop. She had transformed it into a withdrawing room these past few weeks, with chairs and a tea table. Somehow, without ever saying it, she had made it clear that this was her room, not mine. I could *withdraw* to bed, or to the kitchen, or to the roof if I liked. But not here. I had even taken to knocking before I entered. In my own home!

I told her about our supper invitation.

She pulled a face, but even she knew better than to argue with Felblade. 'Milk thistle tea,' she said. 'Before we leave. And when we return.' She frowned. 'What does he want, the old devil?'

'Company?' I put my arms around her waist and drew her close. She stiffened for a moment, then sighed, and leant into me. I kissed a freckled patch along her jaw. 'Change to your green dress tonight.' It was her favourite gown, and mine. She had not worn it in weeks.

She shifted, uncomfortable. 'It's past noon. Are you not late for Moll's?'

I kept my hand upon her waist. 'Who would venture out in this weather? I might as well stay here with you.' I kissed her neck. 'Do you remember the last time we lay on this floor . . .'

. . . the morning Gonson rapped on our door. Ugh. My mistake.

She shuddered at the memory, and pushed herself free of my embrace. 'You might lose a client. They could be waiting for you.'

'I don't care about that. Kitty, please—'

'I can't have you under my feet all day.' She placed her hand against my chest and shoved. 'Go!'

I frowned, rejected. 'As you wish.'

I picked up my coat and hat, and left.

I was in a bad temper when I arrived at Moll's. I tried dosing myself with my usual medicine of brandy and tobacco, but it was no use. She had pushed me away – quite literally pushed me with her hand, damn it. As if I were some irritating child and not the man who shared her bed. Well. Quite frankly, if Kitty did not want me, then she could not complain if I took my passions elsewhere. The thought dropped unbidden into my mind. An hour in another woman's bed. One hour. The simple pleasure of a good fuck. Why not? If Kitty did not want me – why the devil not?

'Mr Hawkins?' Betty appeared at my table, clutching a fresh bowl of punch. Her voice held a warning tone. 'Gentleman here wishes to speak with you.'

I glanced up at the man standing behind her.

Richard Strait – the man I had been hunting for weeks. The man who wanted me dead.

He removed his feathered hat, the snow still melting on its crown, and gave a short bow. 'Your servant, sir.'

I smiled, and gestured for him to join me.

Chapter Seven

'The name's Patchett,' he said, sitting down opposite me.

He did not trouble himself to smile – his lined, heavy-jowled face fell naturally into a glum expression, his expression weary and cynical. A man who both accepted and resented his lot in life. Sam's portrait was not a perfect match, but it had been close enough for Betty to recognise him and so warn me – the straight brows, the head like a shovel, and most of all the inflamed, crusted patches that covered his forehead and neck. 'Scuffed,' as Inchguard had put it.

The clothes were different, mind. 'Richard Strait' had worn plain, journeyman's garb. Patchett was dressed in white stockings and a blue satin waistcoat with silver buttonholes – a most unsuitable outfit for the weather. His stockings were spattered right up to the knees. His only concession to the snowstorm was a pair of heavy boots. I felt, instinctively, that there must have been an argument about them, and that he had won it.

'I speak on behalf of my mistress, Lady Emma Vanhook,' he said.

The name meant nothing to me. Presumably she was responsible for his ridiculous attire. I ladled out a glass of punch. 'An unusual name. Dutch?'

'Her Ladyship read your advertisement in the *Journal*. She asked if you would wait upon her this afternoon.'

'I would be honoured.'

And there was our business concluded, but etiquette demanded we sit for a while and talk about the weather, and other trifling matters. Patchett would tell me nothing more about Lady Vanhook – 'She would prefer to explain everything in person' – though he did mention that she was recently returned to England after several years abroad, and finding the climate disagreeable.

'And where has she been?'

'Abroad, sir,' he repeated, refusing to be drawn. Most definitely a West Country accent – Inchguard had been right about that.

'You did not travel with her, I think? You are new to her household?' It was an easy enough guess – beneath the sore patches, his grey pallor suggested long years shivering beneath an English sky. But my observation made Patchett uneasy, so I pressed him no further. I did not want him alert and suspicious – quite the opposite.

We agreed it would be best if it stopped snowing, and hoped we would not have a winter as bitter as last year's. Then came the obligatory complaints about the city's crowded streets and filthy water, and yes, one could barely walk from Charing Cross to Fleet Street without being robbed. Things were not as they used to be, no doubt, no doubt. All of this had to be supposition on his part – if he had spent any time wandering the city someone would have recognised him from Sam's picture. This could be his first outing in weeks – which would explain how his ridiculous clothes were not spoilt. Naturally I kept this observation to myself.

Patchett rose and stared glumly at his feathered hat, which looked more suited to the Drury Lane theatre than the real world. He placed it on his head with a tentative air, like a usurper king troubled by his crown. 'Five o'clock, Jermyn Street,' he reminded me, and left.

I sat back, feeling very grateful for Sam's sketch. Without it I would never have guessed that Patchett – or his mistress – wished me any harm. I would have arrived at my appointment with my guard down, not realising that I was walking into a trap. Well – I would turn that to my advantage.

Lady Vanhook. Who on earth was she? And what had I done to inspire such murderous hate?

I would find out, soon enough.

In the piazza, the street sellers were packing up their wares, surrendering to the blizzard. Only the roast chestnut seller remained, huddled beside his hot brazier. I bought a bag from him, warming my hands as I ate, and hurried back to Russell Street.

I needed Sam. Today was Thursday, so I knew where to find him. He had persuaded Felblade to teach him about poisons. The very last thing one should do was teach Sam about poisons. Felblade, being a contrarian to his marrow, thus delighted in teaching Sam about poisons. Doing so every Thursday afternoon was Felblade's silent critique upon society, the world and God himself, most likely.

Felblade's new servant opened the door. They never lasted long. Sometimes, when I could not sleep, I would recite their names to myself. Reuben, Barnaby, Flincher, Sarah One, Sarah Two, Skinner, Mary. There had been another girl between Flincher and Sarah One, but she had only lasted a day because of the smell, so I did not consider her canonical. Servant number eight was a thin-boned child of about twelve or thirteen, with lank hair and large, soulful eyes fringed with dark lashes.

'Timothy Wigg,' he said, when I asked his name. And then, in quiet resignation, 'People call me Twig.'

I added him to the end of the list.

'We shall be dining here tonight,' I told him.

Twig digested this news, his eyes filled with compassion. I took my last breath of safe air, and ventured inside.

Whatever Sam was doing, he had tidied it away by the time I found him – but there was a lingering scent of *something*. It made the back of my throat catch. I coughed, and told him about Strait, who we must now call Patchett, and my appointment. I asked Sam to pay an advance visit to Jermyn Street to find out what he could.

'Bribe the neighbours if you must. I'll meet you there at five o'clock.'

'A man may swallow the saliva of a rabid dog and not turn mad,' Sam replied. 'If he has no cuts or ulcers in the mouth.'

This was Sam's idea of a decent trade. I provided him with an interesting task and in exchange he presented me with a useful fact. 'Your picture was an excellent match,' I told him. 'Betty recognised Patchett at once.' I handed him my bag of chestnuts. Sam was one of those queer, lean boys who were always hungry but never gained weight.

We walked down the stairs together, discussing rabies, as one does.

'The poison is destroyed through the mechanical actions of the stomach,' he said, peeling a hot chestnut. 'And the corrosive properties of intestinal bile.'

'Let us hope the same holds true for Felblade's cooking. We have been invited for supper this evening.'

Sam absorbed this distressing news without comment. I was surprised by his lack of protest – Sam detested formal meals (*talking! cutlery!*). Distracted by his new mission, no doubt. He headed off into the blizzard, a scruffy black smudge against the snow.

I turned for home, distracted by thoughts of Kitty, and fidelity. If Patchett had not arrived when he did, I might now be lost in some brothel, breaking every vow I had made to the woman I loved.

A hollow space opened in my chest. A man may lose a woman in thought, long before that thought becomes deed. Was this how things would end between us?

I was only a few paces from home when I saw the door to the Pistol swing open.

'My thanks for the pamphlets, sir, and your kind advice.' Kitty's voice. 'I am obliged to you, as ever.'

'A duty and a pleasure, my child. Be sure to read the passages I marked, and remember the prayers I taught you.'

'I will, I promise. God bless you, sir.'

'God bless you, child.'

The door closed with a soft click and Sir John Gonson stepped out into the street.

I drew back, horrified.

Gonson tilted his hat against the blizzard and turned left towards Drury Lane. Had he turned right he would have collided with me. I could tell from the set of his shoulders, the spring in his step, that he was mightily pleased with himself. Thank *God* he turned left. I would have punched him to the ground.

So this was why Kitty had pushed me out of the shop earlier. She had an appointment with *Sir John Gonson*. A prayer meeting, no less. I laughed bitterly, scarce able to believe it. After all my thoughts of betraying *her*, *she* had invited my enemy into our home. Was that not a far greater breach of trust?

I decided it was. And I shall tell you something else – I did not knock before entering her fucking withdrawing room.

Kitty was unpinning her hair, fingers running through her curls. She gave a start when she saw me, and blushed. 'Tom. You are home early.'

Was this sentence ever spoken by an innocent soul? I took off my coat and slung it on a chair. There was a dent in the cushion. Gonson had been sitting there moments ago, revelling in his secret victory. The thought made me want to vomit.

'Tom? I'm sorry we argued before, sweetheart,' Kitty said. 'I was tired. Forgive me.' She ran her hand down my waistcoat, her fingers snagging upon the band of my breeches. A familiar gesture, and an invitation.

How could she lie to me about *Gonson*? Even if it were some stratagem to keep me safe, she should have told me. I felt like a cuckold. Like a fool! How many times had he visited my home without my knowledge? Had she asked for his advice? Was this why she'd been so cool and distant of late? Had he turned her against me?

Kitty slipped a hand beneath my breeches.

'Your hands are cold,' I said, pulling away.

She looked surprised. It was not like me to reject her advances.

'I must venture out again shortly.'

'Oh, where are you going? Shall I come with you?' She offered me a hopeful smile. 'I am sorry we quarrelled Tom – truly.'

'It's a matter of business,' I said. 'I must go alone.'

Her smile faded. I had hurt her. But if she would not be honest with me, then why should I confide in her?

A petty decision, and – like all decisions of that nature – soon regretted.

Chapter Eight

On Jermyn Street the blizzard had passed, with just a few flakes drifting on an icy breeze, as if reluctant to touch the ground. Sam was waiting for me outside the church of St James, leaning against a snow-topped wall, hands shoved deep in his pockets. Someone was practising the organ; I could hear it faintly across the churchyard.

'They arrived two months ago,' Sam said. 'Three of 'em. Patchett, Lady Vanhook and a black girl. No one knows her name. They stay hidden indoors most of the time.'

We walked down the road until we drew close to a three-storyed house with grey railings and a dark green door. All the windows were shuttered, save for a room on the second floor. 'Only three of them. And such a large house.'

'There's a parrot,' Sam said, as if this explained it.

'How old is the girl?'

Sam placed a hand at hip level, indicating her height, then stuffed it back into his pocket.

'We must buy you some gloves.'

This insulted him, in some inexplicable way.

I heard a hacking, phlegmy cough from across the road. Two beggars were huddled together by the Bell Inn, caught in the lantern light.

'Spoke to 'em, paid 'em,' Sam said, anticipating my question.

The men held up the gin he had bought them and toasted him, their own personal Dionysus. Threaten and reward, threaten and reward. Another Fleet family motto. 'Lady V takes a chair to church every day, with the girl. Wears a hood. Doesn't go nowhere else.' His gaze slid back to the beggars. 'Never gives them nothing.'

I had spoken to Sam before about double negatives, but now was not the time to repeat the lecture.

I glanced back towards St James's. Why would she take a chair when there was a *very* fine church – designed by Sir Christopher Wren, no less – right here upon her doorstep? 'Is she a dissenter?'

Sam shrugged. Religion bored him. He was Jewish on his mother's side, Christian on his father's and Indifferent on his own.

'Any visitors?'

'Never.' Sam's gaze shifted back to the beggars. 'Then two days ago, black gent sits with them all morning. Middling height. Strong.' Sam curled his fists to indicate a broad, thick-muscled man. 'He says nothing, just stares at the house.' He acted this out too, glaring intently at the door.

'And?'

'Chair arrives, door opens, he heads over.'

Another pause.

'*And?*'

'Frozen.' He mimed the same hard-muscled man held firm in an invisible vice, eyes wide, teeth clenched. Struggling against the air, it seemed.

'Then what?'

'Nothing. Chair leaves, he leaves.'

Interesting. And only two days ago. I did not think the timing was a coincidence. *Something* was afoot.

I walked up to Lady Vanhook's door and rapped the lion's head knocker three times.

Patchett opened the door, dressed in his gilded livery. His dark brows lifted when he saw I was not alone.

'This is Sam, my ward,' I said. 'He's an honest lad. You may trust him.'

I could feel the air vibrate with the intensity of that lie, but Patchett didn't seem to notice. He ushered us in.

The doors on the ground floor were closed, the hallway shadowed and dim. The panelling over the staircase was carved with fruit patterns and prancing cherubs – expensive and well made, though too ornate for my taste. The walls were bare, darker patches left where the previous occupant had once hung pictures.

Patchett led us to the unshuttered room on the second floor, at the front of the house. He tapped upon the door.

We waited. And waited. Patchett flexed his fingers, fighting the urge to knock again. At last, just as I had given up hope, one word floated languorously through the walls.

'Enter.'

Patchett opened the door and a dense, musky perfume wafted out – a smell of late nights, and flowers on the turn.

The drawing room was large, with high ceilings and two windows to the street. It should have been airy and pleasant, but the walls were too dark and covered with heavy oil paintings, and there was altogether too much furniture, as if the contents of a shipwreck had washed up in one room. Porcelain figures clustered in walnut cabinets, silver candelabra glinted on marble-topped tables. The fire, roaring and spitting behind an embroidered screen, only added to the room's oppressive air.

At the window, a green and orange parrot perched in a golden cage. It flew to the bars as we entered, pulling itself along by its beak and talons. '*Devil take you,*' it cawed, fixing me with a flame-bright eye. '*Devil. Devil.*'

'He likes you.'

Lady Vanhook reclined upon a gold damask sofa, her long, slippered feet drawn up behind her. She was younger than I had expected – no more than forty – and very handsome indeed, with striking pale blue eyes and dark auburn hair, touched with grey. Her face was dusted with white powder, her lips touched with rouge. Diamonds sparkled at her ears and throat.

She was immaculate, in a studied fashion – as if one of the portraits had peeled itself from the wall and settled here, waiting to greet us.

Patchett gave a clumsy bow. Honestly, I had seen trained bears make a better shift of it. Where had she found him? 'Mr Thomas Hawkins, my lady. And his ward.' He suffered a moment's panic, realising he had forgotten one half of Sam's name, and failed to ask for the other half.

Luckily for Patchett, Lady Vanhook was distracted by my arrival. Without breaking her gaze from mine, she swung her feet to the floor, draping her arms along the back of the sofa. Her bodice was set very low, not even a wisp of muslin for modesty.

I bowed into her silence. 'Your servant, madam.'

Her fingers traced a line along her collarbone, her lips parted in a half-smile. I could see her pulse beating at her neck. And still she stared, as if I were a delicious feast she had ordered after a very long fast. The sensation was not entirely unpleasant.

'Patchett,' she said, without shifting her gaze. 'Where's my little Nella?'

'Preparing tea, my lady.'

'Why does she take so long?' Lady Vanhook rolled her eyes at me, as if I knew Nella of old, and her inadequacies. 'Run along and help her.'

Patchett bowed again and left us.

Lady Vanhook did not invite me to sit down. She seemed . . . enraptured, somehow. But why? We had never met before, not even fleetingly – I would certainly remember her. How could we be enemies? I rested upon my swordstick, one foot turned out, my hand on the fox's head. If I wished, I could draw the blade and place it at her throat – demand answers from her. I dismissed the idea. I would rather keep my advantage for now, and let the meeting play out as it would.

'Stand perfectly still,' Lady Vanhook commanded me, transforming from portrait to painter. 'Just as you are.' She slid her gaze slowly from my ankles to my calves, up my thighs to my crotch, settling there a fraction too long for comfort. Then her journey recommenced, up my chest to my face.

'*Yes,*' she murmured, when she was done. 'I see it now.' She rose, smoothing her gown, and crossed to a tea table awaiting its tray top. As she moved, she brushed her fingers over the figurines and candlesticks and embroidered cushions, caressing them briefly. She likes to touch, I thought. *To possess.* I imagined those long fingers running along my skin, then pushed the thought away, unsettled. Odd. I was rarely embarrassed by such notions.

'Do join me, Mr Hawkins.' Her voice held a smile, as if she had read my thoughts.

There were two chairs set beneath the table – one plain with no cushion, the other padded in green velvet with gilded wood. No question which was mine and which was hers.

Sam was inspecting the parrot. 'What would happen if you let it go?'

'It would die,' she said.

Sam – without invitation – dragged a stool up to the table. He was quite clean for Sam, his black curls oiled and tied with a ribbon. Lady Vanhook ignored him.

A young black girl entered, struggling with the tea tray. Nella, I presumed. She was tiny – no more than five or six years old – with a round, sweet face. A fraction too thin, I thought.

Patchett lumbered in behind her, carrying a kettle on a silver stand.

'I don't want *you,*' Lady Vanhook scolded. Patchett, apparently inured to her ill humour, put down the kettle and left.

I rose to help Nella as she approached, but her eyes flashed in alarm: *no*! Startled, I retreated to my chair. She set the lacquered tray on to its base, breathing hard with the effort, cups rattling precariously in their saucers. She was dressed extravagantly in a peacock blue turban and a blue velvet dress but what I could not bear, what my eyes kept returning to in horror, was the wide silver band wrapped tight around her throat. As she poured the tea, frowning in concentration, I saw that the collar was closed at the back with a silver padlock. I'd heard of this practice, but had never seen it before. The inscription engraved across the front was too small to read clearly, but I could guess the words. They would state that this young girl was the property of her mistress, Lady Emma Vanhook.

A child slave serving tea, chained in silver, as if this were the most natural thing in the world.

'Nella. My little pet,' Lady Vanhook cooed. 'She is not as dark as I should like,' she added, as if describing a bolt of cloth. 'The darker ones are more the fashion, and easier to sell. Not that I will sell you, Nella, unless you misbehave.'

The tea poured, Nella sat down at Lady Vanhook's feet, cross-legged.

'You disapprove, sir,' Lady Vanhook said, revelling in my reaction. 'But you enjoy your tea, and your tobacco no doubt, and would not see the price rise on either. You enjoy the spoils of perpetual service, and accept none of the burdens.' Her words sounded rehearsed, as though she had planned this entire meeting in her head.

'We pride ourselves on our liberty in this country, madam.'

Lady Vanhook laughed, scornful. 'Spoken like a true English*man*. How you adore your liberty, and trample over everyone else's to maintain it. D'you know, Mr Hawkins, if I wish to buy a new gown, I must go to my husband upon my hands and knees,' she leant forward, 'and suck his withered old cock till it's dry. How is that for freedom? Milk?'

I could find no answer to this. Sam, grinning, picked the currants from a bun as if they were musket shot. He was enjoying himself, the wretch.

Afraid my tea might be poisoned, I waited for my hostess to drink first.

'Your husband has not joined you in England, madam?' Perhaps I had offended *him*?

'No. This is the first time we have been apart since we were wed. I am sure he is celebrating our separation in the company of his whores. Thank God his seed is as worthless as he is.' She blew across the rim of her cup, and took a sip.

'And where is home?'

'This is my home,' she snapped, suddenly angry.

Curious, that this should rouse her. *So she has been in exile. And upon her return, remains in hiding ...* 'Well, you have chosen a fine spot for your new lodgings, I must say. And one of the most fashionable churches in London, just across the street. I hear the congregation is so laden with jewels that they pay a man to watch for thieves when they're at prayer.'

I'd hoped to draw her on her daily visits to another church, but she sipped her tea, and looked bored. 'I suppose you take an interest in such things,' she said, 'as the son of a clergyman.' And then she dropped her cup into its saucer, realising her mistake. We were meant to be strangers. I raised my eyebrow.

'Your story is well known sir,' she said, recovering swiftly. She was a clever woman.

'Your servant said you wished to engage me upon some matter?'

'Indeed.' Lady Vanhook pulled Nella on to her lap, circling her arms about the girl's tiny waist. 'Now, my little doll. I am going to tell this *fine* gentleman a story about you,' she whispered in Nella's ear. 'You must be brave. No tears, do you understand – remember how I detest them. And no fidgeting. Yes?'

Nella nodded, and gave me a curious glance before lowering her gaze once more.

'We arrived here in October,' Lady Vanhook began. 'A family matter. We keep to ourselves. London is a *sewer* of vice.'

'Is that why you hired Patchett in Bristol?'

She blinked, ungrounded.

'I recognised the accent.'

'What a fine ear you have. A fine ear and a silver tongue ... Mr Hawkins, pray tell your boy to stop staring at me as if I were some specimen in a jar.'

So she had finally noticed him. 'Pray don't be offended, madam. He looks that way at everyone.'

'Impertinent brat.' And before I could stop her, she smacked Sam very hard across the cheek.

The speed and ferocity of the strike was astonishing. Even Sam – so used to fighting – did not anticipate it. By the time I had jumped to my feet, Lady Vanhook had returned her hand to Nella's waist, as if nothing had happened. Sam himself did not move an inch. But he would store that slap in his mind – no doubt of that.

'Lady Vanhook!' I snapped. 'I am your guest, madam. You will treat my ward with respect.'

She sniggered into her cup, looking at Sam properly for the first time. 'Your *ward*. Did you pluck him from the gutter? And for what sordid purpose, I wonder? Look at him, the ghastly black-eyed creature—'

She stopped dead, horrified.

She knew him! At least, she knew he was a Fleet.

I watched, fascinated, as she struggled to regain her composure.

Was that why she had fled into exile? How on earth could their paths have crossed? Within the underworld, the Fleets were notorious, but they were invisible to the rest of us. I used to trade information for coin, gathering news at gaming tables, brothels and drinking dens. I never once heard tell of them – not until Fate put me in a cell with Samuel Fleet himself. Even then, the old devil never mentioned that his brother was the captain of a criminal gang. Lady Vanhook had looked into Sam's eyes and recognised him at once, which suggested that she knew the family intimately.

She did not strike me as a child of St Giles, but life is remarkable, and people may rise and fall within society in the most surprising ways.

And still – none of this explained why she hated *me* with such a violent passion. She'd clearly had no idea of my connection to the Fleets until this very moment.

A coincidence, then? Surely not. I looked to Sam, but his face was a mask. If he knew anything, he would wait until we were alone to share it.

Lady Vanhook placed her hand upon Nella's head and breathed deeply.

'Are you quite well, my lady?' I asked. I confess I sounded a touch smug, even to my ears.

It was enough to bring her to her senses. I would not triumph over her – she would not allow it. 'Quite well,' she said, and forced a smile.

'Would you continue with your story?' I prompted.

'Of course.' To refuse would be a defeat. 'Are you a pious man, Mr Hawkins? Like your reverend father? Oh!' She put a hand to her mouth. 'How thoughtless of me to mention him again. He disinherited you, did he not? In favour of your brother?'

'Step-brother,' I said, without thinking, then frowned.

She smiled. *A hit, a very palpable hit.* 'My faith is my great comfort,' she continued. She leant down and kissed Nella's cheek. 'We attend church every day, don't we dearest? And thank God for our happy little life. Well. Two days ago, we stepped out at noon, as we always do. The chair was waiting in the usual place, but I had the strangest feeling of being *watched*. I glanced along the street and there he was. Staring at Nella.' Her arms tightened around the girl's waist.

'Who?'

'Jeremiah,' she said, with a false shudder.

'Jeremiah?'

ANTONIA HODGSON

She looked almost surprised I did not know him – as if his reputation were so monstrous, the whole world must quail at his name.
'One of my husband's slaves. A fiend.'

I lifted my eyebrows at the description.

'A *fiend*,' she repeated, defiantly. 'My husband treated him like a
son.' She looked sickened by the idea. 'And he repaid that *unnatural*
honour with treachery. My only comfort was knowing that he had
suffered and died for his crimes. Now I find that he survived and
sailed here, to England. *My home*! He plans to steal my darling
Nella from me, I know it. Snatch her up and devour her.'

Nella gave a sharp gasp. Lady Vanhook looked pleased.

'What did you do when you saw him?' I asked.

'Oh, I kept my composure.' She straightened her back, tilted her
chin at the memory. Everything with a flourish, as if I were sitting
at the back of the theatre, and not across a small tea table. 'I looked
straight through him, as if he were not even there. And then I
stepped into my chaise, and we raced off down the street. I held you
very close, Nella, do you remember? All the way to church? And I
promised I should always protect you, and keep you safe from him.
And you believe that, don't you, *cherie*?'

Nella nodded, her expression solemn.

'I should rather see you dead,' Lady Vanhook added in a light
voice, 'than let him touch you. You are mine, and mine alone. Say it.'

'I am yours and yours alone,' Nella repeated, in that sing-song
way of young children, when they have learnt something by rote.

Lady Vanhook slid Nella from her lap. Nella – understanding at
once that she was dismissed – gave a curtsy and left. Lady Vanhook
brushed imaginary specks from her gown.

'Madam,' I said, growing tired of her performance, 'what do you
want of me?'

'Have you not guessed? How dull of you.' She poured herself a
fresh cup of tea. 'I want you to kill him.'

I laughed. She did not.

86

I sat back, astounded. 'I am not a killer, Lady Vanhook.'

'You were accused of murder.'

'And proved innocent.'

She shrugged, as if this were incidental. '"A swift, discreet service guaranteed, with no provoking questions asked",' she said, quoting from my advertisement.

'That . . . You thought that meant *murder*?'

'Name your price,' Lady Vanhook persisted. 'Twenty pounds. Thirty. How much would tempt you?' She was genuinely curious.

I stood up, too offended to reply.

'Very well,' she sighed, disappointed. 'Then you must find him for me. No more than that. Jeremiah is a dangerous brute. At the very least he must be sent back to Antigua in chains. At the very least.'

'I will not help you, not for any price,' I said. Had she really thought I might say yes? I doubted it. This encounter had been nothing more than a game for her amusement.

'*Not for any price*,' she mocked. 'Those are the words of a wealthy man. But you are not rich, are you Mr Hawkins? Who paid for your fine clothes, I wonder? Your jewelled walking stick?' She laughed.

Ignoring her, I headed for the door.

'She grows tired of you, I hear,' she called after me. 'Your pretty whore.'

This was too much. 'How dare you—'

Her eyes flashed with pleasure. 'What will you do when she leaves you? Poor Mr Hawkins. Will it break your heart?'

'I will find Jeremiah,' I said.

That silenced her.

'I will find him, and I will reunite him with his daughter. Nella is Jeremiah's daughter, is she not?'

She drew back, stunned. I had made a guess, but a decent one. Jeremiah – a runaway slave, presumed dead – would not risk confronting his old mistress without very good cause. Lady Vanhook had told me herself that he wanted to *steal* Nella.

As if a father could steal his own child.

Until this moment, our meeting had felt like a scene from a play. My threat to take Nella from her swept away that pretence. She stared at me with undisguised hatred, her pale blue eyes glittering with malice. 'I will destroy you,' she hissed.

I gave her a short bow. 'Madam. You may try.'

I followed Sam through the door, freed from the room's cloying heat, its musky perfume, the horrible dark spell of its owner. How long had we spent there? A half-hour at most. And yet I felt disorientated, as if I had woken from a long and potent dream. I paused in the corridor to gather myself, and heard a noise above me, on the next landing.

Nella. She was looking down at me with a wide, intense gaze, her fingers gripping the stair rail. Had she been listening at the door?

Nella is Jeremiah's daughter, is she not?

I took a step towards the stairs. 'Nella,' I whispered.

'No,' she whispered back, so quiet I barely heard her. Then she vanished.

What had she meant? *No – it's not safe? No – I don't believe you?* Either way, I was sorry. This was not how a young girl should learn such profound news.

I had promised to reunite Nella with her father in a fit of spite, not even thinking to lower my voice. That was Lady Vanhook's poisonous influence. How swiftly I had lowered myself to her base level. How easily she had provoked me, playing upon my pride, and my love for Kitty.

I had underestimated her. But she had underestimated me, too.

On my way through the house I opened each door in turn and found what I had suspected – that every room save for the drawing room was stripped bare. The gilded opulence was a facade, a stage dressing. I'd heard the bitterness in Lady Vanhook's voice, when she spoke of having to beg her husband for a new gown. I'd noted her resentment of Patchett, her boorish servant. That was how she knew to mock me for my clothes and gifts. She knew how it would sting.

Caught up in my thoughts, I left Jermyn Street with Sam at my side. I still had no idea why Lady Vanhook wished me dead, but the meeting had at least yielded some useful information.

I paused outside a gaming house on Piccadilly where I had whiled away many an evening, winning and losing on the reveal of a card, the throw of a die. What had we learnt? She knew the Fleets somehow, and was terrified of them. And yet she had returned from exile, risking her life in the process. For what purpose? To murder me? Then why had she not made a second attempt? And why the devil had she invited me to her lodgings? That was the great mystery. She appeared transfixed by me. Obsessed, even. All words we use when we fall in love. Only in this case, she had fallen in *hate* – if that were possible.

'She slapped me,' Sam said.

'She did. And before you could dodge her.' A woman used to giving swift, unexpected punishments, with no consequences. 'She recognised you as a Fleet. Perhaps your mother will remember her.'

By which I meant – go now to St Giles and speak to Gabriela. Sam knew that, but stayed where he was.

I stared at him in surprise. 'What is the matter? Do you have some other pressing engagement?'

Sam gave me a reproachful look.

'Oh . . .' I groaned, remembering. Felblade. The one person who would not accept apology or delay. '*Must* we?'

Sam looked stern.

'Very *well*. An hour or two will make little difference, I suppose. You may leave early, if need be.'

Sam nodded his head, vigorously.

We turned for home. Somewhere in this cold, snow-covered city, a father was dreaming about his daughter, a young girl locked in a silver collar. 'Tomorrow,' I said, 'we will search for Jeremiah.'

We smiled at each other, at this simple plan and its possibilities, and walked on.

In the dark green drawing room, Lady Vanhook sits at the tea table, cursing herself.

It had been grand, operatic folly to invite him here. But once she had conceived the idea, it had become irresistible to her. She must meet him face to face one time, before she destroyed him.

'I am a woman of impulse,' she says aloud, forgiving herself as she always does. 'I must do as my heart bids.'

He's a handsome devil, she has to admit. Clever, too. She had not anticipated that.

But the boy . . . the boy . . . She has seen those eyes before, in another face. Samuel Fleet. The devil who forced her into exile. This could not be his son, no indeed. A nephew, then . . . ?

Gabriela's child. Thomas Hawkins had brought Gabriela Fleet's brat into her home. Another reason to hate him – as if she needed one.

If the Fleets guessed who she was . . . If they discovered that she had come back, before she had the power to protect herself . . .

It is no longer safe, she decides, to let things spool out slowly as she had agreed. As she had promised. Thank God. She has spent too long hiding in this dreary room, drinking tea. Too long on her knees in church, pretending to be good, ruining her favourite gown. She is sick of it. Sick, sick, sick. Bored beyond endurance.

She picks up her porcelain teacup, admiring its translucence, its delicate blue and white flower pattern – and throws it against the wall.

'Call a chaise,' she orders Patchett, when he comes to sweep away the fragments.

'Sir John's house?'

Where else? She nods absently, already imagining her next dramatic scene. Finally, after all these years, she will have her revenge, her victory, her reward. She closes her eyes and conjures it in her mind. At last. At last.

Tonight, her favourite dream will come true.

Chapter Nine

There is a particular, weighted silence that hangs upon the air when two people are feuding. It is made all the heavier when they are forced into society together. Kitty and I dressed for supper without a word, our backs to one another. I had asked her again to wear her emerald dress, so she spited me with a bright yellow wrapping gown, matched with a black modesty piece, black stockings, and a black cloak. She looked like a disgruntled bee.

'Go away!' Felblade yelled through the door when I knocked.

'It's Thomas,' I called back. 'With Sam and Kitty.'

'I may speak for myself,' Kitty muttered.

'Well you have not said a word *all evening*,' I muttered back. (It was not yet seven.)

Sam stared at us.

The door swung open. Felblade greeted us *sans* wig, in a leather apron covered in brown and mustard-coloured smears. Supper, I feared. Stripped of his towering headpiece, he seemed half the size and oddly nude, his liver-spotted skin stretched taut across his ancient skull. We followed him to his workroom. Twig, his new servant, had stacked the room's bottles, jars and assorted implements neatly in one corner, and was now scrubbing the shelves with boiled vinegar water. I guessed that he had taken this task upon himself. I could not imagine Felblade asking him to clean anything.

Felblade abandoned us immediately and without explanation, thundering upstairs in the wooden clogs he wore to annoy his neighbours upon either side, both of whom he despised. It was astonishingly easy to become his enemy. Heaven knows how I had not yet offended him – I was like some lone soldier who survives a battle without a scratch, while everyone around him perishes.

We settled around the table, which was clean and also smelled of vinegar. Twig must have washed it on our behalf. I was about to thank him when Kitty folded her arms and frowned at me, and I remembered – just in time – our silent feud. Kitty was much the superior sulker – I always forgot halfway through and started chattering gaily about something or other, at which point she would twist one half of her face up in an enraging smirk because I had spoken first, while she was still demonstrably seething in wounded silence and had thus *won*.

So I did not thank Twig for cleaning the table. Instead I reminded myself of how furious and hurt I was by thinking very hard about Gonson and Kitty's secret meetings in *my home*. Had they clasped hands as they prayed? I imagined them doing so, kneeling and holding hands. How could she? The *duplicity*. The *betrayal*.

Yes, that was much better. That would fuel a good hour of silent resentment. I folded my arms in turn, and gave a weary sigh.

Some time passed. Twig scraped black, sticky patches from the shelves with a palette knife, while Sam occupied himself by sniffing his way down a line of bottles he'd placed on the table. Kitty and I did not speak a word. When she looked up I looked down, and vice versa. When I stood up to stretch, and pace the room, she tutted as if this were the most disgraceful act the world had ever witnessed. When I sat down she stood and paced herself, and now it was for me to shake my head in disbelief.

I had spent six lifetimes in that workshop before Felblade clomped his way back to us, twin-horned wig now firmly secured.

'By the devil, boy – you're right,' he declared.

Sam sat down. 'Bad.'

'*Abominable!*' Felblade corrected him.

'What's this?' I asked. 'What are you talking about?'

'We have been conducting an experiment, sir. An empirical study. The boy is worried.'

'About what?'

'About you, sir!' Felblade cried. 'And *you*, missy.' He poked Kitty in the arm with a sharp finger. She winced but did not look up. 'I am perfectly well,' she said in a dull voice.

'Oh, *perfectly*.' Felblade snorted. 'You spent the summer drooling over each other like a pair of simpering puppies.'

Sam shuddered, remembering.

'And now it is "pray do not look at me sir, or I shall vomit". God in heaven!' Felblade cried. 'Where's the equilibrium?' He prodded Kitty again, then pointed at me. 'That bimble-headed fool has been fretting over you for weeks. Boring us to death with his incessant wittering.'

Kitty unfolded her arms. 'You were worried, Tom?'

'Of course I was worried,' I said gruffly.

We looked at each other. And in an instant, magically, all was forgiven.

'Tom . . .' Kitty rubbed her palm with her thumb. 'I have to tell you something. Pray, don't be angry . . .'

'You've been meeting with Gonson.'

She gave a jolt of shock, then stared at me in utter dismay. 'Yes. Since the fire. I had to, Tom. I had to . . .' Tears sprang in her eyes. She looked so downcast I wanted to gather her up in my arms and comfort her.

So I did. I moved around the table and sat down beside her on the bench. I took her hand, and kissed it.

'*Oh* . . .' she said, with such relief and exhaustion it almost broke my heart. And then she burst into tears.

I wrapped my arms around her, holding her tight as she sobbed. After a while, I heard her mutter something about Gonson, but her words were muffled by my chest. 'What was that, sweetheart?'

She lifted her face so I could hear her. 'He's such an *arsehole*!' She rubbed the tears from her cheeks. 'He thinks he can save me. I don't want to be saved!' she yelled.

Twig jumped, startled. Sam grinned at me, and I grinned back. We *loved* Kitty when she yelled. We'd missed it.

'It's been *torture*,' she moaned. 'He makes me read all his sermons and speeches . . .'

The fiend! No wonder she had been so gloomy.

'Then he tests me, and if I make a mistake he says: "Hold out your hands, Miss Sparks", and then . . .' She mimed a stick striking her palm.

I took her hand and stroked it. 'Does he,' I said, feeling murderous.

'And I couldn't say anything! We had an agreement. A secret pact.' She looked revolted. 'He promised to leave you in peace. And in return, I must close the Pistol, and visit him every day for "spiritual lessons".'

Every day! So she had not been drifting about the city, as I had thought. Damn it, I should have realised.

'I hated lying. But I know you, Tom – if I'd told you, you would have stomped over there and confronted him.'

'I wouldn't—'

'Yes you would, and he'd have set his guards on you and you would be *dead* or in *prison* or *transported* and I would be alone with . . .' She stopped, and bit her lip. 'I told you, Tom – I would not lose you. No matter the cost.'

I sat back, stunned. All this time, Kitty had been protecting me. *No matter the cost.* And I had watched her suffer without knowing the cause for weeks. It must have been terrible, dissembling for so long. For all his faults, Gonson was no fool. If Kitty appeared too penitent, he would be suspicious, or insist that she threw me out of the house. Not penitent enough and he might break the pact entirely. She had been forced to play a subtle role, with no one to confide in.

'You should have come to me, missy,' Felblade said.

Sam frowned. 'Or me.'

'I don't need help,' Kitty said, then relented. '*Thank you*. I knew he would give up, eventually. I just had to be patient, and wait . . . But I didn't realise how exhausting it would be, listening to his endless sermons. And doing *nothing* all day.' She bunched her fists and shook them. 'Gah! I was *dying* to join in your new venture, Tom – but how could I? Hardly a respectable trade for a *virtuous young lady*.' She pouted. 'Well, you have done very well without me . . . I suppose Betty has been helping you instead.' And she flashed a very sharp green look at me.

Good Lord – was she jealous? I smiled. I couldn't help myself. A man likes to be valued and I had spent the last few weeks convinced that Kitty did not love me anymore. 'My darling,' I said. 'There is *no one in the whole world* but you.' I leant down and kissed her. She kissed me back.

Sam groaned and pressed his forehead against the table.

'*Equilibrium!*' Felblade cried. He grabbed Twig's vinegar-soaked cloth and flapped it in our faces. 'No fondling in my workshop.'

We settled back, and smiled at each other.

'How did you find out?' Kitty asked. 'Oh! You saw him today, didn't you? At the Pistol. *That's* why you were so cold with me.' She rubbed her face. 'I *hate* him. I promise that was the first time he came to the house.'

That made sense – if Gonson had been a regular visitor, Mrs Jenkins would have seen him, and told me.

'He said that he feared I was selling books again, but that wasn't the true reason he came. He wanted to inspect the house. He scolded me for keeping it in such a poor state. Tom, do not laugh – I think he plans to marry me.' She clutched herself in horror at the thought. 'He says if I would only repent, and follow his guidance, I should make *someone* a very good wife. He thinks he can transform me into the perfect woman: a meek, obedient little mouse.'

'That,' Felblade said, 'is beyond the powers of alchemy. You would make an atrocious wife.'

Kitty smiled at him. 'I agree. Anyway, he will tire of me soon enough.'

She sounded very certain about that. I was not so sure. Perhaps Kitty would make an atrocious wife, but she would make Gonson a very rich husband. Whatever lies he might tell himself about his honourable intentions, he would not have lavished so much time on her if she were poor. No – it was a powerful confluence of elements that had brought Kitty to his attention. Her fortune, her *vulnerable* state, her youth, her beauty, her spirit (which he would long to bend to his will). And a chance to take his revenge upon me. 'He will not tire of you, Kitty,' I said. 'But there is no need for you to submit to him for another second. You are free of him.' I waved my hand about her, as if lifting a curse.

She frowned, confused.

'Gonson was not responsible for Inchguard's attack.' I told her about my meeting with Lady Vanhook.

'Why does she hate you, Tom?' Kitty asked, puzzled.

'I have no idea. It is as if she is caught in some dark obsession. It *burns* through her. She wants to torment me, to have me suffer. She knows all about me. She even knew we were estranged.' I stopped. A cold, unpleasant feeling crept over me.

She grows tired of you, I hear. Your pretty whore.

My stomach lurched as I realised the truth.

'What is it, Tom?' Kitty asked. 'What's the matter?'

'She has formed an alliance with Gonson,' I said. 'How else would she know we were not on good terms? She keeps herself tucked away in her house on Jermyn Street. No visitors.' I clicked my fingers at Sam. 'The church! I'll wager ten guineas they meet at Gonson's church to exchange news. And she pretends to be a good Christian woman. He would not ally himself with her otherwise. He has to convince himself he is doing God's work.'

Kitty shivered. 'All these weeks, they have been toying with us. Trying to divide us. And it almost worked, Tom! I *wondered* why he made me keep our meetings secret. It seemed unlike him.'

True enough. Gonson was not a sly, manipulative man. Without question, this had been Lady Vanhook's idea. She may not have realised that I loved Kitty, but she did know how much I relied upon her.

It was unsettling to think how much time and effort Lady Vanhook had spent trying to destroy us. Finding Gonson – my great enemy – and drawing him to her side. How could a stranger hate me so much?

The answer to that question must lie in her past or mine. Had my father known her? I could not imagine it in a thousand years. And in any case why attack the son, when the father remained alive? And what of this strange exile of hers? Had she been forced to flee abroad because of me? Some scandal that I had unintentionally inflicted upon her? And how on earth did that involve the Fleets?

I needed more information. I needed to know Lady Vanhook's history. I needed to know her secrets.

'Sam and I will visit Gabriela tonight,' I said.

'I will come with you,' Kitty said.

I beamed at her. I had grown so used to the counterfeit Kitty, I had almost forgotten the real woman beneath. Of *course* she would come with us.

'Friends again, are we?' Felblade asked. 'Very good. Now bugger off home.'

'Are we not to have supper?' I asked, hope blossoming.

'Of course not!' Felblade looked disgusted. 'Supper parties are the invention of the devil and his most conniving minions. Go on, get out, all of you. Not you, Twig,' he said to his servant, who had made no attempt to move.

Back upon the street, Sam led the way home, pleased with himself. Once again I marvelled at the strange contradictions in the boy. In so many ways, he did not seem to care for or even understand the most basic human connections. And yet he had orchestrated this evening in order to bring Kitty and me back together.

I laced my fingers with Kitty's, pulling her to a stop. She looked up at me, her eyes sparkling. 'We are fucking idiots, aren't we Tom?'

'*Bimble-headed fools*,' I agreed.

We both laughed. The ill feeling that had grown between us was gone. Felblade had drawn it out like a poison. Perhaps he was a decent apothecary, in the end.

I put my arms around Kitty's waist and kissed her, feeling a great wave of relief. All would be mended, all would be well.

Kitty hugged me, pressing her cheek against my chest. And so she did not see the black and gold carriage rolling towards us through the snow, lanterns blazing. 'Tom,' she said, her lips to my heart. 'There is something else I must tell you. I did not want to say in front of the others . . .'

The coachman drew up at a slant by the Pistol, blocking the road ahead. Our eyes met. Something about his expression, and the position of the coach, sent a warning through me. I nudged Kitty from my arms.

'Tom?' she said – then saw the carriage.

'Do you have your blade?'

She shook her head. I thought of my swordstick, leaning against the wall in our bedchamber. I had my dagger, at least. I slid it from my coat.

Sam had reached the carriage. He peered through the window, trying to see who was inside. Suddenly the door slammed open, knocking him to the ground. He sprawled in the snow in a daze. A guard jumped out and pinned him in the back with his knee, as if Sam were a sheep ready to be sheared.

I ran forward, but Kitty grabbed my coat. 'Wait,' she hissed.

Gonson stepped from the carriage, smiling in satisfaction. At his nod five constables ran up behind us with their cudgels raised.

We were trapped.

Kitty tightened her grip, holding me back as Gonson strode towards us, boots crunching the snow. 'Hold your temper,' she whispered.

'You would raise a dagger to a king's magistrate?' Gonson called out, hot breath clouding the freezing air.

I tossed the blade upon the ground. 'Forgive me, Sir John. I feared you were a gang of thieves.'

Gonson scowled at the insult. 'Hold him,' he told his constables. Two of them grabbed my arms, separating me from Kitty.

I held my nerve and did not struggle. I knew from experience they would only beat me to the ground if I did. 'Am I for the lock-up, sir?' I asked, mildly. 'Upon what charge?'

'I have no interest in *you*, Hawkins,' Gonson replied. He reached a hand out to Kitty. 'Miss Sparks. You will come with me.'

Kitty stepped back, away from him.

'*Miss Sparks*. I would bid you remember our conversations on obedience. I should hate to use the guards upon you.'

'You cannot snatch her up against her will,' I said. 'She has not committed any crime.'

'Do not lecture me upon the law, Mr Hawkins. I act within the bounds of my authority, you may depend upon it.'

Kitty's black hood had fallen about her shoulders, red curls sparkling with melting snowflakes. 'Sir John. Will you not honour our agreement?'

He gave her an indulgent look. 'There can be no delay when a soul is in peril. Fresh news compels me to act, before you are lost from me. From God's path,' he corrected himself.

I lurched forward, and had my arms yanked in their sockets as his men dragged me back. One of them lifted his club to my face in warning.

Kitty stood alone. 'What more do you want of me?' she cried, exasperated. 'I learnt your prayers. I read all your sermons.'

'It is not enough to recite the words, child. They must penetrate your soul. We shall work upon this, in good time. When you are more compliant. Free of evil influences.'

'You promised you would leave us alone,' Kitty snapped, the fire rising in her. She had contained it for too long. 'You swore an oath to me, sir. Upon the Bible.'

Gonson faltered. Above all things, he believed himself to be a man of his word. 'I promised not to prosecute Mr Hawkins. I will remain true to that promise. Let him stew in sin if he wishes. But you, my dear – you *will* come with me.' He beckoned her towards him.

Kitty stood firm. 'No.'

The word fell on Gonson like a slap. 'Come here at once. Before God punishes you for your defiance.'

I did not like the sound of that. When Gonson spoke of God, he usually meant himself. 'You have no claim upon her,' I said. 'She does not belong to you.'

'Nor you, sir,' Gonson countered. 'And she never will. You may count upon it.'

'I belong to no one but myself,' Kitty said, her hands tightening into fists.

The guards sniggered at her defiance. Gonson joined in their laughter. 'Here is a warning to you, gentlemen,' he said. 'This is what happens when a young girl is granted too much liberty. See how her freedom unmoors her.'

'I am not unmoored,' Kitty said.

'The fault does not lie with this poor creature,' Gonson spoke over her. 'Blame the master, not the dog.' He waggled his finger. 'Remember this lesson sirs, with your wives and your daughters. Man serves God and Woman serves Man. That is the natural order of things. If you allow a woman her own authority, nine times from ten she will fall to wickedness and despair.' He swung his hand out to Kitty, as if she were on display. 'Or in the worst cases – madness.'

'Oh enough, enough! I cannot endure another *second*!' Kitty cried, bursting free from weeks of frustration. 'I am not mad!'

'I'm afraid you are, my darling.'

The words rang out through the night air – a woman's voice, laden with false concern. The carriage tilted as Lady Vanhook opened the door and stepped down, her pale face framed by a fur-trimmed riding hood. 'Quite mad,' she said, and smiled.

Kitty stood paralysed, her mouth open in horror. 'No. Not you. You're dead. He promised. He *promised*!'

'Catherine,' Lady Vanhook said, gliding down the street with her shoulders back, as if she were parading to her own coronation. She stretched out her arms. 'Come to me, my darling.'

They had met before. How was this possible?

Kitty, with no thought, no strategy, staggered back and ran. She was blocked at once by the guards. She scrabbled at them, trying to squeeze past. 'Let me go,' she cried, '*let me go*.' They laughed at her. The leader grabbed her by the waist and lifted her off her feet. She screamed in a desperate fury, kicking out and tearing at him with her nails. The guards laughed harder.

I had seen Kitty fight three men together, and win. Now, seized with panic, she forgot herself, biting and scratching like a cornered wildcat.

'Kitty,' I cried, afraid she would hurt herself as she lashed out. She didn't hear me. I struggled against the two guards holding me. 'Hold still,' the one with the club snarled. 'Or I'll knock you dead.'

It took three men to push Kitty to the ground, pressing her face into the dirt as she screamed and struggled against them. Lady Vanhook watched from a short distance, a soft smile upon her lips. My mind spun. Why was Kitty so afraid of her? And why did Lady Vanhook take such satisfaction in that terror?

She saw my confusion and her smiled deepened. 'Have you not guessed yet?' she gloated. 'Perhaps you're not so clever after all.'

I stared at her. Something about the tilt of her head, the sharp jut of her chin . . . Lady Vanhook. Lady Emma Vanhook.

Kitty's mother was called Emma.

Not you. You're dead. He promised me.

Samuel Fleet had promised Kitty that her mother was dead. But Samuel Fleet was a liar. He'd told me Emma died in the gutter, her body ruined by the pox. Lies, lies. Now he was in his grave, and she was here, alive – a phoenix, rising.

All this time I had thought that I was being punished for some forgotten crime. But this was never about me. I was nothing more than a troublesome rival, a stone in the shoe, a fly to be swatted. Hated, despised, but never the object of desire.

She did not want me. She wanted Kitty.

And Lady Vanhook did not share her treasures. Not with anyone. Oh, God.

She clapped her hands, thrilled by the effect she had on me. Then she turned her gaze back to Kitty. And – oh! – the endless devouring need of that gaze. The delight, the triumph. The anticipation for what would follow. It was sickening.

The guards pulled Kitty to her knees. Her lip was bleeding, her face scratched. My heart cracked in two. My love. My ferocious angel.

'Sir John,' she cried. 'Don't let her take me. Please. I would rather die. I would rather *die*.'

'Blasphemy,' Gonson murmured, but even he looked troubled. 'Miss Sparks, your mother is alive and well! You should rejoice to see her!'

Kitty was sobbing. 'Please . . . please . . .'

'My dear child,' Gonson said, almost kindly. 'You have suffered a shock, no more. You *will* rejoice, once you have rested, under her care and protection—'

'No, no!' Kitty howled. 'You can't. I won't go with her. Tom! Tom, stop them. Please!'

But there was nothing I could do.

Gonson signalled to his men, who picked Kitty up and lifted her towards the carriage while she cried out for help. Lady Vanhook stepped in front of them. Kitty was breathing so hard and so fast I thought she might faint.

Lady Vanhook peeled off her glove and placed a long hand upon Kitty's head, fingers trailing through her curls. Kitty shuddered and tried to pull away. Lady Vanhook tightened her grip. 'Catherine. My darling girl. How I've longed for this moment.' She leant down and branded Kitty's forehead with a kiss. 'Take her to the carriage.'

The guards dragged her away.

'Throw this man in the lock-up,' Gonson told the men holding me. He looked shaken, but covered it with his usual bluster. 'And the boy. This is God's work, gentlemen. We are all His instruments tonight.'

The guards pushed Kitty into the carriage. I caught one last glimpse of her pale, frightened face before she disappeared inside.

'Kitty!' I shouted. 'Don't be afraid. I'll come for you, I swear it!'

Lady Vanhook laughed at me, her foot upon the carriage step. 'Poor Thomas. You will never see her again.'

She stepped into the carriage, closing the door neatly behind her. The driver shook the reins and they raced off into the night.

PART THREE

The Cage

Chapter Ten

There is a house in Bethnal Green with a pretty walled garden. In spring, sweet roses scent the air and bees buzz from flower to flower, gathering nectar. Even now, in stark winter, the garden is a fine sight: the tall shrubs neatly clipped, the paths swept clean, everything in perfect order. An ash tree stands in one corner, its grey branches stretching over the wall. Clouds drift apart and reform, shifting in the wind.

Someone screams.

At the entrance, under a magnificent iron gate, a robin hops along the ground, hunting for food. Sometimes it skips through the gate to the road beyond; sometimes it flutters up and perches on the lock. When it sings, its red throat ripples.

The scream descends to a low, desolate moan. The robin cocks its head to listen, then returns to its work, pecking at the frozen earth. Its feet leave delicate prints in the snow.

There is a house in Bethnal Green with a pretty walled garden, and bars upon the windows, and iron spikes along the roof. Something terrible is happening inside. It is happening to you, my love. It is happening to you now.

The guards chained my wrists and threw me in a cell without a window, no candle, no furniture. I sat on the dank floor until I felt something, some *things*, crawling over me. Cockroaches, stirring from hibernation to greet the new prisoner. I stood up and walked the narrow confines of the cell, back and forth, thinking of a black carriage racing through the moonlit streets. How far could they travel through the night? What if I was locked up in here for a week? Kitty could be on a ship to Antigua by then. She could be anywhere.

No – I would not give in to such black thoughts. This was a lock-up, not Newgate. They could not keep me here without good reason.

But how far could they travel through the night?

I paced until I was exhausted and then gave in to the floor, and the cockroaches, and whatever else was creeping about in the dark.

I fell into a half-sleep, where memory and nightmare took turns to torment me – Kitty's face as she saw her mother, her screams, the guards dragging her to the coach. And through it all, like some ghastly melody, Lady Vanhook's mocking laughter.

Poor Thomas. You will never see her again.

The door swung open. I blinked as lantern light spilled into the room, cockroaches scurrying back into the shadows. Behind the lantern a woman's face, a scar running from temple to jaw. Gabriela.

I staggered to my feet.

'Dormouse,' she said in a low voice, as I stumbled out into the corridor. 'What shit is this? Where is my son?'

I held out my manacled wrists.

She unlocked them with a thin pick, catching the chains before they fell to the floor. 'Why am I helping this arsehole?' she grumbled to herself.

'They took Kitty.'

'So?' She shrugged, but she didn't mean it. 'Who took her?'

'Gonson.' I followed her down the corridor. 'And her mother.'

'Emma Sparks is dead,' Gabriela said, then stopped in her tracks. '*Filho da puta!*' she cursed, under her breath. 'He *swore* she was dead.'

So Samuel had lied to his sister-in-law too. She breathed out hard through her nostrils. 'Emma Sparks is alive. *Foda-se.* That woman's a *witch.*'

'I know. She tried to kill me.'

'A shame she failed,' Gabriela said, but her heart wasn't in it. Preoccupied, she moved from cell to cell, tapping a particular rhythm at each door until she heard a low whistle in response. Her face softened. Within moments Sam was released.

We moved on in silence. The turnkeys were asleep in the guard-room, I could hear them snoring. Dead drunk, most likely.

Gabriela had broken in through a storeroom overlooking a narrow alley. We escaped the same way. I had to strip to my shirt to squeeze through the window. I landed as softly as I could and hurried after them, pushing my arms back through my coat sleeves as I ran. Dawn was breaking, the last revellers of the night stagger-ing home as early morning servants and traders headed for work. Everything and everyone looked grey.

I found Sam and his mother two streets away, arguing in low voices. I thanked Gabriela for rescuing me.

'I came for my son, not you. You are . . .' she gave me a withering look. '*Appendage.*'

'Well – my thanks to you nonetheless.' I bowed and turned away. I had lost hours in that stinking lock-up and could not afford to stand idle now.

Where to begin my search? Jermyn Street, I decided. Never ignore the most obvious place, especially when dealing with a devi-ous mind.

Gabriela grabbed my arm, fingers digging into my flesh. 'Where are you going? You run after that *bruxa* with no plan? All alone?'

'Not alone,' Sam said, fiercely. His face was covered in scrapes and cuts from his struggle with the guards.

Gabriela glared at him, and then at me. Sam stood resolute. After a moment, Gabriela sighed. She knew her son. 'Where are you going?' she asked again, resigned.

'She rents a house on Jermyn Street.' Where I had sat drinking tea, only a few hours before, making threats and thinking I had the better of her. What a fool.

'*So*. We go there and on the way I tell you about Emma Sparks.'

'Very good.'

'*Very good*,' Gabriela muttered, and flung her hood back over her curls. '*Very good*.'

Much of what she told me next – the older history – I already knew. Emma had married Kitty's father Nathaniel when she was not yet twenty. 'He loved her,' Gabriela admitted, grudgingly. 'But he loved Samuel more. He does not admit this to himself for a long time. Years. He fights it, you understand.'

I understood. Even if the world allowed such passions – and it most decidedly did *not* – there was the question of Samuel Fleet himself. I had only known him briefly, and had never felt so ill-at-ease, so discombobulated, so fascinated, so . . . well, for want of a better word – *seduced*. Poor Nathaniel – no wonder he struggled against his feelings. One does not fall in love with the devil lightly.

We walked through Leicester Fields, the birds calling in the trees, the gardens strewn with rubbish from the night's crimes and debauches. A woman passed by with a basket of apples. Gabriela stole a couple on reflex, throwing one to Sam.

'Nathaniel does not love his wife by this time,' she continued. 'He sees behind the mask. Too late. But still he does not want to hurt her, or Kitty. So he pretends. He wears his own mask.' Gabriela bit into her apple. 'Everyone is wearing a mask,' she said, sounding bored. 'But Nathaniel is too open, too honest. The mask slips, and Emma discovers the truth. And then,' Gabriela took another bite, 'Nathaniel dies.'

'My God. She *killed* him?'

Gabriela tilted her hand back and forth.

We paused on Whitcomb Street to let a carriage pass. Gabriela glanced at me. 'Samuel was a spy, you know this.'

And an assassin, I thought, but did not say. It felt impolite, somehow.

'Nathaniel helped him sometimes. Samuel loved this. Danger, travel, fucking – all his favourite things.' Gabriela crossed the road with her low stride. 'But then Nathaniel dies on some mission.' She waved her hand, not bothered by the details. 'Samuel . . . It destroys him. He blames himself. But *I* blamed Emma. Think of it. Emma discovers her husband is fucking Samuel, is *in love* with Samuel – and two months later he is dead. She did not kill him, but she betrayed him somehow. I *know* this, *here*.' She pressed her stomach.

I thought of Lady Vanhook's cold, winter-blue eyes. The way she had manipulated Gonson, and fooled me. Yes, I could believe her capable of plotting Nathaniel's death. The only wonder was that Samuel had not reached the same conclusion. Too busy torturing himself, I suppose. What had he said to me, that bright autumn day when we lay on our backs in Snowsfields? His last day on earth.

Grief can drag you to some dark places. But guilt is like a whip upon your back, urging you on.

Samuel had felt responsible for Nathaniel's death, and that guilt had consumed him. There had been no room left to blame anyone else. And more than that – he was the arch-schemer, Machiavelli's most diligent student. The idea that he could have been tricked by Nathaniel's wife – impossible!

Gabriela threw her apple core in the gutter. 'I warned Samuel – Emma Sparks is *dangerous*. A spider full of poison. We must kill her.' She caught my look. 'You don't like this?'

'Well . . .'

She stopped in the street, and faced me. 'Listen – when I kill you, I will take my blade and push it in your heart. And you will think, "Oh no, I am not happy about this, but perhaps I deserve it."'

I wasn't sure those *would* be my dying thoughts, precisely, but I let it pass.

'I kill when I must. I take no pleasure in it. But Emma plays games. She is clever with men, most of all. She sniffs out what they want and pretends to give it to them. Then she takes everything. *Everything.*' She placed a hand on her heart. 'There is nothing here, you understand? Empty. So she takes and takes. But it is never enough.'

'A void,' Sam said, making us both jump. He had been silent all this time.

'What is that?' Gabriela asked, with a frown.

'An empty space. A vacuum.'

Gabriela looked cross. 'That is what I said. Empty. This is your fault, Dormouse. You teach him this, this ... *gentlemen's cant*, and now I cannot understand my own son.'

We had reached the Haymarket. It was a market day, and the carts blocked the road. The street smelled of horse, and horse dung. It made me think of that black and gold carriage, racing away in the night. *I should have fought harder.*

Gabriela returned to her story. 'Samuel says no, we cannot kill Emma. He promised Nathaniel he would never hurt her. Idiot. Samuel goes away on business, to France. Or Scotland.' Gabriela shrugs, as if there is no difference. 'I can't remember. He comes back a few months later, Emma has lost Nathaniel's fortune and Kitty has run away. Disappeared. Perhaps she is *dead*. I say, Samuel if Kitty is dead, that poison spider witch is to blame. I told you to kill her. And he says, yes, yes Gabriela, you were right, I shall kill her now, don't worry. He told me he cut her throat. That fucking liar! She is alive, all these years.'

'In Antigua,' I said. Samuel couldn't kill Emma without breaking his promise to Nathaniel. So he had sent her into exile. I could just imagine him saying it, his black eyes hard with threat. *Leave the country or die – your choice.*

But then Samuel himself had died. It would have taken months for the news to reach Antigua, and yet more time to arrange a passage back to England, which explained why Lady Vanhook had not arrived in London until early October.

Why had she waited almost two months after that to abduct Kitty? What was her agreement with Gonson?

I was missing something. A plot within a plot.

We turned on to Jermyn Street. Sam and Gabriela walked side by side ahead of me, step matching step. From the back, they looked like twins: the same height, the same narrow frame, the same catlike poise.

We reached the house with the dark green door. I sensed that it stood empty, but I had to try. Sam and Gabriela stood by the grey railings while I slammed the lion's head knocker, over and over, to no reply. At last a neighbour in the next building opened his shutters, dressed in his nightcap and gown.

'Go away, damn you,' he shouted. 'I'll call the watch.'

'You call the watch, I'll stuff that nightcap down your fucking throat and rip it out your arse,' Gabriela called up.

There was a short pause while the neighbour contemplated this disagreeable prospect. 'There's no one home,' he said. 'They left in the night.'

'Where?' I asked.

'How should I know? Made more racket than you did. Some mad girl screaming and swearing like the devil.'

'So why did you not call the watch *then*?' I snapped.

'None of my damned business, is it?' He slammed the window closed.

I returned to the pavement with a sinking heart. I had not really expected to find them here, but now I must face the truth: they could be *anywhere*. 'I will visit Gonson,' I said. 'Could you ...'

'You want me to help steal another child from its mother?' Gabriela said. 'I am *joking*,' she added, when she saw my expression. 'This is family business. We work together.'

My eyes welled with tears. The shock, the exhaustion, the worry.

'Oh my God,' Gabriela said, disgusted.

'Forgive me,' I said, recovering myself. 'It's just ... she said I would never see Kitty again. I'm afraid she will take her back to Antigua.'

'No,' Gabriela said. 'Not until the baby is born.'

I felt the world pivot. 'The baby?'

Gabriela gave me a strange look, then glanced at Sam. 'You didn't tell him?'

Sam looked aggrieved. 'You told me not to. You said it was *Kitty*'s business.'

'Since when do you do anything I say?'

'The baby?' I repeated, stupidly.

'Idiot,' Gabriela said, almost gentle. 'You think you fuck like rabbits and nothing happens?'

'She's ... Kitty ...'

I thought of her changing moods, her exhaustion and loss of appetite. Her certainty that Gonson would 'tire' of her. He might overlook Kitty's past transgressions, but he could not overlook a child.

My child.

Why did she not tell me? How could I not have guessed? My God, even her clothes – replacing her sharp-boned dresses with loose wrapping gowns.

I looked at Sam. 'She confided in you?'

He shook his head. 'I know the signs. Ma's *always* pregnant.'

'What – I am a cow?' Gabriela snapped.

'I'm going to be a father,' I said, standing taller. *I'm going to be a father*.

'Yes, congratulations Dormouse,' Gabriela said. And then she reached out and plucked a cockroach from my shirt, and squashed it under her boot.

I ran home through the quiet streets, chest burning. The sun was rising over the rooftops as I sprinted through the market, early risers browsing the stalls and sharing their stories of the night. Did they talk of Kitty and her abduction? The news must have spread through the neighbourhood by now. Did anyone see or hear something useful? I would ask them, as soon as I had changed from these filthy, verminous clothes. I would start with Mrs Jenkins – our conduit of news.

I hurried down Russell Street, eager to reach home – only to spy two of Gonson's men standing in the road outside the Pistol, laughing and sharing a pipe.

I drew back and watched them closely. I recognised them both from the night before. The older one had been holding me when they dragged Kitty away. The younger one had opened the carriage door and knocked Sam flying. Now he was kicking at something on the ground with his boot. For one awful moment I thought it was a body, then I realised it was a pile of clothes – my clothes, in fact. A third guard appeared at the doorway, carrying my favourite chair from the kitchen. He dropped it on the pavement and disappeared back inside.

They were clearing the Pistol, my home. Furniture, clothes, books – everything.

I took a breath to calm myself. It would serve no purpose to escape prison, only to be locked up again within a quarter-hour. Gonson would not order this done without some bit of paper to show that he could.

If I could hold my temper, the guards might be useful. They might even know where Kitty was being held.

I sauntered up to them, hands in my pockets. 'Good morrow, sirs,' I said, pleasantly.

The two guards returned the greeting, then recognised me.

'No need for alarm,' I said, spreading out my hands in a gesture of peace. 'Sir John and I have reached an understanding. We are all friends here.'

The guards looked doubtful, but I was here, freed from the lockup, and it was easier for them to believe me than to bother with an argument. I picked up my hat, brushing away the dirt and snow, and placed it on my head at an angle. No one suspects a man who wears his hat in a jaunty fashion.

'Quite the fracas last night.' I smiled at the older guard. 'You near ripped off my arm, sir.' I rolled my shoulder and gave a rueful wince.

He laughed. Tell a fellow he is stronger than you, and he will always believe it.

'So you have come to empty the house,' I said in a conversational tone, as if I were perfectly at ease with the matter.

'We have papers,' the younger guard said.

'Yes, Sir John released me in person this morning. He has explained everything.' I thought quickly. How would Gonson justify stealing my belongings – not only to the world, but to himself? There would be some twisted logic to it. I picked my way through to an answer. 'This house is part of Kitty's inheritance, and she bought a large proportion of its contents. I have no claim upon it.'

The guards were nodding. Good. The hours I had spent contemplating Gonson's infuriating character had not been wasted.

'Everything is to be sent on to Lady Vanhook, is that so?'

Their faces closed. I'd made a mistake.

'Wait, no – is it to be sold?' I corrected myself. 'Forgive me, I did not sleep well.' I rubbed my eyes. 'I believe there was some debate upon the matter.'

The guards could not know if this were true. More importantly, they did not care.

'Sir John said that I might collect one or two personal items,' I said. 'Nothing of any great value, you understand.' I picked up my swordstick, covering the golden fox with my palm, and used it to poke through the heap of clothes growing damp upon the cobbles.

I picked up my leather bag and gathered a few items: a razor, a couple of pairs of breeches, a shirt, shoes and my grey cloak, which I put on. My silver pocket watch. All personal items any gentleman would own. I knew better than to retrieve my dagger. The older guard gave the razor a narrow look. I tucked it firmly out of reach, and slung the bag over my shoulder.

'Are you not vexed by all this, sir?' he asked, suspicious. He was more cynical than his friend, presumably from experience.

I gave a rakish grin. 'The perils of being a kept man,' I shrugged, then lowered my voice, conspiratorial. 'It was always a temporary arrangement.' I winked at them. 'God save us from interfering mothers, eh?'

They both laughed, reassured. It was easy for them to believe that I had conned Kitty for her fortune. What other reason could there be – that I loved her?

The third guard trudged out, carrying a rug on one shoulder and Kitty's portmanteau under his free arm. He dumped them on the ground. 'Am I to do all the work? While you stand about gossiping like a pair of old tarts?'

'You told me to stand guard!' the younger man protested.

'Well there's a trunk upstairs full of books and papers and other bollocks, I'm not carrying it out on my own.'

'I'll help you,' the older guard said, stamping his feet and rubbing his hands. It was snowing again. 'Best for my joints if I keep moving. Reeves,' he called to the younger guard, and gestured to the jumble of bags, boxes and furniture. 'Put this in order for the cart.' He nodded to me. 'No hard feelings.'

'None at all,' I lied smoothly, leaning lightly on my cane. They had dragged Kitty to the carriage, screaming and terrified. She could have been hurt. She could have lost our child. No hard feelings? My feelings were harder than granite.

The two older guards headed inside, while Reeves set to work. A lone tradesman trundled by with his hand cart, the wheels leaving tracks in the snow. When he had passed from view, I slid the sword-stick from its ebony case, the steel blade coming free with a whispering scrape.

Reeves had his back to me. Well, that was foolish of him.

I stole up behind him and pressed the blade under his chin. 'Say nothing,' I hissed in his ear. 'Or I'll slice your head from your neck.'

I pushed him against the wall. 'Where have they taken her?'

'I don't know,' he stammered, his eyes wide with fear.

Kitty had been frightened – and he had laughed at her. They all had.

I pressed the swordstick across his throat, cutting into his skin. A thin line of blood welled up over the blade. '*Where is she*?'

'I don't know, I swear. They didn't tell us.' An acrid stink filled the air between us. He'd pissed himself. 'Please don't hurt me. Please.'

Kitty had said please, when they took her away. She had said please, and put a hand to her stomach.

'Think, damn you!' I spat. I needed an answer before his friends came back. 'Did they mention a ship? Bristol? Antigua?'

'No, no. Wait!' His eyes brightened as he remembered something. 'The Lady told her daughter she was sick. She was taking her somewhere safe, so she could rest and get better. That's all I know, I swear to God.'

I could hear the other guards cursing as they shifted the trunk down the stairs. I should leave. But I kept the blade pressed against Reeves' throat. Let him be afraid. Let him beg for mercy. He deserved it.

'Thomas!'

Mrs Jenkins stood a few paces away, her face death white. She must have come from the market – she was carrying a basket filled with parcels.

I lowered the swordstick, my hand still pressed against Reeves' chest.

'What have you done?' she whispered.

I turned back and saw the scene afresh – a young man cringing against the wall, blood trickling from his throat, a wet patch spreading across his breeches.

'They took Kitty,' I said, and stepped away.

Mrs Jenkins picked up one of Kitty's handkerchiefs and held it to the cut on Reeves' throat. Blood seeped scarlet through the white cloth. 'You're safe now, love,' she told him. 'Press down hard. It will stop the bleeding.'

Reeves did as he was told. His hand was shaking. 'Th-thank you.'

'They took Kitty,' I said again.

Mrs Jenkins ignored me. 'Wash the wounds in liquor, soon as you can,' she told Reeves, before rounding on me. 'I know they took Kitty. I saw it. I have just spent the last two hours tramping through the market, searching for news of her.'

'Oh,' I said, dismayed. 'I'm sorry. I'm so sorry. Hannah—'

'I thought better of you, Thomas.'

'You don't understand . . . She's carrying my child.'

'I thought better of you,' she said again, and walked away.

Chapter Eleven

You have never seen your mother so happy.

You sit on the floor in a rough linen smock. They stripped you of your yellow dress last night, ripped and filthy from your fight outside the Pistol. If you are good, if you behave, they might return it to you in a week, or a month. You have always hated that yellow wrapping gown, you only wore it last night out of spite. Now you long for it.

Your left foot is chained to an iron ring in the floor. The iron shackle is cold and rough – it has scraped a raw patch on your ankle that stings when you move. You may walk to the bed and to the chamber pot, but the short chain halts you three paces from the door. Nor can you reach the barred window where your mother stands, her auburn hair glowing in a thin shaft of light.

Six years have passed since you ran away from her. Every day you woke with the fear she might find you. You fled London, her playground – not knowing that Samuel Fleet would soon after force her to leave England. You spent two years hiding as a servant in the country, another eighteen months further north, always working and saving. Learning how to protect yourself. A blade tucked under your skirts. In the end London called you home, but you stayed vigilant.

Then Samuel found you at last. He told you your mother was dead and you wept with relief. You were free. You could stop running. She would never hurt you again.

But here she is, alive and looking very well, only a few grey hairs to show the passing of time. Of course she looks well. It is everyone else who suffers, and fades. You have been in her company for only a few hours, and already you feel drained.

Your mother tells you that you are safe here. She says she forgives you for running away. Lies, lies. She knows you don't believe her, and that is one of the reasons she is so happy. It is one of her favourite things, to say one thing and mean another.

She smiles at you, and you hate her so much you feel the acid bile rising in your throat.

'I escaped you once,' you say. 'I will escape you again—'

She steps forward and cuffs you with the back of her hand, swift and hard. Your teeth cut against your mouth and you taste blood.

'Catherine,' she says, moving back out of reach. 'Darling. Don't be tiresome.'

Tiresome, troublesome, insolent, scheming, petulant, wilful, obstinate – these are her favourite words for you. So many failings to punish. The wounds faded from your skin years ago but you can map them still. They flare up now along your back and thighs – a memory of pain.

The doctor arrives. He is short and neatly dressed, in a fastidious way that sits at odds with the squalid room. The buttons of his waistcoat and the buckles on his shoes are polished to a high sheen; his skin looks as though it has been buffed and polished too, his cheeks smooth, no lines on his face.

He is flanked by two nurses in grey fustian gowns. One is holding a tin bucket. The other is carrying a bowl filled with a thick, rust-coloured liquid. She has a deep scratch on her cheek. You remember her now. She held you down last night while the other one stripped off your dress. You must have caught her with your nails. She gives you a resentful look.

No one here will speak for you. You must save yourself. You must convince the doctor that you are sane.

You stand up and smile at him, your lip throbbing from your mother's slap. 'Good morning, Dr Mackay.'

He doesn't look at you. 'It is as you feared, madam,' he tells your mother, as if you are not there. 'Your daughter has succumbed to a form of lunacy.'

'That's not true,' you say.

'I have seen it before. Young girls who reject propriety and indulge themselves in base, animal passions. And turn savage, as a consequence.' He gestures to the nurse with the scratched face.

'Can she be cured?' your mother asks.

The doctor glances at you. You stand straighter, hands neatly linked. But your smock smells stale, your hair is loose and wild. Your lip is bleeding. Even without a mirror, you know how you must appear to him.

'Nothing is certain in such cases,' he says. 'We shall do our best.'

'Naturally.'

'Dr Mackay,' you say, smiling, smiling. 'I assure you, I am quite well—'

'Is she prone to fits?' he asks your mother. 'Or fainting?'

'No indeed. Catherine has an iron constitution. You must not be timid with her, Dr Mackay. She is not to be coaxed or coddled. I fear that to cure her, we must first break her.'

Mackay is nodding, pleased. 'Quite so. We shall begin with a course of emetic syrup and blood-letting to balance her humours.'

The nurse with the scratched face smirks to herself. She is carrying the emetic, to make you vomit up . . . what, exactly? Your disobedience? Your spirit?

You're afraid for the baby. You want to warn them, but you don't know how your mother will react to the news. Her moods are as unpredictable as the weather and just as destructive. 'Dr Mackay, please, there is no need for this. I am well. You must see that—'

Without warning the other nurse grabs you and pushes you to your knees. She places the bucket on the floor and kneels behind you, wrapping her arms tight around your chest.

You want to fight free of her, but the doctor is studying you intently.

The nurse with the scratched face shoves the wooden bowl to your mouth. Brandy, and underneath that the musty, bitter tang of the emetic. Ipecacuanha. You know it well, its violent effects. You spit it out. 'No. Stop. My baby. My baby.'

The nurse hesitates, then probes your stomach with her fingers. You grit your teeth and endure it.

'Can't feel nothing,' the nurse says.

'I am four months gone. Please.'

The doctor looks to your mother. 'Is this true?'

Your mother puts a steadying hand to her heart. Her eyes are hectic, her breathing jagged. They think she is overcome with shock, but you know better. She is enraptured. This is what she desires, more than anything in the world: to hold your fate, your baby's fate, in her hands. To stand at the centre of everything. You stare at her, pleading silently. This once – oh, God – this once. Be kind.

'A delusion, I'm afraid. Continue.'

'No – please!'

The nurses hold you down and force you to drink the foul mixture. You try to spit it out again, but they clap their hands over your mouth until you swallow. Within moments, it begins to work. The nurses don't need to hold you now. You bend over the tin bucket and vomit, over and over.

'Good girl,' Dr Mackay says, as he leaves. 'Let it out. All the sickness. Let it out.'

Your mother stays and watches, the lightest of smiles upon her lips. You have never seen her so happy.

I walked away from my home, from my belongings scattered in the dirt and slush of the street. Nothing mattered except finding Kitty.

I knew where I must go next, but it would do no good if I arrived filthy from the lock-up. I paid a brief visit to a *bagnio*, renting a room for the hour. I lit a fire while one of the girls filled the bath with buckets of hot water. She looked vaguely familiar. I had visited this place many times before – but never sober, and not strictly for bathing.

'Need a hand, sir?' she asked, as I pulled off my shirt.

'Thank you, no.'

She shrugged – *your loss* – and left. I lowered myself into the bath. The water was scalding hot, as I'd requested. I scrubbed my body hard, turning the water brown. Then I took out my razor and shaved my head close to the scalp. That should take care of any lice that had escaped the lock-up with me.

Once I had dressed in my fresh clothes, I looked much better. I looked, in fact, like a gentleman. I wiped the blood from my sword-stick and set off for Westminster, and Sir John Gonson.

To my surprise his servant let me in without argument, ushering me into a large study, the books ordered with precision in great oak cases, the walnut bureau set with fresh blotting paper and quills. I could have been led blindfold to this room and guessed the owner. Even Gonson's furniture seemed pleased with itself.

'Is there a young woman kept here?' I asked the servant. 'Red hair? A yellow gown? She would have arrived last night.'

He looked so scandalised I would have laughed, in better circumstances. 'This is a *respectable* house, sir,' he said, and left before I could taint him with further disgusting questions.

I searched the bureau – of course I did. The drawers were locked save for the bottom one, which was filled with copies of Gonson's sermons and speeches. Laid on top of these was a broadsheet, of the sort pasted on to walls around the town. The ink smelled fresh.

Let it be known that MR. THOMAS HAWKINS, a Notorious Libertine late of NEWGATE and MARSHALSEA gaols, has persuaded an impressionable young woman, C.–INE S–KS, of his Affections, whereas his Sole Concern is for her considerable Fortune. With no Father or Guardian to protect her, this *most Unfortunate Creature* has fallen under the Spell of the aforemention'd VILLAIN, permitting him to Defile her Body and POISON her Soul. For this Reason I Suspect her to be *non compos mentis*.

As Magistrate for the Borough of *Westminster* and a Founder of the Society for the Reformation of Manners it is my Duty to protect the Innocent and the Vulnerable. The Lord *in His Wisdom* has Provid'd me with the means to do so in this Matter.

Some weeks ago a pious, dignified Lady approach'd me with a Vexing problem. She was, she avow'd, the *mother of* C–INE S–KS. She claim'd her Daughter had been stolen from her in the most Distressing circumstances, by a degenerate rogue named SAMUEL FLEET. This black-hearted creature had made it his Business to turn the Child against the Mother in a most cruel and unnatural manner. So fearful was the LADY V–K of this wicked fellow, that she fled the country, only returning when she learned of his MURDER in *prison*.

She arriv'd in England longing for Reconciliation with her estrang'd Daughter – only to Discover she had fallen into the hands of the Villainous MR. H – MR. FLEET's former cellmate.

Fearing her Daughter would take Flight, or Refuse to Recognise her own Mother out of Ill-judged Spite, this good Gentle Woman came to me for Guidance.

For the past two Months I have studied Woman and Child in Close and Attentive detail. There is no Doubt that they are Mother and Daughter: the Similarities in Complexion and Figure are most Striking. Furthermore, as the Lady is a woman of considerable wealth and Status – being married to SIR F– V–K, a distinguish'd Plantation Owner in Antigua – I am Satisfied that her Motives are both pure and *Natural*.

Thus assur'd, I endeavour'd to prepare the Child for this *Miraculous Reunion*, through Prayers and Instruction. Alas – before this education was complete, LADY V K discover'd that the False and Cunning HAWKINS intend'd to Force a Betrothal upon her Daughter, putting her Beyond reach of Rescue.

To prevent this imminent Disaster, I ordered the Child placed with all Speed into the Loving care of her Mother where, remov'd from the aforemention'd *Evil Influence*, she will assuredly Repent her Sinful ways and recover her Sanity. It is for this Reason that I protect her Identity within this Document, conscious of a Day when she might make a *Respectable connection* with an Honourable Gentleman, able to Tame her Wilder instincts and set her with a firm hand upon God's path.

Let it be known herewith that MR. THOMAS HAWKINS has no Right under Law to C–INE S–KS' property or Fortune & that he is remov'd at once and Entirely from the house and business on Russell Street.

I had no doubt that Gonson had left this nonsense in the open drawer so that I might find it. Was it libellous? Possibly. It also confirmed what I had suspected – 1) that Lady Vanhook and Gonson had been in alliance for weeks, and 2) that the Magistrate for Westminster was a First-Class Idiot when it came to women. I slid the broadsheet back in the drawer and crossed to the window, where I waited an excruciating half-hour, grinding my swordstick into the floor to contain my rage.

'Mr Hawkins.' As usual, Gonson's voice entered before he did. 'I trust a night in chains has cooled that hot temper of yours.' The guards at the lock-up must have been too embarrassed to mention my escape. He gestured to a chair and sat down behind the bureau, smoothing the ends of his long brown wig to be sure they hung in perfect symmetry.

I remained standing. 'Where is she?'

He rolled the quill under his fingers, back and forth. 'She is safe.'

'You dragged her away against her will. That is kidnap, sir.'

'Nonsense. She is suffering from delusions. They will pass. She will be grateful to us, when she has recovered her wits.'

'That was no fit of lunacy, Sir John. You saw her, the same as I. She was terrified.'

He shifted, uneasy. 'The violence of the rescue was unfortunate,' he conceded. 'But that was your fault, sir.'

'*My* fault?'

'Do you deny visiting Lady Vanhook at her home on Jermyn Street yesterday—'

'At her request!—'

'Where you demanded a fortune to give up her daughter?'

'Did I?' I laughed in disbelief.

'Eight hundred pounds, or you would elope with Miss Sparks the same night.'

'That is absurd. Sir John, you must see that—'

'Lady Vanhook has no reason to lie.'

But of course she did, the viper! She was one great lie, from the tips of her dainty fingers to the depths of her blackened soul. She had played the role of the rich, pious gentlewoman beautifully – dressed in her fur-lined hood, transported by Gonson's spiritual lectures. *She finds out what men want and pretends to give it to them.*

'Tell me something, Mr Hawkins,' Gonson said. 'I am genuinely curious. You claim to care for Miss Sparks.'

'I love her.'

He laughed. 'Very well. You imagine an attachment. Can you swear – be honest – that you are a good influence upon her?'

'I believe—'

'No, fie – *be honest, sir*! You hail from a good family. You have studied Divinity. You can recognise the contours of a decent, Christian life. Now consider the troubles you have pulled down upon your head, and hers. Prison, debt, scandal . . .'

'*You* put me in prison! You charged me with murder!'

'And the whole town believed you guilty. What does that say of your reputation? If you walk with the devil, you must face the fire, Hawkins. I have saved Miss Sparks from burning with you. And I rejoice in that fact, sir. I *rejoice* in it.'

I dug my palm into the top of my swordstick, letting the fox head bite into my skin. I must not lose my temper. 'Where is she kept, Sir John?'

He leant back. 'I do not know. I have no wish to know – for my own safety. You have friends, sir. Connections at court, and in darker places. Now – I have given you more time than you deserve. Do not visit me again.' He picked up his quill and made a great show of composing a letter, as if I were no longer in front of him.

I gave my swordstick one last twist, splintering the dent I had made in the board. It was either that or drill it through his wretched head.

Gonson's quill scraped across the paper. It put me in mind of my father, head down, writing another of his interminable sermons.

They were of an age, Gonson and the Reverend Hawkins, and they shared a number of maddening traits. But my father would have believed me when I said that I loved Kitty. He had known love and he would recognise it in his son.

My fingers moved to the chain at my neck, and the gold cross fixed upon it, hidden beneath my shirt.

'Do your parents live still, Sir John?' I asked.

He lowered his quill and frowned at me. 'That is no business of yours.'

'My mother died when I was young.' The cross had once been hers. 'How would it feel to see her again, I wonder? So many years later. What would I do if she stepped out before me one night, with no warning? What would I say?'

Gonson puffed out his cheeks. 'There is no knowing. The shock could disturb the strongest mind.'

But I could tell that he was thinking back, to the moment when Lady Vanhook stepped down from the carriage, and Kitty saw that her mother was alive. There had been no mistaking her horror, nor her fear.

'Lady Vanhook has tricked you, Sir John. Please, in the name of God, help me find her – if only to correct your mistake—'

'Enough!' Gonson snapped. 'I have made no mistake here, sir. And this is not your business.'

'Of course it is my business!'

'No, sir! You are not her husband. You are not her family. You are *nothing* of consequence. Miss Sparks will be restored to the world when she is cured. Her attachment to you is merely a symptom of her illness. Be assured, sir – there will be no place for you in her new life.'

'But there will be a place for you, I suppose? Once she is meek and compliant?' I laughed, I could not help myself. 'My dear sir. You could keep Kitty locked away for a hundred years, and she would *never* choose you.'

Gonson slammed his fist on the bureau, sending the ink pot flying. 'Get out!' he spat. 'Get *out*!'

I gave a short bow, and did as I was asked.

It is productive, in such moments, to find a wall and to kick it. I found the ideal spot a few streets away and gave in to my fury, cursing God and Gonson and the world in general. When I was done I collapsed upon the same wall, pulled out my tobacco and built a pipe.

They had locked her away in a madhouse. I was sure of it.

I cursed to myself. There were scores of private madhouses in the city, and many more rooms with barred windows and doors that served the same purpose. Kitty could be hidden away in a cellar on this very street and I would not know it. My heart sank. How would I ever find her? I thought of the gruesome tales I'd read of innocent people locked away for years. Whispered stories of asylums where the treatment turned sane people mad.

I shook that fear away. I *would* find her. I *must*.

Wherever they were, it would not be some pestilential hovel. Lady Vanhook would not tolerate the squalor on her own account, and she could not risk Kitty falling sick, for one very important reason.

If Kitty died, her fortune would come to me.

Kitty had written her will following our trip to Yorkshire. We had almost lost our lives at Fountains Abbey and she had realised that in the event of her death, her fortune would go to the Crown. 'Unless we marry,' I said, a suggestion she ignored (again). She wrote her will, and save for a few small bequests to Alice and Sam and some other friends, left everything to me.

This, I realised now, had created a dilemma for Lady Vanhook. If I married Kitty, the fortune was mine. If Kitty died, the fortune was mine. No wonder she had wanted me dead.

Her solution, clearly, was to persuade the world that Kitty was *non compos mentis*, and become her guardian. This was why she had spent the past two months coaxing and flattering Gonson, the old fool. For his signature. *'Yes, yes, your daughter is mad, signed J.G. PS I should like her hand in marriage once she is fully subdued.'* Eventually, he would realise Lady Vanhook had no intention of giving up her daughter – or more to the point, her daughter's wealth. Kitty must remain *insane* for ever, so that she might feed upon her fortune.

I finished my pipe, my heart aching for Kitty. Now I understood why she refused to speak of her mother. Even as a child it had been safer for her to survive on her own than to live at the mercy of such a monster.

Monster. A vicious name to give a woman. But what else to call her?

Sam was waiting for me outside the Pistol. The windows and doors were boarded up, and there were bloodstains in the snow from my altercation with Reeves.

Gonson's men had pinned a notice on the door from their master explaining that the shop was closed indefinitely. It ended with a verse from Ephesians:

> For this ye know, that no whoremonger, nor unclean person, nor covetous man, who is an idolater, hath any inheritance in the kingdom of Christ and of God.

I rubbed my forehead, trying to compose my thoughts. I must find a fresh place to live, while I continued my search. Felblade would offer me a room, but the apothecary was much like his medicines – best taken in small doses. Sam suggested a place he knew in Soho, but I needed to stay close to the Pistol. This seemed vitally important, for some reason – as if leaving Russell Street meant abandoning Kitty. What if she escaped and came home? My spirits lifted at the thought. That was possible, was it not? She had escaped her mother before.

I crossed the road. The bakery was closed, but I tapped on the door until Mrs Jenkins opened up.

'I'm sorry,' I said, before she could speak.

She narrowed her gaze. 'You put a blade to that poor man's throat, Thomas.'

'I know, I—'

'No excuses,' she said, sternly.

'No.' I hung my head.

It is a strange truth that one may hold two conflicting opinions at once. I *was* ashamed, when I considered things from Mrs Jenkins' perspective. But then I thought of Kitty, and felt justified again in what I had done. I swung back and forth between these two points – shame and defiance – like a sign creaking in the wind, never settling.

'I put my faith in you, Thomas,' she said. 'Don't disappoint me again.'

'I won't,' I promised with great sincerity, while a voice whispered in my head: *What you did to that* poor man, *you would do again in a heartbeat.* 'I know this is not the best of times ...' I added, 'but Gonson has locked me out of the Pistol. Might I stay with you – just for a few days?'

She shook her head. 'Thomas – there's no room, with my sister here, and the children. And poor Mr Jenkins ...'

'I understand,' I said, feeling wretched.

'Oh!' she relented at once. 'My poor boy, all alone in the world. Not a soul to help you.'

Sam did not count, apparently.

'How can I call myself a good Christian woman, and leave you to freeze on the streets?' she continued. 'Imagine if you were attacked, *murdered*, and I found your body battered and bleeding, right there on my doorstep, a great gash across your throat, imagine that Thomas – how would I ever forgive myself?'

I am not sure why I had been murdered on her doorstep, specifically, but if it convinced her to let me stay, so be it.

'Come with me,' she said, and led us to a cramped storeroom at the back of the house, lined with shelves and sacks of flour. A window about the size of four bricks let in a weak light. Mrs Jenkins, who was broad of hip, could only just fit between the shelves. I had to stoop to keep my head from brushing the ceiling.

'This will do me very well,' I said, hiding my dismay. Sam and I would have to buy a mattress and squeeze it between the shelves. There would be mice. Inevitably, there would be mice.

The only good thing about the storeroom was that it had a second door, leading out to the yard. This meant that we could come and go without disturbing Mrs Jenkins. Sam nodded approvingly at this. *A room with only one exit is a trap* – another Fleet saying.

Mrs Jenkins gave me the key to the outer door and left to attend to her husband. The house had the hushed, reverent feel that comes with impending death. I had found myself whispering, and Mrs Jenkins moved with a careful tread on the stairs. Sam was unchanged, but then he always spoke softly, and moved quietly. And death was an intimate friend.

'You could stay with your mother,' I said, when we were alone.

'No,' he said, simply. 'I'm staying with you.'

I was bone weary, but there was no time to rest. We headed back outside.

'I'll start on Fleet Street,' I said, thinking glumly of the thousands of private rooms from here to the edge of the city. The search could take weeks.

Sam set off for St Giles. I couldn't imagine Lady Vanhook hiding away in the slums, but the servants who worked in the finer asylums still came home to the rookeries to visit family and friends. All of London's secrets rolled their way down into the slums, eventually.

Eventually.

Chapter Twelve

I had promised Kitty I would find her. I had failed.

Two nights had passed since she was taken. I had barely slept, barely eaten. Sam found me just before dawn on the third morning, wandering along Cheapside, banging on doors that would not open. He brought me home to Mrs Jenkins' storeroom, footsore and rambling with exhaustion.

'No use to her dead,' he said, and who could argue with that.

The straw mattress we shared filled the entire floor. I flung myself upon it, face down, still wrapped in my cloak. 'Wake me in an hour.'

Oblivion.

When I woke I was alone. I pulled out my pocket watch and cursed. It was almost three o'clock – I had slept through the day.

There was a tap on the door. I groped for my swordstick. 'Who is it?'

No one answered.

The handle turned. In my near-delirious state, I had forgotten to lock the door.

'I'm armed!' I warned.

The door swung open. A short black man of about my age stood in the yard, clutching his thin coat tight against the cold. His broad chest was rising and falling so fast I thought he must be out of breath from running. Not so. He was struggling to speak.

'Mr Hawkins,' he stammered. 'Jeremiah Patience.'

I lowered my cane. Jeremiah – Nella's father. I confess I had scarce thought of him since Kitty's abduction. He removed his hat,

133

holding on to his brown wig as he did so. From the awkwardness of the gesture, I guessed he had borrowed the wig from a friend, or hired it. A man who struggles to speak must find other ways to express himself. He wore the wig to assure me that he was here on respectable business. Of course the world is full of villains wearing wigs but I appreciated the effort.

I invited him in. He took off his shoes and stood upon the mattress, gripping his hat as if it anchored him somehow.

'My apologies for the lodgings,' I said, embarrassed.

Jeremiah didn't respond. He had seen far worse, no doubt. 'Lady Vanhook. She . . . she . . .'

'She kidnapped Kitty. Cath . . .' No, I could not say that name, it felt like a betrayal. 'Her daughter.'

He nodded – he had heard. 'Thief,' he said, and then, after a moment's struggle: 'Murderess.'

I will never forget the way he said that word. It made the hairs rise upon the back of my neck. 'I met *your* daughter,' I said. 'Nella.'

'Affiba,' he corrected me. 'Affie.'

'She knows you are her father. That you came to rescue her.'

He flinched in shock. There were a thousand questions in his eyes, questions he could not ask. After a short struggle he gave up the fight, and pulled out a letter addressed to me. The paper was of a poor quality, but the hand was elegant and firm.

Sir

I wish that I could speak these words to you directly, but alas my thoughts do not transfer easily to my tongue when I am among strangers.

Some days ago I stood outside a house on Jermyn Street, watching in helpless silence as my child was carried away from me for a second time. I realised in that moment that I could not defeat my old mistress on my own – the risks were too high, the potential consequences too grave. I must find an ally.

I have known of Miss Sparks for some time, but never dared reveal myself to her. And yet the more I learnt of her, the more I believed she might be sympathetic to my plight, if I might only explain it properly. As I could not rely upon my broken voice, I decided to write an account of myself, and most particularly my trials at the hand of her mother. A painful endeavour, completed last night by candlelight.

Imagine my dismay, sir, when I arrived at Miss Sparks' door this morning to find it barred, and the house deserted. Imagine that dismay turning to horror when I learnt that she had been kidnapped some days ago. Worst of all that – had I arrived sooner – I could have warned her of the danger.

Grasping upon your name, sir, written upon the door of her shop, I realised we shared a common cause.

And so – if you will permit me, Mr Hawkins – I wish to present to you the account I wrote for Miss Sparks. Consider it a reference of sorts, in the hope that we shall become partners against a shared enemy.

Most of all, consider it a warning: the woman we are hunting is cunning, ruthless and utterly without pity. Do not underestimate her as so many have done before. And have no doubt that – if we are not clever, and prudent – our pursuit of her might very well cost us our lives.

I am, sir, your humble servant.
Jeremiah Patience

I lowered the letter and looked at Jeremiah, still standing by the door, straight-backed as a soldier. I found it hard to connect the man in the letter to the man in front of me. Only the eyes matched: expressing the same fierce intention and focus I saw in my own, whenever I glanced in a mirror.

Seeing that I had finished his letter, he pulled out a sheaf of paper – the same poor quality, the same fine handwriting. 'My story,' he said.

I took it with both hands.

'I will search,' Jeremiah said, touching a hand to his chest. He attempted another sentence, then faltered. 'Tomorrow.'

His frustration was palpable. His letter revealed him as an eloquent man, careful in his choice of words. But I understood him perfectly well.

I reached out my hand. 'Tomorrow.'

Jeremiah shook it, and left.

The storeroom was freezing, and I had not eaten all day. I wrapped myself in my cloak, shielding Jeremiah's pages beneath it, and headed to Moll's to read his account.

PART FOUR
The Island

THE HISTORY
OF
J— P—
RELATED IN HIS OWN HAND
NOVEMBER, 1728

Miss Sparks – would that I had the capability to tell my story out loud and not within these sheets, which I fear are too thin for their heavy purpose, but my life has been one of great turbulence, and perhaps it is fitting if the paper tears and the ink bleeds beneath my hand.

I was born upon a slave ship in the middle of the Atlantic; a man would be hard pressed to imagine a more dolorous cradle. My mother – may God rest her faithful soul – was stolen from her village in Guinea, ripped from my father's arms and clapped in chains, never to see her family or her home again. What few words are these, to recount her story! Imagine, madam, an ocean beneath this brief paragraph, and it will not convey the depths I must sail over in these meagre pages.

My first months were spent in Barbados – my mother told me I was very sick and almost died. I have no memory of our arrival in Antigua, nor do I recall my first master as we were sold again when I was scarce three years of age. This I do remember. We were sent to auction in St John's, displayed beneath a sun so bright my cheeks ached from squinting at the sky. The vendue master told us to stand on a table so we might be inspected by his customers.

One of the men said he would like to take the mother but not the child, and was that possible? I grew so afraid at the thought that we might be parted that I began to weep. My mother took my hand and said, 'Look straight ahead, Miah. Pretend you are not here.'

Pretend. The word was a golden key.

I closed my eyes, and an image came to me of a great bird with dark wings and diamond eyes. It circled the crowd once, twice, then swooped down, piercing my shoulders with its talons and lifting me into the sky. I felt my stomach drop, but within moments I was soaring through the clouds and I found that I *was* the bird, wings stretched wide. Exhilarated, I rose higher and higher as the world shrank beneath me. Everything was small, the people, the square, the harbour, everything but the endless sky, and the sea sparkling on to the horizon.

It was at this very moment of transcendence that fear found me again. Mother had always told me that when I died my spirit would escape its cage and be reborn in its homeland; the land of my ancestors. Was this what was happening now? What if I could not find my way home and must drift forever upon the ocean, where I was born?

With that dreadful thought I plummeted back to the square and to my body, with such velocity that I sank to my knees. My mother caught me just in time – and what a fine scene that must have appeared to the buyers, a young woman and her child clinging to one another for comfort. I learnt later that they like to see such a bond – believing a woman will be less inclined to end her life if she has a child to protect. Our old master sold us quickly, and for a price that made him smile, and shake the hand of our new owner.

With the auction ended, we were pushed on board a small boat and sailed to the other side of the island, to the small plantation that would become my home for the next twenty-two years.

My new master was an Englishman by the name of Frederick Vanhook. He was an old man to my young eyes, though he was not yet five and thirty: the constant sun of the West Indies is not kind to men of his complexion. His brows and lashes were so pale they appeared translucent.

Mr Vanhook's wife had died on the voyage out to Antigua but he did not seem to grieve her loss; the house slaves said that he never spoke her name nor kept mementoes of their life together. It was a solitary existence he had created for himself: he had no children, nor any wider family on the island, and he lived a long walk from his nearest neighbours. He preferred it that way, I believe. Mr Vanhook owned more than a hundred slaves, and employed an English overseer called Cradduck to run the plantation. As far as I was concerned, he might have been named King Frederick the First, sole ruler of our little world of two hundred acres.

Within a few months of our arrival my mother married Eustace, a strong, even-tempered man, respected by the other slaves. My mother was soon big with my brother, who I shall speak of again when the moment arrives. I have a regrettable tendency, Miss Sparks, to hop from past to present like a frog upon a lily pond, but within these pages I shall do my best to follow a straight line.

Eustace was concerned by my nature. 'Jeremiah is a dreamer,' he would say, and it was true – ever since that day at the vendue, when I had felt my spirit leave my body, I had often sought to escape this world for imaginary realms. A track into the bushes became a path to a land of fantastical creatures; a pile of rocks transformed into a vast mountain range; a piece of driftwood became a sword, or a wise man's staff.

When Eustace caught me in my games of fancy, he would tap the back of my head to wake me up, or hold me upside down by the legs until I agreed that I was Jeremiah, a slave boy in Antigua, and not a warrior, or a pirate, or an eagle. There was no malice to it. Eustace had a talent for survival, that he wished to pass on to me.

Dreaming would only land me in trouble. As it turned out he was right to worry, but here I am getting ahead of myself, which as I say is a habit of mine.

The trouble was I had been seduced by my own imagination and grown reliant upon it. In a cruel and brutal world, it became my sanctuary. I did my best to hide my dreaming from Eustace, not wishing to be slapped or shook ten times a day. But once my brother Michael was born, his attention slipped away from me to his son, and, in the rare and precious moments when I was not put to work, I was left to my own devices.

I soon grew bold in my adventures, venturing closer and closer to Mr Vanhook's house, which he had named Belmaison. To my child's eye, it was a palace. Stone steps swept up to a raised ground floor, shaded by a veranda. The second storey had a painted balcony, where Mr Vanhook would sit as evening fell, reading and drinking rum, and swatting away the insects that buzzed about him.

I dreamt up diverse stories about Belmaison long before I ever stepped through its doors. My favourite conceit was that I was a banished prince, returning home from exile in disguise, so that I might surprise my father the king.

Dangerous, potent fantasy!

Early one Sunday morning I wandered down the path towards Belmaison. The cordia trees were in bloom, and the hummingbirds crossed over my head, darting from flower to flower. I was nine years old. I walked slowly, my limbs and back sore from the days spent digging holes for this year's planting. Perhaps it was because my legs were so heavy, and the birds so light upon the air, that I was clumsy. This much is certain: one moment I was walking down the path watching the hummingbirds feeding from the cordias' bright red flowers and the next I had fallen to the earth, twisting and tearing my ankle as I fell. The pain was terrible. I told myself to flee before I was caught so close to the house, but my body would not obey. The slightest turn of my foot was enough to make me cry out in agony.

Now I was in trouble! Belmaison was no more than fifty paces away – someone might step on to the veranda, or the balcony above, at any moment and see me sprawled upon the path, where I had no right to be. I would be beaten, for certain, and my mother would be whipped.

I closed my eyes and took two deep breaths. 'Rise, Jeremiah,' I said, as if I were an angel, sending a message from God. 'Before the wolves catch you.' For in my tumbled, anxious mind I had become the lost prince, hunted for days as he tried to reach home. My ankle was not torn in a clumsy fall, but savaged by the fangs of a great wolf. I had never seen a wolf, but there were dogs on the plantation, trained to attack on command. Trained to attack us. I had seen what their teeth could do to a man's flesh. That did not take any imagining at all.

'Rise prince,' I intoned, 'and return to your kingdom.'

I heard a high, hiccupping laugh above me. Twisting round, I saw to my horror that my master Mr Vanhook was standing on the path behind me, his shadow stretching over my body. I tried to drag myself away but the pain was terrible. And still Mr Vanhook was laughing.

'You are a prince?' he said, as if it were the funniest notion he'd ever heard.

My throat closed in fear. My mother always told me: do not trust the laughter of white men.

'What happened,' he asked, pointing at my foot with his cane, 'your Majesty?'

'Wolves,' I replied.

To this day, I do not know what possessed me. The word left my tongue and I could not snatch it back. Mr Vanhook stood confounded for a moment, then he laughed again. 'Wolves!' he said, and shook his head. 'Can you stand?'

Mr Vanhook was my master. If he wished for me to stand, I

must do so. Gathering all my strength, I endeavoured it. Pain flared up my leg and my head spun. I collapsed back on to the path, whimpering.

'Well,' Mr Vanhook sighed, and then he kneeled down and gave me his cane. 'Hold this,' he said, and to my astonishment he plucked me up in his arms and marched on down the path towards Belmaison. He was soon sweating from the exertion. By the time we had reached the house his face was bright red.

The interior of the house was dark and cool, and smelled of tobacco smoke and boiled vegetables. Mr Vanhook left me in the hallway, muttering something about the state of my clothes, but in truth I don't think he could have carried me another step. He called for Julius, who looked after the house along with Mary, another slave. Julius gave me a look to say, *Your mother will learn of this*, then carried me to a large room at the back of the house. This room was brighter, with large doors opening on to another veranda. The furniture was very fine. Julius told me that – save for a grandfather clock – he had made it all. Not being an *utter* fool, I made sure to admire his work. He liked me better after that.

I should say that I remained very fearful, sitting in this grand room with Mr Vanhook's ancestors glaring down at me from the walls as if to say: *You? A prince? Insolent wretch!* I still thought I might be beaten, and when Julius left I considered crawling to the veranda and hopping away into the bushes. But that would have been rebellion, for which I had been taught the punishment was a hundred lashes or maybe death.

Mr Vanhook returned and with him came Mary. She looked at me and her eyes said, *problem*, though she didn't say so in front of our master. I was to be scrubbed, Mr Vanhook said, and my ankle bandaged. Julius would fashion me a pair of crutches.

'How did this happen, Jeremiah?' Mary asked, for she knew me too, very well, and would be queuing impatiently behind Julius to speak with my mother.

'Wolves,' Mr Vanhook replied, and winked at me.

And so began my fateful relationship with Belmaison, and Mr Vanhook. Before I left, swinging along on my crutches, he told me I must come back the next day – for what purpose he did not say. I'm not sure he knew himself. When asked, 'But *why* did you bring the boy into your home?', his answer would change depending on his mood, and the person asking the question. To the more scientifically minded enquirer, he would declare that I was an experiment. To the more Christian-like, he swore it was an act of charity. To Mary, and Julius, he snapped: 'Because I can.' He never once gave what I thought to be the most likely answer: that he was lonely, and bored.

Whatever the reasons – and it is my observation that a man can have many, often conflicting and occasionally absurd – for the next ten years I was a daily visitor to Belmaison. Mr Vanhook taught me to read and write in his quiet, humid house, to understand accounts and the management of his business.

Despite my master's curious patronage, I still lived with Eustace and my mother, and my brother Michael, in a tiny hut in the slave village. For the first few years I continued to work alongside them as well, tending the cane, stirring juice in the boiling house and looking after our own small plot when there was time. But as I grew, and learnt, I became too useful to Mr Vanhook and his affairs. Eventually, I took almost no part in the back-breaking work of the plantation.

I grew proud: show me a boy who would not. I had been set apart – told that I was unique and worthy of attention. Promises of freedom were made, or if not promises, then allusions.

'No good will come of it,' Eustace said once, quietly, when he thought I was asleep.

As for my brother Michael – he hated me with a passion. The baby I had once resented for taking away my mother's attention had grown into a strong-boned boy of fifteen. If I had not been so blinded by Mr Vanhook's praise, I would have recognised that of the two of us, Michael was blessed with the better mind. There was a clarity to his thoughts – an ability to see a thing and grasp its meaning at once, and so turn it to his advantage. Had he been of a different complexion he would have been hailed as a prodigy. As it was, Mr Cradduck called him cunning, and watched him with narrow eyes.

'You think you are above us,' Michael said one day, when we were fighting. 'You live in Jeremiah's Land, and think that nothing can touch you.' Then he punched me in the mouth. At fifteen he was already stronger and taller than me. 'See?' he sneered, standing over me. 'You still bleed, brother.'

Michael's curse was that he could see the world too clearly. Mine was that I could barely see it at all. When I was not at Belmaison I lived within my sanctuary, that magical realm of my own imagining, elaborate in its composition. Michael's exposure of it embarrassed me. *Jeremiah's Land*. I denied its existence with the indignant rage that comes from shame, and for a few weeks forced myself to live solely within the real world. My eyes saw only what was put in front of them, my fantastical thoughts were banished, buried, burnt.

And how empty and bitter the real world felt! How hard and dull the endless days. Within a month I had snuck back into my own secret realm again. It was the only place where I felt at home, save within the pages of Belmaison's small library of books. My real home, my family, were drifting away from me, or perhaps I had pushed them away.

In the spring of 1721, Mr Vanhook announced he would be sailing to England for an extended trip. In a curious twist of fate, he had inherited both a title and enormous debts from his uncle, who had lost his fortune to the South Sea Company. *Died suddenly* was the phrase; I suspect he took his own life. At one and the same moment, our master became both Sir Frederick Vanhook and a potential bankrupt.

As his slaves we shared in his misfortune. Sir Frederick worked us hard, but we all knew there were far worse masters in the world, and we feared them. *Better the devil you know*, as the saying is. As for me, I had placed all my future hopes in my master, and my fate was tied to his.

Sir Frederick's great plan was to sail to England, settle his finances and find a rich woman to marry. I was not convinced that the lure of a title would be enough to secure him a wife. He had grown stout in the last ten years, and his teeth were not good. Too fond of his own sugar.

He was gone for over ten months. During his absence, I was charged with examining our accounts. I discovered several ways to make savings, if Sir Frederick was prepared to inconvenience himself a little. Meanwhile Mr Cradduck was conducting enquiries of his own down in the cane fields, at the windmill, in the boiling house. He measured the small plots given to us for growing our own food, and he visited plantations across the island, and each time he returned he wore a private smile, and a determined expression. He looked at me, too – and when he did, I was a small boy again, standing on a wooden table, wishing I could fly away.

For many months, Sir Frederick's letters were brief and empty of news. We were surprised, then, when he sent word in November that he had found a wife – a rich widow who had tired of London society and wished to begin afresh in Antigua. Emma Sparks was an angel, a kind, patient-hearted angel, and we would all love her. Such protestations were so unlike him I should have been suspicious. Instead I rushed to my mother and delivered the good news.

'Well then. I suppose we are saved,' she muttered, and slid her gaze to Michael. He snorted and said nothing.

'I did not have to come tell you,' I said, hating the petulant whine in my voice.

'We are indebted to you, sir,' Michael said with a smirk, and a light curtsy. My mother laughed.

I turned away, hurt.

'Miah, Miah,' my mother called. 'Come back. We are only teasing.'

I knew that – but it was the fact they teased me together that upset me, and that I was excluded from their laughter. When I think of what could hurt me back then, and what I would soon suffer ... I shake my head now, as I write. There is no hell that cannot be made worse – that is the awful truth of it.

Christmas passed, and in late January the whole plantation was ordered to gather at the shore to welcome our new mistress. By chance, I found myself standing close to Mr Cradduck, sweating in his best coat. The boat appeared around the bend, and we could soon hear the oars cutting the waves, the spray of water at the prow. We craned our necks for our first glimpse of Lady Emma Vanhook, and were rewarded with the image of a queen of ancient times, approaching her adoring subjects. She sat in the middle of the boat, her back very straight, beneath a cream parasol that gleamed bright in the sun. Sir Frederick sat behind her, fatter than ever and hot-faced. The closer they came to shore, the less likely it seemed that they could be of the same species, never mind husband and wife.

On the sand, Lady Emma smiled at us all, and declared herself delighted with everything. 'How happy I am,' she said, 'to have left the poisonous airs of London for this quiet heaven.'

I did not dare look at Michael, standing with my mother and Eustace on the opposite side of the crowd. Lady Emma drifted by, inclining her neck slightly towards Mr Cradduck, who bowed in return. I lowered my gaze as she passed. I saw Sir Frederick's shoes, his plump legs, following behind. He paused in front of Mr Cradduck.

'She is a witch,' he murmured. 'A penniless witch.'

He continued on his way, hands clasped behind his back, fingers twirling.

The next morning I hurried over to Belmaison, curious to meet my new mistress, and to greet Sir Frederick after so many months away.

Mr Cradduck was waiting for me upon the steps, a short cart whip in his fist.

He had never liked me, or the position I held within the household. He planted his legs wide. 'Where do you think you're going, boy?'

With that one question, I knew my old life was over. The truth of it hit me as if a building had fallen down upon my head. My legs began to shake.

Sir Frederick and Lady Emma were sitting on the balcony above, taking their first breakfast together. Though I kept my eyes to the ground I could sense them looking down at me, hear the tink of a tea cup on a saucer.

'Well, boy?' Cradduck snapped.

My heart was pounding so hard it felt like an iron fist against my ribs. I had to fight the urge to call out to Sir Frederick for help – appeal to the man who had lifted me up on this very path and carried me into his home. But I learnt now what my family had tried to warn me of for years – that what our master could lift up he could just as easily throw down again. He would not help me now, and to ask him to would only make matters worse.

Cradduck was still waiting for an answer. I knew that he wanted nothing more than to punish me. I was the one slave he had never beaten or whipped. I must not give him the satisfaction. But when I opened my mouth, I found that I could not speak. The words would not come.

Cradduck saw my struggle and revelled in it. 'Answer, damn you!'

My new mistress rose from her breakfast and leant over the veranda. 'Why does he not speak? Is this not your favourite? The *clever* one?' She sniggered.

Sir Frederick muttered something from his seat, some muted protestation.

ANTONIA HODGSON

'Well, clearly you were deceived,' she drawled. 'An unfortunate habit of yours, my dear.'

I tried again to speak, and still nothing came. I was trapped inside a nightmare, the sweat pouring down my face.

'What a sullen, disobedient creature!' she declared. 'Do they all act in such an insolent fashion? No wonder your profits are so dismal.'

Again, Sir Frederick muttered something feeble, from his chair.

'That is demonstrably untrue, Frederick,' she replied. 'If they are working so hard, why are they so rarely whipped? We spur our horses to race faster, do we not? Why, here is the perfect proof. How long has he idled his time here, when he should be out in the fields where he belongs? And see what a Cicero you have created, from all these years of indulgence! Will you not recite a speech for me, Cicero, in honour of my arrival?' She laughed, amused by the idea.

I bowed my head, humiliated.

She saw that I had lost my tongue, I am sure of it, because her voice took on a cruel tone. 'Cicero. I *command* you to speak. Welcome your mistress to her new home.'

I could not, she knew I could not.

Cradduck, furious, shouted in my face. 'Speak, damn you!'

I tried once more, my chest convulsing with the effort. One word heaved itself from my mouth. 'I . . . I . . .' No more would come.

Cradduck lifted his whip. 'You had best withdraw, my lady.'

'No, indeed, sir,' she said. 'I shall stay.'

When he was done with me, Cradduck forced me to walk to the cane fields. I collapsed three times upon the way. Each time he kicked me to my feet.

By the time we reached the fields my left eye was swollen shut and my shirt was soaked in blood. He had conducted the beating with an evil precision born of much practice. My skin was covered

in welts and bruises, but not a bone was broken, not one. My body
was too valuable to destroy. It was my spirit he wanted.

Cradduck prodded me to the steps of the boiling house, calling
everyone to witness my fall from favour. My mother put a hand to
her mouth when she saw me, and tears spilled down her face – but
she did not make a sound. Everyone else looked away or down at
the ground, though they were kind to me later. Only Michael held
my gaze.

This was what happened, Mr Cradduck said, when a slave tried to
rise above his station. Now the natural order was restored, he said. Sir
Frederick had placed him in sole command of the plantation. His
word was law, and we would obey it as if he were God Himself. 'And
let me warn you,' he added, gripping my shoulder. 'If I catch this boy
reading or writing a single word, every one of you shall pay for it.'

That night I sat on my sleeping bench, my head in my hands.

'Why does he not speak?' Eustace asked. I had not said a word
since my return from Belmaison.

'It is the shock, from the beating,' my mother said, sitting down
next to me and drawing me into her arms. I collapsed into her like
a child, not a man of nineteen.

'It was not the beating,' Michael said.

I thought perhaps he would take some pleasure in my fall, and
his prediction of it – but he never did. Michael's view upon the
matter was simple: I had been dreaming and now I was awake, and
there was an end to it.

And what a brutal awakening! I was returned to the fields at once,
at the hardest time of the year. For the next three months I dug
holes and planted the cane, and harvested last year's crop. When I
was not in the fields I sweltered in the heat of the boiling house,
stirring the sugar. I was no longer accustomed to the work and
suffered further under the new regime. Cradduck revelled in his
new power and took great pleasure in punishing us for the smallest

ANTONIA HODGSON

transgression or accident. We were forced to work when we were sick, mocked and humiliated in countless ways.

At night – the only time we might speak freely – we cursed the new mistress, for the changes had come with her arrival, and her lack of fortune. Michael disagreed.

'Let her take a portion of the blame,' he said. 'But do not forget those who look away. Curse Lady Vanhook. But curse Sir Frederick, too. Curse the world. Curse God.'

People hushed him at those final words, but I caught his eye and nodded my agreement. I still said very little. I could speak a few words with my family and those who lived and suffered alongside us. But when Cradduck commanded me to speak, my tongue froze, and the words choked in my throat. Knowing this, he would challenge me for his own amusement, and use my 'insolent silence' as an excuse to punish me. This only made it harder for me to speak the next time, and so the hell continued, and I saw no reason why it would ever stop.

At least I was young and strong enough to survive. Eustace was not so lucky. He collapsed one morning in the fields and died two days before Christmas, 1722. Quietly, patiently, Eustace had become a father to me, and I mourned him as a true son. With that grief came something more dangerous: despair. I looked at Eustace, his body stretched out upon his bench, worn and aged before its time, and I saw my own bleak future.

'Jeremiah,' Michael said to me the next day. By chance we were working side by side.

I glanced at him, without breaking from my work.

'If you kill yourself, our mother will follow you.'

There was Michael's curse and gift again – to see what others missed. He had guessed my intentions without asking me a single question. I didn't answer him. But later, when we walked back to the huts, I put a hand upon his shoulder, to show that I understood. He spun about and embraced me.

'You and me, brother,' he said fiercely, in my ear. 'You and me.'

152

One night soon after that, Michael shook me awake and whispered that he had something to show me. We crept outside together. The forest rustled softly with night creatures and the insects buzzed and fluttered.

Michael took a small package from his shirt and thrust it into my hands. I could feel from its shape that he had brought me a book. I unwrapped it from its cloth and stared at it in amazement. He had taken a fearful risk, bringing it to me.

'It is good?' he asked, anxious. He could not read, so did not know what he had taken, only that it was slim enough to hide beneath his shirt.

The Tempest. I could just make out the title in the moonlight. I pressed my nose to the cover and breathed in the scent of paper, spotted with mildew. My mind filled with wild storms, ships tossed and broken on the rocks, a father and daughter, and a spirit unchained. I suppose I must have smiled.

Michael was laughing at me in the dark. 'There you are, Jeremiah,' he said. 'There you are.'

I buried the book under a kapok tree, a long walk from the huts. I only dug it up on three occasions; the danger of being caught was too great, not only for me but for everyone else – I had not forgotten Cradduck's warning. But knowing it was there, and that my brother had risked so much to bring it to me, gave me both strength and solace.

A year later, I was married at the order of Mr Cradduck. At six and twenty, Sara was five years older than me, and a hundred years wiser. She had lost her son in childbirth and her first husband to an accident at the boiling house. She was a fine woman, admired for her quick wits and sharp humour. No doubt Cradduck thought it amusing to shackle her to me, a man who could barely say his own name.

Sara, who was still grieving her husband and son, would not tolerate my touch, not even in the lightest way. And what more could I offer her? Nothing but silence, which she filled readily enough with her complaints.

I could not speak, but I could watch and listen. One day, when she had berated me for the thousandth time, and railed at her fate – as a slave, as my wife, as a woman – she sat down upon the mattress and wept bitterly.

I knew not to touch her; my clumsy attempts at comfort never helped. Instead I sat down at her side and wept with her, silently. Sara had never seen me cry before.

'Jeremiah,' she said, rubbing her own tears away.

I dragged the words from my lips. 'I am sorry.'

She stared at me, then hissed out her breath as her surprise changed to anger. 'This is not your fault,' she said, grabbing my hand. '*They are to blame*! They took a proud, clever boy and broke him. Broke him *because* he was proud, *because* he was clever.'

But when she took me in her arms I did not feel broken. And when, a year later, I held my daughter for the first time, I did not feel broken.

We named her Affiba, as she was born on a Friday, but everyone called her Affie. She shared her mother's strong and curious character, screaming through the night and staring in wild fascination at everything around her. Affie. My light in the darkness.

Two years passed, and life on the plantation was worse than ever. Sir Frederick had retreated to his quarters and was rarely seen, save by those unfortunate souls he summoned to his bed. It was said he suffered from gout and could barely walk. Mr Cradduck was in all ways but name our master. We hated him, but it was Lady Emma we feared the most.

Cradduck was a dull, brutish man, but we knew his cruelties of old and were at least prepared for them. Lady Emma's moods were unpredictable and far more dangerous. Once, we had envied Mary and Julius for their lighter duties up at the house. Now we pitied them. The only safety was distance, and everyone agreed we should rather encounter a venomous snake than our mistress. She had come to the island filled with delusions of a grand existence, where every whim and fancy was answered, where she would be admired and respected. No doubt the realities of life at Belmaison came as a tremendous shock. Sir Frederick had exaggerated his standing on Antigua, in that he had led her to believe he had any. She was scorned by island society, or at least she was not worshipped. This was unbearable to her.

She could not punish her neighbours, and so we suffered the full force of her disappointment. To say she was petulant sounds too mild, but you must imagine a Grand Petulance, in the manner of an ill-tempered goddess, where the punishment was always too severe.

She hated the house, the heat, her husband; she was bored, she was angry, she was lonely; why should she not buy things to make her happy, why should she not beat Mary for no reason, or wake Julius in the middle of the night for some petty whim? Why should she not come down to the huts and make us sing for her, and then have us beaten when we did not know her favourite songs, that were all the fashion in London?

'I am in *hell*,' she wailed, throwing her hands to the sky. 'Cruel Fate! Why must I suffer so? Why imprison me here, so far from those who love me?'

I've heard it said that when a man turns blind, his remaining senses grow more acute to compensate for his loss. Nature, I believe, seeks balance. I had lost the power of speech, but gained the ability to *hear*. When Lady Emma spoke of being kept from those who loved her, I knew that she was lying, not just to us but to herself. No one loved her, no one.

This was her tragedy, not that I could pity her for it. She was without doubt a beautiful woman, but the more she revealed her true nature, the uglier she became – as if she lived under a dark spell, one that she had cast upon herself.

'Why does she stay?' I asked Sara one night. Affie was sleeping and the air was still and hot. If I chose, I could imagine that the three of us were alone on our own small island, with nothing but peaceful days stretching ahead. I *could* imagine this, but then Sara would flick my arm to wake me, for she could always tell when I was slipping away from the world and into Jeremiah Land. At least she did not tip me upside down, as Eustace had done.

'She stays because she must,' Sara replied. 'She has a great enemy back in England. He swore that if she ever returned home, he would kill her.' Sara had heard this, she said, from my mother, who had heard it from Mary, who overheard Sir Frederick flinging it in Lady Emma's face. 'Go back to London whenever you wish my dear, on my shilling and with my blessing! Let that devil do what I cannot, but wish that I could!'

'She is used to having whatever she wants,' Sara said. 'The longer she stays here, the worse it will be for us.' She reached for my hand in the dark. 'Jeremiah. Look down when she passes, always. She must never know that you see through her; it will shame her, but you will take the punishment.'

My wife was a wise woman, but it was hard to avoid our mistress. *Idle hands are the devil's tools.* With nothing to do, and with a spoilt child's need for attention, her only pleasure became the misery of others, which is to say us. For who else was there to torment?

Her visits became more frequent, her demands more fanciful. We must kneel as she passed – no, we must prostrate ourselves. She laughed as we did so, clapping her hands as if this were a tremendous joke.

Some of the younger men became brief favourites, and that was the worst fate of all. She played with them, whispered dreams of freedom, gave them hope where no hope existed, then crushed them beneath her heel. Of the four men she *noticed*, two were later whipped for 'insolent behaviour' when in truth she had simply tired of them. A third hanged himself.

The fourth was my brother Michael. He did nothing to encourage her interest, but he was strong and tall as his father had been, and handsome with it. She came to visit him every day in the fields. And then she came to visit him at night, against his wishes, but since when is a slave allowed wishes?

I knew that something terrible would come from it, but nothing could have prepared me for the catastrophe that followed, so swift and so brutal.

My mother, God rest her, was the first casualty. Michael was the rock she clung to, solid and sure like his father. The strain of watching him suffer, the constant fear that he might be whipped or even hanged, was too much for her heart to bear.

One morning she could not rise from her bed – within hours she was gone.

I was toiling in the fields when I learnt the news, and the shock was so great that I dropped my shovel and sank to my knees in the dirt. Mr Cradduck came over and kicked me in the ribs until some brave friend cried out, 'Sir, his mother, his mother', and for once he stopped and let me alone. I remember being grateful, and surprised. Imagine such a wretched existence – that I should think well of a man, and consider him generous, because he did not kick me when my mother died?

She is gone, I thought, *she is gone* – and returned to work.

For the first seventeen years of her life my mother had been free; the first months I grew inside her, she was free. She was my mother, and she was also my thread back to another, better life. With her death, I felt that thread break. I was a slave, and always would be.

That night I held Affie in my arms as she squirmed and giggled, and felt the weight of our future lives press down hard upon my chest, like a great stone slab on a tomb. This was why I fled into books and imaginings, why I had soared into the sky as a young boy, holding my mother's hand as the white men sold us. To live in this world was a burden, the chains were heavy even when they

were not visible to the eye, and what brought me the most sorrow
was knowing that one day soon Affie would feel them pressing
down upon her too. So I let her play while she could, and grieved
in silence.

My mother deserved a grand funeral. In days past, we had
honoured our dead with a torchlight vigil, singing, dancing and
sharing rum, but Mr Cradduck had banned such gatherings years
ago, saying they bred rebellion and a 'sullen spirit'. He was a coarse
man in many ways but he understood the message that death sent
to us – how it could provoke anger, despair, even envy. We buried
my mother at dawn in a plain box with no ornaments, and no one
spoke in remembrance.

That night I dreamt of her as a young woman, her hair in long
plaits, wrapped in a bright blue and yellow scarf. She was walking
away from me down a dusty track fringed with high grasses.
Somehow I knew, as is the way with dreams, that this was my mother's homeland, and that she was going to meet my father in the vast
forest ahead. I called to her, but she did not turn until I thought to
use her true name, which they had taken from her years ago.

'Benneba.'

She paused on the road and looked towards my voice, brows
furrowed. I called her name again and she tilted her head, as if she
heard it only as a whisper in the wind. She could not see me, or if
she could I was very faint to her, like a mist.

'Miah,' she said, and smiled. 'My son.' I felt her love sweep
through me, strong and sweet. Then I watched her walk away, until
she disappeared into the forest beyond.

In my dream, my mother's love filled me up like water on a hot
day, but when I woke I felt empty and thin, as if I were the ghost.

When I left my hut that morning, Michael was waiting for me.
His lip was cut, his cheek marked with deep scratches.

'I refused her,' he said, with a look that said, *ask no further*.

Working side by side in the fields, I told him about my dream, hoping it might bring him comfort, but my brother did not share my interest in visions and portents.

'No mystery, brother,' he shrugged. 'She told you her spirit would return home, and so you imagined it.'

'It did not feel like a dream,' I protested.

'That is your trouble, Jeremiah,' he said. 'You never could tell the difference.'

We might have spoken more on the matter, but there was a commotion in the distance, and raised voices. I knew better than to lift my head, so I did not realise it was Sir Frederick until he crashed through the sugar cane. 'Where is he, the devil!' he thundered.

I had not been this close to him in years – and was shocked by his appearance. His swollen face was mottled like a diseased fruit, his teeth black or missing. Liquor had played its part in his ruin, but there was no doubting what had hastened his descent. She followed behind, her hand upon her chest as if she were afraid. An act, of course.

Sir Frederick wiped his brow, panting heavily from the heat and his walk from the house. I could smell the drink seeping from his skin. 'You,' he said, pointing at Michael with a weaving hand. My stomach dropped.

Michael bowed his head. 'Yes, master.'

'Oh, you remember now! Insolent boy.'

'Frederick, please!' Lady Emma sobbed, but she was only pretending to cry. Her eyes were dry and bright. Michael had dared to *disappoint* her, and this was her revenge. She had whispered poison in her husband's ear, knowing he would retaliate.

'One hundred lashes, Mr Cradduck,' Sir Frederick said.

A hundred! I caught Sara's eye, frightened.

Even Cradduck looked concerned. He took Sir Frederick to one side and they began to argue. I had never seen that before. Cradduck was defending Michael. 'He's a good worker. They'll turn surly ...'

Sir Frederick's mouth twisted in a petulant frown. He had come out here in a blaze of anger; retreat would be a gross humiliation. Our master was a weak man, and a vain one.

'I shall thrash him myself,' he said, snatching the whip from Cradduck's hand and limping forward.

Lady Emma flicked a blade of grass from her gown. 'My dear,' she said. 'Pray don't be foolish. You know you do not have the strength.'

Lady Emma had a talent for saying one thing, and meaning another. When she told her husband *he did not have the strength*, you must imagine the mocking inflection to her voice. Her eyes lingered over his breeches, and she pinched her lips, conveying both disappointment and amusement. And be sure to remember that Michael stood between them, brave and fit and everything that Sir Frederick was not.

This is the moment that haunts me. I feel the heat of the day upon my skin, the scorching earth at my feet. I see Lady Emma patting her skirts, Sir Frederick holding the whip. My brother stands with his shoulders back and his chin high. I steal a glance at my mistress and I understand, with a deep dread, that she has planned this – the punishment of one man, the public shaming of the other. Sir Frederick knows it too, and he wants to kill her. He wants, desperately, to kill his wife. But this he cannot do, so he takes out his pistol and shoots my brother instead.

I did not speak to anyone after that, not even Sara or Affiba, not for six months.

It was a Sunday when Lady Emma returned to the village.

I was alone upon the forest path – on my way to dig up *The Tempest* and find a safe place to read it. Most Sundays I would walk with Sara the long distance to market to trade what we could, but today she had come up behind me and rested her chin on my shoulder.

'Go read your book, Jeremiah,' she said, wrapping her arms about my waist and drawing me close. 'Perhaps it will help you.'

She had been so patient with me, my impatient wife.

Lady Emma had not come this way since the day Michael was killed, she was forbidden to visit on her husband's orders, but he must have changed his mind for here she was in a new dress, holding her cream silk parasol and humming lightly to herself, followed by Mr Cradduck, then Mary, in a short procession.

'Cicero!' she cried. I remembered her expression when Sir Frederick shot Michael – shock, and then a dark delight. The blood on her dress, her skin.

She smiled, because she knew what was about to happen. 'Tell me. Where is your daughter?'

The ground fell away beneath my feet. *Affie*. By the time I had recovered Lady Emma had passed me on the path and was picking her way towards the village, twirling her parasol. Mary touched my arm as she passed. 'It is decided, Jeremiah,' she warned me, softly. 'It is done.'

By the time I reached the village, Lady Emma had found Affie, playing with the other children. 'There she is! My little pet.'

Frightened, Affie ran to Sara, hiding in her skirts.

Lady Emma smiled as I put an arm around my wife's shoulder.

'It is so quiet up at the house,' she declared. 'I simply *must* have a companion or I will turn mad. Sir Frederick agrees.' She sighed. 'You see, Cicero – I had a daughter once, but she was taken from me. I shall never recover from the loss. It is a scar across my heart.'

She would have said more, she was preparing for some grand soliloquy, but Mr Cradduck interrupted her. All this time in her company, I suppose he had grown to hate her almost as much as we did. He strode over to Sara and peeled Affie from her arms.

'Affie,' Sara moaned. I could hear the grief in her voice – she was already preparing herself for the loss. First her son, now her daughter.

Lady Emma reached out and stroked Affie's cheek. 'What fun we shall have,' she said.

'Please, she is too young,' Sara begged. 'Don't take her away. Not yet. She is too young.'

'Do you dare challenge me?' Lady Emma snapped, her eyes very bright.

Sara knew better than to reply. Her heart was breaking but she said nothing.

Cradduck handed Affie to Mary.

Lady Emma was displeased. 'I shall carry her home.'

'She is too heavy,' Cradduck replied.

'Yes . . .' Lady Emma pinched Affie's arm. 'We must see to that.'

Affie howled, furious. She reached her hands out for her mother, and when Sara did not come, she howled even harder. I could not bear it. My daughter was not yet three years old – younger than I had been that day at the vendue – and she was being stolen from me.

'Such a noise,' Lady Emma tutted. And then, as if she were being generous, 'You may say goodbye to her, if you wish.'

Sara ran over to Affie and kissed her many times. 'Affie, Affie,' she said. 'Never forget your mama loves you.'

'Enough,' Lady Emma said.

I feared Sara might argue, I think we all did. But she wiped her face, and withdrew.

Mary turned to go, Affie wailing and calling for her mother. Lady Emma picked up her skirts and followed them. She seemed disappointed.

They are leaving, I thought. *Will you do nothing, Jeremiah? That monster is stealing your daughter.*

This was the way of things, this was the life of a slave. Whatever I thought was mine could be taken from me. They could work my mother to death, shoot my brother in front of me, snatch my daughter from my wife's arms. This was the way of things.

'No.'

It was the first word I had spoken since Michael's death.

No. The word was a key, unlocking things I had kept buried. Pain, humiliation – and rage. It travelled faster than I could catch it.

'No?' Lady Emma turned, and smiled. This was what she had hoped for, some drama, some cataclysm to help her pass the time. But she had pushed too far. She had provoked something within me that I could not control. I strode forwards and grabbed her arm.

Even as I touched her, I knew I would pay for it with my life. For a slave to put a hand on his mistress – it was unthinkable. I didn't care.

Lady Emma screamed as my fingers clasped her arm. 'Let go of me!'

I did not strike her. I thought only to stop her – as if I might freeze this moment for eternity, and spare my daughter the suffering I knew must await her.

I could hear Sara calling my name, the way a widow cries the name of her dead husband. 'Jeremiah. Jeremiah.'

And still I could not let go. In the end, Mr Cradduck took out his club and beat me to the ground.

They locked me in a wooden cage. Cradduck would have hanged me the same day but Lady Emma was too eager for a spectacle. She insisted I must be taken to St John's to hang on the scaffold in front of the whole town. *An example*, she said. *The island will speak of this for years.* By which she meant, they would speak of her. Already she had exaggerated the story, saying I had seized her by the throat and tried to throttle her. 'For no reason,' she said. 'No reason at all.'

She came to visit me that night, trailing her fingers against the bars of my cage.

'Your daughter is very young,' she said. 'I promise you this,

Cicero. She will forget you, and the name you gave her. You will be nothing but the shadow under her bed, the branch tapping against the window, the nameless fear that wakes her in the night. You will become her nightmare.'

It was a pretty speech, no doubt she had practised it in front of the glass. I wondered how she could think up something so cruel. I learnt the answer to that question much later, on the other side of the world.

But I run ahead of myself.

It is ironical that Lady Emma's demands for a public execution saved my life. I must be transported in my cage, and that required a larger boat, brought from the other side of the island. And word must be sent out, to ensure a large crowd at my hanging. I was to be flogged first; there was a good deal to plan. So I waited in my cage, locked in a hut where old Julius made his furniture, breathing in sawdust and preparing myself for death.

My heart ached for my wife and daughter and the lives they must lead without me. Poor Sara, now she had lost two husbands and two children. As for myself, I was afraid of dying and eager for death. Let my pain be over, let me join Michael and my mother in the next world. If I could see the path in my dreams, then surely my spirit could reach it. Or if it did not, would the ocean be such a terrible place to rest, deep in green, the storms many leagues above?

It was in this state of resignation, something akin to peace, that Sir Frederick found me.

'That damned witch,' he said, sitting on an unvarnished chair. It was the first time he had spoken to me since his return from England four years ago. 'What did I do to deserve her? She has won again, taking my favourite from me.'

I was his favourite, even now? I felt sick at the thought. How extraordinary, that I had once yearned for his approval! Now, he revolted me. My master the coward, the fool, the murderer.

'Devil take her,' he spat, mopping the sweat from his face. 'Well, I shall not have it. I shall not have it!'

The door opened and Julius entered, carrying a great stone jug filled with oil. He began to douse the walls and floor of the hut.

Was I to be burnt alive? God spare me such a fate!

Sir Frederick pushed himself back to his feet. 'Jeremiah. If you are caught I shall blame Julius for this. So you had better succeed, for both your sakes. D'you understand?'

Julius gave me a tired look, one that travelled back to our first meeting at Belmaison. Then he unlocked the cage.

I sat stupidly for a moment, unable to believe what was happening.

'For God's sake, man,' Sir Frederick cried. He threw a small purse of coins into my lap. 'Run!'

Later, looking back from a high hill, I saw the fire blazing bright against the night sky. I sent out a prayer to my little family and everyone I had known and cared for, and continued on my way.

There was no time to dig up the book buried in the forest. Strange, the things we leave behind.

I could not stay on the island, no more than I could free my wife and daughter. Luck or Providence brought me safely to town, where I heard rumours of a murderous slave who had tried to kill his mistress, only to die in a terrible fire. 'God's vengeance,' a sailor said, in a dank tavern by the harbour. I stowed away on his ship, bribing the captain with every last penny in my purse.

'Won't ask where this comes from,' he said. 'And you won't tell me.' As I still could not speak, I'd been forced to write my offer upon a piece of paper, an act he had found most diverting. 'Your hand's neater than mine!' he laughed, as if such a thing were a miracle, rare as a mermaid. Sailors are a superstitious breed and he decided that I was lucky. Praise heaven the passage to England was a smooth one, or he might have changed his mind and thrown me overboard. I feared he should do so in any case, once I'd paid him, but he said he found it amusing to bring so many slaves across the sea, only to smuggle one back again. He had a singular sense of humour, that captain.

I was hidden away with the cargo when we left Antigua, and so was afforded no final glimpse of my island prison, no farewell as it faded upon the horizon.

My story began on board a ship and here I am at its end, disembarking at Bristol. From there I made my way to London, and to Limehouse, where I found work at the docks.

My first weeks in the city were scarce more than bare-boned survival. I was alone, and lonely. For all the horrors and indignities of my life on Antigua, I had at least been surrounded by family and friends. Now I had no one.

Then one evening I was invited to a country dance arranged solely for black folk. The leader of this gathering was a man called Marcus Brown, a freed slave. He welcomed me as if we had been friends for years. 'Dance, drink, enjoy the music!' he said. 'Or do nothing! As you wish.'

This was the company I had been missing. In time I was able to find my tongue, and tell some of my new friends what had happened to me.

One night, several months later, Marcus arrived at my lodgings, clutching a bottle of rum.

'Emma Sparks,' he said, removing the cork. 'That was her name, was it not? Emma Addington afore that.'

Without my knowledge, Marcus had been making enquiries around town about my former mistress. A woman of such wickedness must have a past, he decided, and enemies with it. He did not have to search long to find them. People did not forget Lady Emma, nor forgive her. Marcus had picked his way back through her story, betrayal by betrayal, learning of promises broken, debts unpaid, lives ruined.

He discovered that Lady Emma had squandered her first husband's fortune and that her daughter – you, Miss Sparks – had run away to escape her cruelty and neglect. Your story helped me to solve an old puzzle. Your mother had promised that Affie would remember me only as a monster of nightmares. She knew at first-hand how that would torture me, because she had drawn inspiration from her own family. She wanted Affie to hate and fear me as much as you hated and feared her.

'What of the man who threatened her?' I asked. 'Her "great enemy"?'

Marcus shook his head. 'I could not find him. And no one had heard such a story. That is not to say he doesn't exist, my friend. Only . . . he is a ghost.'

I bowed my head. My one hope had been to find this man, and beg for his help. If he would permit Lady Emma to return to England, she might bring Affie with her. My wife, I knew, was lost to me for ever. But I had dared hope I might see Affie again. It was my one dream: to hold my daughter again, and to set her free.

Marcus patted my arm. 'She'll come back one day. Be patient, my friend.' He laughed. 'There, have you not been looking for a surname?' He raised his bottle in a toast. 'Jeremiah Patience.'

And so I waited. The seasons turned. I worked hard and saved what I could, and I kept out of trouble – which is not easy for a poor man in this city. When a ship came in from the West Indies I would find a hiding place and watch the passengers disembark. I did not dare approach the sailors with my story, but my friends listened out for fresh news in the taverns. Those who arrived from Antigua would sometimes speak of Lady Emma. She had grown infamous on the island, sweeping into St John's like a hurricane, causing scandal wherever she rested, until her husband came and dragged her home again. She kept a young slave girl at her side always, they said, who she spoilt and punished as the mood took her.

Another winter passed. The old king died and a few months later the new king marched in procession through the streets, under a golden canopy. I stood silent amid the cheering crowds, the kettle-drummers and trumpeters, and thought to myself – so *this* is a prince? He looked more like a frog, an ill-tempered frog dressed in ermine and purple velvet, and a scarlet cap that kept slipping over his eyes. Why would God appoint this man to reign over us, what qualities did he possess that set him apart? I walked home to my lodgings through the rain, thinking of the heroes in my own fantastical realms, wise and generous princes and noble warriors. I thought of Michael.

I did not see Marcus until he jumped in front of me, waving his hands in front of my face.

'Jeremiah! Heaven save us, are you deaf as well as dumb?' He grabbed hold of my arms and shook me, putting me in mind of Eustace shaking the dreaming out of me. 'I have found her, Miah.'

'Affie?' I asked, hope rising.

He looked crestfallen. 'No, no my friend. Catherine Sparks. Lady Emma's daughter.'

'Oh,' I said. How would this help me?

'It is the talk of the town. She has inherited a great fortune.'

It took me a moment to realise what this meant. 'She will come back!' For the money, if not for her daughter. Whatever the threat to her life, she would not be able to resist it.

I knew it would take several months for the news to reach her, and a few more for her to arrange her voyage. I kept a close eye upon the docks, but no one saw or heard of her arrival. For once, she had forgone a dramatic entrance and crept back unannounced.

In fact I might never have discovered her at all, had I not fallen into a piece of good luck. An elderly lady who came to Marcus's Limehouse dances attended church in Westminster. One day, she was struck by two new members of the congregation – a handsome woman dressed in fur, accompanied by a pretty black girl. When she tried to speak with the girl, the woman was very rude to her, and promptly left the church. The lady was put in mind of my story, which was well known by everyone who came to the dances.

And so – with some further investigation – I found that my daughter had at last arrived in London. You can imagine my joy, and agitation.

I could not sleep that night and so I rose early, walking through the city as it woke around me. How many times had I imagined this day, and dreamt of taking Affie in my arms and carrying her home?

Dreams and imaginings are not a good preparation for a kidnapping.

After a long wait in the bitter cold, the door opened and they stepped out into the street, Lady Emma first, in a fur-lined riding coat. And then – Affie.

She had grown, of course she had grown. She was looking down, pleased with her shoes and in her smile I saw her mother.

I had planned to take Affie into my arms and run. But now I realised the truth – I was a stranger to her. Or worse – the monster Lady Emma promised I should become. What if Affie screamed? How far could I run with her struggling against me? If we were caught I would be sent back to Antigua in chains, and hanged along with Julius. Affie would be condemned to the life of a slave for ever, with no hope of rescue.

And so I did nothing.

I stumbled home, shouting my daughter's name into the wind like a madman. Now I could speak! Now I could move! I reached my lodgings and flung myself on to the bed, weeping. At last, exhausted, I slept.

For once, I did not dream. When I woke my mind was clear and sharp. I could not save Affie on my own.

I must approach Catherine Sparks, I decided, *and ask for her help.* I was fairly certain that Lady Vanhook had only pretended not to see me on Jermyn Street. Surely she had recognised me. As I had lost the advantage of anonymity, I might as well reveal myself to her daughter.

Miss Sparks – we are strangers to one another, but I believe our destinies are intertwined. You are not to blame for your mother's sins, and yet I dare hope that you feel stirred to assist me, nonetheless.

I shall await your reply and remain, Madam

Your dutiful servant

Jeremiah Patience

* * *

I placed the final sheet of paper on the pile and rubbed my face. It had taken me two hours to read Jeremiah's account, and in that time I had felt myself transported to Antigua, and the brutal world of the plantation.

I left Moll's with his story tucked safely in my coat. I spent the remainder of the night visiting brothels, *bagnios*, coffeehouses and taverns, seeking information on any private madhouses I might have missed. By the time I was done I had a list of at least thirty new places to visit in the morning – including a house in Bethnal Green, run by a Mr Mackay. I don't know how long it would have taken me to reach it. As I say – I had at least thirty places to visit, most of them closer to town.

In any case, my endeavours proved unnecessary. While I was busy searching for new information that night, Kitty gave up hope of being rescued, and decided to free herself.

PART FIVE

The Hunt

Chapter Thirteen

When the nurse comes, you pretend to be asleep. She holds a lantern to your face – you feel the warmth of it on your cheek.

Yesterday, she fed you the poison. This morning, when the doctor sliced open your arm, she held the bowl, catching your blood as it streamed from the cut. You have spent the day in bed recovering.

You slide a hand upon your belly, imagining the spark of life growing inside. No, it is more than imagining, you sense it in a way you cannot explain.

If you do not escape this place, that spark will sputter out. You both will.

Tomorrow, they will feed you the ipecacuanha again. You will sweat and sleep for hours, growing weaker and more confused. Then the next day – another blood-letting. This will happen over and over, day after day, night after night, until you forget who you are. You will vanish – not just from London, and your friends, but from yourself. Kitty will cease to exist. You will become Catherine. Daughter. You will be as mad as your mother wants you to be.

You must escape, tonight.

In another life you would attack the nurse and snatch her keys, but the risk of failure is too great. You must find another way, quiet and stealthy. So you keep your eyes closed and your breathing steady. Let her think that you are sleeping. Let her think that you have given up.

A thin shriek pierces the air. 'A demon! A demon has come to take me!'

You open your eyes, startled. No point pretending you could sleep through that.

'Lord save me from hell!'

Another woman, locked in another cell. You hear crashing in the cell above and then a heavy thud – the sound of furniture being smashed and overturned. She is destroying her room. Good for her.

Is it rebellion? Delusion? Whatever the reason, the noise sets off a chain reaction on the next floor – a cacophony of moans and shouts, prisoners thumping on the walls.

'Save me!' someone cries. 'Save me!'

Are they mad or desperate? Impossible to tell the difference.

The nurse grabs you by the hair, and digs her fingers into your cheek, just under your eye.

'Stay in bed and don't make a peep,' she snarls. 'The scratch I'll give you won't heal so pretty.'

She leaves, slamming the door behind her. You breathe out. She has taken the lantern, but the shutters are open to the night and the moon is full. The room is flooded with silver light.

She did not lock the door. She did not lock the door.

You stand quickly, your bare feet cold against the rough stone floor. The drug has wrung you dry, like an old rag, your sides still ache from vomiting.

You can't free your ankle from its shackle – you have tried. You follow the chain to the iron ring on the floor, searching frantically for some weakness in the links. The ring is melded to an iron plate, and the plate is bolted to the floor. You test and pull, but everything is fixed tight.

You sit back upon your heels.

This is where most people would have stopped – defeated, broken. But you, my love, are a stubborn creature, and practical with it.

You cannot break the link, you cannot pull up the ring, you cannot unscrew the plate. So you must dig up the flagstone.

There is a thin seam of dirt between the stones. If you can gouge out enough of the dirt, the stone might come loose. You need something sharp, and narrow. There are no sharp, narrow things in a mad woman's cell.

Then you remember the chamber pot. You break the lid against the floor and pick out the sharpest shard, ignoring the stink.

Above you, the protests have grown violent. Servants yell to one another as they hurry up the stairs.

You scrape around the flagstone, chiselling and slicing the earth packed around it. You will need to gouge deep to release the stone. The broken shard cuts your fingers. You keep chiselling, urging yourself on. The house is in pandemonium all around you, but for how long?

At last, with one final tug, the flagstone comes loose. You can't believe it. The ring is still attached to the plate. The shackle around your ankle remains fixed to the chain. But you can hold the flagstone in your bloodied hands.

You carry it to the door and turn the handle. The door swings free.

The corridor is empty. You creep to the end, back pressed against the wall, chain clinking. There are more shouts on the next landing, a heavy thud as an inmate is shoved to the ground.

You hear footsteps further down the corridor and duck into the nearest room, holding your breath. You have to succeed, you have to. If they find you half-freed like this, they will wrap you in a straitjacket. They will put guards on your door. You will never escape.

The footsteps fade and you breathe again. You have stumbled into the nurses' room, abandoned in the riot. You gulp down a cold cup of tea and search the room quickly, finding a small knife. And then you leave, before your luck runs out.

You stumble out into the garden, barefoot in the snow. The air is fresh and the moon is a bright silver disk, magical and unreal.

In the corner of the walled garden, there is an old ash tree. You clamber up into its bare, freezing branches, holding the iron plate in one hand, chain flung over your shoulder.

When you reach the top of the wall, you look back. There are candles flickering in the house, and the sound of muffled cries. A window is pushed open and you're afraid it's your mother.

You jump without thinking.

You throw out your free hand as the ground rises to meet you. The weight jars your wrist, spraining it. You stifle a cry, then stagger to your feet and run.

You don't know where you are, but it feels a long way from town. What if this is the road to Tottenham, where decent folk are robbed by brutal gangs, Macheaths, murderers? You stop, and scold yourself. You are not decent folk. You did not survive on your own for years through sheer luck. You will survive this.

You look up at the sky, reading the stars. North or south? You don't remember crossing the Thames on your way here. Heading south seems a better gamble. If you can find the river, so much the better.

You limp a wandering mile down that road, wrist throbbing, the iron plate tucked under your arm, the chain swinging against your leg. Twice you hear a rider up ahead, and consider calling for help – but who would be riding this empty path in the middle of the night? You hide until they pass, then drag yourself onward.

You are so cold now you have begun to shake, and your feet are numb. Your ankle is bleeding, the shackle chafing it. Your wrist has started to swell. You limp onwards, talking to the baby for company. This is an adventure, you say, to be told one day in front of a blazing hearth: how Mama escaped the wicked queen, carrying a treasure beneath her skin.

And then suddenly without warning you stumble upon a long street with a stretch of houses and shops, and a tavern, still open. There are candles flickering in a few windows, despite the late hour, and a man pissing against a wall, and a woman standing on the corner, waiting to sell herself to him.

Not quite the city, but near enough.

You edge close to the woman. 'Mistress,' you whisper. Your voice is hoarse. 'Where are we?'

She glances at the man, and then at you – as if you might steal him from her. 'Fuck off.'

You hold out your knife, ignoring the pain in your wrist.

She smiles, liking you more. 'Whitechapel.'

Whitechapel. Less than an hour's walk from home. 'Please – I need to send a message—'

'I'm not your fucking sister,' the woman says and walks off.

Who will help you here? What good Samaritan will be awake so late in Whitechapel? You have nothing to sell, except for the blade, and your body. You should keep walking. But the iron cuff cuts into your ankle with every step, you are barefoot and bleeding and sick with cold and exhaustion. You fear the winter night will kill you.

One more step, and then another, to the door of the tavern. You push it open and step inside, almost crying with relief at the light and heat. Men turn to look, then look away again, and mutter to each other. One of them spies the blade in your hand and scrapes his chair back, alarmed.

No sense in hiding now: you want everyone to see you, and hear your story. Someone in this room will take pity on you.

You drop the iron plate to the ground and transfer the blade to your good hand.

'Gentlemen. My name is Kitty Sparks. I was kidnapped from my home two nights ago, and locked up against my will.' You push out your foot to show them the iron band, and the chain. 'I promise that I am a good, innocent woman. Please, sirs. I beg you for help. Please send word—'

And then you see him, striding towards you. Dr Mackay, his face flushed from drinking. 'My God,' he splutters. 'How did you escape?'

You stumble back. No. No, no.

'Gentlemen – this girl is my patient. Quite mad, I'm afraid – as you can see. Catherine, put down the knife.'

*'I'm not mad,' you say, but the men are staring at you, your bare
feet, the chain around your ankle, your tattered gown stained with
sweat and blood and crusts of vomit. The knife in your hand.*

*It can't end here, not so close to home. Fate would not be so cruel.
'Please sirs,' you try again. 'Please help me. My name is Kitty—'*

The world explodes in a white flash, then goes black.

'Thomas?'

Mrs Jenkins woke me with a tap on the storeroom door. I was alone
– Sam still out searching the town. I had been dreaming of Antigua,
hummingbirds and buried books, and blood.

I opened the door and was enveloped in the smell of freshly
baked bread. Mrs Jenkins smiled kindly at me, but she looked
exhausted, distracted by her own troubles. She had brought me a
bowl of coffee, bless her, and fresh tobacco.

'You're baking again?' Mr Jenkins had taken a turn for the worse
several days ago, and she had not opened the shop since. But as I
left the storeroom I realised my mistake. The air was stifling from
the ovens, but the windows were shuttered, the shop door closed.

Mrs Jenkins turned away from me, busying herself with her
work. She pulled out a loaf to test, then slid it back into the oven.
'He said he missed the smell. So I thought . . .'

She could not bear to say her husband's name. Her grief had
already begun, even as he struggled to breathe in the room above.
He could no longer eat solid food. The bread was not for eating, it
was for remembering.

There was a tap on the shop door.

'Jeremiah?'

'Message for Mr Hawkins,' a voice replied. I unbolted the door.
A young lad handed me a letter, then ran off before I could stop
him.

The note was addressed to me care of Jenkins' bakery, and dated
the day before.

Sir. Give up your search, or Catherine will suffer for it. As will all those foolish enough to help you. E.V.

I crumpled the note and tossed it on the stove.

'You have been very kind to me,' I told Mrs Jenkins. 'But I have imposed upon you long enough.' I would not be threatened by Lady Vanhook, but I would not put my friend at risk, either.

She protested, but only a little. 'In better times . . .' she said, wistfully. 'What fun we might have had.' She hugged me (oh, her hugs – what marvellous things they were) then headed back upstairs to her husband. We shall not meet her again in this story, I am sorry to say.

I could not leave until Sam and Jeremiah returned, so I wandered about the empty shop, smoking and drinking coffee, and devouring slices of fresh bread and butter. I had not had a decent meal in days. Eating always put me in mind of Kitty. I promised myself that when I found her – any day now – I would treat her to a great feast comprised of her favourite dishes. Caught in my reverie, I wondered if her appetite had changed, with the baby. And once I thought of the baby, I had to sit down upon the dusty floor, and smoke another pipe to stop myself from tearing the shop apart in fury and frustration. If Kitty were harmed . . . if she lost our child . . . What would I do then? What would I *not* do?

I closed my eyes, and my mind turned again to Antigua, and Jeremiah. How many lives had Lady Vanhook ruined, was it even possible to count? Well – sitting on the floor cursing to myself would not help them, or me.

I was packing my belongings away when Sam arrived. He had nothing to report, save that Lady Vanhook had left unpaid bills across town – food, clothes, perfumes, furniture, rent. She had bought everything on credit.

'That is no surprise,' I said, but I could tell Sam was holding back the best part. 'Go on.'

'The bills aren't in her name,' he said, and grinned.

I thought for a second. '*Gonson?*' Please, God.

Sam nodded, still grinning. 'Gonson.'

'Hee!' That is the precise noise I made, high-pitched and gloating. I had never made such a sound before in my life, one assumes it is only found in books. I am not a petty man, but this was too delicious. *Epikhairekakia*, Aristotle called it – joy upon evil. Punishment justly served. 'How much?'

'Hundred guineas.'

A hundred guineas! 'Does he know?'

'Not yet.'

I clapped my hands. Oh to be there in the room, when Gonson learnt the truth. The great man, duped. Defrauded. Humiliated. This was the first good news I'd had in days.

Sam settled down to read Jeremiah's account. I lit another pipe and opened the shop door, propping myself against the frame. My gaze drifted across the road to the Cocked Pistol. We had been so happy there, Kitty and me. Gonson's order – still pinned to the door – flapped in the wind. He had lost a hundred guineas, but I had lost something far more precious. There is so little happiness in this world.

A neighbour, seeing me in the doorway, came over to shake my hand and ask for news. I was about to answer him when I saw Jeremiah sprinting up the street, clutching his hat to his head. No wig today, no time. He appeared to have run all the way from Limehouse, his stockings mud-spattered, his shirt drenched in sweat. He skidded to a halt in front of me.

'Found them!' he panted. 'I've found them.'

Chapter Fourteen

It was long past noon when we arrived at Dr Mackay's private madhouse in Bethnal Green. The iron gate was locked and cast sharp black shadow lines on the snow. I rattled it back and forth, summoning two large hounds from the rear of the house. They raced towards us across the garden, barking wildly. I stepped away, and Jeremiah jumped back even further, though we were safe behind the gate. The dogs leapt at us in frustration, hurling themselves at the railings. When they had exhausted themselves, they dropped back on to four paws. The larger hound glared at us through the railings, pacing and growling, while its partner sat down with a soft huff, and proceeded to scratch itself, eyes closed with pleasure.

'Wolves,' I said to Jeremiah, thinking of the path to Belmaison, where he had tripped and hurt his ankle as a boy.

He tucked his hands under his armpits for warmth and frowned. We had suffered the same problem upon the road – my familiarity cooled by his distance and wariness. Having read Jeremiah's account, I felt as though I knew him well, but in truth we were strangers. It did not help that he was unable to speak more than a few words at a time. I missed the Jeremiah I had met on the page, which was odd, given that the real Jeremiah stood not two paces from me.

An old man appeared from the side of the house and called to the dogs. They cringed at his voice and grovelled towards him, bellies low. He rewarded them with sharp cracks from his stick, driving them away. Jeremiah winced.

'What do you want?' the man shouted across the garden. He kept his stick high, as if we might be next.

'We are expected,' I lied.

The man snorted. 'Not by me you ain't.' He turned towards the house, with no indication of whether he would pass on our message.

I stared up at the barred windows. Kitty was locked inside one of those rooms. I had to fight the urge to climb over the gate and smash my way into the house.

Jeremiah, as if reading my thoughts, put a hand on my arm. *Wait.*

'It does not look like a madhouse,' I said. It was a handsome building in the modern fashion, fit for minor gentry or a successful merchant, with neat brickwork and fresh-painted windowframes. Only the iron bars, and the spikes along the roof, suggested the truth behind the facade.

Dr Mackay was making a fortune from the misery of others.

The quieter of the two dogs had slunk back into the garden, unobserved by its master. And here I'm afraid I must pause and describe the beast, for reasons that shall become clear.

The Bible assures us that God created everything. Without wishing to blaspheme, I would contest that this was not one of His Great Works. Curiously, it resembled the sort of hound I used to draw as a boy, before I understood the laws of proportion and scale. Its long legs did not match its solid, meaty body, and it had borrowed its shaggy tail from another breed entirely. Its mud-brown coat, patched with black smears, gave the impression that it had just rolled in something filthy. (To be fair, it often had.) It had a rather sweet white flash on its chest, and its ears, I concede, were good – alert and pointed – but much too big for its head. Even as a child I would have scrubbed the whole thing out and tried again, but then I am not God, and His ways are mysterious.

The dog cocked its leg and pissed on a bush, the hot stream

melting the snow. Its master arrived back to give it another savage crack about the head and dragged it away by its spiked collar.

'Sir!' I called out to him, annoyed. 'Have you passed on our message?'

He ignored me.

I rattled again at the gate, drawing fresh howls from the dogs, but the old man must have chained them in their kennels, as they did not return.

At last a nurse came out on to the front step, clutching a ring of keys. She put a hand to her eyes and squinted at us, then decided to venture closer for a better look. She was a narrow, long-necked woman, and as she tottered towards us down the icy path, she resembled nothing so much as a skittle, about to be knocked over. Her cheek was scored with scratch marks.

'Who are you?' she demanded as she arrived at the gate, glaring in particular at Jeremiah. 'We're not expecting no one.'

'Damn your impudence!' I bellowed, slipping into the role I had prepared. It was not difficult – I had met enough arrogant pricks in my time and was not immune to the condition myself. 'How dare you speak to me in such a shameless manner? Who do you think you are?'

She flushed. 'Sir, I'm a nurse—'

'*I* am Charles Buckley, of Hanover Square,' I shouted over her, clanging my swordstick against the gate. Jeremiah flinched. 'I am here at the behest of my patron, Sir Philip Meadows, Knight Marshal to His Majesty the King. You will let me through at once.'

Charles Buckley: my oldest friend. The man who had betrayed me, lied to me about Kitty, and almost cost me my life. I had taken to using his name whenever I did something nefarious. I sincerely hoped it brought him a good deal of trouble.

Charles's name could open doors – quite literally on this occasion. I had barely reached 'Sir Philip Meadows' before the nurse was scrabbling to unlock the gate, full of apologies and simpering deference. She locked it again as soon as we passed through.

A robin watched us from the stump of a newly cut ash tree as we skidded down the path. The tree's trunk and thicker branches had been chopped up for firewood, and lay in a pile along the garden wall.

'Forgive me, sir,' the nurse apologised again, jingling her keys. 'One of our patients escaped last night. Climbed right over that tree, if you can imagine such a thing. Never happened before,' she added hurriedly. 'And she won't do it again.' There was something in her tone I did not like when she said that.

'She was punished?'

The nurse gave a pleased smile. The scratches on her cheek puckered. 'She was *corrected*.'

I fought my temper as she opened the front door. Thanks to Jeremiah, I knew the full story of Kitty's capture in Whitechapel. Dr Mackay's servant had struck her from behind with his club, and then they had tied her up and carried her away, the damned, contemptible cowards. The cruel luck of it, when she was so close to freedom. At least she had thought to shout her name before she was taken. And so the news of her recapture had travelled down the eastern roads to Limehouse, and to Jeremiah.

The nurse waved me forward, but now it was Jeremiah's turn to play his part. He clasped his hands behind his back and glided past her.

The nurse scowled. 'What does *he* think he's about? Sir – pray tell your servant he must wait outside.'

Jeremiah paused at a framed map of the world, examining it with a studied curiosity. 'I am no servant, madam,' he said, without taking his eyes from the map. 'I am a prince.' There was a slight hesitancy to the words, but he did not stammer. He prodded a finger in the middle of the Atlantic ocean. 'Here is my kingdom.'

The nurse sniggered, and threw me a conspiratorial look. 'I'll fetch the doctor.'

We waited for him in the drawing room. It was very much like the exterior of the house: neat and well proportioned, with the occasional flash of wealth – a gaudy bracket clock, a lacquered cabinet.

I complimented Jeremiah on his performance.

He shrugged. 'I call myself prince, so must be mad. There are princes in Africa.'

'Aye. But not in the middle of the ocean.'

He smiled at the idea, some echo of the child who had dreamed up strange and fanciful stories.

The door opened with a flourish. Dr Mackay was a short, spirited man with a carrying voice – the sort of fellow who claps his friends too hard on the back. 'Mr Buckley!' he exclaimed. 'An honour to meet you, sir.'

I bowed lightly, leaning on my swordstick.

'Why – your lectures at Hanover Square are the talk of the town! I have read your excellent pamphlet upon the virtues of ambition several times! D'you know, sir, that it was once considered a sin to be ambitious, a form of madness, even?' He laughed, astonished by the idea. 'Thank heavens we live in more enlightened times . . .'

I let him barrel on. The longer he spoke the better. I was relieved he had not attended one of Charles's interminable lectures, gladder still that he had not seen me hang at Tyburn. He was not in the least suspicious of me – accepting me at once for what I said I was.

Jeremiah picked up a discarded book and flicked through it, fingers brushing the pages as if they were made of velvet.

Mackay lowered his voice. 'Your servant, sir?'

'He is attached to Sir Philip Meadows' household. I am here on His Lordship's behalf.'

The doctor's chest swelled as he savoured this proximity to greatness. 'And he calls himself a prince? A common delusion. You have heard of the King of Bedlam?' He trailed away, still watching Jeremiah. 'He believes he can read. Fascinating.'

I assured him this was no delusion. Mackay, reluctant to disagree with a wealthy customer, allowed himself a private smile.

'How secure is your establishment, Dr Mackay?' I asked. 'I hear that one of your patients escaped last night?'

'Do not concern yourself upon the matter,' he replied smoothly. 'She was a most *particular* case, not at all typical of our usual guests.'

'Was?' I said, but he did not hear me, or chose not to.

'Tell me, is your man prone to violent fits? I am experimenting with a new treatment involving iced water—'

'I hear she walked barefoot and bleeding to Whitechapel. Your *particular* guest. You only captured her again by chance.'

Mackay, unused to being challenged, looked vexed. 'Well, as I say – a unique situation, never to be repeated. But please be assured, sir, I have ordered new locks and thicker chains for every cell. *Room*,' he corrected himself. 'Peace of mind for friends and family. And you have met our new hounds, arrived this very morning . . .'

How long since we had arrived at the gate? I glanced at the bracket clock on its shelf. Long enough. 'Your servant struck her to the ground.'

Mackay frowned at me, puzzled. 'How did you . . . We cannot always be as delicate as we would wish, with the violently insane—'

'You tied her up like an animal, threw her in a cart and dragged her back here.'

Jeremiah put down his book and moved forward.

The doctor, realising that he was trapped between us, rubbed the back of his neck. At last, he was beginning to suspect he was in trouble. Not a perceptive man, this doctor of the mind. 'Mr Buckley. Now I think upon it . . . I fear I cannot help you today, sir. "No room at the inn", you see . . .' He laughed weakly.

The door opened and Sam entered, holding the odd-looking

hound by its spiked collar. I had not asked him to befriend the dogs, but Sam had a knack with them. He shook his head.

'You have searched everywhere?' I asked him. 'Outhouses? The cellar?'

Sam gave a sharp nod. 'She's not here.'

'You . . .' Mackay drew back, staring at me. 'You are not Charles Buckley.'

'No, sir. I am not.'

He looked behind him at Jeremiah, and then at Sam and the dog. I watched him consider calling for help, then decide against it. Not a complete fool, then. 'Mr Hawkins?' he guessed.

I smiled grimly. 'Where is she?'

'I don't know.'

I punched him hard in the stomach. He had no warning, no time to protect himself. He folded into himself, then dropped to his knees, fighting for breath.

The dog barked in excitement, pulling against its collar. Sam fed it a piece of meat to quieten it.

Mackay put out a hand. 'Please. I have money. Whatever you want—'

'I want Kitty. *Now.*'

He cringed. 'I can't . . . She is gone,' he said, in a small voice.

Gone? I drew the swordstick from its case and aimed it at his heart. *Do not say she is dead. Do not say it.*

'She is alive, sir!' he said, catching my meaning. Eyes fixed upon the blade, Mackay continued in a tumble of words. They had left this morning, just a few hours ago. Lady Vanhook was furious with him. She had trusted him to keep her daughter locked up. He had failed her, so she must arrange matters herself. 'She has hired men from town, well armed.'

'She has her own carriage?'

'Yes, yes!' he cried, desperate now to give me anything he could. It was a large black carriage with yellow doors and wheels, and matching yellow curtains. The horses were brown or dark chestnut – four of them. 'But you may catch them, on horseback,' he said eagerly. 'If you leave at once. It is slow work for a carriage in this weather.'

'A child,' Jeremiah said. 'Was there a child?'

Mackay nodded vigorously. The young slave girl? Yes, she was still part of the company. 'You should leave at once, sirs,' he said again. 'They will have to rest the horses tonight, or change them. If you follow the coach road, you should find them …'

'Which way did they head?'

'North. I believe it was north.' He let out a long, shuddering breath. 'Please. That is all I know.'

I was still aiming my swordstick at his chest. 'You hurt her.'

His eyes bulged. 'She was my patient. I was trying to protect her—'

I pressed the tip of the blade against his heart to shut him up. 'You knew she wasn't mad.'

He licked his lips, spoke carefully. 'She was distressed. Unbalanced. That was my honest opinion, sir.'

'*Your honest opinion.* And how much were you paid for that?' I gestured about the room – taking in the lacquered cabinet, the ornate clock, the silver sconces. 'That's why you brought her back. Not to protect her, but to protect your investment.'

I was truly angry now. Kitty had made it all the way to Whitechapel and this vain, avaricious fool … Why should he escape without a scratch? He should suffer, as she had.

The dog was growling softly, as if it were an extension of my own rage. I sheathed my swordstick. 'Perhaps I should lock you in here together,' I said, indicating the dog.

Mackay shrank back even further, slithering across the floor on his arse. 'No, please. I'm sorry,' he whimpered. 'I'm sorry.'

I took the dog from Sam, gripping its collar. I could feel the power of the animal under my fingers, straining for release. It didn't know Mackay, it felt no loyalty to its new master. I doubted it would do him much harm, its friend was the ferocious one, but I couldn't be sure. There were scars on its muzzle and notches on its ears from old fights. I felt my fingers loosen against the collar. The dog shifted and looked up at me, licked its chops.

It was tempting. My fingers loosened further.

'Stop,' Jeremiah said. 'Enough.'

I caught the collar at the last moment.

Mackay began to sob with relief.

'If she is hurt, I will come back here for you,' I warned him. 'If you speak of this to anyone . . . I will not need the dog, sir. I will tear you apart myself. Do you understand?'

Mackay nodded vigorously. 'Not a word. Not a word. I promise.'

Back in the walled garden, I told Sam to go back to London and speak with his mother. We would need her help against Lady Vanhook's hired gang. 'I will send word when we've found them.' They could not have travelled far in the snow. We could ask people along the road – they would remember such a mismatched group of travellers, in a coach with bright yellow doors and wheels.

Sam set off at once, taking the dog with him.

I touched Jeremiah's arm. 'You did well, sir.'

He shifted, and moved his arm away.

'You are not afraid of me?' I stared at him in surprise. 'It was an act, Jeremiah. With the dog. I was playing a part.'

He did not answer. But then, he spoke very little.

Chapter Fifteen

You have no memory of your return to the madhouse. When you woke, your head throbbing, it was morning. You were back in your cell, bound up in a straitjacket, your mother's servant standing guard over you. Patchett – that was his name.

He lifted you out of bed and carried you downstairs. Outside, by the gate, a coach with yellow wheels stood waiting, flanked by six guards.

'I'm too sick to travel,' you said, as he set you down inside.

He joined you on the cushioned bench, sitting too close. The carriage was spinning – you feared you might be sick.

'Mr Patchett. Please—'

He put his hand around your throat. 'This is your fault, you spoilt cunt,' he said. 'We could have stayed here nice and quiet. Now I have to risk my neck on the roads, in the freezing cold.' He gripped harder, and stars flashed before your eyes. 'You run again, I'll choke the life out of you, d'you understand? I've had enough of the pair of you.'

You heard your mother's voice on the path.

Patchett squeezed your throat again, to be sure you understood, then left. You gasped the air into your lungs, eyes streaming.

'No indeed, Dr Mackay,' your mother said as she reached the gate, 'there is no bill to settle. You promised me this was a discreet, secure establishment. You have failed me on every count. If I were not in such a hurry, I would sue you down to your last farthing.'

You set off – your mother on the seat opposite, holding Nella in her lap. 'Crying Catherine?' she said. 'You have only yourself to blame. Perhaps now you will behave.'

Three hours have passed since then. The roads are terrible, the carriage lurches and sways with every turn of the wheel. Your mouth tastes sour, and your arms are stiff and sore, tied up in the straitjacket. It is impossible to sit comfortably.

'Dreadful. Useless,' your mother says for the hundredth time, glaring out of the window. She could be speaking of the roads, or the horses, or you. Most likely all three.

Nella looks at you. You offer her a secret smile. She smiles back, delighted. Words are not always needed. You can guess what her life must be like with your mother.

The carriage rattles along, too fast in the snow. 'We are running away,' you say, because you know this will make your mother angry. You have grown tired of being compliant. 'Like scared rabbits. Who are we running from, Mother?'

'Be quiet,' she snaps, unable to resist the bait.

'Tom will find me.'

'He will not,' your mother says, furious. A small victory.

You try to stay awake, but eventually you slide into a half-dream. The carriage slides in the ice. Splintering wood, yellow carriage wheels spinning, the scream of horses. Your mother lies dead in the snow, her auburn hair spread out beneath her. The world is safe again.

The carriage lurches and you wake. You pray, silently, that the life inside you is strong.

Your mother is looking out of the window again.

'Mother,' you say. You have to lift your voice over the noise of the carriage. 'Mother. Do you love me?'

'Of course,' she says, without turning her head.

'Then let me go.'

She slides her cold blue eyes over you. 'Don't be ridiculous.'

'You can take my fortune. All of it. Just leave me at the next inn.'
You will find a way to help Nella, once you are free.

The horses whinny as the driver urges them on. If they go much faster, that dream of an accident will come true.

Your mother is considering the idea, you can tell. Whatever she had hoped from this reunion, it has not lived up to her expectations. Nothing ever does. She shifts, deciding.

'Your place is with me, Catherine,' she says firmly. 'I will never let you go.'

You cry then – really cry. You can't help yourself.

She has broken you again.

'Don't cry,' a voice whispers. Nella has slipped across the carriage to sit next to you. You look down at her. Her silver collar gleams against her brown skin. Your own throat, still sore from Patchett's attack, tightens in sympathy. Nella shuffles closer, keeping a wary eye on your mother. You can't hold her, tied up in your straitjacket, so you lean down and kiss the top of her head.

'How charming,' your mother says, but she is not charmed at all.

We were at least two hours behind the carriage.

'The driver was whipping the horses hard,' a farmer told us, leaning over the wall. 'Guards clinging to the sides. Mean-looking fellows.' He described another man standing in a basket at the back, who sounded like Patchett. 'Thought there was something queer about them,' the farmer said. 'They was travelling too fast for the roads.'

So Lady Vanhook had chosen speed over secrecy, emboldened by the addition of her mercenaries. She must have hired them in tremendous haste and at tremendous cost.

'She is using Kitty's fortune against her,' I said to Jeremiah, when we set off again.

He circled his thumb over the tips of his fingers: *money*. Then with a *pffft*, he stretched his palms, flinging out his fingers. *Gone.* She would spend it all.

Had they been travelling on horseback like us, we might have lost them across country – too many winding lanes and shortcuts through fields to choose from. But they were restricted to the carriage roads, which made them easier to follow. I could almost sense Kitty up ahead of me, as if she were calling to me. I asked Jeremiah if he ever felt the same with Affic.

'Sometimes,' he replied. And then, almost under his breath, 'Dangerous.'

At Leytonstone, we learnt they had stopped briefly at the Green Man Inn to eat and buy some blankets. I told the landlord my story and he nodded. Like the farmer, he had suspected something was amiss. 'Aye, I saw her,' he said, when I described Kitty. 'Poor girl. I told them she wasn't fit to travel. *Mind your own business*, they says. You'll catch them, sir,' he added, kindly. 'They'll have to stop before nightfall. Only a fool rides through Epping in the dark – there's more robbers than trees out there.'

'Where will they rest, would you say?'

He didn't hesitate. 'Walthamstow. Any further and they'll be *murdered*.'

As we were leaving the Green Man, we passed a group of merchants riding back to the city, anxious to reach home before the light faded. I paid one of their servants to deliver a message to Sam, telling him to meet us at the Nag's Head in Walthamstow. He would be safe enough travelling at night, given the company he was gathering about him.

'We could meet them here,' Jeremiah suggested.

I shook my head. It might be safer to wait and travel together, but I was too restless to sit warming my hands by the fire, letting the miles stretch between Kitty and me. If she was in Walthamstow, that was where I must go.

We returned to our saddles and set off upon the high road, the sun sinking below the trees and taking with it any warmth from the air. As the last of the houses disappeared, I listened hard to the darkening world. Low marshes stretched out to the west, deep forest to the east. This was where gentlemen of the road lay in wait for those foolish or desperate enough to travel at night. I kept a tight hold upon my swordstick, expecting an ambush at each new bend in the road.

My horse, sensing my unease, began to share it, flaring her nostrils and breathing hard. When an owl called from a branch overhead she panicked, and I had to grab hard on the reins to stop her from bolting. She snorted and almost lost her footing on the ice. After that she refused to move another inch. I could feel her flinching and trembling beneath me.

Jeremiah rode up alongside, singing a sweet, melancholy tune. My horse's ears lifted. After a moment she settled and we continued on, side by side.

'I have not heard that melody in a long time,' I said. 'Fair Angel of England' was my sister's favourite ballad – she used to hum it to herself when she was sewing. How long ago, how distant. I had not seen Jane in four years, but now here she was, travelling with me on this wintry road.

Jeremiah was singing different words from the ones I knew, something about his true love, stolen away by a tyrant, and a promise to remain constant. 'Till then I'll retreat to the forest and mourn,' he sang, his voice clear and strong.

'Lights,' he said, after a time.

We had reached Walthamstow.

The Nag's Head was an old inn and very popular that night, with travellers and villagers gathering together for warmth and company. We led our horses round to the yard, where I looked in vain for the black and yellow carriage. I called to a stable boy and described it to him.

'Been and gone, sir,' he said.

My shoulders sagged in defeat. I had been so sure they would be here, I had felt it in my bones. I asked the stable boy if he had noticed a woman with freckled skin and red hair, and if she was well. He told me that he had, and that she had stayed in the carriage. She had looked weak, and very tired.

'Did you speak with her?'

He shook his head. 'Wasn't allowed near,' he said, regretful.

I described Lady Vanhook, and he snorted. Oh yes, he had spoken with her. Very haughty and ill-tempered, shouting at everyone and demanding service with a click of her fingers. After months of pretence, hidden away in her dark green sitting room, she was free to be herself at last.

Inside the inn, the air was thick with pipe smoke and the smell of roast meat. One or two fellows stared at Jeremiah on account of his complexion, not in a welcoming way. But most paid us no mind, until a serving maid slammed her tray on the bar and pointed at me.

'Half-Hanged Hawkins!'

At once, everyone turned and stared. Oh God, not now. I steeled myself for the inevitable comments. *I saw you on the cart, sir! I watched you twist upon the rope! I saw them lay you in your coffin!* As if I were an actor and it had all been some marvellous spectacle we might laugh about now that it was done. Here was the first of them, weaving towards me – some drunken merchant beaming from ear to ear.

'Well now, sir – and how do you do? Much better than the last time I saw you, I'll wager,' he guffawed. 'By the devil, I shall never forget you dangling from that rope, legs kicking—'

An older gentleman in a black coat stopped him. 'Good heavens, sir, let the poor man be!'

No one had ever stepped in to save me before. The merchant looked disappointed but did as he was told. I thanked my rescuer.

'Thomas Hawkins,' he said, his eyes bright with amusement. 'Do you not remember me?' He smiled, and at once the stranger became familiar.

'Mr Chishull!' I said, astonished.

Edmund Chishull was an old friend of my father's – a traveller and antiquarian, and a fellow clergyman. He had aged well in the years since we had last met – he had the clear complexion and lean build of a man who walked a good deal in the fresh air, and ate and drank in moderation.

'*Mr Chishull?*' he chided me. 'Uncle Edmund to you, Thomas.'

He led me to an empty booth, where we sat opposite one another, Jeremiah sliding on to the bench next to me. I introduced them to each other, and they shook hands. It may have been my imagination, but I thought Jeremiah liked me better, having met my friend. We are judged by the company we keep, are we not?

'My dear boy,' Chishull said, 'you look as though you have staggered from a battlefield.' My clothes and face were spattered with mud. Jeremiah looked no better. 'Stew and ale,' Chishull declared. 'That's what you need. When I was in Ephesus, I would *dream* of stew and ale.'

I laughed, remembering our old, shared joke. Chishull had travelled extensively as a young man, and never lost an opportunity to speak of his adventures. Being an insolent little wretch, I would tease him for it. 'When *I* was in Ephesus,' I would say, and then add something foolish, such as 'I grew an extra toe', or 'I lived on goat droppings for six months'. Chishull, ever-amiable, was happy to join in and laugh at himself. He understood that children needed silliness as much as they need food, or air.

It was strange, I had not thought of him in years, but I had been most attached to him as a child and had indeed called him uncle. He had visited our home in Suffolk on numerous occasions. He had a knack for persuading my father to release me from my studies so that we might walk the coastal paths together. I had not questioned this – the ways of adults are so often a mystery to a child – but looking back I realise he was being kind to a lonely boy, who missed his mother. She had walked the same paths with me, letting me run and explore. Chishull must have known that, too.

As I grew older, he would send long, lively letters to me at school, full of encouragement and advice. Knowing I was destined for the church, and that I had misgivings, he did his best to prepare me. *There are many paths to the Lord, Thomas,* he wrote. *I am sure there is a way for you to honour your father's wishes without giving up your own ambitions. Did I ever mention that I travelled extensively as a young chaplain?* [Our silly joke again.] *Perhaps you might find a similar position and thus see the world?*

When I suggested the idea to my father he snorted. 'A travelling chaplain? And where should you like to set up your mission – the moon? Chishull should know better, filling your head with foolish notions. No, no – once you are ordained you shall stay here with me, Thomas, where I might keep an eye upon you.'

As for Mr Chishull, he was never invited to our home again. I had not seen him in fifteen years.

He explained that he was now rector of St Mary's, the church across the road. 'Not an easy parish,' he said, with a smile that suggested this was an understatement. 'Old feuds and factions.' Which sounded like every parish and every neighbourhood, to me.

I lit a pipe, and told him about Kitty's abduction and my search for her. Chishull listened attentively, and if he disapproved of my unconventional life with Kitty (and surely he must), he did not say so. Kindness first, always.

'Such wickedness,' he said, when I had finished. He rose to his feet. 'Allow me to ask about the inn on your behalf. I know these people very well. Someone will have heard something. And if they lie to me, I shall know it.' He squeezed my shoulder. 'I am glad to find you here, Thomas. I am only sorry it is under such dreadful circumstances.' He disappeared into the crowds.

'Some good fortune at last,' I said to Jeremiah. Our stew had arrived, along with the ale.

'A thing is not a thing until you grasp it,' he replied.

The way he spoke the words, reflexively, made me think it must be an old, familiar phrase – an antidote to wishful thinking.

'Is that something your brother used to say?'

Jeremiah lowered his spoon and stared at me in shock. 'How . . .?'

'Your account,' I explained. 'I feel as if I know you very well. You and your family.'

'And yet I do not know you at all,' he said.

I shrugged. 'I am as I seem.'

Jeremiah did not appear convinced by this.

We ate our supper in silence, side by side, looking out into the room. It was a snug, cosy place, with low ceilings and plenty of candles. I thought of Kitty begging for help in that Whitechapel tavern. If only she had found a welcoming place such as this, instead. I imagined her sitting upon the opposite bench, enjoying her stew and ale. She had been gone only three days, but her absence was a physical pain in my chest. I knew it would not leave me until we were together again.

I was about to make some idle comment to Jeremiah, that this was a pleasant spot, when I noticed a couple of men glance in his direction and mutter to each other. Jeremiah shifted and sighed. He had seen them too. Vigilance, always.

A man of about fifty years pushed his way through the crowds, clutching a tankard of ale. He had a florid face and the bulging middle of a committed glutton.

Chishull followed close behind. 'This is—'

'Bunnell, George Bunnell, esquire,' the man interrupted, squeezing himself on to the opposite bench. He extended his hand.

'Bunnell lives a quarter mile from a family called the Conyers,' Mr Chishull explained.

Mr Bunnell took a deep breath. 'Yes, damn their eyes, and—'

'Yes, yes, there is a great deal of nonsense between the families,' Mr Chishull said, wearily. 'The short of it is, they have taken rooms here tonight, the entire household. They said it is on account of the snow—'

'Hah!' Bunnell swigged his beer. 'As if John Conyer would pay for rooms if there's no profit in it. Miserly old goat.'

Mr Chishull frowned at Bunnell. 'It appears that Mr Conyer has been induced to abandon his home for the night. And he is certainly keeping quiet about it. They have already retired upstairs, the whole family.'

'Villains—' Mr Bunnell began.

'Not an inch of it,' Mr Chishull interrupted. 'There are plenty of decent families around here with debts to pay. I dare say if a fine gentlewoman materialised at *your* door, Mr Bunnell, and offered *you* a small fortune to rent your house for the night, you would agree with alacrity.'

Mr Bunnell frowned and drank his beer.

'Where is the house?' I asked Chishull.

'West of here, across the river. Too dangerous a journey in the dark, in this weather. Rest here for a few hours, and we shall visit them at dawn, together. I'm sure we may settle this matter in a peaceable fashion.'

I nodded my agreement.

Chishull was not fooled. He knew me too well. 'Thomas. Promise me you will not rush up there tonight on your own . . . Please,' he said, when I didn't answer. 'It is my duty to protect you, in your father's absence. He would not want you running headlong into danger.'

Mentioning my father was – as always – a mistake. 'My father would not have me do *anything*.'

Chishull looked pained. 'He does love you, Thomas.'

'If he loved me, he would not . . .' I stopped myself. What was the use of reliving old miseries? The endless days spent cramped at my desk, the constant criticism and vigilance? Once, when I was no more than ten years old, I had signed my name with a flourish on the final 's'. When my father saw it, he caned my writing hand.

Such embellishments were a mark of vanity and rebellion. I could not move my fingers for three days.

'He was too strict with you,' Chishull conceded. 'But only because he was afraid.'

'Afraid of *what*?' I was too tired, and worried about Kitty, to keep the impatience from my voice.

Jeremiah was listening intently.

'He was afraid,' Chishull said, 'that he would lose you, as he lost your mother. You are so like her, Thomas. Bright, generous. Reckless.'

Instinctively, my hand reached for the cross around my neck. 'My mother died of a fever.' And my father took her portrait down from the wall, and never spoke her name again.

Chishull winced. 'Of course. I only meant . . . he wished to keep you safe. From yourself.'

I drank my ale and looked to the door. Sam would arrive soon, surely. He would rescue me from this.

'Thomas,' Chishull said. 'I must confess something to you. Something terrible.'

Oh, Lord, what now? I had been so pleased to meet him after so long a time. I stuffed some tobacco in my pipe.

Chishull reached over and put a hand on mine, holding me still. When I had stopped fiddling, he continued. 'Last spring, I wrote to your father. You were in prison, condemned to hang. I told him I was sorry. He had recognised the evil in your heart when you were a child and tried to correct it. I should not have stood in his way. I should have realised that he knew you best.'

I pulled my hand away.

'Your father wrote to me, by return,' Chishull continued. 'Four words. *My son is innocent.* Do you understand Thomas? Your father had faith in you, when the world did not.'

I covered my face.

Seeing my distress, Chishull turned his attention to Jeremiah, enquiring about his health, and how he came to be in my company.

Jeremiah did his best to answer. The conversation was stilted, but it gave me time to recover. I lit my pipe and took a long draw.

Bunnell leant forward and spoke into my ear. Heaven knows what he had made of the conversation. It did not seem to interest him. 'I'll take you up to the house tonight,' he said. 'For three guineas.'

I nodded and the deal was done, right under Chishull's nose.

The room in which we were seated had a thick red velvet curtain across the door to trap in the warmth. I had been keeping a close eye upon it, watching customers and servants come and go. At last the curtain drew back to reveal Sam, muffled to his nose in a scarf. Still no gloves, though. Dr Mackay's stolen guard dog stood at his side, nose twitching at the scent of roasted meat.

I followed Sam up the stairs to a pair of private rooms overlooking the stables, the dog padding ahead of us and sniffing everything with great interest. 'You know most of 'em,' Sam said, as he opened the door.

Gabriela sat by the fire, eating a roast chicken. She had brought two members of the Fleet gang with her. They nodded at me, and returned to their meal.

I had expected Gabriela and her men. I had not expected Felblade's new servant. He kept himself apart from the Fleets, shoulders hunched about his ears. 'Master Twig!' I said, pleased to have remembered his name.

He gave me a doleful look.

'Felblade insisted,' Sam said. The apothecary – hearing that Kitty was sick and injured, and that we would be facing armed guards – had filled a leather satchel with salves, tinctures and other remedies. Apparently Twig had been schooled in their uses, though he did not seem confident about his skills. As I talked to Twig, Sam slid a pistol into my coat pocket, and some powder. There was no reason for him to be surreptitious about it, given the company, it was simply a question of habit. Nor had I asked him to bring me the weapon. I had no intention of using it . . . and yet the weight of it in my pocket felt both unsettling and reassuring at the same moment.

The door opened behind me and Finbar Inchguard lurched in, carrying a tray of drinks. 'Mr Hawkins!' he cried, almost tripping over the dog, which snapped half-heartedly at his ankles. 'Good evening to you, sir!'

I glanced at Sam, who shrugged. 'He owes us.'

'Should you not be in Durham by now?' I asked him.

Inchguard looked at me blankly.

'Herding sheep?' I prompted.

'Oh, that's a fine idea!' Inchguard beamed, as though he had never considered the notion himself, nor told me of it. He was a vague fellow. Still, he added to the gang, rather as a stick of celery adds to a hot pot. Flavour and bulk, at little expense.

I explained what I knew of the Conyers' house, and the guards. Including Patchett, that made seven men on their side.

'So.' Gabriela fed a piece of chicken to the dog. 'You have a plan?'

I considered our company. Our enemy held the better hand, without a doubt. We should bide our time, and wait for a better opportunity. That would be the sensible choice.

We should wait, most definitely.

Chapter Sixteen

The river was frozen over.

The ferry boat was trapped firmly within the ice and covered with a dusting of fresh snow. On the western bank, the forest stood waiting, silent and still. I sighed, my breath clouding the night air. We would have to walk across.

'How long has it been frozen?' I asked Bunnell, who was standing several inches too close to me. He had turned anxious when he met the rest of the company, and had not left my side on our walk to the river. I couldn't blame him. We looked like the sort of gang they hanged all together at Tyburn, including the dog.

'A few days now,' Bunnell replied. 'Send the boy over first if you're worried,' he suggested, when I didn't move. He meant Twig. But Twig was nothing but skin, bone and misery – of course the ice would hold for him.

'Oh!' Gabriela huffed. 'I'll go.' She hoisted the dog over her shoulder – it looked more surprised than anything, it had had a peculiar day – before stepping out on to the ice. Her men hurried after her, then Sam.

Inchguard followed, with much windmilling of arms and legs. After a moment's hesitation, Jeremiah slid off after him.

'I'll be going then,' Bunnell said, rubbing his hands against the cold. That had not been the deal, and it struck me that he had waited until the most dangerous members of the gang were halfway across the river before suggesting it. He pointed at the woods on the far bank. 'Walk through the trees and up the hill and you'll find it.'

He ran off bow-legged down the track towards the village, snow scuffing up behind him. Three guineas and the bastard had abandoned us.

Twig looked up at me with big, worried eyes. 'Go back with him,' I said. 'You can wait for us at the inn.'

Twig clutched the leather satchel filled with his master's bottles and implements. '*Mr Felblade insisted*,' he said, bravely, and stepped on to the ice.

I caught his elbow. 'Hide in the woods when you reach them.' I would not have him caught up in any trouble. With luck Lady Vanhook's guards would be sleeping up at the house, and we would catch them by surprise – but I did not want to be worrying about Twig in the midst of everything else.

Twig nodded, relieved, and began his slide across the river.

A fresh squall of snow peppered my face. I took a deep breath, and stepped out on to the ice. It felt solid. I prayed that it was.

It was not an easy journey. The ice held firm, but it was hard to walk upon without slipping. I was forced to slide forward in short bursts, arms outstretched. When I reached the middle I stopped for a moment to catch my breath. As I did so, I chanced to look upriver and saw a wooden platform jutting out from the bank, black against the ice. An old jetty perhaps, or the remnants of a ruined bridge. I squinted at it through the falling snow. There was something odd about it, but I could not say what.

I looked harder. *Black against the ice.* The whole world was covered in a blanket of snow – the woods, the ground, the river. The air itself was sparkling with ice crystals. But the surface of the platform was dark.

Someone was lying on top of it – waiting, and watching.

An ambush.

My heart punched against my chest. From the corner of my eye I saw Twig struggling up the frozen bank.

'Run!' I yelled. 'Twig! Run!'

The figure on the platform stood up.

For a second, it was as if everything stopped, even the snow.

Then he jumped down on to the ice and made his way towards me, silent and steady, like something from a nightmare.

I hurried forwards, slipping to my knees in my rush to escape him.

Patchett.

He was going to reach me before I made the bank. There was nothing I could do about it. I stumbled to my feet, sliding on the ice.

He was almost upon me.

The silence was broken by shouts from the woods. 'Ambush!' Gabriela screamed. As I glanced towards the woods I heard a pistol fire, followed by an answering shot, close enough to make my ears ring. Something tapped my left arm, near the shoulder. For a moment I felt nothing, and then pain burst through, searing hot.

I had been shot.

Patchett lowered his pistol. He was no more than six feet away from me on the ice. I could see the smoke drifting from the barrel.

I staggered with the pain, but didn't fall.

In the woods beyond, I could hear more pistol fire. 'A child,' I said, clutching my arm, feeling the blood stream over my fingers. 'There's a child out there.' And Sam. Jeremiah. Gabriela. I'd led them all into a trap.

Patchett was reloading his pistol, struggling in the cold and dark. Before he could finish, I pulled my own pistol free and aimed it at his head. My injured arm was burning, but I kept my right hand steady. 'I'll shoot you dead before you can reload.'

He stopped, watching me closely.

'Throw it away.'

He did as he was told, and lifted his hands.

His calmness infuriated me. 'Where's Kitty?'

'They left hours ago.' He grinned. 'I've been waiting for you.'

'How did you know ... *Bunnell.*' No wonder he'd run off when we reached the river. The whole night had been one great trap, to make us think they were up at the house, and not travelling on through the night. Patchett had been left here to slow us down.

'Where are they headed?'

'Let her go, Hawkins,' he drawled. 'Plenty more whores in the sea.'

'Thomas!' Gabriela called from the bank. 'Where the fuck are you?'

I turned, distracted and Patchett leapt at me. Before I could think, I squeezed the trigger.

The shot hit his chest.

There was no time for his expression to change, no fear, no confusion, no surprise. He fell hard at my feet, dead. A knife fell from his hand and skittered across the ice.

I had killed a man.

The scent of gunsmoke filled the air.

The pistol felt heavy in my hand. My wounded arm no longer hurt, but as I thought about it, the scorching pain returned, as if I'd called for it.

'Thomas.' Gabriela had reached me on the ice. She looked at the body at my feet, then prodded me towards the bank. 'Go.'

I moved without thinking. The snow fell softly on my face.

I had killed a man.

Sam was crouched at the edge of the river, cleaning his blade. He stood up when he saw me. 'Three guards,' he said, giving his account as if I were a general. There was a smear of blood on his cheek. 'One dead. The other two ran.'

'Is everyone safe?'

'You're bleeding.'

'Is everyone safe?'

He didn't answer. I stumbled past him into the trees. I could hear voices up ahead. Gabriela's men drew their blades when they heard me crunching through the snow, then lowered them when they saw me. I pushed past them into the clearing, towards a lantern light. Inchguard was kneeling down in its glow, holding on to the dog by its collar. The dead guard was sprawled at the foot of an oak tree, his neck twisted at an odd angle. The snow in the clearing was muddy and broken up from the battle.

'Bad business, Mr Hawkins,' Inchguard said.

'Where's Jeremiah?'

Inchguard gave me a sombre look and handed me the lantern.

I followed a pair of fresh footprints through the snow, ducking under low branches. I could smell blood in the air. I wasn't sure if it was mine.

I found Jeremiah kneeling beneath a weeping willow, its empty branches draping to the ground as if in mourning. He was muttering something beneath his breath. Praying, I realised.

'Jeremiah. Are you hurt?'

He sat back upon his heels. Another body lay stretched out upon the ground. A guard, I thought, because the alternative was too terrible. It must be a second guard. But the body was too small, and slight. The hand reaching out, lifeless, was a boy's hand.

The shot had torn straight through his throat.

I stumbled away from the willow, refusing to believe what I had seen. It wasn't possible.

I had spoken to him on the river. He had turned to look at me. How long ago? Two, three minutes? Five at most.

It wasn't possible.

I was struggling to remember his true name. He didn't like Twig but we had called him that anyway. He would have died in an instant and without pain, silenced for ever. Twelve. Thirteen at most. *Mr Felblade insisted.* I should have insisted. God help me. I should have sent him back to the inn.

Gabriela kicked her way through the snow, trailed by Sam and the rest of the company. Her eyes flickered to the willow. 'The boy's dead?'

Jeremiah stepped out to join us. He gave me a long, angry look – but said nothing.

'God rest his soul,' Inchguard said. 'Poor little sod.'

'His bag.' Gabriela pushed Sam towards the willow. 'Thomas. Take off your coat.'

'I need to reach the house. Kitty—'

'She is gone. Think, idiot! That bitch tricked us.'

My shirt was soaked in blood. Gabriela tore the sleeve to reach the wound beneath. Blood was streaming down my arm, patting lightly on to the snow. She put her fingers to the wound and pulled it wide. I gritted my teeth.

'No shot,' she said. 'And it missed the bone. Lucky.'

Gabriela saw my expression and slapped me once, very hard. 'This is not your fault,' she said.

She wrapped a strip of cloth round my arm and tied it tight. I swore with the pain – I couldn't help myself. Her men laughed, half sorry for me.

'Good enough for now,' Gabriela said, cleaning the blood from her hands with snow. She turned to her men and they began to discuss Patchett and the dead guard as if they were sacks of corn. The men would take the bodies back to the city. Sam knew a surgeon's assistant who would pay good money for two fresh corpses, no questions asked. 'Take the boy too,' Gabriela said. 'We'll give him a decent burial. He is Christian, Thomas?'

I had no idea. I didn't even know if he had a family. I knew almost nothing about him. A child. Gone for ever.

Gabriela was wrong. This was all my fault.

I walked up the hill to the Conyers' place with Jeremiah. The dog trotted at our heels, snuffling at the ground. I knew I would not find Kitty at the house, but we had come this far – and lost so much. I could not go back to the inn yet.

I had wanted to make the trip on my own. Gabriela and her men had accepted that, and Inchguard was happy to do as he was told.

Sam wanted to join me of course, but he needed to help with the dead. *The dead.* He insisted on sending the dog in his place and gave me a small parcel of meat to keep in my pocket. After the ambush, the raw and bloody flesh made my stomach turn, but I fed a piece to the dog and became, at once, the most magnificent and fascinating creature on the planet, to be followed to the ends of the earth or until the meat ran out, whichever came sooner.

This had left only Jeremiah, who stood to one side with his arms folded across his chest. He had not said one word to me since the attack. I had suggested that he go back to the inn, that I would prefer to visit the house alone. He had ignored me.

The front door was barred shut, so we headed to the back yard. The stables were empty save for one lonely horse. I marvelled at the money Lady Vanhook was prepared to spend to keep me from Kitty. She had paid an entire family to leave their home, just to draw me into her ambush. Or perhaps she'd expected me to wait until morning, just as Mr Chishull had advised. Either way, she and Kitty would be long gone, travelling through the night to remain ahead of me.

We broke in through the coal cellar. The house creaked and sighed, as empty houses do. In the hallway, a clock chimed ten.

We toured the quiet rooms together while the dog made its own private search, claws clacking on the stone flags. I followed it up the stairs, feeling weaker and weaker with each step. My arm had felt numb on the walk to the house, but now the pain was awake again, burning down to the bone.

I stopped in the middle of a dark-panelled bedroom, defeated. What was I doing here? Kitty was gone, there was not the faintest sign that she had even rested here. I sat down on the nearest chair, filled with despair.

'We should leave,' Jeremiah said quietly, from the doorway.

I nodded, and closed my eyes. At once, I saw Patchett's body stretched upon the ice, the blood seeping out beneath him, his rough red face empty of life. Had I truly seen that, in the dark? Or had I invented it? No matter, it was now inked indelibly in my mind. Blood red ink. Blood . . . The room spun.

'I'll fetch some brandy,' Jeremiah said.

The dog pattered in and pushed its wet nose against my palm. In a half-trance, I leant down and stroked its ears. A dog would forgive me. Dogs forgive everything. It licked my face then wandered off again, snuffling its way to the bed. It had probably spent its entire life chained up outside. Everything was new and exciting, a mystery to be explored. It jumped on to the bed.

'Get down,' I said, wearily.

It woofed at me, turning circles and settling down with a contented huff.

'*Down*,' I said, forgetting that we were both interlopers in this house. 'We are leaving, as soon as Jeremiah comes back.'

There was an oak chest under the window, covered with an embroidered cloth. As I scolded the dog, the lid shifted slightly. I stood up in alarm. Had I imagined it? No. The dog was staring too, its ears pricked.

A small face peeped out from the box. 'Thomas?'

'Nella!' I hurried over, scarce able to believe my eyes. 'What on earth—'

'Kitty promised you would come,' she said, standing up. She was shaking – more from shock, I think, than the cold. She put her hands up and I lifted her out, wincing as pain tore through my arm. The dog, tremendously pleased with itself for absolutely no reason, gave a joyous bark.

'Nella – is she here? Is Kitty hiding somewhere?'

She looked sad, and shook her head. 'She put me in here, and told Mistress I had run away in the snow. There was no time to search for me, so they left.'

I draped a blanket around her shoulders, fighting back my disappointment.

'Kitty said you would come, that I should stay quiet until morning. But then I heard your voice . . .'

'You were very brave.'

She smiled, proud of herself.

'*Affiba*.'

Jeremiah stood in the doorway, holding a bottle of brandy. It fell from his hand.

Nella stared at him. She clutched my fingers in her hand. 'Thomas?' she said, uncertainly – but her eyes were fixed upon Jeremiah.

He kneeled down to her level. 'Affie.'

There were perhaps ten steps between the child and her father. She took each one slowly, heel to toe, heel to toe. I had to fight the urge to lift her up and carry her to him. Jeremiah waited, smiling in encouragement.

When Nella— when *Affie* was one step away, she hesitated. The blanket slid from her shoulders. She looked at me, then back at Jeremiah.

'Affiba,' Jeremiah said, still kneeling. 'Affie. You do not remember me . . . but I am your father.'

'I remember,' Affie said, and walked into his open arms.

Chapter Seventeen

Jeremiah carried Affie all the way back to the Nag's Head. We passed the willow, we crossed the river. I was shaking with pain, barely able to walk, and sweating despite the cold. Affie peered at me over her father's shoulder, her fingers locked around his neck.

'Thomas is sick,' she said.

Jeremiah's pace did not falter.

When we arrived, the whole company cheered. After the ambush in the woods, honour had been restored. No one mentioned Twig.

Affie was kissed and hugged by the gang. Inchguard offered her some wine, which Jeremiah refused on her behalf. Then he carried his exhausted daughter away to rest.

'Thank you,' he said, bowing to the room. He did not look at me.

'That collar. *Bárbaro,*' Gabriela muttered, when father and daughter had left. 'Tomorrow we will take her to St Giles. Cut her free.'

'Ten guineas melted down, I reckon,' Sam said. 'Solid silver.'

Gabriela frowned at her son. 'You wish her neck to be wider, Samuel?'

Sam shrugged. He was satisfied that we had accomplished at least part of our plan, and pleased for Jeremiah and Affie, in his way. But they weren't *family.*

'We need more ale,' Inchguard declared.

This was something the entire gang could agree upon. I used the distraction to steal away into the adjoining room and sat alone in the dark, by the cold, unlit hearth. My hand was empty, but I could feel the weight and heat of the pistol in my palm; the window was closed, but I could smell gunsmoke and blood in the air. When I closed my eyes Patchett's scuffed, angry face appeared before me, unbidden.

He'd called Kitty a whore. Was that why I shot him?

No. He had run towards me, with a blade.

But had I seen it?

Sam slipped into the room and without a word began to build a fire. Some distant part of me knew I should thank him, not just for this but for all his help over the past few days. He had been true and loyal – and had almost lost his life as a consequence. I thought again of Twig lying under the weeping willow, his throat torn by the pistol shot. So much promise and potential snuffed out, in an instant.

'Does it hurt?' Sam asked.

I was so wrapped up in my guilt, I thought he meant Twig's death, or maybe Patchett's murder. *Does it hurt? To be a murderer?*

'Your shoulder,' he prompted.

This was odd. Sam was not given to asking questions to which he already knew the answer. Of course it bloody hurt. He was asking, I realised, because he had learnt this was the sort of thing one should ask, when a friend was shot. This question, the fire – he was trying to show his concern for me, in a way that I might understand.

'I killed a man.' My voice fractured.

'He shot you!' Sam exclaimed, exasperated. He rarely showed strong emotions, but really – I was being ridiculous. He stoked the fire then stood up, clapping soot from his hands. 'It *is* a shame,' he relented. 'Murder don't suit you. Sits on you too heavy.' His black eyes hardened. 'I should have done it.' He sounded cross with himself.

'No. Sam.' God, no. 'That is not the lesson . . .' I trailed away, too sick with pain and grief to argue. The room was lurching around me, I could barely keep my eyes open. 'You should go back to the city tomorrow. Help with . . .' *Help with the dead.* I shifted, sucking in my breath as a searing pain stabbed my arm. 'Mr Chishull will look after me. I'll send word when I'm recovered.'

Sam nodded. This was a good plan. 'Tom,' he said, awkwardly. 'We will find her.'

Such a curious boy. He treated most people with contempt or more often indifference. But those he loved – he'd fight wars for them. 'Thank you,' I said, and closed my eyes. I must have drifted, because when I opened them again, he was gone, replaced by his mother. She had brought willow tea for the pain and of course I thought of Twig again, lying under the tree. This is the way with death. Everything reminds you, you cannot help it.

'Your shirt,' Gabriela said.

I undressed. My arm was coated in streams of drying blood, I had to peel my shirt free. Gabriela untied the bandage and examined the wound again. 'Yes. Straight through,' she said. 'You'll live.'

I drank the tea as she cleaned and stitched the wound. Once she was done, she made up a poultice.

'It was Bunnell who betrayed us,' I said.

'*Yes,*' Gabriela replied, with such menace she could have plucked the word from the air and used it to stab someone.

'I would consider it a favour, Gabriela, if you did not kill him for it. There has been enough death tonight.'

She rolled her eyes. 'You feel guilty?' She scooped out the grey, lumpy poultice and smeared it on my arm. A thousand bee stings jabbed into the wound.

'Oh fuck the stars! Fuck the fucking stars!'

'There's your punishment,' Gabriela said. She wrapped a fresh cloth around the wound, holding the poultice – and the pain – in place.

'Fuck,' I muttered again, stamping my heel to distract myself.

Gabriela cackled. 'Now – you listen to me. You want to blame someone, blame that bitch Emma Sparks. I *told* you she was dangerous! Now I am going to drink gin and you are going to sleep. Good night.'

'Gabriela,' I said. 'Bunnell . . .'

'Yes, yes! He lives!' Gabriela said, generously. 'But I tell you this. Very soon, *someone* will creep into his house at night and take his clothes, his money . . . *everything*.'

I considered this for a moment, hovering on the edge of sleep. 'Very good,' I said. 'Very good.' And then I surrendered to the dark.

When I woke the next morning the rooms were quiet. I knew before I'd swung my feet to the floor that the company had gone, and left me sleeping. The room spun when I stood up, but after a few deep breaths I found my balance. *I am well enough*, I told myself, *for what I must do next*.

I had lied to Sam. I had no intention of staying in Walthamstow with Mr Chishull. I could not squander my time lying in bed when Kitty was on the road ahead of me. Gabriela had cleaned my wound, and it was no longer bleeding, or at least not much. I would recover en route. True, the sheets had been soaked with sweat when I woke, but that was a good sign, was it not? I was sure I had read that somewhere, that sweating was a good sign.

In the adjoining room, I found a note from Jeremiah. I read it as I dressed, my arm thrumming with a soft, persistent pain.

Mr Hawkins

Pray forgive me for leaving so early but I must return at once to the city – my daughter still bears the mark of her bondage and I am anxious for its swift removal.

How glad I am to hold Affie in my arms, and know that she is safe! I thank God for our reunion. And yet – alas – my joy is tempered by sorrow. A young boy is dead, who would still be alive had we been more careful. Your low spirits last night suggest that you feel the same – but feeling is not the same as doing. What will you do now?

I hesitate to counsel you, sir. We are little more than strangers. But I fear for you, Mr Hawkins – and so I shall be plain.

I believe that you have reached a crossroads in your life – a most dangerous one. Take the right path and you will find good, decent folk standing ready to assist you: Mr Chishull, Mrs Jenkins. Your father. Turn the wrong way and you will find yourself upon a dark and solitary road, that will lead only to further misery and despair. I know it well. It tempted me many times. Do not take this path, sir. For the sake of your soul, do not take it.

If you remain unpersuaded, pray think upon this: if you and I had only rested until dawn, and approached the Conyers' house with Mr Chishull as he had suggested, we would have found my daughter safe and well, waiting for us. There would have been no ambush in the dark. You would not have fired your pistol on the river. A young boy would still be alive this morning.

I am told you plan to stay in Walthamstow until you are strong enough to continue your search. I hope that you will recognise this enforced rest as a gift – an opportunity to set yourself upon that better path. If you do so, be assured that I shall be at your service when you are recovered, ready to repay my debt.

You are hunting a monster, Mr Hawkins. Do not become one yourself in the process.

I am, sir, yours
J.P.

P.S. We have left the dog as company. I have seen many hounds trained for cruelty – but I believe this one is good and faithful in its way. I have named him Gonzalo, after the faithful servant in *The Tempest*. I thought this would make you smile.

I crumpled the letter into a ball and tossed it on the fire.

How dare Jeremiah lecture me, with his daughter safe in his arms? We had joined together to find Affie *and* Kitty – but now that his half of the bargain was complete, he had abandoned me.

Well – I was better off without him.

As for the dog, it would only slow me down. Some kind soul would give it a home, no doubt.

And I had rested long enough.

It was a bright morning; the snow clouds had vanished with the night. I bought some provisions from the chandler's shop and set off down the road, swordstick in hand. I had not walked ten paces when a servant from the Nag's Head called after me.

'Sir! Sir!' he shouted, and waved. 'Your dog!'

I wasted a good five minutes explaining that the dog was not mine, but he would not be persuaded. My friends had been clear upon the matter. Gonzalo belonged to me, and wherever I went, he must follow.

'We had to kill the last dog abandoned here,' the servant said with a heavy sigh. 'We can't afford to feed a stray.'

I was certain he was lying . . . *Almost* certain.

Devil take it.

The servant led me to the kennels. Gonzalo's big, stupid ears pricked up when he heard my voice, and he barked a greeting when he saw me. How was this possible? I had barely spoken three words to the wretched creature.

'Look how pleased he is to see you,' the servant said, happily – as if he had just reunited two star-crossed lovers.

Gonzalo wagged his tail in agreement.

I didn't want a dog, least of all one spawned in some ghastly debauch between a mastiff and a bloodhound. And a spaniel. A spaniel had certainly sprung in there at some point. 'I am not your master,' I said. 'You are not my dog. Is that clear?'

Gonzalo wagged his tail even harder.

The servant handed me a bag of meat. 'A few bones,' he said. 'And a couple of chops.'

I opened the bag. There was enough to last the dog for at least two days. 'I thought you couldn't afford to keep him?'

The servant smirked. I had been conned. *Conned.*

I decided to return to the Conyers' house, just to be sure I had not missed anything in the confusion of the night. I could not bear to walk across the ice again, and pass the willow. Instead, I walked along the riverpath until I found a bridge, adding another hour to my journey.

The house offered up no new secrets. If the carriage had left wheel marks, they were long buried in the snow. The lonely horse was still locked in its stable. I would have been tempted to steal it, but could not ride with my injured arm.

Go back to Walthamstow, and Mr Chishull, a sane voice whispered in my skull. I ignored it.

I walked north along the coachway. The road was in a terrible state, which gave me hope that I might catch up with the carriage before nightfall. At midday I reached a large crossroads, with an inn set back upon one corner. I asked there for news – but no one remembered a coach with yellow wheels.

They had not taken the southern road back to Walthamstow – this much I knew. North, east or west, then? I stood there stupidly for a while, trying to decide, the dog looking up at me with a quizzical expression.

East, I decided. They had been heading east from the beginning. I would do the same – and pray for luck.

I walked on, for several hours. No one had seen them. They might as well have been snatched from the earth.

The sun was setting, casting an eerie, golden light across the winter fields. A gentleman and his steward rode past, their horses splattering me with icy mud. They paused at the top of the hill, the steward leaning forward in his saddle, listening and nodding before riding back on his own. I took the dog's collar and brought him to heel.

The steward touched his hat. 'Good morrow, sir. Are you lost?'

A polite way to enquire who I was, and what the devil I might be doing. This was not the city, one could not wander about without attracting curiosity – suspicion, even. I told him of my search. 'But I fear I have taken the wrong path. I must turn back.' A weariness overtook me as I spoke these words, heavy as a stone slab. The thought of returning to that crossroads and beginning again ... A whole day gone to no purpose ...

The steward shook his head. 'It's almost nightfall. There's an inn three miles ahead. I should rest there tonight, sir. Hire a horse for tomorrow's journey.'

I gestured to my injured arm. 'I cannot ride.'

He threw me a sympathetic look. 'My horse can carry you as far as the inn, at least. She's a placid old thing. You'd be quite safe.' He patted her flank.

It was a kind offer to a stranger, but I could not bear to ride another three miles in the wrong direction. I thanked him, and turned back the way I had come.

And what a miserable journey that was, plodding back past the same woods and fields. Even the dog looked weary. I stumbled several times on the ice and once fell into a ditch, only just saving myself from landing on my injured arm.

Three hours later I had arrived back at the crossroads, and the inn on the corner. I tottered to the fire as if I were a man of ninety, aware of the sidelong stares I was drawing from the other customers. I smoked a pipe, which helped, and ordered some brandy, which helped still more. I took a room, slept fitfully, and set out again at dawn. The dog came with me.

*　　*　　*

Another endless, hellish day followed. In the afternoon I met an old journeyman who swore he had seen the coach, or perhaps not seen but heard of it. He was drinking with two of his friends, and his speech made little sense. There would have been two women, I said, struggling to hide my impatience. The younger woman with red hair, the older tall and evil. (I did not say evil. I do not think I said evil.)

'Maybe, maybe,' he said thoughtfully, then held out his hand for payment. When I ignored him his two friends stood up with clenched fists. The dog growled at them, but I was not strong enough for a fight. I threw coins at the ground and hurried away, while they laughed. *When I have found Kitty, I will return and break your jaws. Insolent devils.*

That night the maid who brought me supper offered to ask about the inn for news.

'You should rest, sir,' she said. 'Begging your pardon, but you do not look well.'

I retired to my room, while she made enquiries on my behalf. But no one had heard or seen anything of Kitty, or Lady Vanhook. The maid told me again that I did not look well, and asked if I had family or friends nearby, who might help. I assured her I was tired, nothing more – tired and distracted.

Once she had left, I removed Gabriela's bandage, rinsing my injured arm with hot water. It was not healing as I'd hoped, the wound was leaking beneath the stitches in an ugly way and the flesh surrounding it was taut and tender. I would call for a doctor in the morning, I decided, and with that, collapsed into a deep sleep.

When I woke I was sure I felt much better and did not need a doctor after all. The sheets were soaked through to the mattress – I must have sweated myself free of the infection. As I had no appetite I left without taking breakfast.

I had been walking for two hours or so when I saw the figure standing in the middle of the road, some distance ahead. It surprised me that the dog had not barked a warning. 'Who is that?' I asked him. Gonzalo looked up at me in confusion.

The figure was too small to be a man, I thought. It took me a long time to reach him, he seemed to shift further away whenever I drew close. When at last I caught up with him I was delighted to see that it was Twig, his lank hair loose about his face.

'How strange to find you here,' I said, but now that I thought of it, I was sure I had told him to meet me along the way. He said that he was worried about my wound and that he would like to fix a fresh plaster, and I promised we would do so once we arrived in Cambridge, for that was where we were heading. I tried to introduce him to Gonzalo but the dog kept nudging my hand and whimpering; I wasn't sure why he was doing that.

'I shall hire a coach in town,' I told Twig. There was some reason I had not done so yet but I could not remember it. Twig looked at me with his large, soulful eyes and said nothing.

A little further down the road I found that I was very hot, so I gave Twig my coat. After a time I grew very cold and needed it again, but Twig had disappeared and when I found him waiting for me further up the road he said he had lost it, or perhaps someone had stolen it from him. He said it was no matter, I would be warm enough when we hired the coach. It was then I remembered that I did not have the funds to hire my own carriage, which was why I was on foot.

'How many days have we been walking?' I asked Twig. He was clutching his bag close to his chest. Strange – I was sure Sam had taken it back to London.

Twig opened the bag to show me a white dove. Its neck was broken.

I walked three more steps but the road was moving beneath my feet, lithe as a snake. I staggered sideways into a ditch.

Gonzalo trotted over and licked my face. Twig watched me from the road, impassive. Blood was pouring from a ragged hole in his throat, was that why he didn't answer? Something was moving in the bag, the dove was trying to break free. Twig held the bag tight.

You should rest yourself, sir.

I lay down in the ditch. The ground was very cold. Was I lying on the river? Yes, that was it, I was lying on the frozen river, and here was Patchett stretched out beside me. He was bleeding on to the ice. So much blood, thick and cloying – I could feel it soaking into my clothes. Why could I not move?

Patchett's face was white, his lips blue. There was a gaping wound in his chest.

He opened his eyes and grinned.

I heard a sharp crack, and then another. The ice was breaking beneath me.

Somewhere in the distance, I could hear a dog barking.

The ice broke and I plunged into the water. It was not as bad as I had feared. I slipped deeper. The light of the world dimmed. No pain. No feeling. Nothing.

I sank slowly to the river bed, to the dark, and was grateful.

PART SIX

Recovery

Chapter Eighteen

The light when it woke me was soft. I was no longer on the road, and when I probed my memory I remembered other wakings: a hard, jolting ride on a cart; sweating and shivering on a narrow bed; the stink of my wound turned putrid. Pain. *Looks like a gentleman. Pistol shot. A duel most likely. Damned fool.*

The room was small and plainly furnished, with lime-plastered walls and a wooden cross above the bed. The window contained sections of stained glass, fractured images jumbled together – a bird's wing, an angel's face, a saint's hand raised in blessing. They cast jewelled colours on the stone floor. Had I woken in a different age, I would have said this was a monk's cell.

A church bell rang out and doors opened in response. Voices, and shadows passing the window. Perhaps I *was* in a monastery. I sat up, slowly.

The dog was asleep by the bed, its long legs twitching as it dreamt. Its name slid into my mind with surprising ease.

'Gonzalo.'

The dog lifted his head sleepily and our eyes met. He lumbered to his paws and woofed in greeting, sniffing my hand. I pulled back the blanket and swung my legs off the bed. My feet flinched as they touched the cold floor. Every movement was an effort, every muscle ached in protest. Gonzalo wagged his shaggy tail in encouragement, as if I had just performed some extraordinary feat of acrobatics.

How long had I lain sick in this room? A day? A year? Dream, delirium, memory were all muddled together.

The door opened and a tall, lean woman of about sixty entered, carrying a bowl of steaming water. She was a stranger, and yet I recognised her. Her grey hair was tucked and pinned under a plain mob cap. She considered me with stern, kind eyes. I was to be scolded – this too I knew, before she spoke. Clearly we had spent a lot of time together, though I could not remember any of it.

'Sitting up. *Marvellous*. Now lie down.'

'I must—' I tried to stand. The room spun, and my stomach twisted.

'You must not! Fractious boy. Lie *down*.'

She helped me back into bed and tucked me in tight as an oyster, snug in its shell. Martha, that was her name. My nurse was Martha, the dog was Gonzalo.

'How long have I been here?'

'Six weeks. Through Advent and Epiphany.' She dropped a flannel cloth in the hot, rose-scented water.

Six weeks. I had lost the whole of December, and made a decent start on January. I groaned and shifted beneath my blanket. The movement brought a slight twinge of pain to my arm. I was dressed in a stranger's shirt, and could not see the scar. 'Who—'

'A couple of woolmen found you face down in a ditch. He was standing over you,' she nodded at the dog, 'howling like a fury. Saved your life, bless him.' She had answered these questions before, I could tell from her tone. She scrubbed at my face. I had grown a thick beard in my sleep. It rasped against the cloth.

'Where—'

'Oh, heavens! No more, not today. You have fallen three times into a fever, I won't see it take you again. I doubt you would survive it.'

I sank back against my pillow and slept. In my dreams I searched for Kitty, and never found her.

*　　*　　*

Another six days passed before I was strong enough to leave my sick room. Until then I slept, and ate, and slept again. My monk's cell was in fact a room in an almshouse. I had been found on the Cambridge Road on the outskirts of Saffron Walden and brought here to die. Then, to everyone's surprise, I had lived.

'I suppose you needed to,' Martha said, on the day I left. 'Unfinished business. That can save a man, when prayer and medicine fail.'

We looked at one another. I must have said things in my fever – dark, disturbing things.

Somewhere amid those ramblings I had told her that my name was Thomas, and that I was searching for my wife. (I had called Kitty my wife: interesting.) Beyond that I was a mystery. My coat, which might have offered some clue, was lost upon the road, along with my purse. My hat and swordstick, by some miracle, had survived. Martha had spent all these weeks nursing me, borrowing from the almshouse's funds to keep me alive, and the dog fed.

'I'm sorry,' I said. 'I have been nothing but a caterpillar, chewing my way through your precious stock.'

Martha laughed. 'And now you will fly away.' She held out a thick woollen cloak. When I tried to refuse the gift she shook it out, and draped it around my shoulders. 'More bat than butterfly.'

I flapped the cloak and she laughed again. 'I knew I liked you,' she said. 'You come to know a man. We have been on a journey together, Thomas. Through the valley of the shadow of death.' She stroked my shoulder. 'You must take care of yourself.'

She opened the door and I stepped outside for the first time in almost two months, the crisp air like a slap upon my skin. Sparrows pecked at the wet earth until the dog startled them away. Snowdrops had pushed their way up in clusters beneath the trees. Winter was almost over. I had wasted so much time. 'I am a fool,' I said.

'You are *young*,' Martha said. 'That is the very best time to be foolish. And when you're old. That's a good time, too.' She smiled to herself. 'How old are you, Thomas?'

'Six and twenty. No!' I corrected myself. 'Twenty-seven.' I had missed a birthday in my fevered state.

We walked along the path, past the old chapel, the dog tacking back and forth in front of us. A blackbird eyed us cautiously under a hedge, a fat worm twirling in its beak. 'The coach will stop at the Eight Bells, just past St Mary's.' Martha pointed to the church spire that poked above the rooftops a couple of streets away.

'Will you not wait with me? I would be glad of the company.'

'Oh, no. This is my little world. I am content within it.'

I studied her for a moment. She was almost as tall as me and stood like a soldier. 'There's a story tucked away in there,' I said, pointing at her heart.

'There always is,' she replied.

I promised I would send money, when I could, and tried to offer her my swordstick. It should fetch a good price. She said she was not in the business of selling weapons. In any case, I would need it to lean on. I was not recovered yet.

'Well then.' I felt reluctant to say goodbye. It felt too abrupt. I thought she was sorry, too. 'Should you ever need help . . .'

'My dear boy.' She buttoned my cloak. 'A gift needs no reward. Find your wife, live a good life and be happy.'

She put a hand on my shoulder, and pushed me gently on my way.

London, after my long absence, felt both strange and familiar. I was home, and there was relief in that. But when I reached Russell Street I found the bakery closed and shuttered, and when I enquired, I was told that Mr Jenkins had died, and his widow was in Staffordshire with her family.

Oh, what would Hannah Jenkins think of me now? A dark, limping spectre returning home to haunt the neighbourhood. A ruined man with blood on his hands.

She'd had such faith in me.

I walked on, through the piazza. As I passed the open door of Moll's I caught its quintessential scent of coffee and liquor mingled with pipe smoke and a trace of vomit. I was tempted to venture inside and find Betty – she might have missed me. (Had anybody missed me?)

I turned instead towards Long Acre, the dog padding at my side. It would not do to reach St Giles in darkness.

The rookeries were as riotous as usual, an ever-shifting web of alleyways, ladders, balconies, ropewalks and rooftops. I trudged a conservative path along the middle of the street (never step into the shadows in St Giles, they will eat you and spit out your bones). The air was not so bad in winter, by which I mean one could breathe it without fainting to a dead heap.

I had always stood out in St Giles, which was a bad idea. This time I made my way without any trouble or even much attention. The street boys didn't call out for money, or try to jostle my purse free. No one offered me their body for sale. It was only as I reached Phoenix Street and caught my reflection in a window I realised why. I was a wreck, a looming skeleton in an antique cloak and ruined boots, with a great hound at my side and no purse to jostle. (*And I had killed a man.* Did they smell that on me?)

Phoenix Street. I had arrived, unmurdered. One of James Fleet's boys was watching me from a doorway across the road, I could feel his stare upon my neck. He sauntered towards me and I realised my mistake. Not one of his gang but a daughter – one of Sam's five sisters – dressed in old breeches and a patched shirt. She looked about twelve or thirteen, her features rougher than her brother's – her nose had been broken at some point – but like all Gabriela's children, she had inherited her mother's black curls and olive skin. This must be Becky. Or Sophie. I always muddled them.

'Fuck off stranger,' she said, showing me a knife.

I looked at her, and smiled.

Her eyes widened. '*You.*' She stood amazed, mouth open, too shocked even to swear.

'Becky?' A toss of the coin, an easy gamble.

She grinned and pocketed her blade. Becky it was.

James Fleet's den stood within the centre of a square of houses, like a castle within a moat. No one entered that square without being seen by half a dozen of his men. Becky led me through, still grinning, as if she were leading a prized horse back to its stable. I felt more like an old nag clopping to the knacker's yard. Perhaps they would shoot me out of kindness.

'Sam!' she yelled, as she approached the house – a square, three-storeyed building with warped balconies wrapped around each storey. 'Sam!' she yelled louder. 'Come out you scrub. Look what I brung you!'

Sam emerged from the top of the house and peered down. 'Who is it?'

I took off my hat and looked up at him. 'It's me, Sam.'

He stared at me.

I had lied to him, the last time we spoke. Perhaps he had not forgiven me for it. 'If you're angry—'

With a sudden leap, Sam jumped over the balcony, clambering down a rope to the next storey. He swung down to the next level, then sprang to the ground. I was still marvelling at his agility when he ran at me, almost knocking me to the ground. He flung his arms around me, burying his head in my chest. And then he burst into tears.

He was *hugging me.* And *crying.* Good God. Miracles and wonders. I put my arms about him as he sobbed, great heaving hiccups of relief.

'You're alive,' he said. 'You're alive!'

Becky was pissing herself laughing. Sam didn't care. He wiped his face and grinned up at me. Gonzalo, caught up in the mood, pounced and leapt at thin air. He truly was a ridiculous creature.

'Ma!' Becky yelled. 'Come look. Ma!'

Gabriela was already on her way, her dark hair loose about her shoulders. Two of her men followed close behind. I recognised one of them from the fight at the river. Gabriela looked at her son, who was gripping my shirt in his fist, as if I might fly away. Then she looked at me.

'My God, Dormouse. What is this nonsense on your face?' She rubbed her jaw, mocking my beard.

The man from the river nodded in greeting. 'Thought you was dead.'

'*Hoped*,' Gabriela corrected, but there was a glint in her eyes. At least, I liked to think so.

I couldn't wait any longer. 'Did you find them? Is there any news?'

Gabriela did look sorry then. 'They ain't in London. This much we know. The men *she* hired came back. We asked them. Very polite.' Her men smirked.

Six weeks and no news.

I told Sam about Mrs Jenkins. 'I must find a room to rent.'

'I have lodgings,' he reminded me. 'Soho.'

Gabriela told him to fetch something from inside, and scolded her daughter back to her post on Phoenix Street. 'You pester me for this a thousand times, so go!' she said, shoving Becky with the sharp blade of her hand. Another glance dismissed her men, which left us alone. She put her hands on her hips.

'My husband,' she said, 'was happy to hear of your death. Well.' She clicked her tongue. 'A problem for another day.'

That was something to look forward to.

'Gabriela, did you ever meet a woman called Martha ...' I described my nurse, as best I could.

Gabriela scrunched her nose. 'What, you think I have a big book of women I can look through? No, I never met a tall Martha. Why?'

'She saved my life. I thought perhaps there was some reason, some connection.' But there wasn't. I'd been betrayed so many times in recent months, I'd forgotten that there were kind people in the world, who would help a stranger for charity, and nothing more.

I expected Gabriela to laugh at this, and offer some cynical argument. Instead she shrugged. 'Of course.'

Sam returned, still smiling. He was carrying a bag over his shoulder. He handed it to me. Clothes, a dagger, a full purse. All stolen.

I thanked Gabriela for the gift, trying not to think of their previous owner.

'Stay away from St Giles,' she said, before turning to her son. 'And you . . .'

But she had no orders for Sam, only wishes. She tangled her fingers in his hair, then let go.

The walk from St Giles took no more than ten minutes and yet – as is the way with London – we might as well have walked into another city. Soho had been sliding down the scale of respectability for years, but compared to the slums we had just left, it was the Palace of Versailles.

Sam's secret lair lay on the first floor of a narrow, crumbling house. How he had secured these rooms, and when, he wouldn't say. But there was no rent to pay, and no one to ask questions. The air smelt of mould, and fifteen-year-old boy.

There were two connecting rooms, one very small, the other much bigger, with a balcony overlooking the street. This larger room was an Aladdin's cave, heaped not with gold, perfumes and silks, but with Sam's macabre possessions. Sam was a collector. Bones, clocks, books and weapons. Poisons. The faces of friends and strangers, captured in charcoal. I had always wondered what had happened to all his missing treasures at the Pistol, and now the mystery was solved. They had gone forth to Soho, and multiplied.

Sam pulled back the curtains, spilling light on to this hidden world. 'Don't sit on the bed,' he said, without turning. I lifted back the sheet to discover a well-stocked arsenal of blades and pistols.

Gonzalo, curious, poked his nose towards a bayonet. Sam dragged him on to the balcony for safety.

I sank down into a low chair, hand resting on the top of my swordstick as I surveyed the room. My eyes caught upon a rat's skeleton. A detailed sketch of a man's sneer. A microscope. Sam was obsessed with the hidden workings of the world – what lay under the surface. If he could pull something apart, he could put it back together again.

He returned from the balcony and stood proudly in the centre of the room.

It is necessary, upon visiting a person's home, to say something pleasant. I cast about me. 'Well, you have made a very sensible use of the space.' I considered the row of skulls displayed in descending size along a high shelf. 'And so neatly ordered.'

Sam smiled shyly.

'Is there a bed one can sleep on without being stabbed?'

He led me to the connecting room where I lay down upon a mattress mercifully free of knives. I fell at once into a deep sleep, still wearing my cloak.

When I woke, I was alone and starving. I left Sam a brief note, and stumbled out into the darkening streets. I had lived in Soho before I met Kitty, and when I dipped my head in the tavern on the corner I was remembered and welcomed. I ordered a bowl of mutton and greens and a bottle of wine, though I was so weakened from my illness I could barely finish a glass of it.

I built a pipe, watching the room from my shadowed corner. I had played cards with people here, not so long ago, traded stories of court life and street scandals. The master tailor dining three tables from mine had been a great friend for a month or two. We had raised toasts, proclaiming our undying fraternity. Now I could scarce remember his name.

This had been my life, before I met Kitty. How false it had been, what a thin facade. The same men who had slapped my back and called me friend back then had jeered and shouted 'Villain! Murderer!' when the constables dragged me to the gallows. If I asked my dear companion the tailor of it now, no doubt he would protest. *By God, sir – I always knew you were innocent! All's well that ends well, as the saying is . . .*

I finished my supper and headed back on to the street, thinking of friendship, and debts owed.

It is quite possible to live in London and never once venture to Limehouse. Ask any coachman to take you there after dark and he will shake his head, as if denying its very existence. As for walking the Ratcliff Highway at night, I would not dare it even if I were dead and returned to haunt the living. The river is best for such journeys.

My boatman set me down at the Kidney Stairs. My back foot had not touched shore before he rowed off again, oars splashing the night-black water. I could hear him whistling to himself, in the way men do to cover their nerves.

The anchored ships out on the Thames were quiet, their crews on shore. I took a breath and smelt barrelled fish, wet timber, the faint salt tang of the sea – invoking old memories of my childhood on the Suffolk coast, walking along the sand with my mother. I felt an old ache in my chest, a longing for something lost years ago.

It started to rain.

Turning my back on the docks I headed into the dense web of alleyways behind them. There were plenty of people out upon the streets, and I was soon directed to Jeremiah's lodgings. He was not at home, and nor was Affie. I stood confounded, until I remembered Jeremiah's story of his friend Marcus, and their gatherings in a room above a tavern.

My enquiries led me nowhere, only round and round in circles in the drenching rain. I was afraid to stay out much longer in my weakened state – I was soaked from the top of my stolen hat to the bottom of my worn-out boots. And yet a familiar compulsion drove me forward.

At last, trudging down yet another dingy alleyway, I caught the sound of music under the pounding rain. Following the faint melody, I discovered an ancient tavern, the long room above it lit with lanterns, windows propped open despite the weather. The noise seeping out into the alley was unmistakably that of a country dance: music, singing and the constant thud of feet.

Shaking the rain from my hat and cloak, I ducked into the shelter of the tavern. The room was almost empty – who would sit drinking beneath a large group of dancers? The thumping along the floorboards was bad enough, but given the ruinous state of the building, the ceiling might well collapse one ill-fated evening – and what an ignominious way that would be to leave the earth. Death by gavotte.

I followed the noise up the steep staircase, leaning upon my swordstick. I had to pause and catch my breath on the landing – six weeks of fever and sickness had left their mark. When I was recovered, I pushed open the door to the private room and a great wave of sound crashed over me. A large company of men and women – all of them black – were engaged in dance and conversation. They were a mixture of ages, including children and elderly folk, but most were of about my age or a few years older. The dancers were midway through a longways set, adding flourishes I did not recognise.

Jeremiah was watching the dance from a far corner, and talking with a friend. He seemed at ease here, and happy. Well. *Good for him*.

As the dance came to an end I pushed my way into the crowded room. Two men standing close to the door barred my way, frowning in unison. 'Private meeting, sir,' one said over the loud chatter, while his friend placed a hand upon my chest, nudging me back. They would have closed the door on me, had Affie not seen me.

'Thomas!' she cried, weaving through a forest of legs to reach me. She was wearing a simple gown and a plain cap. The silver collar was gone, along with the bright silks. No longer a plaything, no longer a slave. Although, when I looked closer, I noticed a lighter band of skin around her throat, where the collar had been set for so many years.

I kneeled down so that she could hug me the better. She wrapped her arms about my neck, just as she had done the night I'd lifted her out of the oak chest. My injured arm ached at the memory.

'Where have you been? Have you found Kitty?' she asked eagerly. 'Is she here? Oh, how scratchy you are!' She giggled and rubbed my beard.

'I am so glad to find you well, Affie.'

'I am learning to read!' she said, rattling along in that excited way small children do. 'A, B, C . . .'

'Mr Hawkins.' Jeremiah stood over us, his face grave.

I rose and bowed lightly. Affie smiled hesitantly at her father. She could sense his tension but could not understand it.

Jeremiah leant down and kissed the top of her head. As he did so, he shot a glance to the man who had tried to push me from the room. Without a word being spoken, the man took Affie's hand.

'Come and dance, Affie,' he said.

'Yes!' She jumped upon the spot, excited. 'Come dance with us, Thomas! Marcus, shall we all dance together? Pa too!' She looked pleadingly at her father.

Marcus and Jeremiah exchanged looks.

'Another time, Affie,' I said, sparing them an awkward discussion. 'I am a little tired.'

'Oh,' she said, disappointed – but the dance had begun. She skipped off with Marcus and had soon forgotten me, too busy trying to remember the steps, and laughing when she made a mistake.

'How well she looks,' I said.

Jeremiah frowned and left the room, picking up a lantern on the way.

Hurt by this cool reception, I trailed after him to a room in the attic filled with bottles and barrels. The rain pattered hard against the sloping roof. It sounded like a thousand fingers drumming in irritation.

Jeremiah opened a window that looked out on to the street and sat upon the ledge. I could not understand why he sat there, soaking his back with the rain, but that was his choice. He folded his arms. 'You have been ill?'

'Aye, for several weeks. A putrid fever. I was close to death.'

I'd hoped for some sympathy, but he merely nodded, as if two plus two had made four, as usual. 'When did you return?'

'This morning. Jeremiah, please – I must speak with Affie about Kitty. She may remember something useful, some small detail—'

'No.' He spoke the word softly, but his expression was firm, and fixed.

I glared at him. 'We had a deal, sir. We swore an oath to help one another.'

'That is my debt, not my daughter's.'

I put a hand to my heart. 'And what of *my* child? I have lost six weeks, damn it.'

'Your fault, not mine, sir! I tried to warn you—'

'Yes, yes. You were right! Will that appease you? I have learnt my lesson.'

'You have learnt nothing!' Jeremiah snapped. 'You come to a strange neighbourhood at night, through the rain. When you are sick, and weak. Reckless man! You could not wait one day? You could not write, or send word?'

I covered my face, weary to the bone. 'Please. Save your lectures for another time. I am here now, let me speak to her. What harm would it do?'

'She knows nothing. Do you think I did not ask? Now go home. You look half dead.'

'Jeremiah—' I shuffled forward, leaning on my swordstick.

With a swift movement he drew back and stepped out of the window. There must be a small balcony below – I had not seen it in the dark. 'Go home, sir!' he said. 'Or I shall call for help.'

'Jeremiah,' I said, dismayed. 'Why will you not help me? I am no threat to you. Why do you treat me as if I am the enemy? *I am no wolf*, sir.'

'But you are, Mr Hawkins,' he replied, sadly, the rain drenching his clothes. 'The most dangerous kind. You are a wolf who thinks he is a man.'

He would not be persuaded. I left with nothing, a journey wasted, and waited a sorry hour for a waterman to take me back to the city.

It was only later, when I thought back upon the encounter, that I realised Jeremiah had not stammered once.

Chapter Nineteen

I woke the next morning feeling ill at ease and oddly ashamed of the night's misadventures. Jeremiah's words had mingled with my dreams, tormenting me. Was I a wolf, to be feared? Was I no longer myself? What had Lady Vanhook done to me? What had I done to myself?

I dragged myself from my bed, searching for any sign of a chill. What had I been thinking, walking through the drowning rain at night, when I was still not well? *Reckless man.* I stared at myself in the glass, inspecting my appearance with new eyes. A wild, desperate fellow stared back, with hollow cheeks and the black beard of a pirate. My God. It was a wonder Affie had not screamed when she saw me.

Sam and I ate breakfast together before he hurried off upon some mission of his own. I had asked how he had spent his time in my absence, but his answers were – as usual – evasive. We agreed to meet again later.

'*Shave,*' he said.

Another sign of my lamentable state – that *Sam* should scold me for *my* appearance. But he was quite right. I paid a visit to the barber's and then I walked to Westminster and presented myself at Sir John Gonson's house.

His man servant slammed the door in my face.

I retreated to the nearest coffeehouse and wrote a note, pipe clenched between my teeth. The trick was to strike him at his weakest point: his pride.

Sir John

By now you must suspect the truth: you have been tricked and used by a creature of infinite cunning and wickedness – and are now discarded. Will you hide behind your servants like a coward, and do nothing to repair the damage you have wrought? Shame on you, sir!

If you refuse to come to my aid, know that I shall make it my business to humiliate you. You were fooled by Lady Vanhook – the world will know of it. You wished to possess Kitty for yourself – the world will laugh at you for it. Pamphlets will be written, sir. Ballads will be sung. Your name will be mocked down through the ages – you may depend upon it. I shall make it my life's work.

The law is on your side, Sir John, but the town is on mine. The next time I knock upon your door, I will not be denied entrance.

T.H.

P.S. You should know, sir, that Kitty is with child. If nothing else will stir your conscience, think upon that.

I waited an hour, smoking and drinking coffee, then knocked upon his door again. This time the servant led me to the study, where Sir John was waiting for me at his writing bureau, my note folded in front of him. Almost two months had passed since we had last met in this room. He looked tired and irritable. No doubt I looked much worse.

He stared at me, making his own observations. 'You had better sit down,' he said, waving me to a padded leather stool by the fire. I think this was the first piece of kindness he had ever shown me. I lowered myself down slowly, clutching my swordstick for support.

He lifted my letter between finger and thumb. 'I could have you thrown in gaol for this.' He dropped it back upon his desk. 'I did not know she was with child.'

You do not know her at all, I thought, but held my tongue.

'I should not have placed my trust in Lady Vanhook,' he said, as if this were some great concession. 'Villainess! She emptied half the shops of London in my name. Clothing, furniture. Jewellery! I have spent a small fortune appeasing her creditors.'

I tried very hard not to laugh, and failed.

'Yes, yes,' Gonson said, as my laughter turned into a coughing fit. 'I can see how that would amuse you. You think me a zealot, deserving punishment.'

Two months ago I would have corrected him. Yes, he was a zealot, but what I hated most about Gonson was his damnable hypocrisy. He had the same appetites as any man, and yet he acted as though he were some crusading saint, soaring a thousand feet above us all. He had wanted Kitty, and he had wanted her fortune. But instead of admitting that base truth, he must pretend he was *protecting* her. *Saving* her. And what a fine job he had made of that.

'Will you help me find her?'

Gonson puffed out his cheeks, frustrated. 'Really, Mr Hawkins. Do you think I have stood idle? Lady Vanhook has committed a great fraud upon the *state*.' He patted his chest, venerating himself. 'I have spent a *considerable* sum conducting my own search. When she is found – *and she will be found* – I shall ensure that she is punished as the law demands.'

'Then we must work together.'

'For heaven's sake, man – you can barely stand! Go home and rest. I will send word when I have it.'

'That is not ... I cannot wait. I cannot ...' Oh Lord, I must not break down, not in front of Sir John Pisspot Gonson of all people. I looked away, pressing the gold fox head into my palm to distract myself from a deeper pain.

I heard the chink of a bottle, the glug of liquor. A moment later Gonson pushed a glass into my hand. I took a sip and then another. Brandy. It was rather fine. So he did indulge in the occasional pleasure.

Gonson watched me drink. 'I was wrong about you, Hawkins. I thought you were a cynical man. A shallow, empty-hearted libertine.'

I raised my glass to that, grimly.

'But you suffer from the opposite affliction. You are too passionate, too swayed by feeling. You are not in command of yourself. It is ... unmanly.'

I gritted my teeth.

'Your mother was Scots, I believe.' He nodded to himself, as if this explained everything. 'A rebellious breed.'

Only Gonson could aim for conciliation, and become more insufferable in the process. I knocked back the last of the brandy and rose to my feet. 'Give me your word. If you find her, let me come with you.'

'You have no right to demand—'

'For the sake of my child. Please, Sir John.'

He let me dangle for a moment, no doubt enjoying his power over me. I didn't care. 'Very well,' he said, at last. 'If you can learn to control your impulses.'

'Thank you,' I said, controlling the impulse to punch him in the nose.

He clapped his hand upon my shoulder (*ugh!*) as if all were well between us, as if his own failings had not brought us to this sorry pass. This is the way men such as Gonson forgive themselves. They simply ignore their many outrages and press on, unburdened and unchanged.

'Upon another matter,' he said, surprising me. Kitty was missing – what other matter was there? 'There is to be an enquiry into our prisons, did you hear? Sir James Oglethorpe will lead the committee. He wishes to speak to you of your time in the Marshalsea. What is the name of the keeper there ...'

'Acton. William Acton.' A thousand horrors spilled into my mind. Corpses piled up and rotting. A boy flogged to death, and nothing to be done. Blood sprayed on the walls and ceiling of my cell ...

'That was it. Brutish fellow, by the sound of it. But this is what happens when butchers and stock dealers rise above their station.'

'Indeed. A gentleman would never use his power in such an infamous fashion,' I said drily.

'Well, quite.'

In other circumstances I would have visited Oglethorpe that same morning to offer my testimony. Too many souls had suffered and perished under William Acton's hellish regime. The sooner he was brought to justice the better. But I was too preoccupied with Kitty's disappearance to give it much thought that day. In truth, by the time I had left Gonson's house and walked back to Sam's lodgings in Soho, I had forgotten all about it. You may forget it too, if you wish. It is a story for another time.

If this were a tale of adventure, or an Italian opera, there would now follow a divine intervention, or at least some clever coincidence, perhaps involving twins. It would transpire that Martha, who had nursed me back to health, was in fact Lady Vanhook's long-forgotten cousin. Or Mrs Jenkins, staying with her sister in Staffordshire, would stumble upon a remote and mysterious house and see Kitty staring out from a barred window.

And even in real life, are we not – upon occasion – confronted with such miracles? Some extraordinary gift of fate presents itself, with such perfect timing that it stretches credulity. We exclaim: why, who would believe this, if it were written for the theatre, or in a novel? *Surely this is God's work.*

This is what happened in truth: nothing. *Nothing.*

Oh, I searched. I knocked on doors. I placed advertisements in the papers. I paid ballad singers to hand out broadsheets across the city, with portraits of Kitty and her mother. I waited each day for the coaches to arrive from out of town and begged the passengers for news. I visited Gonson every week and submitted myself to his pompous sermonising so that he would never forget his promise to me.

The days passed. January turned to February.

Nothing good ever happens in February.

Each day, I fought a rising fear that I would never see Kitty again. Each night, I stared at Sam's portrait of her, afraid that I would forget her face. I thought of her scent, the feel of her skin against mine, her terrible singing, her laugh, her temper. The way her nails scraped against my back. The taste of her.

I missed her terribly, and my loss felt like grief.

Was she dead? If so, how would I bear it? First my mother, now Kitty . . . Was I doomed to lose everyone I loved?

What if I never learnt the truth? How would I bear *that*? The agony of not knowing?

What if this were my penance for Twig's death?

Ahh, there it was: that vicious, predatory thought, returned again to devour me.

A boy was dead, and I was to blame.

I had been too ashamed to visit Felblade at first, and when I did he did not spare me. 'He was a *boy*, damn it, under your care. You might as well have shot him yourself. I shall never forgive you for it.' His words cut me like a blade, and I relished them. Something terrible *had* happened. It *was* my fault – thank God someone recognised it. I deserved to be punished. And so I went back, more than once.

Felblade, shrewd creature, soon realised what I was about. 'If you wish to be flogged, visit the brothel,' he snapped, and slammed the door in my face. The next time I tried to see him, his new servant (oh, God, a new servant to replace the old), said I was no longer welcome.

I had not realised Felblade was a friend, until I lost him.

And still, there was no news.

*　　*　　*

By late February the last of my savings were gone, along with the stolen purse Gabriela had given me. Worse still – beyond my daily trips to the coaches, and visits to Moll's to collect fresh news and correspondence, there was nothing for me to do but wait alone in Sam's macabre lodgings, with no one but the dog for company. I drank too much wine, smoked too much tobacco, and thought too often of that dreadful night on the frozen river.

One morning I woke on the floor by the bed, surrounded by bottles and cradling a skull. I must have taken it from the shelf – in fact I had a dim recollection of talking to it the night before, as if I were Hamlet. *Alas, poor me.* I sat up, shielding my eyes from the light, and caught a strong whiff of vomit. To my utter shame, I found that I had thrown up on the bed. That must be why I had slept – well, passed out – on the floor. Even worse, I knew that Sam had found me like this in the night, because I was wrapped in a blanket from the other room.

Feeling sordid and humiliated, I cleaned up my mess.

Sam arrived home an hour or two later, through the window.

'I'm sorry,' I said.

He nodded.

'Any news from Moll's?'

He shook his head.

'Letters?'

As Sam's lodgings were a secret, I conducted my correspondence through the coffeehouse. Sam fanned out a collection of letters, including one from my sister Jane. 'Dear brother,' it began. 'It has been too long since we have had news from you. Are you well?'

Oh, I am very well, sister. I have lost my beloved Kitty, my home, my belongings and, just this morning, the last shreds of my dignity.

I had not told Jane or my father of Kitty's abduction. I had scarcely told them of Kitty at all. They understood so little of my life in London, and approved of still less. In my darker moments I imagined confessing what had happened to Patchett, and Twig, and watching them recoil in horror. *My son is innocent*. No longer, father. No longer.

The rest of the letters were from prospective clients. I had not advertised my services in the *Journal* since Kitty was abducted, but that had not dissuaded people. Like it or not, I had earnt a reputation as a man who solved mysteries. With Kitty still missing, that struck me as ironical, to say the least.

Over the past few weeks Sam had taken up one or two enquiries himself. He had a natural affinity for the work. I had convinced myself that I must spend every waking hour searching for Kitty, but the truth was that simply wasn't practical. There were great swathes of time when I could do nothing but wait – and drink. I would be better served trying to earn a living, and keeping my wits fresh.

I picked up a letter at random, from a Mrs Pamela Lightborn of Brook Street. She was convinced that her maid servant was stealing from her, but wished to be certain before making an accusation. *Most* considerate of her, given that the girl could hang for such a crime. There followed many flattering phrases about my talent and reputation, and a request for discretion.

Kitty had been a servant, when I first met her. Perhaps I could help this poor woman from the gallows. Assuming, of course, that she was innocent. Something about Mrs Lightborn's eagerness to accuse her made me suspect that she was. We would see.

At the very least it would be a distraction from my own troubles – and my screeching banshee of a headache.

Mrs Pamela Lightborn lived at the fashionable end of Brook Street, in a brand-new house in the brand-new style. Her rose gown fanned out in artful pleats and made the wonderful rasping sound of vastly expensive silk. Whether she was pretty or not was quite beyond the point – she was immaculate, groomed and sleek and glowing with wealth.

Despite my swift scrub at the *bagnio* I felt like a grubby wretch by comparison – but Mrs Lightborn was *thrilled* by my visit, *honoured* and *thrilled*. What *tragedies* had befallen me, and how *nobly* I had endured them! Such an admirable quality in a man, endurance. And who was this young gentleman with me, an apprentice? What a solemn boy, but then this was a serious business, no doubt, no doubt. Well, we must have tea, and cake, and Mr Hawkins you must meet the twins, they were sleeping bless their angelic hearts, but they would be roused at once.

She picked up a fine crystal bell and rang it briskly. This would summon Sophia – the servant in question. 'I have not told her of my suspicions,' Mrs Lightborn said, and tapped her delicately powdered nose.

'What is her position within the household?' I asked.

'*Well.*' Mrs Lightborn sagged her shoulders, as if wars had been fought upon the matter. 'I say she is a maid. Mr Lightborn insists on paying her the wages of a housekeeper. My husband,' she added, in a grim tone, 'is a very generous man.'

Sophia was a good fifteen years older than her mistress, with pale blonde hair and a blotched complexion. She looked anxious, and kept her eyes fixed upon the floor. Mrs Lightborn had perhaps not been as discreet as she'd thought.

'Sophia, this is Mr Thomas Hawkins.'

Sophia curtsied. 'An honour to meet you, sir.'

'You are German?' I asked, catching her accent.

'Yes, sir, from Bavaria—'

'Mr Hawkins has no interest in such petty details,' Mrs Lightborn decided for me. 'He is a man of great discernment and wisdom . . .'

Sam, who had found the cake, shoved a slice in his mouth.

'. . . with a keen eye for deception,' Mrs Lightborn finished. 'He can sniff out a villain like *that*.' She clicked her fingers.

Sophia flinched. 'I shall wake the children,' she said.

While we waited, Mrs Lightborn told a well-rehearsed anecdote about the Earl of Coventry, in which she was able to mention that he was a close neighbour. 'And of course Mr Handel lives just down the road. The composer,' she added, in case I had been thinking of Mr Handel the street sweeper.

She picked up a slim red book with gold lettering. 'This,' she said, presenting it to me with a little shiver of excitement, 'was a gift from the Viscount Mountjoy.' (Another neighbour – goodness, she could rattle them off.) I turned to the title page, and stifled a groan. It was an account of my trial and hanging, illustrated with sketches of me locked in a prison cell in Newgate, hanging on the gallows and – this I had not seen before – leaping from my coffin, the skeleton figure of Death pointing at me as if I were a naughty child. 'You must write a dedication,' Mrs Lightborn insisted. 'I attended the hanging with my dear husband and sister. One cannot *bear* hanging days, but one must go, it is a moral duty, and Mr Lightborn was so kind to purchase tickets for the gallery, with the very finest views. Oh, Mr Hawkins, when the cart pulled away and left you kicking the air – I thought I would *die*.'

Mercifully, I was saved from any more of this torture by the arrival of the Lightborn twins, Emily and George, tear stained and fretful from being woken from their afternoon nap. Emily clung hard to Sophia until she spied Sam, at which she tottered over at once, clambering on to his lap and chattering away gleefully in some three-year-old approximation of conversation. Sam – to my constant surprise – was a powerful magnet to small children, though I'm sure the spread of cakes and buttered rolls were an added inducement. As Emily seized a sugared bun in her grubby fist, Sam told her in vivid detail how I had been accused of murder and hanged, then brought back to life. This was certainly one reason why children adored Sam. He told them all the things that adults kept hidden from them.

Emily's twin brother, meanwhile, skewered me with the haughty stare of a jaded courtier, and found me lacking. Quite apart from the ravages of my lonely debauch the night before, my long illness and slow recovery had marked me. I looked older, and tired, and my borrowed clothes did not fit me as well as they should. But still, what a condescending glare!

Once George had wilted me with his disdain, he crawled on to the sofa to sit next to his flawless mother. The sofa – upholstered in green-and-gold cut velvet – received his approval where I had failed. He traced his fingers back and forth, relishing the change from rough to smooth, the intricate flower pattern.

Sophia, unsure if she were now dismissed, stood awkwardly at the door, hand curled around the handle. She did have a furtive look to her, I had to admit.

'Mr Hawkins has come to solve a *mystery*,' Mrs Lightborn said, arching her brow as if to say there was no mystery here. 'We have a thief in the house.'

Sophia gave a start, and placed a hand upon her stomach.

I asked Mrs Lightborn what had been taken. 'Oh . . . small things. I did not notice at first. They are so easy to misplace in such a large house. We have eight bedrooms, you understand.'

'Could you list the items, madam?' I asked again.

'Trifles, trifles . . .' she murmured. 'My favourite yellow handker-chief with pink roses. A white kid glove I wear for riding. A diamond earring.' She pulled her son closer and kissed his head. He had stopped stroking the sofa and was regarding me with a sullen air.

'No money?'

'I don't *believe* so . . .' she said, vaguely. Too wealthy and careless to notice one way or another. But judging by the nature of the other stolen pieces, I thought it unlikely.

Sophia was clutching the door knob so hard that her knuckles had turned white. 'Mrs Lightborn,' she said, in a faltering voice. 'I have served your husband's family for eighteen years. I would never steal from him, or from you.'

Ah, now that was interesting. Sophia had been part of the house-hold far longer than her young mistress. That might cause resent-ments and rivalries, if Sophia had Mr Lightborn's confidence. Mrs Lightborn might not accuse her servant out of open spite, but there could be subtler prejudices at work. 'Is your husband away at present, madam?'

Of course he was; she would wait until Sophia was alone and vulnerable. Mrs Lightborn's eyes narrowed. 'How sharp you are,' she pouted, not liking me as much as before. She had hired me to remove a stone from her shoe, not to unpick the shoe itself. 'How shall we proceed, Mr Hawkins?'

'The swiftest way to resolve the matter is to search her room,' I said.

'I have already looked,' Mrs Lightborn replied. 'I found nothing.'

'Because I'm innocent!' Sophia cried. 'I swear it – upon my life!'

'She has sold them, I suppose,' Mrs Lightborn said. 'Devious creature.'

Sophia muttered something under her breath in German. *Verdammt*, I think.

'One must never underestimate a cunning thief,' I said, smoothly. 'My apprentice has a talent for discovering the most unexpected hiding places – if you would permit . . .'

'Of course!' Mrs Lightborn said, liking me again. 'How kind of you to be so thorough.'

With a look, I signalled to Sam what was needed. He lifted Emily from his lap and left, chewing his lip to cover a smile.

Five minutes passed. More talk of grand neighbours and court gossip from Mrs Lightborn. Was it true I had met Her Majesty the Queen? Pray, how did I find her? In her private rooms, eating bon bons, I told her. Mrs Lightborn gave a fluttering fake laugh. 'No, but in earnest sir . . .' George, growing restless, pulled a ribbon loose on his mother's gown. Mrs Lightborn was delighted by this act of sabotage. George was a prodigy, so *clever* of him to untie a bow, do you see that Emily? You could not attempt such a feat, could you my darling? Emily, who was eating a second bun with intense concentration, did not answer. Sophia stood mute, her eyes darting about the room in panic. She really must practise her expressions in the mirror – the poor woman looked positively shifty.

Sam returned with the missing yellow handkerchief, its corners tied together in a knot. He shook it, and it rattled. There was more contraband inside.

'Oh, *Gott*!' Sophia cried. 'I did not take these things, I swear!'

Sam handed the handkerchief to Mrs Lightborn, who opened it out. There was the kid glove, the diamond earring, and other items – a pearl button, a red silk ribbon, a silver trinket box inlaid with tortoiseshell. 'Good heavens,' Mrs Lightborn exclaimed, lifting the box up to the light. 'I had no idea this was missing. What else have you stolen from this family, you ungrateful jade?' she demanded of Sophia, who looked as though she might collapse in terror. 'Poor Mr Lightborn. This will break his heart. To be deceived in such a cruel fashion. And he holds such strong views on thieving. He will be forced to take this to the magistrate and demand the most severe of sentences . . .'

Sophia dropped to her knees, hands clasped. 'Mercy!' she sobbed. 'I am a good, honest servant, I swear—'

I had witnessed enough. 'Peace, Sophia – I know you are innocent,' I assured her, helping her to her feet. 'There is no question of it.'

Mrs Lightborn sat rigid on the sofa, glaring at me. George buried his face in her gown. 'I don't like him, Mama,' he whined.

His mother was inclined to agree with him. 'Explain yourself, sir.'

'Why would Sophia steal one glove? One earring?'

Mrs Lightborn pursed her lips. 'I don't—'

'And if she would steal a silver trinket box, why not coins as well?'

'But you found them in her room!'

'No, madam,' I said, more gently than she deserved. 'Sam? Where did you find them?'

He smiled his wolf's smile. 'Nursery.'

It was diverting to watch the parade of emotions that passed across Mrs Lightborn's face. Confusion, indignation, denial. Embarrassment. No shame, though, for accusing an honest woman. 'Well,' she said, uncertainly. 'She might have hidden them there . . .'

'Consider the items that were stolen,' I said. 'Such small, pretty things. Something a child might covet.'

Mrs Lightborn absorbed this news, blinking hard. '*Emily!*' she said, at last. 'How could you! See the trouble you have caused! You shall be punished for this, young lady, most severely.'

Emily looked up from her bun in bewilderment, while her brother bit his nail, his guilt obvious to everyone but his adoring mother.

'George Lightborn,' I said, sternly. 'Will you let your sister take the blame for this?'

George, to his credit, burst into tears. Dear Lord the noise a three-year-old can make. They must have heard him in Kensington Palace. 'I didn't . . .' he sobbed, lying as little children do, because they are scared and ashamed.

Sam, standing behind the sofa, reached down and poked a finger in George's pocket, pulling out a silver hair pin.

Mrs Lightborn stared at it. 'But . . . how did you know?'

Because your son adores you. Because he loves bright ribbons and the feel of cut velvet, and the smell of your perfume. Some of us find comfort in pretty things. I did not say this to Mrs Lightborn. I wasn't sure she would understand. In any case, I would rather take the opportunity to help Sophia.

'I shall tell you, Mrs Lightborn. But first you must promise not to tell a soul, not even your husband.'

Irresistible! 'I shall not breathe a word,' she said.

She was lying, but it did not matter. I put a hand to my breast, and called upon my father's best sermonising tone. 'As you know, madam, I was hanged for a crime I did not commit. For a few brief moments, my spirit flew free from its mortal cage and reached the celestial gates.'

I feared I might have gone too far, but Mrs Lightborn was enraptured. She was, after all, a crashing snob. A visit to paradise was – beyond question – even better than an audience with the Queen. 'God be praised,' she murmured.

'Now that I am restored to life, I can sense the innocence and guilt of others, as if the Lord Himself were shining a light upon their soul.' I raised my eyes towards heaven. 'This is the great gift bestowed upon me, that I brought back from my brief encounter with the Divine.'

Mrs Lightborn clasped her hands in rapture. 'God be praised,' she said, again.

'You may trust your servant implicitly, Mrs Lightborn. Treat her with kindness and grace.' I lowered my voice. 'For imagine, madam, if she had been arrested for this crime. She might have been hanged on your word. Sophia would ascend to heaven of course, but you madam, with her death upon your conscience . . . Who can say?'

Mrs Lightborn shuddered, probably at the thought of a servant rising above her. 'Mr Hawkins. How can I ever repay you?'

'Two guineas,' Sam said, 'will cover it.'

Sophia guided us to the front door. 'Thank you, sir,' she said, wiping away her tears. 'I have been so afraid . . .'

I touched her arm. 'You had best leave this household before they learn your secret,' I said, quietly. 'You are with child, are you not?'

She stiffened in shock, then drew an arm across her stomach. 'How . . .'

I had spent many hours thinking about the signs I had missed with Kitty: the way she carried herself, the way her hand drifted to her belly when she grew anxious, the subtle change in her complexion. I had failed to notice these things, and the consequences had been catastrophic – so it was near impossible for me to miss them in Sophia. I had even spied the way the pleats of her skirts did not fall evenly, suggesting that she had let out her gown at the waist.

'It won't be long before Mrs Lightborn realises the truth. Take advantage of her remorse. Ask for a reference, and any wages she owes you – and leave.' With a good reference and such long, loyal service to the Lightborns, she would soon find a position in another home. Assuming she could bear to give up her child. Well – I could not solve all her problems. 'Do you have friends? A place you may go until . . .'

She nodded. 'Sir. Is it true you reached the gates of heaven?' She stared up at me, her eyes wide and earnest.

It was not true, of course it wasn't. My death upon the scaffold had been a counterfeit. But there was such longing in her voice, it would have been cruel to disappoint her. So I simply smiled enigmatically, and wished her well.

Sam contained himself until we had turned the corner. Then he sat on a wall and laughed so hard he had to clutch his sides. I had just provided him with a peerless hour: human folly, free cake and the chance to sneak about a grand house.

And I had rediscovered my vocation.

'My day began badly,' I told Jeremiah.

It was later that evening, in Limehouse. After some persuasion, Jeremiah had agreed to join me for a drink at the Bunch of Grapes. The tavern leant out over the water, and some brave souls were standing on the river steps, preferring the stink of the Thames to the stink of their fellow revellers. We had found a table under the staircase, where we would not be disturbed. A cheap tallow candle flickered between us, greasing the air.

Jeremiah looked remarkably well. He had secured a clerk's position at the docks that paid twice as well as labouring, and offered better hours. Finding Affie had not only brought him joy, it had restored some lost confidence and pride – he sat straighter in his chair and he stammered less frequently too. I was pleased to see that he had spent some of his earnings on a thick cloak – heaven knows how he had survived the previous winter in that thin coat of his. It may have been my imagination, but I felt he was closer to the Jeremiah I had met in his account. On our walk to the tavern, he had told me how he would make up stories for Affie at night, imaginary tales full of wise spirits and talking animals. They helped soothe her to sleep. She suffered from night terrors, sometimes, he'd said, before adding firmly, 'They will pass.'

I told him how I had woken that morning upon the floor, cradling a skull. The stink of vomit. I explained how this had been the culmination of weeks of misery and frustration. Then I told him of my visit to Mrs Lightborn on Brook Street. I talked for perhaps a quarter-hour. Jeremiah listened without interruption, sipping his punch. When I was done, he leant back.

'You saved a woman's life today.'

'Yes.'

'That is what you wished to tell me.'

'No. Not really.' I drew my punch towards me, then pushed it away again. I had not yet recovered from my lonely debauch the night before. 'I wished to say . . . I am sorry, Jeremiah. For my poor conduct, my recklessness. My arrogance. For what happened at the river.' I paused, as the memories rose again to assault me. 'I have no excuse for it. You tried your best to warn me.'

Jeremiah shrugged. 'A man can only listen when he's ready.'

I wondered if that were another of Michael's sayings. It sounded like the sort of thing he might have said to the young, dreaming Jeremiah. 'I saved a woman and her child today. And I was jubilant – for an hour. I had found my path. My vocation.'

Jeremiah waited.

'But that is not the hard part, is it – finding a path? It is staying upon it – day after day, night after night, with no promise of reward, or even resolution. What if I never find her, Jeremiah? How will I bear it?' I broke down.

Jeremiah leant forward and squeezed my arm. And that was how our friendship began.

I learnt a great deal in the cold, empty days that followed – lessons of resilience and humility. Most of all I learnt patience. It did not come easily – why would it? True patience requires more effort and more courage than a thousand bloody battles.

But it can be learnt. It must be learnt. Without it, we are mere creatures of impulse. Little boys who steal glittering trinkets, and do not consider the consequences.

So I continued my search, with no promise of success. In the long spare hours left over, I distracted myself with work. I walked through the city with Gonzalo and helped Affie with her reading. I taught Sam how to win at cards without cheating. I wrote cheerful lies to my father and sister, and made peace with Felblade. I visited Twig's grave, and prayed for him.

'If only Kitty were here,' I found myself thinking, a thousand times a day. Every time, a knife in the heart. Then the moment would pass, and life continued.

And still winter held us in its grip, long after it should have released us. It had been, they said, one of the worst on record. All I can remember of that time is ice and snow, and thick, freezing fog. Poor Affie, used to the mild winters on Antigua, could hardly bear it. 'When will spring come Thomas?' she would demand, in an accusing way, as if I were somehow responsible for the weather. 'Very soon,' I replied, but spring was exceptionally late that year, and March was only a fraction warmer than February. Affie wrapped herself in blankets and sulked by the fire, and I learnt a valuable lesson – do not promise gifts to small children unless you can deliver them. They will judge you harshly.

On a damp, freezing afternoon in late March, I returned to Twig's grave with fresh flowers. Alone in the churchyard, I prayed for his soul, and mine. For once, Gonzalo did not try to eat the flowers. As I walked back to Soho, I felt something lift within me. I was not the man I was before the night on the river: I never would be. My actions and their consequences would stay with me for the rest of my life, faithful as the hound trotting at my heels. Well: so be it. I would bear their company, and accept the man I had become.

I told Gonzalo this, because the man I had become liked to walk the darkening streets of the city, talking to his dog. 'Not in a brooding way,' I said. 'I am not a brooding, melancholy fellow, you know that. But there are things I cannot say to anyone, that I may say to you. I can say them every day and you will not grow tired of hearing them, or worry about me, or suggest I take up a new pursuit to pass the time.' (Felblade had suggested alchemy, Sam boxing. Jeremiah thought I should join a choir.) 'I miss my friend, Gonzalo. With all my heart. I'm afraid I have lost her for ever.'

Gonzalo nuzzled his foolish, misshapen head against my hand, and licked my fingers. We walked on.

Seventy miles away, on that same spring evening, Kitty sat down to supper with her mother.

Chapter Twenty

How many days have passed since you last saw your mother? Or is it weeks now? The memory is as distorted as a dream.

You know you have been trapped in this attic room for months – ever since that terrible journey through the snow, when you thought you would die. Is it still winter? The weather has not changed, each day drags by like a year, but the swell of your stomach reveals the inevitable passing of time. Surely you cannot grow much bigger. The baby will come any day now. The thought is both thrilling and terrifying.

A guard visits each morning to unlock the shutter in the eaves. You are expected to be grateful and say thank you for this gift of daylight. If you stand on the bed you can look out of the window. You can see a river like a silver ribbon and water meadows, and pasture in the distance, dotted with sheep. No houses. For as long as you have the strength to stand, you watch the birds skimming from tree to hedgerow. Their singing wakes you in the morning and soothes you as the light fades to evening.

On good days you are given a book to read. On the best days a guard will lead you down the stairs so you can walk along the corridor, back and forth, the floorboards creaking under your toes. This is for the baby's sake, not yours. Your mother insists you must exercise, so that you are strong enough, when the time comes.

On bad days the shutters remain closed and you are left in darkness.

There is no reason for the good days and the bad days, you cannot predict them. Your life is dictated by your mother's moods. That has *always been the way, save for the six blissful years you were free of her.*

This morning, when the guard comes, something is different. He has brought a woman with him, an old drunk with little sense in her. Your mother has paid her to wash you, to tend to the sores on your skin and the tiny pests crawling through your hair. She doesn't trust you to bathe yourself – perhaps she fears you will drown yourself and the baby, just to escape her.

The woman combs your hair as you sit in the tub, killing lice with her fingernails. She gives up in the end – there are too many. She pulls your hair into a long plait, takes out a pair of scissors and cuts it off. This is done in a flash, without warning – too late to stop her. In truth it is a relief when she shears the rest of your hair almost to the scalp. The lice have sent you half mad with itching.

She helps you out of the tub, the water cloudy with dirt. The smock you have been wearing for weeks lies at your feet, streaked and stinking of old sweat. Now that your belly has grown so big, you cannot pick anything up from the floor without squatting, or kneeling. Stifling a groan, you start your long, weary process to the ground.

The woman stops you. She pulls out your old wrapping gown, shaking it to remove the worst of the creases. You stare at it in wonder and start to cry. You are so happy to see it again – that horrid yellow dress you hate. Someone has sewn an extra panel into the gown so that it will fit around your stomach – a wide hessian strip that doesn't match the rest of the material. You don't care – it reminds you of home. It reminds you that you are Kitty, not Catherine.

The old woman helps you with your stockings and a new pair of slippers. Then she leaves, without another word, taking the long red plait with her. You guess that she will sell it – for gin, judging from her breath.

The guard returns, dagger drawn as usual. It is the younger one today. You thought he was kind when you first arrived here, but then he put his hand up your skirt, pressed you down on to the bed. You spat in his face and screamed and fought until the older one came and dragged him away. He has never touched you since but he terrifies you every time he enters the room with his blade.

He leads you down through the large, gloomy farmhouse with its dank stone walls and air of long neglect. Suddenly, on the ground floor, everything changes. The floors and walls are scrubbed clean, the rooms are crowded with furniture and there are candles everywhere, dazzling your eyes. After months locked away in an empty attic room, the opulence is disorientating, almost sickening. You catch yourself in a gilded mirror and your reflection is so changed you flinch and look away.

The guard opens a final door to the dining room, prods you in with the flat of his blade.

And here is your mother – revealed in all her glory. She is seated at the dining table, magnificent in a blue satin gown, candles positioned artfully to show her in the best light. A diamond brooch glints on her lace cap, a sapphire pendant adorns her throat.

You take a breath, knowing of the battle that lies ahead. She will have spent days preparing for it. You can see the fever in her eyes, the excitement, something close to arousal. A familiar dread creeps through you as you sit down opposite her. Somehow you will say the wrong lines. She will be disappointed. She won't beat you, for fear of harming the baby. But she has other, subtler punishments in her weapon chest. Cruel barbs, that stay lodged in your heart like fish hooks.

She has prepared a feast for the occasion. You can't be trusted with a knife or a fork, so you must eat with a wooden spoon, the roasted meat and fish already cut for you. You eat it all, no shame in that, you are starving and there is a simple relief in sitting at a table, with candlelight and good plates. You wonder if you could kill her with a wooden spoon.

Yes – in spite of everything – you are still gloriously, valiantly you.

She watches as you cram the food into your mouth, your hair shorn, your dress shabby. Your skin smells stale despite your bath. Your mother, in contrast, is immaculate, auburn hair dusted with lavender powder, skin soft and smooth. She is enjoying the disparity, you can tell – the sharper the better. Anything to burnish her own beauty. You know her secrets of old – the pots of cream and paste on her dressing table, the lip-salves and perfumes, the linen cloth coated with cream and stuck upon her face at night. There is no end to the care she will bestow upon herself.

'Darling.' She is drinking wine, rather a lot of it, and keeps the glass in her hand like a prop. 'Darling,' she says again, in a needling voice. 'Why do you hate me?'

You can't think how to reply. There are so many reasons, you would need to write a book – several volumes in fact, and even then you are not sure you could capture the depth and intricacy of your loathing.

'It is that vile toad's fault. He filled you with poison.'

She means Samuel Fleet. Your second father. You killed the man who murdered him. Your mother doesn't know that. She doesn't realise that she is dining with a murderess.

'That is the way with inverts.' She gives a false shudder. 'Vile creatures. They corrupt everything they touch.'

Does she even believe this? It doesn't matter. She wants to provoke you, so you ignore her, and help yourself to a lemon syllabub, scooping the cream with your finger. Such small victories sustained you when you were a little girl. They are petty, manipulative and necessary.

Your mother pouts, annoyed – but she wants something from you. 'You look exhausted, darling. Here.' She pours a glass of wine and slides it across the table with a wink, as if the two of you are grand conspirators. Someone else is holding you prisoner, leaving you for days without light, punishing you for no reason until you fear you really have turned mad.

She cups her chin in her hand, and smiles at you. 'Tell me about your bookshop.'

You sip the wine to hide your confusion. Your mother has no interest in your life, she finds other people's passions boring. She is interested in you solely because you come from her flesh. When she stares at you, she *is looking only for traces of herself – the shared contours and self-beloved features.*

You must answer, or she will punish you. So you tell her about the Pistol. You describe the books you sold there, and how you brought in more trade by selling condoms and dildos, and the mercury cure.

Your mother nods her approval. 'Sex is a man's greatest weakness. How clever of you, Catherine, to trade in it.'

She never flatters you without wanting something, but you don't care. Talking of the Pistol – even to her – restores some part of you that had disappeared. The clever, capable you, full of ambition. Alive. Your mother listens attentively, and for a moment you could almost believe that she does care, and is interested in your achievements.

The baby gives a sharp kick, as if reminding you not to be so fucking stupid. You place a hand upon your belly and shift – then wince as your back twinges.

'Not long now,' your mother murmurs. There is a hungry look in her eyes. It sends prickles of alarm down your spine.

For weeks you have dreamt of being released from your room but now you want nothing more than to return to it, to shield yourself and your baby from that devouring gaze. The thought of spending the night in your mother's company is unbearable. She will have composed this evening like an opera. Arias will be sung about the people who betrayed her: family, friends, everyone. And you, most of all you – the ungrateful daughter who abandoned her.

If you tell her you are tired, she won't care. You will be forced to sit and listen to her self-pitying lament until dawn. You must try a different tack. You must make her believe that she is banishing you against your wishes. That she is – always – in command.

'Samuel didn't poison me against you, Mother. You did.' The candles flicker on the table between you. You hear laughter from another room – the guards are drinking together. 'I watched you for years. I sat at your feet, just like Nella.'

She clenches her jaw. She doesn't know of your part in Nella's escape, but she suspects it.

You smile at her. 'Let me see, what comes next? Your mean, treacherous friends? They didn't betray you. You betrayed them. Cheated and stole from them. Fucked their husbands.'

'How dare you—'

'And as for poor Father . . . You tested and tormented him until he couldn't bear to be in your company. And because you kept me so close, I lost him too – long before he died.'

Your mother does not like this. She is the injured party, not you. How dare you steal that precious role from her? She must wrest the story back for herself. 'Your father,' *she drawls,* 'was a sodomite.'

'I know. He was in love with Samuel.'

She laughs. 'In love. Silly girl.' *She pours herself another glass of wine.*

'When Father died, you threw a party, do you remember? It lasted three days. You made me sit at your feet, while you told lies about how cruel he had been to you. You said you were glad he was dead.'

'Nonsense.' *Your mother toys with her earring. She is bored.*

'Every night strangers came to the house to play cards and drink and worship you. Queen Emma. When you came out of mourning, you bought five new gowns to celebrate, and jewels to match. You burnt through our fortune in less than a year. You sold Father's books, his clothes, all the gifts he gave me. Then the furniture. Then the house.'

'I was cheated,' *your mother says.* 'Cheated and robbed—'

'When we moved to the Strand, you sent me out to work and I was glad of it. I was happy to escape from you, and your gentlemen friends.'

Your mother's pale blue eyes glitter, her face twisted with suppressed rage. Here is the tawdry truth, not the gilded fiction. She will not be reminded of it. She lowers her glass. 'You are deluded.'

'There's no shame in being a whore, Mother. I don't judge you for that.'

She throws back her head and laughs. Her tongue is stained black from the wine. 'You do not judge me. How marvellous! Sitting there with your fat belly. You opened your legs to the first man who pretended to love you. And where is he now, your brave hero? Did he come to your rescue? Of course he didn't. He gave up the search months ago. In fact, I hear he is set to marry some rich merchant's daughter. No doubt he is pleased to be rid of you, and his bastard child.'

You know this is not true. You will not let her distract you. 'Do you remember our lodgings on the Strand? The walls were very thin. I could hear everything you said, even in the next room.'

Your mother blanches. Ahh . . . now you have her attention.

'One night I heard you talking with one of your gentlemen. He told you that his friend – some nobleman – was suffering from the pox. He said: "blasted fool believes if he fucks a virgin, he'll be cured."'

She says nothing, only stares at you across the table. She remembers. She remembers.

'This friend of his was prepared to pay a fortune for the right girl. "But where does one find a clean, honest maid in this filthy town?" And you said, "my daughter is a virgin."'

You take a sip of wine. You haven't thought of that night in a long time. You locked the memory away where it couldn't hurt you. Speaking of it now releases not only the memory but all the pain and fear. You are a child again, kneeling against the wall, listening to your mother trade away your body, your life, for money.

'I realised then I wasn't your daughter. I was your possession. Something you could sell, like a silk gown or a diamond ring. So I ran away, that same night. If I died, at least it would be on my own terms. I lived on my wits until Samuel found me. There were times when I thought I wouldn't survive, but I never once regretted it. And when Samuel told me you were dead, I cried. I was so happy.'

The candles flicker again – the wicks need trimming. The baby has stopped kicking. You wish it would start again if only to remind you that you are not alone.

You had hoped your story would push your mother into a grand temper, but you have misjudged her. You have tried before to hold up a mirror to her soul. And every time she sees a brave, beautiful heroine staring back at her. 'What a silly story, Catherine,' she says. 'You must have dreamt it. Now. We were speaking of your bookshop. How much profit do you make from it?'

Your heart drops as you realise the truth. She has spent your fortune, all of it — just as she spent your father's before you. That is why she asked about the Pistol. You had thought, naively, that she could not spend so much while she was hidden away here, far from town. You have underestimated her, and her endless appetite. The terrible, gaping hole where her heart should be.

She will never let you return home to the Pistol. But she could establish it again, hire someone suitable to run the shop and then take the profits for herself. The scheme will end badly — of course it will. Your mother destroys everything she touches. But now, in this moment, she believes she has found the answer to her problems.

She rinses her fingers in a porcelain bowl. 'It is so rare,' she says, 'to be given a second chance. I made mistakes with you, Catherine, I see that now. I was too generous and forgiving. I spoilt you, because I loved you. And now you are broken, beyond repair. But that child you carry . . .' She gestures to your stomach. 'I do hope it's a girl. I shall be so happy to begin again, with a new daughter. I am quite sure she will love me.'

Without your fortune, you are without value.

Without your fortune, there is only one thing left for her to take.

It is at this moment you realise that your mother is going to kill you.

PART SEVEN

Blackbirds

Chapter Twenty-one

The little town of Nayland lies in my birth county of Suffolk, close to the Essex border. It is a steady, prosperous place, with old timber buildings and a cotton mill, and sheep nibbling the grass in the graveyard. The clock on the church tower has told the same time for at least a century, but the bell rings at four each morning to rouse people to work, and tolls again in the evening to encourage them to bed. There are shops, and alehouses, and roads wide enough for two carriages to pass. If one had a favourite aunt, one could imagine settling her in Nayland, knowing she would be comfortable, and surrounded by good neighbours.

This was precisely the arrangement Mr Henry Monke had organised for his beloved Aunt Evelyn, his late mother's sister. Mr Monke – a physician – enjoyed an excellent living in Sudbury, ten miles from Nayland. He would have invited his aunt to live with him and his family, but he knew that she would be more content in her own cottage. Aunt Evelyn was an independent soul, with a great liking for her own company. She also liked to drink liquor, and spit tobacco, and simmer foul-smelling herbal remedies in her cooking pans. Ten miles was, upon reflection, a most suitable distance.

There was no denying that Evelyn Cuddington was an unfortunate neighbour, requiring much forbearance from the townsfolk. They did not mind so much that she erected a gin still in her yard; more that it exploded one night, destroying an ancient yew tree and convincing half the town that the Jacobites had sailed over from

France to burn down their homes. But forgiveness was a Christian virtue, as Reverend White reminded his congregation, before bidding them to kneel and pray upon the new cushions Mr Monke had kindly donated to the church.

After three turbulent years, the town had come to accept Evelyn – she despised titles – much as one accepted a blackened tooth or a persistent rash. They were not pleasant things, but it was hard to recall how life had been without them.

Shortly after her arrival Evelyn had stood up at a town meeting and announced that she was prepared to take in laundry, mend clothes, and undertake other modest chores. Her neighbours, assuming she was short of funds,* made sure to find little jobs to keep her from debt. These she did with an ill temper, often drunk, and seldom to any decent standard. She was, to be scrupulously fair, very good at pulling vegetables. This was fallen upon with some relief, as a truth upon which the whole of Nayland could agree – that for all of Evelyn's failings, she *did* have exceedingly strong arms for a woman.

So when a fellow from Stourbank Farm came looking to hire a servant for the afternoon, it was with an air of mischief that everyone insisted that Evelyn was the perfect candidate. No one else would do. 'And be sure to call her Mistress Cuddington,' they said, hiding their sniggers. 'Or she will take offence.'

This same man and his friend had been the cause of much nuisance since their arrival in November. Whenever they ventured into town they would drink too hard and too fast, pestering women with lewd comments and starting fights. Within a month they had been banned from every drinking hole in a five-mile radius. As for their mistress, she had not deigned to visit the town once, preferring to order endless supplies of food and finery from Sudbury or Colchester. A handful of folk caught glimpses of her

*She was not. She was bored.

out riding and conceded that she was a great beauty with an excellent seat, but very proud and disdainful. Visitors to the farm were dismissed roughly by her men. Even Mr White was turned away at the door.

Yes, it would be amusing to inflict the town's greatest weapon upon these rude, irksome neighbours.

Thus it came to pass that a (somewhat inebriated) Evelyn was dispatched to Stourbank Farm, and brought into the presence of Lady Emma Vanhook, who barely condescended to look at her.

'There is a girl upstairs,' she said, admiring her sapphire earrings in the glass. 'Her condition cannot be disguised. She must be washed and dressed, and you must do something with her hair, I am told it is crawling with lice. You will not speak to her,' she said sharply. 'Not one word. You will be paid five shillings now, and a further shilling a week until we leave the county, to ensure your silence. If you break your word and speak to anyone, I shall send my men to your home and have them burn it down.' She scented her neck and collarbone. 'Do you understand?'

Our flaws destroy us in the end. Had Lady Vanhook thought of Evelyn as a person, and not merely an old baggage, a lumpen thing to be used, she might have been more careful. Indeed if she had washed and dressed Kitty herself, she would not have needed to hire Evelyn at all. But she was too proud to stoop to such menial work as caring for her own daughter.

As for Evelyn, she performed her tasks in her usual desultory fashion and walked home along the muddy paths. It was too late, she decided, to send a letter to Sudbury and in any case she did not trust the post. So she ate her supper and went to bed, thinking about the swollen-bellied girl up at Stourbank Farm with her chapped lips and bruised skin, her wild green eyes blazing from a death-pale face.

The next morning Evelyn rose to the tolling of the four o'clock bell and shoved on her boots. It was a long walk to Sudbury, but she was a sturdy woman not given to dawdling. When she reached Assington she was offered a ride on a pig cart, which she accepted, and was able to surprise her nephew at breakfast.

'I have found your girl,' she said, throwing Kitty's red plait on to the table. 'You had best shift yourself.'

This was how I learnt that Kitty was alive, and being held prisoner at Stourbank Farm.

Evelyn Cuddington and Henry Monke were perfect strangers to me. And yet – somehow – I had engaged them several weeks earlier in the hunt for Kitty. How could this be?

One morning I was crossing a patch of grass behind Devonshire House when I noticed a blackbird pulling a worm from the soil. The jab of its beak was so particular, and the turn of its head so curious, that I was reminded instantly of the one I had seen the day I departed from the almshouse at Saffron Walden. I found myself thinking of all the blackbirds in England pecking for worms and turning over leaves with their bright yellow beaks. There must be hundreds of thousands of them, sifting through the soil at this very moment, searching for the same treasure.

Perhaps I only had this thought because of my own long, painful search for Kitty. When one is fixed upon a singular purpose, one sees signs and portents everywhere. In any case, it gave me an idea.

For months I had fretted over Kitty's health, not realising her condition might help me find her. She was with child. At some point she would require a physician, or an apothecary, or a midwife – *someone* to help with the birth. I turned at once for Covent Garden, and Everett Felblade. He listened to my garbled explanation in silence.

'It might work,' he conceded, and set to work.

Over the next two days Felblade sent urgent letters to every apothecary and doctor he knew outside of London, explaining what had happened to Kitty. If they should see her, or hear some rumour about her, they must write to him without delay. They should also pass word on to any other doctor or apothecary of their acquaintance, and any local woman who might be asked to help with a birth. Should they be 'damned whimpering puppies' and require assurance of the legitimacy of this request, they might apply to Sir John Gonson, magistrate at Westminster.

This had been a great concession from Gonson. Had I not made my weekly visits to him, and suffered his lectures, I could never have borrowed his authority. He saw the merit in the plan at once, and as it required very little effort on his part, agreed to support it. Much as I detested him, his name added the necessary weight to Felblade's request.

And so through late February and into March, news of Kitty's abduction and disappearance spread quietly from village to village, county to county. Discretion, Felblade had warned in his letter, was paramount. If Lady Vanhook learnt that scores of doctors, midwives and apothecaries throughout England were involved in the search, she might not call for their help when it was needed.

Meanwhile my flock of blackbirds worked for me, turning over leaves, poking their beaks in the soil. Mr Monke was not acquainted with Felblade, but when a friend recounted the story to him, he was greatly disturbed by it, and wrote down the details in his diary so he should not forget them. He also told his dear Aunt Evelyn.

When Felblade received the news he ran wigless all the way from Russell Street – people spoke of it in days to come, it became a thing of legend – brandishing Mr Monke's letter in his bony fist. I snatched it from him, hardly daring to believe it.

I had found her. After all this time, I had found her. She was alive.

Now I must rescue her.

'Gonson next!' Felblade said, heading for the door.

I seized a bony elbow. 'No!'

ANTONIA HODGSON

Gonson would insist on bringing a band of men with him, and a carriage. We might as well march in procession with trumpets heralding our arrival. If Lady Vanhook learnt that Gonson was on his way to arrest her, she would run again. Mr Monke's letter had warned that Kitty was not in good health. She might not survive being dragged across the country a second time.

And so, although the restless, reckless part of me was desperate to snatch up my cloak and hat and go, I forced myself to sit down, and think. I pulled out my pipe.

'Only two guards at the farm. That is good news.'

Felblade was browsing a pile of Sam's books. 'Half of these are mine!' he sniffed. 'Sneak-fingered shifter.'

I closed my eyes and conjured an old oak-framed farmhouse set by a riverbank, surrounded by water meadows, and pastureland. Two loutish guards, a sullen boy servant. Lady Vanhook, dressed in a silk gown, sparkling with diamonds and sapphires. And her daughter, locked away in a dark attic. So close, so far.

I scribbled some notes on to a scrap of paper. Felblade fished out his spectacles and read over my shoulder, flapping his hand to beat away my pipe smoke. He hated tobacco – claimed it congested the lungs or some such nonsense. 'Why not send the Fleet gang?'

'Gabriela will kill everyone.'

'Not the servant boy,' he said, then sighed. He was thinking of Twig. We both were. 'She'll spare the guards too, if you reason with her.'

I sketched the farm and its land, the river winding along its southern edge, the small cherry wood to the west. The dogs in the rear yard.

'Thomas,' Felblade said, when I was done. 'Emma Addington is wicked – down to the marrow.'

I stared at him in surprise. 'You knew her? Before she was married?'

'Of course I did. I'm a thousand years old.'

274

I had never thought to ask him, and naturally he had never bothered to tell me. 'What was she like?'

'Oh . . .' He sat down beneath the shelf of skulls, his bony head a living addition to Sam's collection. 'She was enchanting. And spoilt. And vain.' He took off his spectacles and wiped them with a grubby cuff. 'Came to London with all manner of giddy notions – she would marry a duke, and live in a castle with a thousand servants. Half the town was in love with her.'

'Including you?'

He laughed until he coughed. 'I was far too old for such piffle-paffle.'

Too old even then. He really was ancient.

I thought of Lady Vanhook in her room on Jermyn Street, her lean arms stretched along the back of the sofa. A duchess – I could imagine that. 'Perhaps if she had married a duke, she would have been happy.'

'*Happy*?' Felblade almost lost his teeth. He pushed them back into place. 'Impossible.'

He was right, of course. Emma Addington, Mrs Sparks, Lady Vanhook could never be satisfied. Nothing would ever be enough, not even a title and a thousand servants. Or a plantation and a village of slaves.

So much misery and suffering, spreading out from one poisoned heart.

But did she deserve to die? Did I have the right to *execute* her? Felblade thought so, clearly. If I took Gabriela with me, I wouldn't even need to do it myself. But that was a coward's thought. I am many foolish things, but I am not a coward.

'I will need four men,' I said.

Chapter Twenty-two

It took us three days to reach Nayland – myself and Sam, Inchguard and Jeremiah. We rode at a good pace but not a furious one, careful not to attract attention or wear ourselves out. I had learnt my lesson. I would not reach Kitty too exhausted to fight for her. I would not be ambushed a second time.

Jeremiah had agreed at once to join the rescue party. He was keen to repay his debt to me, and there were things he wished to say to Lady Vanhook.

Sam would have preferred to bring Gabriela along, and the Fleet gang – but he approved of our plan. 'Swift and quiet,' he said. 'Good.'

As for Inchguard, we needed someone who was a stranger to Lady Vanhook, and had no connection to the Fleets. And, oddly, his ability to trip over his own feet would be a benefit for once.

I left Gonzalo with Felblade. I'm sure I did not miss him, not at all.

We rode the last mile in silence. It was a miserable night, cursed with that fine, grizzling rain that clings to the skin. There was barely enough light to see – the moon dimmed to a silver haze behind a bank of clouds.

We stopped at the top of a hill, taking shelter under a broad yew tree. Sam dismounted and vanished into the night.

Two hundred yards away lay the dark bulk of Stourbank Farm. Two hundred yards. This was the closest I had been to Kitty in over four months. The urge to rush down there now and take on the guards was almost overwhelming.

I wiped the drizzle from my face. 'How long has he been gone?'

'Five minutes, no more,' Jeremiah whispered.

At last Sam returned from his scouting mission.

'Two dogs roaming the yard,' he said. 'Didn't hear me, but ...' They would hear the rest of us. We were not Fleets.

A fox gave a low, barking cough in the next field. Sam frowned. He hated the countryside.

The time had come. A shiver ran through me; half anticipation, half dread. I stepped out from under the yew tree and walked down the muddy field towards the farm. The others followed.

It was a good plan, I told myself. All would be well. No one would die tonight.

The dogs began to bark as soon as Inchguard approached.

This was a promising start. I had told him to make as much noise as possible as he walked past the yard wall and up to the front door. 'As if you were drunk,' I said. Inchguard, who had been sneaking mouthfuls of liquor from a leather bottle for the past several hours, had promised to do his best.

He banged his fist against the door. The dogs howled, trapped behind the wall. I was glad now that I had not brought Gonzalo with me. He would be howling along with them.

'Let me in, for the love of God!' Inchguard slurred, convincingly. 'Take pity upon a poor man, lost and starving.' And then he began to sing, in a fine tenor:

> O farewell grief, and welcome joy,
> Ten thousand times and more;
> For now I have seen my own true Love,
> That I thought I should see no more.

A wandering ballad singer, drunk and lost upon the road, was unlikely to arouse suspicion. I would like to think he chose that particular song for the occasion, but knowing Inchguard it was probably the first tune that fell out of his mouth. I crouched next to Jeremiah by the yard wall, hefting a rock in my hand.

At last Inchguard's racket roused one of the guards, who cursed through the door.

'Go to hell you son of a whore!'

Inchguard sang louder, and banged on the door with his fist. 'Mercy! Take pity on a poor wandering traveller.'

The guard slid back the bolts, prepared for a fight. He lowered his club when he saw Inchguard. Lady Vanhook would have warned him about Jeremiah, and Sam. Most of all she would have warned him about me. Inchguard – that great flapping crane of a man – was very much himself, and no one else.

'Don't worry,' the guard called up the stairs. 'It's only some drunken arsehole.' He gave Inchguard an almighty shove. 'Sod off you twat.'

Inchguard – rarely stable – crashed to the ground, still singing. The guard stood over him, and raised his boot. Before he could stamp on Inchguard's face, I slipped out from behind the wall and hit him across the back of the skull with the rock.

He crumpled to his knees. 'What—'

I put a blade to his throat. 'I would prefer not to kill you, sir.'

He shared my preference, it transpired. 'She ain't paid us for weeks, the cow,' he said, touching the back of his head where I'd hit him. He didn't struggle as Jeremiah gagged and bound him, and led him into the wood.

I helped Inchguard to his feet. 'Keep a close eye on him.'

Inchguard gave me a cheerful salute and wandered off after his prisoner. He was still singing.

Jeremiah returned with Sam and together we headed through the open door. I bolted it again, in case anyone was listening closely, and called up in a hoarse voice, mimicking the guard's accent. 'He's gone.' There was no reply, but I thought I heard voices higher up the house.

I paused in the hallway, and took a steadying breath. This floor was filled with furniture, gilded mirrors and grandfather clocks, oil paintings and silver sconces. But the air smelled of damp and neglect. Far too much work for one boy servant. Another facade, just like the house on Jermyn Street.

I turned to Sam, who nodded and crept away. He was enjoying himself now, despite the rural setting. A dark house was a dark house, and trouble was trouble. He would find the boy and keep him quiet.

Which left the second guard, and Lady Vanhook.

Jeremiah followed me up the worn and sagging staircase. I clenched my dagger, wincing at each creak and groan. There was no light on the first floor, the doors shut tight.

We groped our way towards a back staircase that led up to the attic. I could hear voices again. The second guard would be standing outside the attic door. We must capture him silently, before he drew his weapon. Once he was bound and gagged, Jeremiah would find Lady Vanhook. I would save Kitty.

A very good plan. Quiet, sensible, and no theatrics. I placed my foot upon the first step to the attic. Tested my grip on the dagger.

A woman's scream filled the air – a raking sound of prolonged agony. Then a shattered, terrified moan.

Kitty. Someone was hurting her.

Someone was killing her.

'Thomas,' Jeremiah breathed, in warning.

But instinct claimed me. I sprang up the stairs, calling Kitty's name as she screamed, a tortured roar of pain.

The guard was blocking the door. He gave a shout as he saw me and reached for his pistol. I leapt upon him in a fury, slamming my fist into his jaw and knocking him to the ground.

Kitty screamed again.

Jeremiah jumped upon the struggling guard, pinning him down. 'Save her!' he cried, as the guard fought beneath him.

The door was locked from the inside. Cursing, I kicked at the lock. It held firm. I kicked again, over and over, until the lock splintered and the door swung open. I lurched into the room, unbalanced.

It was at this moment, with one last throttled scream from Kitty, that my daughter entered the world.

The bare attic room glows in the light of two large candelabra, wax streaming and pooling on to the floor. There is a strong smell of blood, and beneath that the stink of unwashed skin and sheets, and chamber pots.

You lie on the bed, knees wide, thighs smeared with blood. Your hair is cut to your scalp and your cheeks are hollow, but it is your expression that makes you strange – so much pain and fear, and a terrible pleading in your eyes. You are exhausted, but you find the strength to sit up.

Your mother kneels at the edge of the bed, wiping the baby clean with a cloth. The cord is still attached, thick and bloody as it winds back to your body. There is another cord, a chain of iron, running from your wrist to the bed. The baby is screaming for you.

You reach out, desperate. 'Please. Give her to me.' Despite the violence of my arrival you do not see me standing in the doorway. Your attention is fixed upon the baby, helpless in your mother's arms.

Your mother lowers the baby carefully on to the bed, and pulls out a knife.

'No!' I step forward, breaking the tableau. All my hopes and dreams for our reunion vanish. There is no time. Your mother is holding a knife. She lowers the blade before I can stop her.

She cuts the cord.

I sag with relief. Blood oozes from the cord, staining the sheets. You give a low moan, your body trembling. 'Please,' you say. 'Mother – please.'

Your mother rises slowly, cradling our baby in the crook of her arm. She grips the knife in her free hand. 'Perfect,' she whispers. 'My perfect little girl.'

My arrival holds no interest to her. She is enchanted by her new toy. She glides towards the door.

I block her path. 'Madam,' I say, carefully. 'The knife, the knife. I hold out my arms.

She hugs the baby close. 'Do you think I would give her to you?' She curls her lip, contemptuous. 'Better she did not live at all.'

I put out my hands, terrified. 'No! Please!'

Your mother gloats, victorious. Such a perfect scene, better than she could ever have imagined. Her enemies defeated, her perfect child safe in her arms. She seems to grow taller, filling the room with her triumph.

It takes all my strength to stay where I am, feet planted firm. Your mother is lost to the real world and its consequences. She could kill the baby and still cast herself as the victim. I cannot let her leave.

She sees that I am resolute, and adapts – scheming and assessing. Such a clever woman. Such a waste.

'There is no need to be tiresome,' she says, as if none of this were her doing. 'We may both have what we want, if you will be sensible. I'll take the child, and you may keep your silly slut.'

She means you.

'Tom, no.' You are delirious with fear, still reaching for your baby. You look so pale and sick I am afraid for you.

'You would give up your daughter?' I ask your mother.

She looks at you, chained to the bed. Your eyes are so wide and desperate. 'She is nothing to me. An empty vessel.'

'She is everything to me.'

A tear slides down your cheek.

Your mother shrugs. 'Take her, then.' And with that she knocks a candelabrum on to the bed, and then the other. You scream. The sheets catch fire where the candles fall. I rush forward, pulling off my jacket and beating at the flames, calling for help.

'No, no, Tom,' you cry. 'The baby. The baby.'

Your mother has fled the room, the baby screaming in her arms. But what can I do? Leave you to burn? I pick you up and carry you as far from the bed as the chain allows, the links pulling taut against your wrist. I must find something to break it.

'Thomas!' Jeremiah appears at my side. The fire has engulfed the bed and is creeping up the wall. Together, we beat out the flames, coughing as the smoke invades our lungs.

Jeremiah pushes me towards the door. 'I will take care of her. Go!'

'I can't leave—'

You scream along with him. 'Go!'

The front door remained bolted, which meant that Lady Vanhook had escaped out through the back yard. I grabbed a lantern and lit it with fumbling hands, clumsy in my haste. Someone – Sam, I presumed – had chained the dogs in their kennels. They howled as I crossed the yard.

I followed a path leading down towards the riverbank, guessing that Lady Vanhook would not deign to ruin her skirts in the muddy fields. As I ran, I thought of the attic room. There had been a lot of blood on the sheets. Was that the normal way of things? I had no idea.

I heard a thin, piercing wail further down the riverbank. No need to hunt for footprints in the dark when my newborn child was crying. I ran towards her screams, smiling grimly. She sounded *furious*.

Lady Vanhook had not brought a lantern with her, nor a cloak. She walked slowly by the river, back straight, as if she were in some royal procession. A queen of myth and tragedy. Dido. Medea. The stars were her backdrop, the rush of river water her music.

'Lady Vanhook.'

She turned, no more than ten paces from me. Her hair was damp from the misting rain, but her appearance in every other respect was the same as it had been on Jermyn Street, when we had drunk tea together in a room stuffed with too much furniture. There was a smudge of blood on her cheek, nothing more. I thought of Kitty, so changed, and had to bite back my fury. It would not help me here.

'So. You left her to burn,' she said. 'No surprise. All men abandon their whores, in the end.'

'Your daughter is safe, Lady Vanhook. And she will be well again, despite what you have done to her.'

She barely heard me. She was too preoccupied with her new treasure. Everything would be different this time. This one would love her. 'Hush now,' she cooed. The baby screamed even louder.

'She needs her mother.' I took a step forward.

She backed away, closer to the riverbank, the fresh spring reeds pressing against her skirts. The water was running high and fast. My stomach lurched. 'Please.' I held out my hands.

'You will not take her from me!'

'Lady Vanhook. I must. She is my daughter.'

'*Now* you understand!' she cried, laughing wildly. 'Now you know *my* pain. I have lost everything. My little Nella. My sweet Catherine. You *ruined* her. Why should I be left with nothing? Why should I be alone?' Tears streamed down her face. 'Why is everyone so cruel?'

A small, secret voice whispered in my ear. *Reach for your pistol. End this now. Kill her before she hurts anyone else, most of all your daughter. It is the only way to be safe. The only way to be free.*

I felt my hand moving to my jacket . . .

No – I would not stain my soul with another death. I must do better.

'I am sorry, Emma,' I said.

She drew back, surprised. '*Liar.*'

'I am. Truly. I am sorry you are alone.'

She pouted. 'It is not fair!'

She sounded like a child. Perhaps she was, in many ways. Perhaps she had never grown up.

'But this is a fantasy,' I said, as gently as I could. 'Where will you go? How will you survive? You have no fortune, no friends.'

She gave me a condescending look. 'I shall do very well upon my own. I have been betrayed and abandoned before, more times than you can imagine. No one has ever cared for me.'

'But how will you travel in secret with a newborn child? How will you find a wet nurse in time?'

She plucked at the baby's blanket, petulant. She knew I spoke the truth. She was not wholly mad, but she was too proud to accept that she had lost. She had come so close to winning!

I must help her escape the trap she had made for herself. 'You are an extraordinary woman, Emma. Exceptional.'

She lifted her chin, and listened.

'If the world were just, you would be a duchess, with a thousand servants. You would have been magnificent at court. You have ten times the wit and beauty of most courtiers.'

She acknowledged this. 'They are all fools,' she sniffed.

The baby was wriggling in her arms, fingers clasping and unclasping. Each time I caught a flash of skin, a tiny pink hand, my heart skipped a beat. How was it possible to love something so quickly and so deeply? I had not even seen her face, not really.

'You may walk away,' I said. 'With dignity and grace. No one need ever speak of this again.' I paused. 'Are you not tired, Emma?'

She brushed away a tear. 'I *am* tired.' She stared into the baby's face and her expression softened. 'She looks like me,' she said. 'So pretty. She has my eyes, my chin. Such a shame.'

I inched forward, sensing trouble.

'You will not suffer as I have,' she said, and before I could stop her, she lifted the baby out over the reed bank and slipped her into the river.

The baby screamed in shock as the cold water enveloped her.

I did not think, I did not stop. Holding the lantern high I plunged into the river. I caught a high, panicked wail and surged forward, raking the water with my free hand. I couldn't find her. I couldn't find her.

She would drown, not even an hour old.

I waded out further, ice-cold water rushing up to my thighs. The lantern showed up patches of reed bank, and clotted weeds. I called out, hoping the sound of my voice would bring some answer. She had stopped crying.

Had she been carried downstream? The current was fast, I could barely stand in it.

I felt the weight of oncoming loss, and grief. How could I live, if she died?

I plunged my arm again and again into the water, groping down to the silted riverbed. I was chest deep now, my sodden clothes slowing me down. I'd lost her. My daughter. She did not even have a name.

My fingers brushed against the edges of the reed bank.

Was that a cry?

Please God. Please.

I pushed deeper into the reeds, still calling over the rush of the river. As I groped in the water my fingers caught on something coarse and sodden. Cloth, it must be. The edge of a blanket. I lifted the lantern high and saw a tiny bundle caught within the reeds, floating and lifting on the lapping water.

I'd found her.

I snatched her up, water streaming from the freezing blanket, and staggered up on to the bank, clutching her tight. I'd lost my lantern in my panic to snatch her. Was she hurt? Was she breathing?

'Little one,' I said, unwrapping her blanket, searching desperately for some sign of life. I put my hand upon her chest. 'I'm here.'

I felt her take a deep breath. And then she screamed, a high, furious wail that half deafened me.

It was the most beautiful sound in the world.

Chapter Twenty-three

I flew back to the farm, my new-born, new-saved daughter nestled snugly against my chest. I was cold and wet, and overjoyed. Any doubts I might have had about becoming a father had been washed away in the river.

As I approached the house I found Inchguard on the doorstep, swigging from a bottle of wine. He staggered to his feet. 'Did we win?'

How to answer such a question, after so much suffering and loss? And yet my daughter was in my arms. 'Yes . . . I suppose we did . . .'

Inchguard grinned and performed a small, capering dance on the spot. Finbar Victorious – a rare sight.

The baby was growing restless, needing her mother. 'The guards?' I asked quickly, before she began screaming again.

'Locked in the cellar. Sam spoke to them.' Inchguard turned sombre. 'That boy, Mr Hawkins . . . He ain't—'

But I didn't have time to discuss Sam and his more unsettling qualities. I hurried off in search of Kitty.

I found her upstairs in her mother's room, lying on clean sheets in a four-poster bed with silk curtains. Jeremiah had carried her there, and cut the chain from her wrist. She was still pale, and shaking with worry and exhaustion, but she sat up when she saw me.

'Oh . . .' Kitty breathed, as I placed the baby in her arms. Relief, joy, sorrow bundled together in one sigh. 'My angel,' she whispered, kissing her and breathing in her scent. 'What did she do? What did she do? Hush, hush. You're safe now.' She put the baby to her breast, pulling the sheets around them both for warmth. I stood watching them from the foot of the bed. Kitty was too distracted to notice that I was soaked to the skin, water pooling around my feet. I suppose I should have felt neglected. For months I had dreamt of this reunion – what I would say, how it would feel to have Kitty in my arms again. None of that mattered now.

I stripped out of my wet clothes and stood by the blazing fire, shivering under a quilted blanket. I thought of the river, and how close I had come to losing our daughter. If the current had not pushed her into the reeds ...

I glanced towards the bed. Kitty was watching me, the baby drifting to sleep in her arms. 'Tom.' Her voice shook. 'I'm so sorry.'

'No, no, no.' I joined her on the bed, sliding under the blanket. It was blissfully warm.

Kitty gave a tiny shriek as my freezing skin touched hers. 'You're cold as *ice*. What happened?'

I didn't answer. Our stories could wait until tomorrow, or some other time when she was feeling stronger.

I shuffled on to my side, stretched out next to her. We stared at each other for a long moment, not speaking.

'Are we safe?' she whispered.

'Yes.'

'Promise?'

'I promise. Am I warm enough yet?' I asked, touching her arm.

'No!' she yelped. And then she laughed. It was not her old laugh, there were too many shadows wreathed around it, but it was welcome all the same. She smiled at me. 'We have a daughter. Look!'

'I know.' I smiled in return. 'She's perfect. Am I warm enough *now*?'

'Yes,' she said, though I wasn't, not really. These are the accommodations we make for those we love. We shuffled closer, the baby between us. Kitty's eyes did not leave mine. 'Are you sure you still want me, Tom, now I'm penniless? A vagabond whore?' She was searching for herself, for her natural, teasing nature, but she couldn't disguise the doubt in her voice. She had spent too long in her mother's company.

I told her that I loved her, and that I always would. I kissed her forehead, and ran my fingers through the soft tufts of her hair, and told her she was beautiful. She was too tired to disagree. She fell asleep in my arms.

I could feel sleep embracing me too, pulling me down into the mattress – but the night was not quite done with me yet.

I peeled myself from the bed and padded downstairs, every step that took me away from her feeling like a betrayal.

Jeremiah was making soup in the kitchen, warming himself by the range. Inchguard, he said, had fallen asleep in the middle of the hallway, dead drunk. Jeremiah had covered him with a blanket. 'Too heavy to move.'

'And Sam? He's gone to town?'

'Aye, aye.'

Just as we had planned. When we arrived in town earlier that afternoon I had collected Evelyn from her cottage. Together we had paid a visit to the town's vicar, the Reverend John White. He was a brisk, vigorous man of about five and thirty, who opened his own door rather than trouble his maidservant. His desk was strewn with correspondence, but he had swept it to one side, listening attentively as I told my story, shaking his head at the worst parts.

'I am persuaded to support you,' he'd said carefully, when I was done. 'Within the limits of the law.'

'Naturally.'

He explained that the magistrate was out of the county visiting family and not expected back for several weeks. In his absence a squire by the name of Abbott from a neighbouring town was in charge. 'But let us not trouble him unless we must,' Mr White added.

'He's an idiot,' Evelyn explained.

'*Evelyn,*' Mr White protested. 'We have spoken before of the need for tolerance.'

Evelyn snorted.

Mr White promised that if Lady Vanhook came to town seeking sanctuary, he would provide it. 'But I cannot hold her against her will.'

Evelyn, meanwhile, would spread the word about the town – should the lady from Stourbank Farm come demanding help, they must send her to Mr White. In this way we hoped to funnel her to the vicarage – and keep her there – without suspecting a trap.

Jeremiah poured me a bowl of soup and we ate in silence. I'm sure he was thinking – as I was – of Lady Vanhook, and what we must do next.

'She's at the vicarage,' Sam said, appearing silently at the back door. 'Screaming for the High Sheriff. They've sent for that squire – Abbott.'

'At this hour?'

Sam ladled out some soup. 'She insisted.' He drank the soup from the ladle and wiped his mouth with the back of his hand. 'How's Kitty?'

'Come and see,' I said.

Kitty was fast asleep, so deep it felt wrong to rouse her. I lifted the lantern over her to show Sam the baby. Like her mother, she was fast asleep, breathing softly in tiny gasps. She breathed very well indeed, I was very proud.

'Another girl,' Sam groaned. Five younger sisters and now this.

'Is she not perfect?' I said, with scrupulous objectivity. 'Look at her little toes.'

Kitty stirred, then woke. 'What is the matter?' she asked, her face still crumpled with sleep. 'Are we safe?' There was a strained, anxious tone in her voice, that had not been there earlier. Sometimes we do not panic until the threat is over. I had been quite calm when I was carted off to the gallows, but was plagued with nightmares for months afterwards. I feared Kitty might suffer from a similar disorder. I must watch her closely.

'*Are we safe?*' she asked again. 'Where is she?'

'In your arms, darling,' I said, thinking she meant the baby.

'No!' Kitty sat up, then winced in pain. 'Where is *she?*'

'At the vicarage.' I tried to explain the plan I had concocted with Jeremiah. I wanted her blessing for it. If anyone deserved to decide Lady Vanhook's fate alongside Jeremiah, it was surely Kitty. But she was not listening.

'I need a knife.'

'You're safe—'

'Tom. Find me a knife.'

I hunted out my dagger and handed it to her. She tucked it beneath her pillow.

'What shall I say to your mother, Kit? What do you want—'

She recoiled, pulling the baby closer to her chest. 'Nothing. I don't want *anything* from her.'

I tried again. 'I'm sorry, sweetheart – but we must decide together what to do ... she is—'

'She is *nothing*,' Kitty said, her voice trembling. 'I do not wish to speak of her, or think of her. I just want her to go away. For ever.' She turned her back on me, curling into a ball under the blankets.

Sam watched her from the window sill, his face grim.

'You will never see her again,' I promised. The same vow Lady Vanhook had made when she took Kitty from me. I had not meant to echo her.

Kitty shuddered, and curled even tighter. As I left, I saw her hand slide under the pillow, groping for the comfort of a cold steel blade.

Victory is a strange thing, and never quite what one imagines.

Sam offered to keep watch over Kitty. The guards remained locked in the cellar with the boy servant – we would let them go once everything was settled. I felt sorry for the boy, but not for the men. They had kept Kitty prisoner for months. They were lucky to have met me now, when I had grown weary of violence and vengeance. It was revenge, after all, that had caused so much trouble in the first place. Revenge, fuelled by envy and greed.

The night was coming to an end, but I would not risk riding across open ground in the grey, muffled light before dawn. I set off on foot instead, to the sound of a cock crowing in the back yard. Jeremiah came with me.

'We are in agreement?' I asked him.

He reached for a piece of paper tucked in his coat, I heard it crinkle against his fingers. 'Yes.'

'We must be wary. She is—'

'I am always wary.'

True enough.

Chapter Twenty-four

Dawn broke as we reached the town. A milkmaid was guiding her cows along the high street, their bells clanking softly as they made their way to the dairy. We paused to let them pass. By chance we had stopped by the town's pillory, the wood rotting from neglect. Pleasant indeed to live somewhere that demanded so little of its instruments of punishment, but I feared Lady Vanhook would use this to her advantage. It is hard to recognise evil if one has never experienced it. True villainy – irredeemable wickedness – is rare. People do not wish to believe in it – even when it is standing directly in front of them. Most of all when it is standing directly in front of them.

Not that I wished to lock Lady Vanhook in the pillory. She would only cast herself as the victim and weep for herself, and kind people would feel sorry for her.

So what to do?

She was a clever woman. We must outwit her.

Mr White's vicarage stood on Fen Street. The mill stream ran along the edge of the road and each cottage had its own tiny bridge across it. The vicarage, with its three gables, was by far the grandest building in its row. As I walked across the bridge I looked up, and there she was at the window: Lady Vanhook, posed as if she had been waiting for this very moment. (She had been waiting for this very moment.) The glass was latticed, and dark, but I thought I saw her smile.

We had barely exchanged our good morrows with the vicar and his wife when Mr Abbott, the magistrate's proxy, arrived to offer his counsel. He was a man of about seventy years, with a hearty, bluff manner quite unsuited to the occasion. One of those blithe, careless fellows, who blunders against a table, smashes a vase, then blames the vase for being too fragile.

And yet we must humour him. The law is the law and we must appear to abide by it. I was curious too, in a way, to see how this fellow applied it. A test, if you like.

'Great heavens!' he exclaimed, upon hearing our account of the night. 'Are you *certain* she meant to drown the infant? Perhaps it slipped from her arms? These things do happen,' he added, dismissing Lady Vanhook's attempted murder of my child with a flap of his glove.

I assured him the act had been deliberate. It was only luck that my daughter was alive this morning. Abbott nodded absently. 'Her husband is a respectable gentleman of some wealth, I believe? Sugar, is it?'

I felt Jeremiah shift behind me.

'They are estranged,' I said.

'Dear, dear. What a scandal, what a pity. I had best speak with her.'

I moved to join him, but he raised his hand to stop me.

'No, Mr Hawkins, I shall hear her side of events in private. I'm told she is distressed and most fearful of you, sir. And your friend.' He frowned at Jeremiah.

And so we waited. The parlour was directly below Lady Vanhook's room: we heard the squire's bellowed greeting, her muffled reply. This was followed swiftly by Abbott's laughter, loud and sycophantic. I put my head in my hands. Lord help us.

Jeremiah sighed, then picked up a book left open on a chair. He was soon absorbed in it, oblivious to the world. This was not indifference on his part, more a question of sanity.

I fixed a pipe and paced the floor until Abbott came back. His mood was even more cheerful and confident than before. He had the measure of all this nonsense, and the remedy for it.

'Remarkable woman! Such grace and composure. Tell me, sir – is the daughter as great a beauty? No wonder you have been chasing her about the country.' He winked at me.

'Mr Abbott,' I snapped. 'That *remarkable* woman has caused untold misery—'

'Yes, yes – there are grievances on both sides, no doubt.' He poured himself a glass of brandy. 'To families!' he said, and laughed. 'Oh come, let it pass, sir. You are well, the baby is healthy. Is it not better to forgive and forget? The lady is prepared to do the same.'

'She is prepared to forgive *me*?' I laughed. The woman was shameless. 'What have I done?'

'What have you done? Come now, Mr Hawkins! You have ruined her daughter!'

'That is not true—'

'The child is a bastard, sir!'

It still astonishes me that I did not punch him.

Abbott wagged his finger. 'Aha, yes – you did not think to mention that. Or the truth about this fellow.' He turned his finger on Jeremiah. 'A runaway slave, eh?'

'She is lying,' I answered quickly. 'Mr Patience holds a respectable position in town, with references, he is a clerk—'

Abbott yawned. 'The good lady has also accused you of stealing her property.'

I frowned in confusion.

'A young slave girl, brought over from Antigua. She believes you or . . .' he flapped his glove at Jeremiah, 'may have stolen her.'

I could feel Jeremiah's anger raging like heat between us. Somehow, he contained it.

'The law does not permit the ownership of slaves in England, sir,' I reminded Abbott.

'The law, the law,' he murmured, slurping his breakfast brandy. 'Cloudy on the matter, I should say. Well, well. You may continue to press your case against the lady if you wish, Mr Hawkins – and I shall judge it without prejudice, naturally. But be warned, you may find *yourself* judged – and a good deal more harshly than Lady Emma. There is no doubt she acted with excessive passion. But she was trying to protect her daughter from ruin – something you will come to understand, now you are a father.'

He rocked back upon his heels, smiling contentedly, as if he had brought everything to a happy conclusion. The world was good and right, because it had been good and right to him. 'Families!' he said again, knocking back the last of his brandy. And then he left.

I might have hated Abbott's argument, and the way he delivered it, but he was right about our case in law. He was the perfect embodiment of the problem.

If I lost the case against Lady Vanhook – what would happen to me? Very little. I might rail against the injustice of it, the lack of redress, but I would still be free to continue my life with Kitty and our daughter. Affie and Jeremiah might not be as lucky. Their status under the law was precarious, to say the least. If Lady Vanhook sued over the theft of her *property* and won, Affie would be fitted with a new silver collar, and returned to slavery. Jeremiah would be sent back to Antigua and hanged. Even poor Julius back at Belmaison would be punished for aiding Jeremiah's escape.

We had always known – Jeremiah and I – that we could not rely upon the law as it stood. But there were other ways to protect ourselves, and our families.

Mr White emerged from upstairs, where he had been consulting with his unwanted guest. 'She is prepared to speak with you alone, as you requested,' he croaked. Yesterday, he had been bursting with energy. Now the poor fellow looked exhausted. One night attending to Lady Vanhook's needs had been enough to drain him to a husk. 'But I must take your weapons, if you have any.'

I was not in the least surprised to hear that Lady Vanhook had agreed to meet with me. How could she resist such a moment of high drama? I leant my swordstick against the wall, Jeremiah handed over his dagger and then we·followed Mr White up the stairs.

He hesitated on the landing. 'Is this proper? A private conversation of this nature . . .'

'Perhaps you could ask your maid to bring up some tea?' I suggested.

'Oh, of course! I shall see to it at once.'

He hurried off, reassured. Nothing bad could happen over a pot of tea. I was about to say this to Jeremiah, in jest, when I recalled his first meeting with Lady Vanhook, when he was beaten on the path. She had watched from the veranda, drinking tea.

We entered the room together.

Lady Vanhook lay sprawled upon the end of her bed, her stockinged feet tucked beneath her. I call it *her* bed, because that is what happened to objects, and rooms, and people when they fell into her orbit. Mrs White might consider this her bedchamber, but she would be mistaken, as long as her regal visitor remained in state.

'Mr Hawkins.' Lady Vanhook lifted her arm with a languid movement and pulled a tortoiseshell comb from her head, letting her dark auburn hair fall down her back. She said many things with that one small gesture. *Look at me. You desire me. I am not afraid of you. I am unchanged.* I thought of Kitty's hair, chopped roughly to the scalp. I was meant to, that was another unspoken message.

She was dressed in the same blue gown she had been wearing the night before, a tad muddy about the hem. Presumably Mrs White's gowns were not fine enough for her taste. The sapphire pendant glinted at her throat.

Jeremiah closed the door and stood guard in front of it. She glared at him, then with an effort of will decided to find him amusing.

'Cicero. I hardly recognised you in your fine clothes. You have a new master, I see.' She slid from the bed. 'Do you miss your wife,

Cicero? You will be sorry to hear that my filthy husband has become *overfond* of her.'

Jeremiah held her gaze. 'Sara is dead.'

She laughed. 'No, no, Cicero. Did my little Nella tell you that? I may have lied, and told her that her mama was dead, but I promise you – she lives yet.'

Instinct told me this was a lie, another one of Lady Vanhook's cruel tricks. She knew Jeremiah could never sail back to Antigua to discover the truth.

Jeremiah remained silent. He had learnt long ago to hide his feelings from her. As she could not bait him to react, she turned her attention back to me.

'How fares my Catherine this morning? Do you find her much changed? Has she lost her bloom? Perhaps you wish you had never found her.'

This was how she restored herself, feasting on the misery of others. I would not be provoked. I sat down and proceeded to build a pipe.

Disappointed, she took out a fan – she too could fiddle with props – and wafted it at her bosom. 'Mr Abbott is a kind, sensible soul, is he not? One had quite forgotten the simple kindness of a true English gentleman. He plans to offer me a cottage on his estate.'

How quickly she had recovered! She may have lost the battle at the riverbank, but within hours the war was resumed. How long had she spent in Squire Abbott's company – a quarter of an hour? Give her a week and she would have half the county rallying to her side.

I took a long draw on my pipe and breathed out slowly, watching the smoke trail up to the ceiling. 'Are you not in the least ashamed, madam?'

'Ashamed? For protecting my daughter from a scoundrel? I am *proud.* And sorry that I failed.'

'You almost drowned our child.'

She drew back upon the bed, offended. 'Slander! Is this your plan, sir – to spread wicked lies about me? To poison my reputation?'

She was not dissembling. Her outrage was genuine. In a few short hours, she had erased the memory of what she had done. Only a monster would try to murder her own grandchild. She was not a monster, so it did not happen.

'Mr Abbott's offer is most generous,' I said.

She smirked.

'You will refuse it.'

She lowered her fan and laughed. 'Will I?'

The maid arrived with the tea, halting negotiations. We watched in silence as the kettle was set down, the tea poured, slices of bread and butter laid out on dainty porcelain plates. Lady Vanhook sat down and began to eat, licking butter from her long fingers.

'You made a deal with Samuel Fleet, madam,' I said, when the maid had left. 'To leave England and never return.'

'Samuel Fleet is in hell, where he belongs. He has no hold over me.' She touched a finger to the sapphire at her throat. 'I have enjoyed spending his fortune. I deserved it, after all he took from me—'

'We are willing to offer a similar deal,' I said, glancing at Jeremiah. 'Leave England at once and for ever. And promise never to return to Antigua.'

'Take a single slave, and the deal is broken,' Jeremiah added, from his position by the door.

Lady Vanhook sipped her tea. 'You have no power over me. I shall stay here, with Mr . . .'

She had forgotten her new benefactor's name already. 'Mr Abbott?' I offered.

'Precisely. Suffolk is such a fine county. I shall like it here,' she said. 'There are several very good families in the area. I shall enjoy their company, now that I am free to do as I wish.'

Free. As though *she* had been held captive for months, and not Kitty.

'You may keep the gowns and the jewels,' I said. 'Enough so you may settle yourself abroad. No doubt you will find some fool to keep you, until he discovers your true nature. That is how you have always lived, is it not? But you will not stay here. I will have a wide sea between you and the people I love. An ocean would be preferable.'

She was barely listening – too busy thinking of her next insult. 'You are not as handsome as you were, Mr Hawkins,' she decided. 'And your clothes! So drab and ill-fitting. You look like a poor country curate. Like your father, I suppose.'

She picked up her tea and carried it to the window. The light caught her hair, and smooth flashes of skin. Her dress was loose, half falling from her shoulders. She looked – as she so often did – like a painting.

She had not changed an inch from our first meeting. How could she? She only remembered the parts of herself she liked, and shed the rest each night like a snake, revealing the same patterns beneath, fresh and polished. 'There is no deal to be made, sir. I shall do as I please. You have no authority over me.'

'True,' I said. 'But I know someone who does.'

I pulled out a thick, folded letter, written on vellum and sealed with wax. 'You have offended the magistrate of Westminster, Lady Vanhook.'

'Who? Oh ... *him*.' She laughed. She had long discarded and forgotten her old ally.

Sir John Gonson had not forgotten her.

'This is a warrant for your arrest.' I had persuaded Gonson to provide me with a copy some weeks ago, in case I should find her before he did. 'You left a great number of unsettled bills back in London. The rent for your house on Jermyn Street. Food, clothes, jewellery, guards. Over a hundred guineas, it says here. And you named Sir John as your guarantor. He is . . . displeased. "Sins must be punished", and so on. You are to be dragged to London in chains, and thrown into a debtors' gaol.'

She stared out of the window, feigning nonchalance. 'You cannot compel me to return.'

'This is a *warrant*, madam – signed by Sir John himself. Even Mr Abbott cannot ignore it.'

She dragged herself from the window. 'Let me see.'

I held it open, so she might inspect the seal and the signature. I knew better than to hand it to her – she would toss it in the fire.

'A forgery,' she said. But she knew it was genuine. She returned to her seat and picked up her stolen fan. Her hand trembled as she held it.

I must admit, I took some satisfaction in that.

She rallied herself. 'He will forgive me—'

'I doubt that most intensely.'

'Then I shall find new friends—'

'Lady Vanhook. Do you not understand?' I smiled thinly. 'At this moment, I am your only friend.'

She stared at me.

'You made a deal with Samuel Fleet. Yes, he is dead. But he has a brother. And his brother has a wife. You must remember Gabriela?'

She flinched. Oh yes, she remembered Gabriela. *Now* she began to understand. It had taken her longer than I had expected. She was so used to playing the spider, and not the fly. Her eyes darted to the door, and to Jeremiah.

'You broke your promise, madam. You came back. The Fleets are not a forgiving family. Do you think you can escape them again, if you return to London? If you're trapped in a debtors' prison?'

She toyed with her fan, miserable.

I leant in, confessional. 'I was so tempted to bring Gabriela here. She would have stormed into town like an avenging angel and stuck a blade through your heart. Vengeance, madam. *Life for life, eye for eye, tooth for tooth. Wound for wound.* But I will not have another life upon my conscience. Not even one as worthless as yours.'

I sat back.

For a moment she held herself rigid and proud, considering her next step. And then she slumped, defeated. 'Why is everyone so *cruel?*' she said, and started to cry.

I tucked the warrant back into my jacket. It was over. I had won. She would agree to my terms and leave the country. I felt no sense of triumph, only relief. I had kept my promise to Kitty. She would never see her mother again.

By the time we had finished our negotiations, Lady Vanhook had convinced herself that she *wanted* to go abroad. It was her dearest wish. She had so many friends on the Continent; kind, generous, loyal friends who would be delighted to extend an invitation. And England was so miserable and wet in the spring. This was the very best time to leave. 'I am only sorry for the baby,' she added, venomously. 'How will she fare, poor thing? Her mother is a slut, and her father is a devil. She will be meat for the gallows one day, I have no doubt. Such a pity.' And having called down death upon her only grandchild she poured herself another cup of tea, but the pot had stewed and the water had turned cold and honestly, what had happened to English servants? Did they have no standards? 'This would not happen in Antigua,' she said. 'Would it, Cicero? I had Nella very well trained. She would not dare let a pot grow cold.'

This seemed the best moment to rise and exchange places with Jeremiah. I touched his arm as we passed, and he nodded in reply to my unspoken question. *Yes, I am ready. Today, I am ready.*

'Oh what is *this?*' Lady Vanhook rolled her eyes. '*Spare* me from more *torture.*'

'Lady Vanhook,' Jeremiah said, standing over her. He gathered his breath. 'I am alive.'

His old mistress looked bored. 'I dare say you are.'

Jeremiah took the note from his pocket. This document was written on cheap paper, not thick vellum, and it came with no wax seal of authority. But it carried Lady Vanhook's sentence, all the same.

'Is that a speech, Cicero?' she asked, in a mocking voice. 'Did I not ask for one when we first met? Well, you always were slow. Nothing like your brother. What was his name . . .?'

'You remember,' Jeremiah said. 'You remember Michael.'

She bit her lip, and looked away. It was the only time I ever saw her look ashamed. Just for a moment, and then it was gone. Buried.

'Lady Vanhook,' Jeremiah said, reading from his note. With his words written down, he was able to speak without faltering. 'You stole so much from me. For years, I could not understand why, but now I do. You stole from me because you are poor.'

Lady Vanhook choked back a laugh.

Jeremiah ignored her. 'What are the greatest riches on this earth? Love, friendship, family. You have none of these treasures. You have *nothing*. That is your punishment in this world. It will be your punishment in the next. When I die my spirit will find its way home. I will rest with my family and my friends. My Sara, who I know is dead. But you, Lady Vanhook . . .' Jeremiah took a breath, so that his next words came like an invocation, or a prophecy: 'No one will come for you. No one will call you home. Your soul will never know peace, or rest. It will drift alone, all alone, for ever. This is why I do not curse you now. There is no need. You have cursed yourself. I take comfort in that and will think of you no more.'

He folded the note back into his pocket and walked out.

A tear slid down Lady Vanhook's cheek. She threw me a poisonous look. 'You wrote that for him, didn't you? Didn't you? Well, I shall have my revenge on you, sir. I swear it. I will destroy you, and your family, everyone you have ever loved . . .'

Her old refrain.

Jeremiah was right – there was no need to punish Lady Vanhook. She was her own punishment, walking round and round her self-made circle of hell.

I left her alone, weeping for herself, and with each step grew lighter.

I will think of you no more.

Chapter Twenty-five

Lady Vanhook left for the coast the next day. Sam and Inchguard carried her trunk into town, past cows wading through the water meadows. They would travel with her to Harwich and make sure she boarded the packet boat to Holland. It seemed fitting that a Fleet should escort her from the country. A clear reminder of what would happen to her, should she return.

The trunk was heavy with furs and gowns, bought with Kitty's money. Infuriating, but she was more dangerous when she was desperate. Let her put on a show of wealth across the water and snare another man. There were rich fools in every country. She could move slowly down the Continent, a precise and very singular plague.

Kitty did not approve or disapprove of my plan. She would not speak of it. The only thing that reassured her was the blade under her pillow. A few days after her mother left I found her weeping in bed, the baby wailing in harmony.

'What is the matter, Kit? Is it this place?' I had – with reluctance – rented the farmhouse for a few weeks. I'd had no choice – Kitty was too weak to travel yet.

'Yes ... I don't know. Tom ...' She cried harder.

Later, much later, she told me that she had been crying for many reasons. The months of suffering, the fear of raising a child, the worry of surviving without her fortune. Grief for all that we had lost. She didn't know then that I had killed a man, but she had sensed a change in me and was troubled by it. We were not as we were and she blamed herself for it, even though she knew she should not. As

ANTONIA HODGSON

I have said – victory is a strange thing, and can often feel like defeat.

But let me not end on such a melancholic note. Let me dwell upon happier moments and look ahead to better times.

The day after Lady Vanhook set off for the coast, Jeremiah returned to London and to Affie. He did not like to leave her on her own, even in the safe, congenial company of his friend Marcus.

Before he left we shared a bowl of punch in the back parlour of the Queen's Head. The long window behind us offered a fine view of the river below. Jeremiah watched the barges unloading goods on to the bank, and I could tell that he was thinking of Limehouse. *Home.*

I handed him the present I had been saving for this moment: a copy of *The Tempest.* He smiled sadly, turning it in his hands, but thanked me for it.

'I don't mean for it to replace the one you lost.'

'I know, I know.'

I lowered my voice. 'We could have sent her back to London, Jeremiah. To Gabriela. We would both sleep more easily …'

'No, Thomas – we would not.'

'She could return, one day.'

'We shall be ready for her.'

He fell silent for a moment, then poked me with his elbow. 'So. You are a father.'

I knocked back my glass of punch. 'I am a father. God help me.'

He laughed. The sun was streaming through the window. He passed his hand through the light, basking in the warmth. 'Spring. Do you see? I thought it would never come. Yet here it is at last.'

When Kitty was well enough, we walked slowly into town with the baby wrapped up tight in a sling. The day was mild and bright and the birds filled the air with song. Kitty wore a cap and bonnet to hide her short hair, and the yellow wrapping gown we both hated. She looked beautiful.

I told her about a conversation I'd had with the Reverend White.

306

The town was looking for a new schoolmaster. Was that something I might consider? I had never thought of settling down in some quiet country town, least of all in my home county. But everyone had been so kind to us in Nayland, and after all Kitty had endured, I wondered if she might prefer some peace and quiet.

'Is that what you want?' she asked me.

'I don't know. Perhaps.' *If you want it, my love*.

She narrowed her eyes. 'Tom, you would hate it.'

'I would not! Nayland is a very fine town, with plenty of taverns ...'

'A *schoolmaster*.'

'A noble occupation.'

'Yes. One that requires you to sit cooped up in a room for hours—'

'I can do that!'

'Sober, Tom. *Sober*.'

Well that was debatable if my old tutors were anything to go by. We walked on, the baby filling the silence with little grunts and sighs.

'Are you trying to punish yourself for something?' Kitty asked, eventually. She stopped, and punched me in the arm. 'Whatever you did, whatever happened, that is *her* fault, do you understand?'

'So everyone tells me.'

'Well, they are right.'

We had reached the town. People were keen to see the baby and to meet Kitty, or Mrs Hawkins as they knew her. Everyone assumed that we were married, and we certainly did not correct them. We bought a few items from the chandler's and continued on our way.

On Bear Street, Evelyn Cuddington was chopping wood in her back yard. 'Give it to me,' she said, holding her arms out for the baby.

Kitty loosened the sling and handed the baby over as if she were the world's most precious jewel, which of course she was.

The baby, who had been dozing contentedly on her mother's chest, was not at all pleased to find herself deposited in a stranger's arms. She scrunched up her face in protest and let out an ear-shattering wail. Evelyn seemed to approve. She handed the baby back, without saying she was bonny, or had her mother's eyes, or any of the usual compliments. 'It's a good weight,' she conceded.

'You are always welcome to visit us in London,' I said, hoping fervently that she never would.

Evelyn picked up her axe and a fresh log, not dignifying the offer with a response.

Kitty tucked the baby back into her sling. 'We've decided to name her in your honour.'

'Why?' Evelyn asked, bringing the axe down with a satisfying *thunk*.

'You saved us, Evelyn. We are very grateful.'

'Do as you please,' Evelyn said with a shrug. 'But you should know that I *hate* my name. Always have.' She rubbed her nose on her sleeve. 'Do you want your hair back? I still have it.'

'You may keep it,' Kitty said, generously. 'As a memento.'

'I shall probably sell it,' Evelyn said.

We made our farewells. Then we found a quiet corner down the road, looked at one another, and burst out laughing. I'm not sure I have ever laughed so hard, for so little reason.

'I can't breathe,' Kitty said, holding her side. 'Why am I laughing?'

I shook my head. I had no idea. It didn't matter.

When I was recovered I leant down and kissed her full upon the mouth.

'We will be well,' I promised. 'That will be our revenge.'

'Yes, Tom,' Kitty said, pushing the doubt from her eyes. She kissed me back. 'We will be well.'

Epilogue

A packet boat left Harwich for South Holland twice a week, on Wednesdays and Saturdays, carrying post and passengers to the port of Hellevoetsluis. Four boats made the journey, to ensure a reliable service: the *Prince*, the *Dolphin*, the *Eagle* and the *Dispatch*, all sloop-rigged hoys with a capacity of one hundred and fifty passengers and crew. Passage cost twelve shillings and the journey took two days in good weather.

Sam recited this information to himself as he lay in his berth, curtains drawn. Wednesdays and Saturdays, Hellevoetsluis, sloop-rigged hoy, one hundred and fifty, twelve, two. He liked the way the numbers decreased.

After a miserable journey down the River Stour to Manningtree, and then on and on through detestable countryside, with nothing to do but look at cows and fields and other worthless things, it had been a tremendous relief to reach Harwich. Sam said so, and Inchguard had agreed with him, but then Inchguard always did. The streets were narrow and slippery with mud, the gutters clogged with filth. The locals treated visitors in a sullen manner, overcharging as a point of honour. Sam, naturally, approved. Drinking small beer in a rough alehouse, he listened intently to a gang of smugglers as they planned their next crossing. For the first time since leaving London, he felt at home.

At the harbour, he watched Russian traders making deals with English merchants. Tar, wax, tallow, furs. Sam liked this too. It looked, to use one of Mr Hawkins' words, *nefarious*. 'You should stay here for a while,' he told Inchguard. 'Opportunities.'

Inchguard agreed this was an excellent idea. 'Shall I leave you now?'

'Yes.'

Inchguard ambled away, waving once before disappearing down a side street. Sam did not wave back. He might call upon Inchguard again one day, he might not. All men had their uses, even useless ones.

An hour later he was settled in his berth on the *Dispatch* and an hour after that, they set sail.

The boat pitched and swayed and the empty chamber pot slid along its narrow shelf. Sam grabbed it, thinking he might be sick, but the nausea passed. He had not anticipated this problem, having never been at sea before. It was a shame – he liked his little berth with its thick mattress and white quilted covers. He had always preferred small spaces.

He slid open the curtains and dangled his feet over the edge of the berth. There was another box below him, empty. There were only a handful of passengers on board; he'd heard the captain complain about it.

Sam dropped to the ground then paused as the boat hit a wave. Someone in a distant berth groaned and retched.

Up on deck, the night air was fresh and biting. Sam stuck out his tongue and tasted salt. The world was dark and England was lost to the horizon. There was nothing to see but sea and sky, and a boat that had seemed large in the harbour, but now felt small and vulnerable, riding the dark waves. For a boy used to cramped houses and narrow alleys, all this space felt . . . oppressive.

Facts, facts would help, but Sam didn't know the names for anything, except mast and sail, everyone knew those. Which was port and which starboard? What was that rope for? He was embarrassed by his ignorance. When he returned home he would find some books and learn everything he could about boats and navigation.

Home. One more day to Holland, two days back to Harwich, then four days to London – now the numbers were increasing.

He waited behind a barrel as an elderly Dutch couple walked past. The man paused and vomited into the sea, as his wife rubbed his back. Once they were gone Sam made his way up the boat, timing his steps against the roll of the waves.

Lady Vanhook stood at the prow, wrapped in her fur-trimmed riding hood, the cloak lifting and flapping behind her as she stared out into the night. She looked, as always, magnificent.

Sam waited for a moment, studying her closely. It would not do to make a mistake. Yes, there was no doubt – it was her.

He walked up behind her, stabbed her three times in the back, and pushed her overboard.

He tossed the dagger into the sea. A shame, that – it was a good blade.

She should not have come back. *Leave England and never return* – that had been his uncle's deal. She had broken her promise to a Fleet. The first stab.

She should not have hurt Kitty. *I just want her to go away. For ever.* The second stab.

She should not have hurt Mr Hawkins. Tom was Sam's brother and he had almost died. Because of *her.* Unforgivable. The third and fatal blow.

The boat crested a wave, tilting the boards under Sam's feet. He gripped the sides of the prow, steadying himself.

Had she screamed when the blade went in? It was hard to say against the roar of the wind. Sam thought not.

No one would notice she was missing until they reached Holland. She was travelling under a different name. There would be rumours that she was a melancholic, and overfond of wine – Sam would help to spread them. Perhaps she had fallen, perhaps she had jumped. No one would care, not really.

It was cold at the prow. That was the trouble with Lady Vanhook,

ANTONIA HODGSON

Sam thought. She would rather stand here and pose than keep warm and safe. That *had* been the trouble with Lady Vanhook, he corrected himself.

As he stepped away from the edge Sam remembered the slap she had given him, that day on Jermyn Street. He paused, annoyed with himself. Really, that had deserved a fourth stab.

Too late now.

He headed back towards the cabin, already anticipating the snug comfort of his berth. He no longer felt sick, the swaying of the boat no longer troubled him. He would sleep well tonight.

At the harbour, earlier, Sam had talked to an old fisherman, who'd said there were boats that sailed all the way from Iceland to Harwich and then upriver to London. The fishermen would catch the cod and keep them in sea water containers in the hull, so the fish were still alive and swimming about when they reached the city. Ingenious! There really was so much to learn about boats, he would enjoy his research when he returned home.

The *Dispatch* sailed on through night-black waters, and the heavens were silent.

Historical Note

This is the fourth book in the Thomas Hawkins series, but I have been planning it ever since I finished my first, *The Devil in the Marshalsea*.

As with my previous books, I've included below some details about my research and any real characters in the novel. This sort of 'end matter' is not for everyone, I know. In fact some people *positively disapprove* of notes and bibliographies in works of fiction. It enrages them! In which case feel free to snap the book shut/toss your e-reader over your shoulder/turn off the audio now.

Slavery in the 1720s

One word seems to crop up more than any other in my research into 1720s England: liberty. The English were incredibly protective of their freedom. 'They love liberty more than religion,' wrote one disapproving traveller. Voltaire and Benjamin Franklin – both visitors to London in the 1720s – admired the English for their (comparative) freedom of speech and their constitutional monarchy.

And yet. And yet. How often is liberty for some won through the enslavement of others? The Athenians – so proud of their democracy – had their slaves and vassal states. The English, who sang ballads in praise of their escape from absolutism, were at the same time turning an already growing slave trade into a terrible, streamlined industry.

In 1713, as part of the treaty of Utrecht, Spain granted Britain the *asiento*, or contract, to sell slaves to the colonies. The slave trade was a cornerstone of Britain's economic growth in the eighteenth century. The 'triangular trade' between West Africa, Britain and the colonies meant that ships never sailed empty, importing and exporting back and forth from point to point and maximising profits. The unspeakable trade in human beings thus supported many other industries, directly or indirectly, including Britain's rapidly evolving banking system.

As noted in the novel, slavery was not permitted in Britain itself. And while the precise figures are debated, there were certainly thousands of free black men and women living in London in the 1720s (Betty, a servant at Moll King's coffeehouse, being one example). So what happened when a slave ran away in England? This question was deliberately fudged right through the eighteenth century. In 1772 a runaway slave named James Somerset won his case for freedom, when Lord Mansfield ruled that he could not be taken by force from England. But even after that, slave owners continued to hunt down runaways.

I love research – most of all reading primary sources. Prison diaries, memoirs of infamous criminals, housekeeping accounts, family letters, court trials, speeches – anything and everything, high and low society. But primary accounts of the lives of black people in England in the 1720s and 1730s – free or not – are extremely rare. There are glimpses only, in the margins.

There are of course many excellent secondary sources, but I was conscious that my usual research process could not provide all the answers. I'm often inspired by brief asides, the footnotes of history. I had to search much harder and I had to interrogate what I found closely. Clear references can be hard to find for lives 'writ in water'.

For example, there is some debate between historians about a reference to 'blackbirds' living in St Giles. Some point to this as evidence of a black community based in the area. Others query the meaning of the term. It makes a lot of sense to me that runaway slaves and indeed poorer black people in general would gravitate towards St Giles – it was dangerous there, but also cheap and a good place to hide. It also makes complete sense that those with a shared, terrible experience would choose to live close together and protect one another. Runaway slaves would also, in the first instance, need a willing blacksmith to remove their collar and a place to sell the silver, no questions asked. Again, St Giles seems the ideal place for that.

There were, of course, black sailors and journeymen working at the docks out east. The description of the private dance gathering is based on a contemporary account.

One day in the British Library I was reading a collection of advertisements for runaway slaves (in a later period than the novel) and spotted a pattern. Over and over again, a slave would be described as having a stammer, or a similar speech impediment. Not surprising, given the extreme trauma they would have endured.

This disturbing revelation stayed with me and inspired the creation of Jeremiah, an eloquent man with a vivid imagination, who struggles with speech.

Private madhouses

Kitty's experiences in a private madhouse were based on the horrifying memoir of Alexander Cruden, a former bookseller to Queen Caroline. He describes how he was tricked and dragged off to a madhouse in Bethnal Green, chained, purged and forced to sleep in a straitjacket, surrounded by other screaming, terrified inmates. By the end of his account it's hard to tell whether he is entirely sane, or if he has suffered some form of breakdown. The treatment alone – poisonings and blood lettings included – could have tipped him over the edge of sanity.

Eliza Haywood's 1726 novella *Love in a Madhouse* also provided some inspiration, though in that odd way that sometimes happens with research, I read it after I had plotted out my story.

Betty

There was a young black woman called Betty working at Tom King's (or Moll's) coffeehouse in the 1720s, but very little is known about her beyond her name and a couple of illustrations. (Even her name is in doubt, as 'Betty' was a commonly used generic name for a servant.) The character of Betty is inspired by this young woman, but fictional beyond these scant details.

Sir John Gonson

Readers of my second novel may remember the Westminster magistrate. A prominent member of The Society for the Reformation of Manners, he had a penchant for arresting 'lewd women' and sending them off to prison for harsh labour. He also placed informers in molly houses (gay brothels). Sir John would have been about fifty-six at the time of the novel, and at the height of his 'reforming' activities. Alexander Pope referred to 'the storm of Gonson's lungs'. I won't say any more as he may strut into another novel some time. If you'd like to see a picture of him, Hogarth depicts him in plate three of *A Harlot's Progress*, bursting in on Moll Hackabout with a very curious expression on his face.

Edmund Chishull

Mr Chishull was granted a living at St Mary's in Walthamstow in 1708. As a young man he travelled extensively both privately and as a chaplain, and was a noted antiquarian. He was also chaplain to Queen Anne from 1711 to her death in 1714. He spent time in Ephesus, you know.

Almshouses at Saffron Walden

There have been almshouses in the town since the year 1400, although the current buildings postdate the novel. The description of the room where Tom recovers after his long illness is based on a primary source.

Nayland

We now consider Nayland a village, but in the eighteenth century its inhabitants called it a town. Sadly there is now only one drinking hole as opposed to thirteen – the Anchor Inn, which was known as the King's Head in the 1720s. In more cheering news it is very pleasant, there are swans, and pub crawls are overrated anyway. If you have a seat, stay where you are, that's what I say.

In 1729, despite its size, St James's was a chapel of ease for the old and the infirm, which meant that it did not have regular services. It was, however, the focal point of the community and the site of town meetings. The Reverend John White was minister from 1713 until his death in 1755. It was he who campaigned for St James's to become a fully independent church in its own right.

I mention this because it's unclear whether White lived in Nayland or nearby Stoke-by-Nayland, to which St James's was affiliated. But as White is buried in St James's graveyard along with his wife and two sons, I thought it reasonable to place him in the town. This also meant placing him in the vicarage on Fen Street. For simplicity, I refer to St James's as a church, rather than a chapel, which might have suggested something much smaller to modern readers.

The vicarage no longer exists – unusually for Nayland, which is astonishingly well preserved and demands a visit. My thanks to Andora Carver (see also Acknowledgements) for sharing her painting and photograph of this lost building.

Richard Strait/Patchett

Eczema was not recognized as a condition at the time – doctors had not yet connected together all the various types under one name. The idea was basically *not* to treat it, as the flare ups were thought to be poisons coming up from the blood. Anything that soothed the skin was deemed unhelpful to this 'balancing' process and to be avoided. One of those occasions where going to the doctor did you more harm than good. To be fair we still haven't found a cure almost three hundred years later.

Harwich

Apologies to any current citizens, but my description of the town as being thoroughly disreputable and the locals being a bunch of swindling thieves is based on primary accounts. I'm sure there were some very decent locals around at the time too, but Sam wouldn't be in the least bit interested in them.

Select Bibliography

Primary Sources

Anon., *The Laws of the Island of Antigua 1690-1798*

Cruden, Alexander, *The London-Citizen Exceedingly Injured; Or a Journal or Narrative of Mr C—'s Sufferings at Bethnal Green*, 1738

English Broadside Ballad Archive, ebba.english.ucsb.edu

Gonson, John, *The Charge of Sir John Gonson to the Grand Jury of Westminster (April 1728)* and also *The Third Charge of Sir John Gonson, Knt, to the Grand Jury of Westminster (Oct 1728)*

Haywood, Elizabeth, *Love in a Madhouse*, 1726

Hodges, Graham Russell and Brown, Alan Edward, eds, *Pretends to be Free: Runaway Slave Advertisements from Colonial and Revolutionary New York and New Jersey*

Meades, Daniel, *Advertisements for Runaway Slaves in Virginia, 1801-1820*

Prince, Mary, *The History of Mary Prince, A West Indian Slave 1831*

Turner, Daniel, *De Morbis Cutaneis: A Treatise of Diseases Incident to the Skin*, 1726

Secondary Sources

Alston, Leigh, *A Walk Around Historic Nayland*

Álvarez López, Laura, 'Who named slaves and their children?', *Journal of African Cultural Studies*, Vol. 27, Issue 2, 2015

Bhattacharya, Tanya et al, 'Historical Perspectives on Atopic Dermatitis: Eczema Through the Ages', *Pediatric Dermatology*, Vol. 33, Issue 4, 2016

Birch, J. G., *Limehouse Through Five Centuries*

Bowett, Adam, *Early Georgian Furniture 1715-1740*

Chater, Kathleen, *Untold Histories: Black people in England and Wales during the period of the British slave trade c. 1660-1807*

Cunnington, C. Willett and Cunnington, Phillis, *Handbook of English Costume in the 18th Century*

Fryer, Peter, *Staying Power: The History of Black People in Britain*

Fulford, Tim, 'Fallen Ladies and Cruel Mothers: Ballad Singers and Ballad

Heroines in the Eighteenth Century', *The Eighteenth Century*, Vol. 47, No. 2/3, 2006

Gerzina, Gretchen, *Black England: Life before Emancipation*

Gundara, Jagdish S. and Duffield, Ian, *Essays on the History of Blacks in Britain*

Heller, Jerome S. and Jacoby, JoAnn, 'Slave Names and Naming in Barbados, 1650-1830', *The William and Mary Quarterly*, Vol. 53, No. 4, 1996

King-Dorset, Rodreguez, *Dance Parallels in the Ghetto: Parallels Between an Eighteenth-Century London Black Minority and a Twenty-first Century London Black Minority*

Molineux, Catherine, *Faces of Perfect Ebony: Encountering Atlantic Slavery in Imperial Britain*

Scobie, Edward, *Black Britannia: A History of Blacks in Britain*

Shyllon, F.O., *Black Slaves in Britain*

Slade, Dr Sidney, *History of Nayland* (with thanks to Andora Carver for the loan of this unpublished work)

Sparrow, Wendy and Carver, Andora, *Nayland and Wiston: A Portrait in Photographs*

Steer, Francis W., 'The Statutes of Saffron Walden Almshouses', *Transactions of the Essex Archaeological Society*, Vol. 25, Part 2, 1958

Stewart, Graham, *Time and Tide: The History of the Harwich Haven Authority*